LEO, LULU, LOBIE, & MAE

A MODERN DAY FOUR HORSEMEN OF THE APOCALYPSE

ROBIN ANDERSON

To the much-loved FOUR Ms in my life

MARGARET POWELL (PEGGY)
MAI CORDELL
MARGARET KIRKBRIDE (MAGGIE)
MARGARET, DUCHESS OF ARGYLL (MARG OF ARG)

Plus, as always,

BEESLE

LEO, LULU, LOBIE, & MAE

A MODERN DAY FOUR HORSEMEN OF THE APOCALYPSE

THE FOUR HORSEMEN OF THE APOCALYPSE

HORSES' COLOURS & MEANINGS

WHITE HORSE = CONQUEST

RED HORSE = WAR

BLACK HORSE = FAMINE

GREY HORSE = DEATH

WHITE HORSE

FLASHBACK - LONDON 2016 - A LOCAL McDONALD'S

"I *hate* hamburgers!" announced Lulu Mayhew, a scowling, dark-haired twelve-year-old bearing no resemblance to the chirpy singer so admired by her mother Babe, a vivacious, somewhat plump, Jessica Rabbit lookalike.

"So, don't eat it then!" grunted Doug Tindall, a hefty Neanderthal of a man and Babe's latest paramour in a long line of beefy, burly, hirsute, hefty paramours.

"Think of all those poor starving children in those third world countries," added Babe with a toss of her peroxided head.

"At least they don't have to worry about *their* weight like someone else I know," snickered Lulu.

"Lulu! That's quite enough!" said Doug sharply. "You don't speak to your mother like that otherwise you could find yourself with a very sore bum!"

"But I just did," replied Lulu equally as sharply. "And as for you, Mr. Super Shooting Stick - I know that's what my mother calls you! - *you* can't talk to me like that seeing it's what is now known as child abuse! I've got a good mind to call one of those helplines they're always advertising and report you! So there!"

"Jesus, I give up," muttered Doug. Glaring at a defiant Lulu he gave a faux smile and said sarcastically. "Okay, have it your way, *Miss* Lulu. You *don't* have to finish your hamburger. You *don't* have to do anything you don't want to do, and you can speak to your mother, me, or anyone else for that matter, exactly as you wish. So, good luck Lulu. Good luck from your mother and me."

Having expected a sharp comeback from Doug as opposed to a passive "do as you wish", Lulu gave both adults a glare before picking up the now tepid hamburger and attacking it with gusto. Babe and Doug sat in silent bemusement as Lulu, an expression of utter bliss on her freckled face, made a great show of chewing and swallowing in between muffled mumblings of "delicious" and "yummy yum!"

Having eaten everything put down in front of her, Lulu pushed the empty plate aside and said with a strychnine sweet smile. "Now, that was utterly, utterly, delish, Mummy dearest! And a big thank you, *Uncle* Doug, for showing me that there is no harming in being charming! Now, if you'll excuse me, I need to go to the little girls' room so that I can throw up!"

Two days later Lulu was unexpectedly taken to see Mrs Hortense Jenkins, the headmistress, following set-to between her and Miss Watson, their English teacher. The minor altercation taking place after a smiling Miss Victoria Watson, an Alice B. Toklas lookalike, having asked the class which historical, literary female character - imaginary or real - they would have liked to have been.

"Yes, Lulu?" said Miss Watson brightly on seeing Lulu's raised right hand. "Pray tell the class *whom* you would have liked to be?"

"Lady Godiva, Miss Watson," replied Lulu with a sugary smile. "But instead of riding about naked on a horse, I'd prefer to be riding naked on a Harley-David motorcycle. More vroom-vroom and much more exciting!" She gave a giggle. "However, I wouldn't be *entirely* naked seeing I would have sprinkled some glitter on my lady bits!"

Despite the shocked gasps, sniggers and giggles, Miss Watson was not amused, and on instructing the snickering class to read the next few pages in their textbooks, promptly escorted an unfazed Lulu to Mrs Jenkins office.

After listening to an indignant Miss Watson's complaint about Lulu's "vulgar remark" in front of the whole class, Mrs Jenkins - doing her best to suppress a laugh - asked the glowering teacher to leave so that she and Lulu could have "a serious talk".

After Miss Watson had left with a smug, self-satisfied expression on her usually grim face, Mrs Jenkins sat staring at Lulu for a full minute before saying in an exasperated voice. "Lulu, Lulu, when will you learn it is not funny, nor is it nice, to deliberately upset a person? Last week you deliberately upset Mr. Jennings during your history lesson by asking him if it was true that all Spartans were gay, how then was it possible for there to be any baby Spartans! Your words, not mine! And as for what you said to poor Mr. Reynolds in Art Class . . ."

"I only asked Mr. Reynolds if his willy was bigger than Michel Angelo's David's willy," interrupted Lulu blandly, "because I'm exactly like Alice."

"Exactly like Alice? Alice who?"

"Alice in Wonderland," trilled Lulu. "Like Alice, I'm naturally curious! And, unless I'm mistaken, schoolteachers are there to help us broaden our receptive minds. Not stifle them!"

"I think it would be a good idea if I arrange a meeting between you, your parents and myself," said Mrs Jenkins in a no-nonsense voice.

"If that's what you wish, then please do so," replied Lulu. Giving a a dismissive shrug of her tiny shoulders, she added with a hint of a smile. "And if you can get any sense from Mum and her current man of the moment, it will be *exactly* as Alice said. *Curiouser and curiouser!*"

RED HORSE

TWO DAYS LATER

"Lobie, will you *please* get into the car," said Patrick Maseko, a six-foot-two Boris Kodjoe lookalike, in a deep, from the balls voice, to Lobengula, his glowering twelve-year-old son who was standing, arms crossed and legs akimbo next to the gleaming Bentley. "Now!"

"But why?" grizzled Lobie looking up at his father, his lower lip trembling.

"You *know* why!" said Patrick doing his best to control his exasperation. *Christ, Lobie, you may be the light of my life but compared to you, when you wish to be difficult, even my most difficult clients become mere novices!*

(Patrick Maseko, a graduate from the University of Harare, Zimbabwe, and now a partner in one of London's most prestigious Law firms, had met his future business partner while on honeymoon with his new wife, the elegant Melody Mbele, a former Miss Zimbabwe and a top interior designer. After ten days together in the delightful company of Barry and Barbara Bartholomew, the newlyweds showed little hesitation when Barry offered the recently graduated Patrick a junior position in his firm. Patrick's speedy rise to becoming a partner came as no surprise to the ambitious young man, just as it came as no surprise that Melody, through a planned, introduction by Barbara, ended up a director of a top interior design company. What did come as a surprise was the birth of a boy quickly followed by the birth of girl. It was Melody who insisted on naming their son Lobengula, after the famous Matabele chief, while it was Patrick who insisted on naming their daughter Oshun, the African goddess of love and freedom.)

"Yes, I know *why,* but why must I?" muttered Lobie, scraping the gravelled driveway with the toe of his shoe.

"Because it's your little sister's birthday and we still have to collect her and Marjorie, her best friend, from Marjorie's house before we collect Mum from the showroom before we get to the cinema for the six o'clock programme, Oshun's choosing, that's why. Followed by a visit to McDonald's. Again, your sister's choosing. Now, as you know more than even MI5, will you please get into the damn car!"

"Surely, I, as your only son and heir have some say in the matter," said Lobie pompously giving his impatient father a defiant look. "It's not as I even *like* those silly films by Disney, and I am certainly far too choosy to ever deliberately eat at a McDonalds!"

Doing his best to supress a grin, Patrick bent down and looking Lobie directly in the eye said, man-to-man. "I heartily agree with you, Lobie. Like you, I have no wish to eat at McDonald's, but it *is* your little sister's birthday! What's more, Oshun is exactly like your Mama. Which you and I know Lobie, means that what Oshun and your Mama want, Oshun and your Mama get!"

"Okay, Dad," said Lobie, his round, brown face breaking into a dazzling, whiter than white smile. Giving Patrick an unexpected high five, he added conspiratorially in his squeaky, boy's treble. "Let's go for it . . . but, on one condition!"

"Oh, yes? And what's that?" rumbled Patrick, turning on the ignition.

"You take me with you when you go to Wimbledon this year!"

"Done!" said Patrick, releasing his large left hand from the steering wheel and giving his son's small right hand an affirmative squeeze.

"Good," replied Lobie. Looking sideways at his father, he added smugly. "Now I can tell Mama a whopper and say that I've really been looking forward to Oshun's birthday treat, especially seeing Disney's *Incredibles 2* and as for a hamburger at McDonald's. Wow!"

Not giving a bemused Patrick a chance to respond, Lobie said matter-of-factly. "So, Dad, apart from a movie and a Big Mac, what are you and Mama *really* giving Oshun for a birthday present?"

"Your mother and I have it all arranged," replied Patrick with a sidelong smile. "On Saturday we'll be taking an early Eurostar to Paris and from there, take a previously hired cab to Disneyland where we will be staying the night at - so I'm told - the fabulous Disney Hotel New York. Sunday will be spent exploring Disneyland before returning to Paris that evening where we'll be staying at The Ritz." He gave a chuckle. "On Sunday evening we will be visiting The Moulin Rouge where you, I and Mama and maybe Oshun. seeing children of six are allowed and your sister will be a full-fledged ten-year-old, can see the famous cabaret which includes Can Can!"

"That's more like it!" cried Lobie. "I maybe only twelve but, like you, Dad, I'm all for a bit of ooh-la-la!"

BLACK HORSE

TWO DAYS LATER

"Bloody stupid bike!" shouted twelve-year-old Leo Murrain giving his orange Cuda Trace 26 a vicious kick. His face reddening, he said with a haphazard series of further kicks. "Why" kick "did you have to go" kick "and get" kick "a bloody flat tyre" kick "just as I was about to" kick "cycle over" kick "to Jenny Minter's" kick "and then join up with Lobie" kick "Carrots and Kathy" kick "at McDonald's" kick "for a burger and a Coke!" double kick.

Panting from the effort of his kicks, Leo, a doppelganger for Hank Ketcham's *Dennis the Menace*, added between breaths. "Now I'll have to borrow sissy Steve's from next door's bike; but not before repolish my shoes." Glaring down at the dusty, scuffed pair of Clarks as if it was their fault they'd been made to "kick up a storm", he added with a grunt. "And if sissy Steve isn't there to let me borrow his bike, I'll then have to catch a bloody bus which means that by the time I get to Jenny's it'll be time to come home!"

Giving a growl, Leo flung the guilty party against the garage wall and, dusty, scuffed shoes forgotten, marched across the side lawn in his best "man on a mission" mode toward the tall, boxwood hedge separating the two properties, and squeezed through a hidden gap which served as a shortcut when visiting Steve.

"Oh, I thought it could only be you," said twelve-year-old Steven Poulter, a pale, Bart Simpson lookalike, from where he lay, book in hand, on a sun lounger on the paved terrace overlooking a small, kidney-shaped swimming pool - referred to by Margo Murrain, Leo's acerbic mother and double for Patrick Denis's *Auntie Mame,* as the Poulter's *Pissoir.*

He added nasally. "If you've come to borrow my bike - you do have a very loud carrying voice - you can forget it. After the way you referred to me a few minutes ago and after what you called me in front of Harriet Hanley and Lulu Mayhew yesterday, I will never, *ever,* let you borrow my bike again!"

"Oh?" replied Leo nonchalantly. "What was it I called you?"

"You called me a four-eyed twit! That's what you did!"

"Well, with those goggles you call glasses and the way you keep hitching up your pants as they always seem to be falling down, what else am I supposed to call you? A pair of Coke bottle bottoms on top of a saggy sack?" Holding up a placatory hand, Leo added with a disarming grin. "Before you answer, the question is, yes, I need to borrow your bike and I promise, on my Scout's Honour, never to refer to you a four-eyed twit nor even a pair Coke bottle bottoms on top of a saggy sack again. Or anything similar!"

There was a tense moment while the two boys remained staring fixedly at each other. Steven from where he lay supine on the sun-lounger, and Leo from where he was standing. Breaking into his best "this'll melt Mum's heart smile", Leo said cheerfully. "I promise!"

"Promise, promise?" came the surprised response.

"Promise, promise, *promise!*" grinned Leo.

"Okay, you can borrow my bike but remember what you've promised!"

"I promise, promise, I will never call you a four-eyed twit again," said Leo solemnly.

But that doesn't stop me from calling you a four-eyed arsehole next time you piss me off, he thought as he began peddling his way toward the Minter residence. *Or better still, a four-eyed - it looks as if you've just pooped your pants - droopy-drawers!*

GRAY HORSE

TWO DAYS LATER

"I'm afraid but I have no choice but to cut off both your legs," announced twelve-year-old Mae Collison in her sweet, little girl voice. Ignoring her grinning patient lying spreadeagled on the playroom floor, she turned to face her best friend Lizzie Masterson, who, like Mae (a double for Richmal Compton's Violet Elizabeth Bott) was dressed in a nurse's uniform similar to hers. "The saw, please, nurse!"

On Mae being handed a wire coat hanger, twelve-year-old Clive Cordell, the patient, began to make the appropriate groans and moans as Mae proceeded to slowly "saw" off his legs.

"Well done, Nurse Collison, we'll make a surgeon out of you yet!" squeaked Barry Edwards, Mae's popular eleven-year-old neighbour and regular playmate.

"Thank you, Dr Edwards," replied Mae. "So, what do we cut off next?"

"Why not his willy?" snickered Lizzie.

"If you're expecting me to pull down my pants, you've got another think coming!" snorted Clive, an Artful Dodger lookalike. "In no way are you going to even pretend to saw off my willy!"

"Spoilsport," said Mae wiping her forehead with the back of her tiny hand as if exhausted by the surgery she'd carried out. Grinning at Clive now lounging on a bright yellow bean bag chair, and Lizzie perched on a matching mushroom pouffe, she added cheerfully. "Who's for a Coke and a cookie? After all, surgery is thirsty work, plus the fact I'm famished!"

"Me too," sniggered Clive. "Being cut up is also thirsty work plus I'm also hungry and could easily eat a hundred cookies!" Glancing at Mae he said mischievously. "Next time we play doctors and nurses *you* can be the patient and allow *me* to be the one to slowly - and I mean *very* slowly - saw off your arms and legs!"

"As Mummy always says, anything worth doing, is worth doing *slowly*," said Mae loftily. Mummy being Viola Collison who, like her husband Brian, was an avid watcher of Mae West vintage films, with both parents including the actress's pithy quotes in their conversation whenever they could. Hence the unexpected arrival of a squalling baby daughter saw her immediately given the name Mae. "And as for *you* being the doctor, as Mummy also says, what's the point of resisting temptation? There'll always be more!

"Even better, Mummy slipped me a couple of ten-pound notes so that I could treat my medical team to hamburgers or whatever and more Cokes at our local McDonald's seeing she and Dada B (no mere "Daddy" for Mae) have a few people in for drinks and, as she said, I'm a woman of few words, but lots of action."

A LOCAL McDONALD'S

"Don't look now," snickered Lulu, giving Leo a nudge, "but you'll never believe what the cat's dragged in!"

Ignoring Lulu's hissed instruction Leo immediately turned to have a look and said with a snort. "Jesus! Mad Mae Collison and her group of zombies!" He gave a snigger. "I never knew zombies liked hamburgers! I thought they only ate humans!"

"So?" giggled Lulu. "Maybe this is a cover-up. After all, that Clive Cordell looks nothing like a human; nothing at all!"

"You're only saying that Lulu Mayhew, because Clive Cordell is super dishy but, no matter how hard you try to attract his attention, he simply ignores you!" crowed Kathy Carr, a plump twelve-year-old who, having viewed *The Long Good Friday* on Prime Time, saw herself as another Helen Mirren, Bob Hoskin's "right-hand woman", and, unbeknown to Carrots Marsden her present crush, spent hours parading in front of her bedroom mirror perfecting her desired role as Carrots' sultry moll.

"Liar! Liar! Pants on fire!" snapped Lulu.

"What's more, you said he even makes Brooklyn Beckham look 'less dishy!' Your words, not mine!"

"I never did!"

"Did!"

"Didn't!"

"Oi! Stop it, you two!" chided Leo. "Talk about a cat and a dog!"

"I'm not the least bit like a cat!" said Lulu giving Leo a venomous look.

"Really, Miss Meow?" tittered Mathew Marsden, a freckled, ginger-headed Charlie Stewart lookalike, otherwise known as Carrots among his friends.

"Okay, you two, that's enough!" said Leo with a grin, "We're here to enjoy ourselves so let's do that and simply ignore the table of zombies over sitting by the window. So, who's for a Big Mac and a Coke?"

"I'd *adore* a Big Mac and a Coke!" crooned Lulu. "And I *adore* coming to our local McDonald's!" (Her virulent comments to her father two days earlier, tactfully forgotten.)

"Don't we all!" enthused Leo. "Given the choice of coming here or going to some stuffy grown-up place I'd settle for a McDonald's *anytime!*"

(Fortunately for Lulu and Leo there was no errant thunderbolt nearby to overhear their very own whoppers as opposed to those offered by McDonald's!)

*

Pushing her plate aside Lulu announced to nobody in particular. "You know what, that noisy group of zombies sitting over there really annoys me!"

"You said it!" grunted Leo, nodding in agreement.

"Well, before you lot get into another argument, Kathy and I have to get going," said Carrots in a no-nonsense voice.

"Me to," said Jenny giving Leo a coquettish look.

"Oh?" questioned Leo glancing at his Swatch watch. "I thought you wanted to have a quick look in Zara before going home and watching TV? So, why the hurry seeing I was about to order us all another Coke."

"There's no particular hurry and I don't want to have a look in Zara, I simply want to leave!" replied Jenny with a pout.

"We'll walk you home, Jen," interrupted Kathy. Glaring at Leo (whom she had never liked) she added waspishly. "That's if *Leo* doesn't mind,"

"Ouch!" snickered Lobie.

"No, Leo *doesn't* mind, *Kathy*," replied Leo equally as waspishly. "Plus, *Leo* wishes to hear whatever else Lulu has to say about zombie Mae and her team, So, off you go!"

Ignoring the obvious chill in the air, Lulu, Leo and Lobie watched as the other three made their way toward the exit, but not before Lulu had calculated and demanded Carrots hand over their share of the bill.

Making sure the trio had left and Leo had ordered another three Cokes, Lulu turned to a grinning Leo and Lobie and said with a Cruella de Vil smile. "Now, as I was about to say before I was so rudely interrupted, that group over there is really annoying me as well as you two from what I can see, so why don't we do something about it?"

"Like what?" asked Lobie with a grin.

"But before doing something to any of them I do think that nerdish Matthew and stupid Kathy need to be taught a lesson for saying such things about me and that equally stupid Clive." said Lulu making a face. "How dare he call me a cat when he is nothing more that stupid Kathy's lap dog! And, as far as he's concerned can do nothing wrong!"

"I'll say it again," grinned Lobie, "like what?"

"Easy-peasy," giggled Lulu. "And this is what I, Lulu Mayhew, tough girl, suggest." Her suggestion, delivered in a clipped, couple of sentences, saw the two young boys staring back at her in disbelief.

"I think - after that - we could all do with another Coke," murmured a stunned Leo.

"I most certainly agree," chuckled Leo. Turning to face a smug Lulu, he said with a grin. "I've heard of dangling a *carrot* before, but never quite like that! Brilliant! Lulu! Bloody brill!"

PLAYGROUND - HALLIDAY SECONDARY SCHOOL - A WEEK LATER

"Just look at him!" hissed Lulu, nodding to where a shaven-headed Mathew Marsden stood regaling an awed group of his recent "terrifying ordeal" in which he was viciously attacked by "a masked gang" who not only stole his mobile but "shaved his head before spraying it with orange gloss paint". A terrifying ordeal from which he emerged "the winner" having finally managed to give them a "seeing to" before escaping.

"Instead of being a victim or a loser, bloody Carrots has ended up a hero! As for Miss Smarty pants, she's wallowing in all the fuss and making sure that *everyone* knows she's also his girlfriend! Pity we never got the chance to shave *her* stupid head!"

"Don't worry, Lulu," said Leo with a placatory smile. "Next time - and there will be a next time - we'll do what you originally suggested and in addition to shaving and spraying his head and willy orange, we really will cut off his willy and leave it in his blazer pocket! Plus, shave Kathy's head and paint it violet!"

"I agree with Leo," added Lobie. "At the present moment we're really too inexperienced to have done something as serious as that but, give us a few years then Carrots' carrot will dangle no more and Kathy will find herself mistaken for a large aubergine!" He gave a grin. "And before you remind Leo and me, *yet again,* of your heroine, Emma, from the TV series *The Woman in the House Across the Street from the Girl in the Window*, and how she got away with murder, practice makes perfect and it's far better to be safe than sorry."

"Practice makes perfect?" repeated Lulu. "What's *that* supposed to mean?"

"Let's face it, Lulu. When it comes down to it and people who annoy, Carrots isn't the only fish in the sea," added Leo philosophically. "Take a look at zombie Mae Collison holding court over there alongside Carrots. Put on your thinking cap and plan what we could do to *her* when we three turn eighteen or, better still, twenty-one!"

"What makes you sure we'll still be friends then?" said Lulu matter-of-factly.

"Because we will be, that's why," said Lobie in a sombre voice. "And, to make doubly sure, let's seal our friendship in blood . . ."

"Seal our friendship in blood?" squawked Lulu. "What do mean? How?"

"By a simple pricking of our fingers, that's how," said Lobie. "Look, give me one of those button pins on your lapels and we can make a blood oath, here and now, to our everlasting friendship!"

"And if one day I want a divorce?" giggled Lulu.

"You'd be a very silly girl if you ever did," replied Lobie deadpan, before breaking into a dazzling smile and adding with a chuckle, "Not that I can see you ever wanting to divorce Leo or handsome me!"

ONE

PRESENT DAY

SCALINI ITALIAN RESTAURANT - WALTON STREET - CHELSEA - LONDON

"At long last a gathering of the *glans*!" crooned Lulu - a walking advert for Gucci - led by the beaming maître 'd, sashayed her way to where a grinning Leo and Lobie were already rising to their feet in greeting. Arriving at the table she added with a throaty laugh. "A touch different from our usual McDonald's of yore, wouldn't you say?"

"Eight years on *everything* is a touch different!" chuckled Leo. Leaning forward he gave Lulu a tentative kiss on her elegant Keira Knightly cheek. "Look at you, for example," he added admiringly. "Tchaikovsky would have been proud!"

"Tchaikovsky would have been proud?" repeated Lulu. She gave another, throaty laugh. "I can see a couple of years spent visiting the wicked world's hotspots still hasn't stopped you talking in riddles!"

"Not a riddle, Lulu, love," cut in Lobie with a dazzling, whiter than white smile. "He's obviously referring to the maestro's *Swan Lake* where the ugly duckling turns into a swan! And not only a swan but a successful author of two bestsellers!"

"Nice try, Lobie," chortled Lulu. "Wrong names all round, plus I don't think Tchaikovsky and Hans Christian Andersen ever met!" Eyeing the two grinning young men she added mischievously. "Nor was I *ever* an ugly duckling, maybe a bit of a tomboy, but I was *never* ugly! Your turn!"

Leaning forward so Lobie could give her a kiss on the cheek before turning to thank the smiling waiter for pulling out her chair, she sat down and said with a further throaty laugh. "Goodness! Lobie love! I always

25

thought your dad a dish to die for in the good looks' stakes, but you are much more of a gorgeous Boris Kodjoe lookalike than he could ever be! Plus, rumour has it you're now a much sought after PR person!"

"And what about me?" said Leo with a chuckle. "A boring but highly successful stockbroker. And before you come up some witty remark you can forget the former Dennis the Menace for, according to my gorgon baby sister, seventeen going on for seventy, Oshun: one of her friends - of uber-intelligence and good taste I might add - said I reminded her of a young Brad Pit!"

"Ha! Oshun must have misheard as I'm pretty sure Miss Uber-Intelligence and good taste surely could have only said a young Brad Shit!" quipped Lobie. His bright riposte causing the three friends to burst out laughing.

Wiping his eyes, Leo said cheerfully. "Instead of yesteryear's Cokes, lovely Lulu, Lobie and I are having a glass of wine. However, in between buying up Gucci and Pucci, you're obviously a martini, champers or G and T girl, so, please feel free to order whatever you wish."

"A glass of white wine would be lovely *despite* it being a celebration," purred Lulu. "The three of us being more-or-less out of touch since fleeing hideous Halliday!"

"As I have a feeling it's going to be a long, fun, catching-up lunch I'll order two bottles of Pinot Grigio," chuckled Leo. "I won't go to three seeing that wouldn't leave any room for those delicious grappas and sambucis to go with our espressos!"

"*Perfecto,*" said Lulu. "As I'm a regular here, I know exactly what I'll have, let's order before we get down to some really serious catch-up and gossip!"

"Hear! Hear!" agreed Lobie. "But, unlike you, Lulu dear, I need to see a menu."

"*Anche me,*" chuckled Leo. "Though when I go Italian, I usually go for *lasagna*, but seeing I'm in fabulous *Scalini's*, I'll go for something much more adventurous."

"So," said Lulu once the waiter had taken their orders, "Carrots and Kathy! Whatever happened to them after our little *Barber of Seville* and unknown artist little escapade." Making finger quotes she added with a mischievous smile. "A still to be continued escapade if my memory serves me well!"

"Carrots - Matthew Marsden - was so taken by the oohs and aahs he received as a result of his shaven pate he decided to keep it billiard ball smooth from then on," chuckled Lobie. "Remember how we often commented on how his hair never grew back and put it down to shock? Apparently, when Mr. Bradley, the headmaster, brought it up with his parents - apparently other parents had complained it showed a lack of discipline as well as a lack of respect for the school and the other pupils - Carrots' parents came up with the same excuse. Due to the shock of the incident, they had taken Carrot's to see a psychiatrist and he had said the same. Carrots' permanent hair loss was due to shock!"

After the three friends had stopped laughing, Lulu said matter-of-factly. "After all that, he surely no longer refers to himself as Carrots?"

"You're absolutely right! He now calls himself Corey after Corey Stoll, that bald actor in that great Netflix series *House of Cards*," said Leo. "So, if we ever *did* decide to finish our unfinished escapade - that's meant to be a joke, nota bene!" - we'd be dealing with Mr. *Corey* Marsden despite him looking more like fucking Humpty Dumpty than heartthrob Corey Stoll!"

"And what about his *other* tell-tale ginger locks," giggled Lulu. "Those carroty locks down below!"

"Shaved!" chortled Leo. "I saw him in the showers after a footie match and the whole of him is as hairless as a newborn baby! And when I say the whole of him that included his arms, legs, and even his armpits!"

"Good God!" camped Lulu clutching her throat. "Have you any idea as to what Carrots-cum-Corey is up to now?"

"Apparently he's now some sort of a whizz-kid estate agent thanks to Daddy Marsden's connections."

"And the constipated Kathy Carr?"

"You'll never believe it but, she too is a success in her own right. She's now an accomplished florist and everyone, and I mean *everyone*, is after her. Albeit a wedding, a christening, birthday party or even a simple bouquet, *Katherine Carr Flowers* is the call of the day!"

"In other words, she's become the veritable rose to his shaven prick!" snickered Lulu. Ignoring Leo and Lobie's guffaws she added waspishly. "To quote a phrase I used to annoy everyone with back at school. Curiouser and curiouser!"

"As for Clive Cordell, I believe he's now a junior doctor at one of the major NHS hospitals here in London whilst Jenny Minter, my on and off schoolboy crush, is now a nursery teacher."

"Nothing curiouser about *that*!" came Lulu's instant, acerbic reply.

"And as for Mae Collison," added Leo ignoring Lulu's obvious response, "curiouser and curiouser doesn't even come into it."

"Oh?"

"And a gigantic oh at that! Still in *Alice in Wonderland* mode, and even more curiouser and curiouser, mundane, and unbelievable. Does the name Maebelle mean anything to you?"

"Not really. Unless you're referring to that ridiculous fashion model everyone's talking about. The blonde bombshell who's supposedly being courted by some Saudi billionaire prince."

"I most certainly am! Maebelle the uber-glamorous fashion model being none other than Mae Collison, or zombie Mae as we used to call her!"

"Jesus!" squawked Lulu, causing the neighbouring diners to visibly jump. "Talk about a mini monster morphing into a catwalk butterfly! I knew her parents were loaded, but in addition they must have won Euromillions more than once to pay for all her plastic surgery and other makeovers! Maebelle the uber-famous model, eh? Talk about adding grist to an almost forgotten mill!"

THE IVY CHELSEA GARDEN - SAME TIME - SAME DAY

"Lovely to see you, Clive," cooed Maebelle on Clive being shown to the table.

"Not nearly as lovely as me seeing *you*," came Clive's gallant reply as he leaned forward to give Maebelle a light kiss on her proffered cheek before sitting down. "An invitation to lunch at Chelsea's most popular to see and be seen restaurant by Maebelle, the glamorous, international fashion model is indeed an honour, hence me wearing my Sunday best, but with a hint of hospital instead of Gucci Guilty or Tom Ford!"

"Flatterer! Plus, it's a well-known fact Maebelle simply *revels* in flattery!" gushed Maebelle giving Clive and the rest of the gawking diners the benefit of a dazzling hundred watt "look at me, look at me" smile. The very fact that you've gone and forsaken your many decaying patients to join me for a mere luncheon is flattery indeed!" She pointed a rhinestone embellished fingernail toward her champagne flute. "I'm having a champers cocktail. Care to join me or would you prefer something else?"

"I'll stick to good old H20 thanks, Mae - or do I call you Maebelle? - seeing I am on duty this afternoon," replied Clive. Staring at Maebelle, whose interest seemed to be fixated on a nearby table where Julian Fellowes, writer of *Downton Abbey,* was busily chatting to an elegant couple, he added, a touch irritably. "Those decaying patients et cetera."

"Oh! Of course, duty before pleasure; to quote one of our gracious queens!" quipped Maebelle, summoning a nearby waiter. "And as you are *so* pressed for time, we'd better order. I always enjoy a simple salad - a girl, in my position, having always to watch her figure, ha ha! - but please order whatever tickles your tastebuds!"

Lunch ordered Maebelle sat back and said with a theatrical sigh. "How long is it since we last saw each other? Six months ago? A year?"

"If you *really* wish to know, we last met on the sixteenth of February, two years ago," chuckled Clive. "We had dinner at The Berkeley. You, me, and your manager. I remember it well because you and your manager had a blazing row over some assignment you weren't happy about. In fact, you stormed out, quickly followed by your manager, leaving me with a sodding great bill!"

"Sorry about that!" said Maebelle with a dazzling smile, the main beneficiaries being the next table as opposed to Clive. She gave a delicate toss of her artfully coiffed head before adding coquettishly. "I promise you today's little luncheon won't be a repeat performance as I can see no reason - as yet -ha ha! - to storm out!"

Halfway through their meal during which the conversation hadn't exactly flowed, Clive placed his table napkin on his side plate and said firmly. "C'mon, Mae. Out with it! Why did you *really* invite me, a dull doctor, to lunch when you literally have London, Europe, the Far East and America at your feet!"

"Okay, Clive. I agree. Time to cut the crap! Remember Lulu Mayhew, Leo Murrain and Lobie Maseko from school? *That's* why we're here as I still haven't forgotten how they used to annoy us and how their pathetic little plan to upset Carrots backfired. How they continued not only to irritate but positively *plague* us." Maebelle was about to give a snort but ended up flashing Clive a faux smile instead for the benefit of her admirers. "I know you'll probably think me childish, churlish, and hopelessly pathetic, but every time I look in a mirror, I remember Lulu Mayhew's scathing catcalls and comments such as zombie queen, zombie slag and more!" Her mascaraed eyes filling with genuine tears, Maebelle added softly. "It may surprise you that despite all my fame, fame doesn't allow me to forget the hurt and now zombie Mae Collison wants payback!"

Clive sat staring at Maebelle, his jaw dropping, a look of total disbelief on his handsome face.

"Better close your mouth, Clive dear. In case there's an errant fly hovering about!" quipped Maebelle.

"Forget any bloody hovering flies!" came the curt reply. "Lulu Mayhew may have referred to you zombie Mae but if she met you today, she'd no doubt refer to you as *mad* Mae! I don't know if you're being serious, but I have a strong suspicion you are." Clive gave a dismissive shrug. "Do as you wish, but I will have nothing to do with it. In fact, as for what you just said, I've already forgotten such utter balderdash!"

"Are you daring to tell me - plus insult me - by saying your answer is a resounding no," hissed Maebelle.

"You're damn right it's a no, Mae!" snapped Clive. "Jesus Christ! The world's already your oyster so why the *fuck* would you want to turn it into a bad one?"

"Typical cowardly Clive Cordell!" snapped Maebelle springing to her feet: her sudden movement sending their drinks crashing to the tiled floor. "Talk about bloody déjà vu!" Giving Clive a venomous glare she turned on her Louboutin heels and began snaking her way out between the busy tables. Pausing for a moment she glanced back over her shoulder and said with a tight smile. "By déjà vu, I mean once again the magnificent Maebelle departs leaving *you* to pay the bill! However, the magnificent Maebelle can assure you there will *not* be a third time!"

Giving the nearby intrigued diners and apologetic smile and a "what can a guy do?" type of look, Clive then apologised to the concerned maître d' and the waiter clearing up the broken glass, water and champagne, and, with a snigger, asked for the bill.

Just as well I was on water and you only asked for a salad, thought Clive on noting the amount. Turning to the next table he said with a mischievous grin. "My apologies again for disturbing your lunch! But then, if you're a superstar who always expects to get their way and then she doesn't, she simply ups and walks away!"

"A beauty as well as a beast! Haw-haw!" brayed the young man at the next table.

"Oh, Bobby! You are *such* a one!" tittered his young female companion. Pouting prettily and fluttering her eyelashes at a bemused Clive, she said squeakily. "Isn't he a one?"

Depends on what sort of a one you're referring to, thought Clive with an inward snigger. *And if it's the one whose elevator never made the top floor, then I'd say bull's-eye!*

"Please tell me I'm not wrong when I say wasn't that Maebelle the fashion model who just left?" trilled the young woman; eyes wide.

"'Twas indeed," replied Clive. He added with a sardonic chuckle. "She never waits for tomorrow but always leaves today!" His answer resulting in puzzled looks from Bobby and this lady friend before vigorously attacking their plates of cooling pasta.

In the taxi on his way back to the hospital, Clive made a quick phone call. "Kathy, it's me. You free for a drink later, say Brinkley's, Hollywood Road, around sixish? You are? Fabulous!" He gave a chuckle. "You probably won't believe it when I tell you I'm on my back to the hospital having been invited to a sort of lunch by the dreaded Mae Collison today!"

"You mean former doctors and nurses Mae Collison now Maebelle, the superstar fashion model?" replied Kathy Carr with a gasp.

"The very one!" chortled Clive. "And when I tell you *why* I was invited, no, make that *summonsed* to lunch, you'll understand why I'll wait until we meet to give you all the grisly details as I you're your reaction would probably lead to all the flowers in your shop losing their petals!"

"I can hardly wait!" laughed Kathy. "And yes, you're right, it wouldn't be right for me to cause the loss of one petal should *I* lose *my* petal! Or do I mean mettle?"

"Ouch!" oohed Clive followed by a cheerful. "See you at Brinkley's."

BRINKLEY'S - HOLLYWOOD ROAD - CHELSEA

"She said *what?*"

"She wants payback!"

"In between travelling the world, staring smugly from endless magazine covers and having every Tom, little Dick, big Dick and Harry salivating over her she still has a bee in her bonnet about Lulu Mayhew?"

"Not only Lulu, but the rest of her little entourage," snorted Clive.

Taking a hearty swallow of wine Kathy said matter-of-factly. "All I can say is Mae Collison - since day one - has always been a firm supporter of *Katherine Carr Flowers,* suggesting we supply any floral arrangements for a show whenever possible. In fact, the complete antithesis to what you've just told me. The Mae Collison *you've* just described sounds like a completely different person. A person *I'd* describe as mad; stark raving mad." She paused to take a sip of wine before saying mischievously. "Have you had a chance to tell Lulu about Maebelle-cum-Elizabeth Bathory's wish-cum-threat-cum-fantasy?"

"No. Since my return from my so-called freebie luncheon I've been rushed off my feet. But what's to stop us ringing her now?"

"Do you have her number?" said Kathy in a surprised voice. "Not that I have any wish to become involved. A sure-fire case of biting the hand that feeds you et cetera, et cetera!"

"Not only do I have this century's answer to Agatha Christie's telephone number, I also am the proud owner of two signed copies of her bestsellers one and two! Here, let's see if she answers."

"Lulu?" said Clive on hearing a crisp "Lulu Mayhew. As I don't recognise the number calling, who is this and, more importantly, how did you get this very private number?"

"Er . . . Lu . . . Lulu . . ." stammered Clive. "It's . . . er . . . Clive Cordell, *Dr* Clive Cordell."

"Clive Cordell? This *is* a surprise," crooned Lulu. "May I ask you again how you got this very private number?"

"You gave it to me a year or two back when we bumped into each other at The Chelsea Flower Show. We swapped cards and said we'd be in touch, but, as we're both busy . . ."

"Of course, The Chelsea Flower Show! You were there with Kate . . . Kristy?"

"Kathy Carr. You *must* remember Kathy Carr?"

"Kathy Carr? Of course! Now known as Miss Flower Power," crooned Lulu. "How could one possibly forget such a bloom despite all the other competitive blooms! Do you ever see her?"

"See her? In fact, I'm looking at her as we speak!"

"Oh!" said Lulu somewhat taken aback. She added in a no-nonsense voice. "I can't quite believe looking at Miss Flower Power has led to you ringing me. If so, pray tell, or else please terminate this call as I'm in the middle of a chapter!"

"I can't wait to read your next book!" enthused Clive, ignoring Lulu's cryptic response. "Is it another chiller thriller?"

"Could be, Clive. Could be," muttered Lulu. "Should I ever be allowed to finish it!"

"Oops! Sorry, Lulu, I didn't wish to disturb you, but the main reason for this out of the blue telephone call . . . I had lunch - or what was supposed to be lunch - with none other than Mae Collison today."

"You mean zombie Mae Collison who now parades along the world's catwalks in her new role as Mae - pure hell - Belle, fashion model extraordinaire?"

"You got it in one!" laughed Clive. Clearing his throat, he said sonorously. "However, let me explain my reason for calling." Eyeing Kathy, Clive gave a quick recap of the conversation between him and Mae.

"And zombie Mae is still harping on about *that*?" said Lulu in disbelief once Clive had finished. "Good God! I'm sure you - like myself - and the others have never given it another thought."

"Mae has not only given it another thought, Lulu. Instead of it being a mere fantasy thought, it looks to me as it's now become a sicko festering thought!"

"Ha! Long may Madam Zombie and her thoughts fester!" chortled Lulu. "Look, Clive. I really must go. Tell you what, Leo and Lobie are here, at Godfrey Street - the address is on the card - for drinks and dinner this evening so, if you're free, why not join us? Bring Kathy is she feels she could cope with the likes of us!"

"That sound great, Lulu! Hold on a sec while l check with her."

Lulu sat, fingers tapping her desk, while Clive had a word with Kathy before saying. "Lulu, Kathy - like me - would love to join the three of you. What time would you like us to be there? Eightish? Perfect! See you then! Oh, white or red? Never mind, we'll bring a bottle of each!"

A BIJOU TOWN HOUSE - GODFREY STREET - CHELSEA

"My, my," murmured Lulu staring at the silent landline. "Mae Collison wants to play dirty, does she? Very well then Miss *Zombie* dear, *two* can play that little game! And whilst Mae zombie Collison is festering, so is an idea for a novel. In fact, such is the suppurating thought, *Mae*-be be I'll set aside the novel I'm currently working on and jot down a few ideas for a wicked, chiller thriller centred around the decline and downfall of a vicious, vacuous, vindictive fashion model. A thriller inspired by Mr. G's searing *The Decline and fall of the Roman Empire* bearing a bestselling title such as *FROM CATWALK TO CATERWAULING* by Lulu Mayhew! Or something equally as eye-catching or appealing!"

TWO

GODFREY STREET - LATER

"Welcome. Kathy! Welcome Clive!" crooned Lulu, resplendent in a colourful Moroccan kaftan with equally colourful Moroccan slippers, on opening the front door. Eyes widening as a smiling Kathy handed her a large bunch of assorted tulips, she added in genuine delight. "Tulips! My favourite flowers! Goodness, Kathy Carr! You must be telepathic!"

"No, not a all, Lulu!" laughed Kathy. She added, a touch waspishly. "I simply remembered how the dreaded Mae kept saying you only liked tulips because they came from a country famous for its dykes!"

Bloody hell, Lulu! thought Clive. *You promised to behave!* Giving an overzealous chuckle, he added hastily. "Before you explode - nota bene I did *not* say 'burst a dyke. Ha ha! - and God only knows where Kathy's *colourful* quip came from . . ."

"Oh dear!" interrupted Kathy. "I didn't mean to be offensive. Now I come to think of it, she actually said - and I quote - 'famous for its *windmills'*, and how you envied Tamara Vane because she lived in a converted one. Something you yearned to do!" She added apologetically. "Do forgive me!"

"There's nothing to forgive, Kathy dear," replied Lulu with a tight smile. "We all make mistakes, slips of the tongue, or whatever you wish to call it."

Not that I will, when I have you dismembered in my so-called homage to Maebelle. My present novel now definitely on the back burner, thought Lulu maliciously as a nervous Clive pushed Kathy aside and handed Lulu a Waitrose bag.

"As I said, before you explode, please accept my long time, no see, little gift. Namely two bottles of Waitrose's best. One white. One red."

"Tulips *and* wine?" crowed Lulu taking hold of the proffered bag. "What more could a windmill-loving author wish for?"

"Maybe a bumbling Don Quixote and an equally bumbling Sancho Panza *sans* windmill," chuckled Leo as he and Lobie emerged from the shadows behind Kathy and Clive. "And like our long time, no see, colleague here, we, your 'all the time see' friends also arrive bearing gifts; namely *four* bottles of *Sainsbury's* best!"

"Goodness! And here was innocent, struggling writer *me* thinking I'd invited the four of you to a quiet, get together dinner, which now could have the makings of a *very* drunken orgy!"

"I'll drink to that!" guffawed Leo.

"And as I *have* invited you for dinner, why don't I actually invite you *in* as opposed to the five of us prattling away on my front doorstep!"

Duly seated, drinks in hand, on two Mondrian sofas, topped and tailed by four ubiquitous Barcelona cream leather chairs embracing a sheet of plate glass resting on two lacquer red coffins - wittily referred to by Lulu as "my coffins-cum-coffee table" - there was moment's silence before Lulu, eyeing each guest individually, said with a warm smile. "I'll say it now, so as to clear the Durance enhanced air, it really *is* good to see you, Kathy and Clive, after all this time. When I told Leo and Lobie about your call and you'd be joining us for dinner, they were delighted!" She gave a light laugh. "And, like me, uber-curious to hear more about zombie Mae-what-the-hell-belle and her wicked plans: if any!"

Staring fixedly as Clive, Lulu added mischievously. "So, Clive, the floor - along with is outrageously extravagant V'soske rug - is yours!"

"There's really nothing more to add to what I told you earlier," replied Clive matter-of-factly. "Mae - oops! *Maebelle* - seems to have more of a hornet instead of a bee in her fashionable bonnet about the way you - us – treated her all those years back at Halliday. Apparently, the sobriquet zombie Mae, really hit a nerve. A nerve which continues to pain her to this very day, *despite* all the expected painkillers such as money, fame, et cetera!"

"Good!" sniped Lulu. "And long may her so-called toothache, ache!" Taking a sip of wine, she added with a dismissive shrug. "I suggest we simply forget Madam Zombie. And should she even *attempt* something untoward .. . As the saying goes: 'it takes two to tussle!'"

"You mean *five* can tussle," chuckled Leo. "You, me, Lobie, Kathy and Clive."

"Make that *four*," cut in Kathy sharply. "To be quite honest, I have nothing against Mae - Maebelle -Collison; added to which she has been an avid supporter of *Katherine Carr Flowers* since day one. So, you can count me out. *One hundred percent* out! And if you're going to discuss the matter further, it's best I leave."

"Then Leo had better see you to the door," said Lulu with a tight smile. "As for you, Clive. Should you feel it only right to join Miss Flower Power in her *loyal* flower power bower; feel free to do so!"

"Jesus," muttered Leo.

"Jesus has nothing to do with it!" snapped Lulu. Staring stonily at Clive she said icily. "If *you* feel any sympathy toward the pain of Miss Flower Power abandoning ship, then I suggest you jump overboard as well!"

"I'll see Kathy out," muttered Leo rising to his feet. Looking at Clive he said with a growl. "Are you staying or leaving?"

"Oh, I'm definitely staying," replied Clive with a grin. "I wouldn't leave this ongoing scenario; not even for a heart transplant operation!"

"Careful what you say, Clive, dear," chortled Lulu as Kathy stalked out of the stylish sitting room with Leo hot on her Christian Louboutin heels.

"Now, whilst we wait for Leo to return, how about you play at being Jeeves, Clive, and giving me and Lobie a top-up," suggested Lulu. "Or" - as they most probably say in *your* neck of the woods, 'just what the doctor ordered!'"

About to come back with some equally corny comment, Clive was beaten to the chase by a tut-tutting Leo entering the sitting room.

"*Not* a happy bunny girl," said Leo with the semblance of a smile. "Not only did she refuse my gallant gesture that I walk her to King's Road to find a taxi, but said, in no uncertain terms, I should get back to the lynch mob a.s.a.p. as she would much prefer to call an Uber! Joking apart, I didn't realise how close Kathy had become to Mae. Did you know the meet on a regular basis for a girl's luncheon when Mae-cum-Maebelle is back in town?"

"Perhaps I'll send Miss Flower Power a complimentary pair of Ray-Bans to spare her baby-blues from all those nasty camera flashes!" tittered Lulu. "Leo, dear, another drink as Clive's kindly seeing to any refills?"

"Thank you, a top-up would be great," said Leo holding out his glass for Clive. He gave a self-conscious chuckle. "I don't know if it was the daggers' drawn tension created by you two ladies, Lulu dear, but I'm famished!"

"Good, as dinner should be ready within a few minutes. My *real* gem among my wannabe ones, the lovely Mrs Horsfall, who cooks for me on special occasions, has no doubt conjured up something utterly delish for us simple souls to devour. So, grin and bear it for a few more minutes and then, dear Leo, you'll be able to gorge yourself to your stomach's content!"

"I keep forgetting how you always talk in the same manner you write, Lulu," chuckled Leo. "While most people refer to your books as chiller thrillers, I see them more as a case - ha! - of a chiller thriller-cum-tongue twister!"

"Chiller thriller-cum-tongue twister?" crooned Lulu. "I like it! I like it! Aha! The bell! The bell!" she cried, cupping her ear. "In other words, Mrs Horsfall banging the buzzer which means dinner is served!"

During dinner, a delicious repast of asparagus wrapped in ham, rack of lamb served with broccoli and new potatoes, and sticky toffee pudding with ice cream, accompanied by the wine brought by the three men; conversation tended to be more general with the subject of Mae Collison left until it was time for coffee and liqueurs.

"If I were you, Lulu, I'd just forget it, her, or whatever," said Lobie a touch nonchalantly.

"I agree with Lobie," said Clive.

"While I'm not all that comfortable at assuming this could be a wishful case of pie in the sky, I tend to agree with you both," added Leo, always the diplomat. "Lulu?"

"Simple me? Oh, I see it more as a dark, black, thunder cloud in the sky as opposed to a mere, inoffensive, humble pie," said Lulu drily. "But as it appears to be game, set, and match with three determined musketeers against one and who am I, a mere damsel in potential distress, to disagree!"

Raising her glass of sambuca she said with a cry. "So, here's to forgetting zombie Mae and here's to all of *us*!"

"And here's to your new book, Lulu," said Leo with a wide smile. "Are we allowed to know the title, or is that a secret?"

"The title? Oh, it's no secret. However, due to *very* recent events - I'd make finger quotes, but I don't wish to spill my sambuca - the original title has taken on a completely *new* persona. So, gentlemen, be prepared, be *very* prepared, for the arrival of FROM CATWALK TO CATERWAULING later this year."

Lulu gave a light-hearted laugh. "Should you wish to know anything else, don't ask, as my sculpted, carmine lips are sealed until publication day!"

*

Having bade the somewhat inebriated newly dubbed three musketeers a cheerful goodnight, Lulu went downstairs to her basement study, turned on the lights and booted up her computer. She then poured herself another sambuca before sitting at her desk.

"*This*," she murmured as she typed in the magic word 'Prologue', "this is going to be better than good. It's going to be stupendously, breath-takingly, Oscar-winningly, marvellously, bloody fuckingly *brilliant!*"

Lulu began to type. *Medora Maddox's parents, Gideon and Eleanora (a former fashion model and catwalk queen) were rich. Hideously, obscenely, Midas-equivalently rich. So much so, that when the totally unexpected Medora arrived, her christening saw the small, village church selected for the occasion, presented with a new, gold-plated font, while the baby's christening robes were embroidered with gold thread and decorated with diamonds, pearls and pink sapphires, along with a similarly bejewelled christening spoon.*

Adding further dazzlement to the already present dazzlement was proud mother Eleanora who surely outdid the gold-painted Shirley Eaton of Goldfinger fame by appearing in a gold, diaphanous, shift dress which did nothing to hide the diamond, pearl and pink sapphire-encrusted bikini bottom and top, and similarly decorated, high-heeled fuck-me pumps. The pièce de resistance being Eleanora's hat; a shimmering, diamond, pearl and oink sapphire-encrusted miniature replica of The Shard, London's tallest building.

*

"Good morning, Clive!" said Leo cheerily. "Not too early for you, am I?"

"Early? No, not at all," yawned Clive. "I'm on a late shift tonight so was having a bit of a lie-in." There was a moment's silence before he said softly. "Good to see you last night, Leo, after what? Three of four years? Hopefully, unlike mine, your head isn't *too* painful . . . a reminder of those endless sambuca we so recklessly downed!"

"No, I'm fine," chuckled Leo. "No accusatory head at all!" There was another pause before he said a touch tentatively. "Any chance of meeting of us meeting for a drink - maybe lunch - sometime next week?"

"I'll have to check my work schedule," said Clive, followed by a further yawn. "Lunch is usually a no-go - seeing Mae yesterday was an exception - and as for a drink, why not?" He gave a chuckle. "As long as I clear it with Andy."

"Andy?"

"Andy McCulloch, my husband."

This time the following silence was what some writers described as "thunderous".

"Er . . . did you just say *your* husband?" Leo finally managed to say.

"Yes, my husband. We've been married for almost three years."

Again, there was a notable silence before Clive said with a chuckle. "Jesus Christ, Leo. Surely you must have known, guessed or whatever, I was gay?" He gave another chuckle. "In fact, if the truth be known, I've fancied you *and* Lobie since junior school!"

"No, Clive," replied Leo with a smile in his voice, "I can honestly say I had no idea!" He gave a chuckle. "Like everyone else, I thought you and Lizzie Masterson had a thing for each other! Whatever happened to *her*?"

"Lizzie Masterson?"

"Yes, your supposed childhood amorata!"

"She emigrated to Sydney, Australia, where she works with a team of much-in-demand architects. We talk from time to time." Clive gave a chuckle. "*Despite* me referring to her as Australia's very own Frank Lloyd-*Blight*!"

"So," said Leo, cutting to the chase. "Er . . . when do I meet your . . . er . . . husband? Er . . . Andy . . ."

"His name's Andy, Andy McCulloch, Leo, and why not meet *him* when *we* meet next week." Clive gave a chuckle. "That's if I can drag him away from his computer, of course."

"Er . . . what does Andy do, workwise?"

"Do? He's a writer, rather like Lulu. He writes under the pen name of Robert Apps."

"Robert Apps? Author of *Et Tutu Brute?*!" exclaimed Leo, "He's one of my favourite authors! Yes, *do* let's meet next week as it would be great to see *you* again and great to meet Mr. McCulloch-cum-Robert Apps!"

"Whatever you do, do-no-tell Lulu!" laughed Clive.

"Don't tell Lulu?"

"She'd be livid to hear you were in collusion with a rival! Remember, Lulu Mayhew has only written *two* bestsellers, whereas Andy aka Robert Apps - and a decade or two older than Lulu! - has had at least thirty: several of which have gone on to become popular television series or films."

"My lips are sealed," chuckled Leo. "The thought of Lulu finding out I was meeting a rival being a thought to terrifying to even contemplate! Added to which, I've suddenly developed an acute case of the shivers!"

AN ELEGANT DUPLEX APARTMENT OVERLOOKING EATON SQUARE - BELGRAVIA

"Thinking back to my farce of a luncheon yesterday isn't it depressing how former friends, like candles, simply flicker out and, in some cases, end up totally wick-less!" snickered Mae (referred to Maebelle from now onward) helping herself to a large vodka tonic from the bar wittily created from a former red, telephone box (dubbed the interior decorators' deliberate mistake by Dee-Dee).

"Good Hades! Which latest faux friend has decided to flicker out now?" pouted David - Dee-Dee Devereaux (real name David Donaldson), Maebelle's uber-camp Man Friday, hand holder, soothsayer, secretary and the temperamental super model's loyal, much abused, doting companion.

"Clive Cordell," hissed Maebelle.

"Dr Cunnilingus Cordell?" tittered Dee-Dee, "also known as Dr Death due to those who *have* had the misfortune to experience *the ultimate intimacy* with the man claimed that, during the severely handicapped *small-legged* race, they were quite convinced they were being *bored* to death! Pun, deliberate! Ha ha!"

"Please, *please* don't tell me that *you've* stained sheets with the dismal doctor!" crooned Mae.

"Do I *look* like a corpse?" trilled Dee-Dee. "No, Mae dear. I *have* not been to bed with the deadly doctor; but if it came - ha - to his husband, that would have been a resounding yes, please!"

"Now you've really tickled this super model's frivolous fancy! So, explain - *nancy!*" yodelled Maebelle. "Explain this husband, this magnificent ode to manhood, *despite* him being married to a cowardly cadaver?"

"Hubby is one Andrew McCulloch whose alter ego is - wait for it! - none other than bestselling author Robert Apps; also responsible for that *wunderbar* TV series, *Jan Unleashed!*"

"Yet he's *married* to Dr Death-cum-Dr Dull-cum-Dr No-Can-Do?" snorted Maebelle. "Obviously he must have a gigantic willy in order to keep Mr. Best Seller Andrew-stroke-Robert agog!"

Eyeing Dee-Dee (a plump, blonde version of a young Donny Osmond) over the rim of her glass, Maebelle said in a "don't you *dare* contradict me" voice. "So, let's invite them to dinner. I'm sure, after his fading flower act yesterday, the dear doctor must be anxious to make amends, so amends it shall be." Holding out her glass for a refill, Maebelle added glibly. "First thing tomorrow you will emerge from your usual Toot Braunstein mode . . ."

"I am not the *least* bit like Toot Braunstein!" squawked Dee-Dee; his plump frame, clad in an acid green onesie, bridling with indignation. "Justin Bieber, yes! But Toot Braunstein? *Never!*" (Toot Braunstein being the suicidal, borderline personality in the American animated adult reality show, *Drawn Together.*)

"Emerge from your usual Toot Braunstein mode," repeated Maebelle, regardless, "and morph into your Mr. Charm-cum-smarm persona and call the now dear doctor as opposed to the deadly one, and, on my gracious behalf, invite them both to dinner here at Eaton Square."

"Goodness! What a conundrum!" camped Dee-Dee. "I mean, what does a mere fuck-totum wear as I'm sure I'll look quite dreadful in a shroud!"

"It's ringing!" snapped Maebelle.

"What?"

"Mr. Alexander Bell's irritating little bequeathment! It's ringing! So, don't just sit there, *Toot,* dear. Answer the bloody thing!"

Giving Maebelle a venomous look, Dee-Dee picked up the phone. "Dee-Dee Devereaux, liquorice allsorts to Maebelle, fashion model extraordinaire, speaking. How may I assist you?" Covering the mouthpiece, he said in a stage whisper. "'Tis one of the Valkyries. Miss Katherine Carr, no less!"

"She's brave," sniped Maebelle. "Gimme!"

Snatching the phone from Dee-Dee still visibly smouldering from the Toot Braunstein comparison, Maebelle said breezily. "Katherine dear, what a pleasant, mid-morning interruption!" She gave a madcap laugh. "Sorry, no flower orders or floral tributes required today, but, apart from such trivial news, how may *Mae* - ha ha - help you?"

"It's about Lulu Mayhew and her lot," whispered Kathy in reply. "Are you alone?"

"No. I have the lovely chaotic, angst-ridden Dee-Dee-Toot-Devereaux sitting glowering at me." Maebelle gave a light laugh. "But, as you well know, *my casa* is Dee-Dee's *casa* so feel free to speak. You said something about Lulu Mayhew and her lot. Can you therefore explain your airy-fairy comment?"

"I didn't stay to hear what was actually said," replied Kathy in a conspiratorial whisper, "but, as a friend I thought I'd better let you know."

"Know *what*, Katherine?" snapped Maebelle.

"Yesterday evening, after his lunch with you, Clive Cordell, couldn't wait to tell Lulu Mayhew, Lobie Maseko and Leo Murrain - no holds barred - what you said to him at lunch."

"Oh? The devious doctor did, did he?" said Maebelle with an Eartha Kit purr. "Thank you for letting me know, Katherine, dear." There was a brief pause before she continued. "I know you make pretty Christmas wreaths along with all sorts of other, necessary wreaths, but do me a favour, Katherine, dear. Make one out of poison ivy with a touch of hogweed, then have one of your doting minions discreetly affix it to the front door of Lulu Mayhew's tribute to *Casa Vogue* in Godforsaken Street, or whatever it's called. A nasty hint of nastier things to come."

"Take it as done, Maebelle," replied Katherine with a giggle. "Anything else?"

"Apart from a hydrogen letter bomb to my manager, no, nothing else," sniped Maebelle. "So, no more chit chat as you know what has to be done. Oh! One last thing afore ye go! May I suggest *Katherine Carr Flowers* gets together a substantial offering of kindling and firewood."

"Kindling and firewood?" repeated Kathy.

"Yes, dear. Kindling and firewood. Enough, say, for four funeral pyres."

Smiling to herself at the shocked silence from Kathy's end, Maebelle gave a chuckle. "Joke, Katherine dear! A joke! However, joking apart, take it from me that when I *do* decide what to do with Madam Lulu and her three lapdogs, a funeral pyre would have been seen as a blessing! Oh! Darling Dee-Dee's making faces which means there's another call for busy bee me! Thank *you* for your illuminating call, Katherine dear. Maybe we'll speak again later. Byee!"

"There's no other call," pouted Dee-Dee.

"I *know,* Dee-Dee, dear. It's simply because I couldn't think of anything else to say to Madam Carr!"

"Maebelle at a loss for vitriol? That's a first," snickered Dee-Dee. "What next? No more scorpions instead of pennies in various charity boxes? However, for a giddy moment, it appears as if *I* am back to my correct persona!"

"Tut-tut, Dee-Dee - *see*, your maddening Maebelle got it right! Now, instead of sitting there with what is certainly *not* a pretty pout, why don't you open a bottle of The Widow and then you and I, suitably 'widowed', sashay our way to lunch somewhere like The Ivy Chelsea Garden where we can be seen without being obscene!"

"Wunderbar!" cried Dee-Dee clapping hands. "Good thing I won't be wearing a shroud, but then, maybe see-through gauze-drawers with flashing falsies and flashing high-heels aren't allowed. Oh, dear, dear and damn!"

Staring at Dee-Dee, Maebelle said deadpan. "Toot, dear. Maebelle does not approve of competition; however trite!"

"Okay! Okay! No flashing falsies then!" crowed Dee-Dee!"

"You're on! Macho man!" crooned Mabelle giving him a high five.

GODFREY STREET

"Typical," muttered Maddy Thompson, Lulu's live-in secretary about to close the front door. "Some cranky, do-gooder who obviously doesn't approve of Lulu Mayhew's books. I *told* Lulu that telling some nosy journalist how much she enjoyed shopping in nearby Chelsea Green was a mistake. All someone needed to do was ask one of the shopkeepers if they knew her whereabouts; hence this charmer!"

Reaching for the ugly, thorny wreath that must have been attached to the front door overnight, she ripped the offensive object plus adhesive tape from off the door. Walking briskly toward King's Road before heading for Smith Street and on to the Embankment for her daily jog, Maddy casually drooped the wreath in a nearby litter bin.

"What the eye doesn't see; et cetera, et cetera," she murmured. "And something like that is something Lulu doesn't need to know."

THREE

THE IVY CHELSEA GARDEN

"Hi!" mouthed Maebelle, twiddling her fingers at a table of four elegant women as she and Dee-Dee were escorted past by the beaming maître d' to their table in the garden area of the popular restaurant.

"Who's the blonde, when she's *not* at home?" hissed Dee-Dee in an aside while eyeing the four women Maebelle had deigned to acknowledge.

"Liz Brewer, a top social figurine," hissed Maebelle. "As for the other three, well-heeled hangers on, no doubt!"

Giving the maître d' a gracious smile accompanied by a purred "thank you and we'd like a bottle of Dom Perignon. please", Maebelle sat herself elegantly on the chair pulled out in readiness by a handsome young waiter standing nearby: a worshipful expression on his face,

"Oh, no!" she groaned on glancing across the busy room. "Talk about a sight too painful to even contemplate>"

"Who? What? Where?" pouted Dee-Dee glancing hither and thither.

"Over there! Two tables away from La Brewer! It's the dreadful Lulu Mayhew and the even more dreadful Lobie Maseko, no less!" She added maliciously. "I thought dogs - especially bitches - weren't allowed?"

"Ignore them. Maebelle," said Dee-Dee diplomatically. "Remember, *you're* the star of the show and here, to prove it, here cometh the first of your many admirers to ask for your autograph, no doubt!"

"Miss . . . er . . .Miss . . . Miss Maebelle," stammered the blushing young man, a dead-ringer for Freddie Highmore, famous for this portrayal of young Norman Bates in the TV series *Bates Motel.*

"May I . . . *may* I?" he repeated with a nervous giggle. "Er . . . may I, please. Miss Maebelle, have your autograph?" He nodded toward a distant table where a pretty, young girl sat staring wide-eyed at her boyfriend and

Maebelle as if transfixed. "Er . . . and could you please sign it to Posy and Peter!"

"Posy and Peter?" cooed Maebelle at her most gracious. "Why, of *course*, Peter." Giving Dee-Dee a sly wink, she added playfully. "Are you and your pretty Posy lunching alone?"

"Er . . . yes, Miss Maebelle, we are," gulped Peter (immediately dubbed Pete the Treat by the mentally salivating Dee-Dee). "It's our first time here as we could never afford it before!"

"Well then, Peter," purred Maebelle. "Why don't you and Posy join Mr. Devereaux - Dee-Dee - and me for lunch. My treat of course."

"Join you for lunch, Miss Maebelle?" gasped Peter, followed by a disbelieving. "Really?"

"Yes, really, Peter. So, be a good swain and ask pretty Posy is she would care to join us and if she says yes, please ask one of the waiters to bring over another two chairs.

"Will do. Miss Maebelle! Will do!" gushed Peter. "Golly gee willikers! Nobody, but *nobody*, is going to believe this when I tell them!"

"Oh, they will, Peter; they will," crooned Maebelle.

Watching as Peter scurried back to his table to inform Posy of their impromptu invitation by the legendary Maebelle, Maebelle in turn said briskly to delighted Dee-Dee. "Ring you know who and make sure our usual photographer's ready and waiting outside for another 'Maebelle and two surprised fans' exclusive."

"On it already," pouted Dee-Dee reaching for his mobile. "And, if you hadn't noticed, Lulu and her shady - ha! - sidekick have just left. Not in a snit due to our lauded arrival - they were already on coffees and a liqueur when we glided past - but simply because Lulu Mayhew - author of two tacky novels - knows when to slink out seeing she can't hold a dildo to glamorous you!"

"Welcome Posy! Welcome back Peter!" crooned Maebelle as the nervously smiling couple reached the table. "As introductions appear to have been well and truly made, please take a seat. Dee-Dee and I are gulping our usual bubbly. Do join us or else order whatever libation you'd prefer."

"I'd love a glass of champagne, thank you, Miss Maebelle," said Posy Webber, a chirpy Sandra Dee lookalike, in a quavering voice, her eyelashes fluttering.

"Champers for me too, please, Miss Mabelle! Lovely jubbly! What?" trumpeted Peter making sure the intrigued neighbouring tables could hear.

"As long as it doesn't lead to any double, double toil and trouble later," replied Maebelle with a smile that would have soured milk.

A bored Maebelle and a turnabout Dee-Dee (he'd rapidly come to the conclusion Peter was more a Pete the Prick than a Pete the Treat, after his opening Lord Haw Haw performance and a tirade of Christmas cracker jokes), having managed to endure Peter's ceaseless, irritating prattle over a salad and a main course, saw matters brought matters to a head by Maebelle's sudden: "Oh, my *God*! Dee-Dee! We've been so overwhelmed by our fun, new friends that we've totally forgotten about collecting poor Xiomara from the vet!"

"Oh, my God! Xiomara!" cried Dee-Dee. his hands fluttering to his face in a parody of Edvard Munch's *The Scream.* "Poor Xiomara! And we both know how she hates Mr. Vet doing all those nasty, personal things to her!"

"*Do* forgive us!" purred Maebelle rising to her Jimmy Choo heels. "Order whatever your stomachs' desire as they'll simply put it on my bill. Divine meeting you both. Now, come along Dee-Dee! We don't wish to find the veterinary surgery awash with you know what simply because we were *so* enjoying our lunch with Posy and Peter, time simply stood still!"

"Isn't she *fabulous*?" sighed Peter as he watched Maebelle and Dee-Dee leave.

"No, she's not!" sniped Posy. "She's a stuck-up, sanctimonious, two-faced bitch and as for that poisoned, bleached, overweight little queen . . . Surely, at his or her age and stage" - she made a couple of finger quotes - "he or she should know one gently *applies* make-up. Not plaster it on with a trowel!"

Taking a gulp of champagne, she added acidly. "As for you, Peter Proudfoot, you were so bloody gobsmacked I wouldn't be the least surprised if you've come in your obviously stretched skants!"

Peter sat staring at Posy as if she'd suddenly grown two heads. "Posy!" he finally managed to gasp. "I've never heard you speak like that before! Never, ever! What you've just said was *horrible*!"

"As was having to sit here and watch those two patronise us," hissed Posy. "And as for them having to collect some imaginary Xiomara animal from some equally imaginary vet? Utter bullshit!"

Glaring at a visibly shrinking Peter, Posy bossily summoned a nearby waiter. "I'd like a large Drambuie please and another helping of that delicious chocolate bombe." Daring Peter to interrupt, she added smugly. "As this is going on Miss Maebelle's bill, make that *two* large Drambuies. As for my companion, he'll settle for a glass of Perrier seeing he has an imaginary appointment with an imaginary psychiatrist this afternoon."

"Trouble in paradise?" murmured a smiling diner giving his luncheon companion a mischievous wink as a swaying Posy and a grim-faced Peter finally left.

"Unmitigated *disaster* in paradise, more like it," said his female companion with a tinkly laugh. "Not only was Mr. Poor Sod's lady friend green with envy at his obvious infatuation with the stunning Maebelle she must have downed enough Drambuies to rival the likes of a Lake Como!"

GODFREY STREET

Waving as the taxi carrying Lobie sped away - Lobie having insisted on dropping her off at the before returning to the office - Lulu entered the house and immediately went downstairs to her study where she poured herself a large G and T before settling down in front of the computer.

"Oh, Miss Zombie Mae," she muttered as her fingers began to fly furiously over the keyboard. "You never fail to inspire me in uber-vileness when we have the gross misfortune of suddenly crossing paths. Seeing you desecrating my favourite restaurant with those two fawningcators literally drooling at your designer label shod feet whilst your ghastly shadow of a Billy Bunter in drag sat there stuffing his face as if there was no tomorrow, has set this bestselling author into immediate overdrive! You may think you're tough when the going gets rough Miss Zombie Mae, but you ain't seen nuthin' yet! So, let's see what this bestselling author's poison pen comes up with next thanks to you and your flouncy friend!"

AN ELEGANT DUPLEX APARTMENT OVERLOOKING EATON SQUARE - BELGRAVIA

"Such attractive premises for a veterinary surgery," quipped Maebelle as she and Dee-Dee sat sipping a restorative Courvoisier after what Maebelle had described as an ordeal "tantamount to pulling teeth".

"Such a pity Peter of such potential should end up being a Peter capable of boring for Britain," snickered Dee-Dee. "As for Miss Posy Prim-Prim! Talk about a vacuous vagina!"

"Did my baby blues do me wrong or did I actually see potential Peter surreptitiously slip you his card or was that wishful thinking?"

"Yes, he did," replied Dee-Dee with a puzzled look *What gives with the wishful thinking?* he thought. *But knowing Maebelle, always be prepared for the unexpected!* "Please don't' tell me that in some sicko way you have an even more sicko desire to rub noses with those two Ps who should never been allowed to leave the pod!"

"No, not her! Him!" Maebelle, slipping into Mata Hari mode, added furtively. "Didn't he, amidst all his endless babble, mention how his dozy Posy referred to him as her reincarnated Robin Hood when it came to his favourite pastime; archery?"

"And as archery involves bow and arrows - even poisoned arrows!" squealed Dee-Dee, wriggling with fiendish glee. "This could mean that instead of the former Pete the Treat retaining his latest modus operandi as Pete the Obsolete, he could, perhaps, prove himself useful after all!"

"Bull's-eye!" camped Maebelle. "Let's give Pete the potential *hood* - geddit? Let's give him - that is *you* give him - a call in a day or two and invite him to dinner: but him alone. You simply say Posy made it quite plain she was not amused by his interest in seductive, irresistible me, and - being a sensitive soul - I have no wish to upset her! Therefore, far better to be safe than sorry!"

"Good God, Maebelle! You're not seriously planning on *seducing* the poor hoodwinked Peter?" cried Dee-Dee, clapping hands,

"If it achieves what *we* plan to achieve, why not? If I can grin and *bed* it with the likes of Harold Hasty, my hideous, hirsute, pathetically hung agent, seducing posturing Peter with his little bow and hopefully not so little arrow should be a doddle!" Maebelle gave a giggle. "Maybe you could join in. After all, we both bedded that Neanderthal carpet layer who couldn't stop panting 'you're the best bit of carpet I've ever laid! You're the best bit of carpet I've ever fucking laid'!"

"Ah, yes. The Neanderthal you dubbed 'superbly tufted'!"

"And *you,* my dear, dubbed 'a dream in my seam'!" chortled Maebelle. "Dear Dee-Dee, we *do* have fun, don't we? However, on a more sober note, what I have in mind for Peter-Robin-Hood will be more than fun. It'll be - to use one of your favourite words - *wunderbar*! And while I think of it, why not invite Matthew Marsden who apparently has it fixed in his faux bald pate that he looks like the actor Corey Stoll so now only answers to Corey Marsden. Which means when you do call him at his office..."

"Ask for Matthew Marsden!" cried Dee-Dee joining in.

"If anyone has an axe to grind with Lulu Mayhew, no one could be more *grinding* than Lulu Mayhew!"

DICKENSON AND MARSDEN - ESTATE AGENTS

"Call for you, Corey," announced Clarissa Kemp (referred to behind her back as Clarissa Unkempt) on Corey answering. "A Mr. Dee-Dee Devouring asking for *Matthew* Marsden so I soon him right!" She gave a giggle. "And although he sounds more like a Mr. Donald Duck, shall I put him through?"

"Devouring? Devouring?" muttered Corey/Matthew. "The name doesn't sound at all familiar. Tell him I'm on a call to the States but do *not* say a call to San Fag Crisco as *I* sometimes say when trying to get rid of a tiresome caller whose predilections I actually know about! Ask him what sort of property he's after before I call him back!"

"Will do!" giggled Clarissa, a strapping, blonde (assisted) Brunhilde lookalike desperately in lust with Corey.

"Me again!" trilled Clarissa saying the obvious. "Mr. Donald Duck is not at all interested in a property. He wished to speak to you about a Mae Collison!"

"Mae Collison now known as Maebelle?" quizzed Corey.

"You mean as in fashion icon Maebelle?" gasped Clarissa.

"The very one," chuckled Corey. "She and I go way back! I tell you, Clarissa, this could be something too good to miss! I take it Mr. Quack left a number?"

"Mr. Quack?" replied Clarissa sounding puzzled. "I'm talking about a Mr. Donaldson. I never mentioned a Mr. Quack."

"Jesus Christ, Clarissa! You just referred to Mr. Devouring as Mr. Donald Duck, and in my book Donald Duck equals a quack!"

There was a brief silence before Clarissa said with a squeal. "Mr. Donald Duck leading to Mr. Quack? I get it! Oh, Corey, you can be *such* a tease! Give me a couple of seconds so that I can call Mr. Donald Quack back!"

"Bloody hell," murmured Corey as he sat waiting to speak to Dee-Dee. "Mae Collison after all this time. What the fuck does she want to talk to me about? It can't be a property as I know she recently bought that extravaganza overlooking Eaton Square through bloody Harold Hanna."

Leaning back in his Herman Miller executive chair, a hastily poured whisky soda close at hand, Corey sat, his mind doing cartwheels. It wasn't long before his face broke into a broad smile. "Could it have something to do with the old saying 'what goes around comes around' and possibly be about the much-needed come-uppance of the dreaded Lulu Mayhew and her lot? If it *is* about that constipated, scribbling cunt and her cuntish cronies, then Mae - Maebelle - you can most definitely count me in!"

He was about to take a mouthful of whisky when the phone rang, "Mr. Devouring," crooned Corey on promptly answering. "Sorry about earlier, but I was on a call to the States!"

"It's not Mr. Devouring," said Clarissa in a stage whisper. "It's Maebelle herself. Shall I put her through?"

"No, put her in the fucking waste bin," snapped Corey. His Humpty Dumpty face paling at the thought of Clarissa taking him literally, he cried in a panic-stricken voice. "Jesus! I didn't mean that! Yes! Put her through!"

"Corey dear! Or may I - a mere world-famous fashion model - be allowed to call you Carrots as in days gone by?" cooed Maebelle.

Cow! thought Corey glaring at the phone in his hand. "Mae!" he crooned. "*What* a surprise. I'd much prefer you to call me Corey or, at a push, Matthew, but not Carrots. Added to which there isn't a hint of a hair on my shining pate. As they say, grass doesn't grow on a busy street! Ha ha!"

Surely you mean grass doesn't grow out of your half-witted arse, thought Maebelle. "Corey it shall be," she crooned "So, let's begin again. Does the name Lulu Mayhew ring any distant clangers?"

"Distant clangers?" exclaimed Corey. "She'd make *any* clang sound a mere whisper!" He added craftily. "Why? What's Madam Bestselling Author of Trash up to now?"

"It's not what she's up to, Corey dear, it's what she *did* and please don't dare tell me - like someone else we both know - what's done is done!"

"Meaning?"

"To quote a regularly abused saying; *revenge is truly a dish best served cold*!"

"Hear, hear," murmured Corey,

"Delighted to find we're both still on the same wavelength, Carrots - oops! Corey!" tittered Maebelle. "So, another question. Knowing your former penchant as a super sneak, how about joining us for dinner this evening (said as a statement and not a question). I'll get Dee-Dee Devereaux, my mini knight in tainted armour to email you the address. There may be a fourth person joining us but, if not, then, like Macbeth's charming trio, you, I and Dee-Dee can put our scheming topknots together and revel in matters untoward!"

"I like it! I like it!" chortled Corey.

"Good. We'll see you around eight, then. Love and hisses, Carrots dear - oops! Corey!" Maebelle hung up.

"Clarissa!" yodelled Corey not bothering to use the in-house phone. "Drop almost everything as I need you to make an urgent phone call."

"Dinner with Maebelle? Oh my," gushed Clarissa as she came waddling into Corey's office.

"Those who listen into other people's conversations could be in for a nasty surprise," said Corey prissily. "As you now know I'm dining with Maebelle and friends this evening, will you please call Short and Curly . . . er . . . Mr. Towler . . . and say unfortunately I cannot manage dinner this evening because of blah, blah, blah! You have his number."

"Yes, Mr. Corey," simpered Clarissa. "I take it Mr. Short and Curly Towler can only be the person you have listed as Mr. Short and Curly *Butt Plug* Towler on your computer?"

"How very receptive of *you*, Clarissa, so, please give him a call," said Corey, doing his best to control a snort.

*

Maebelle gave Dee-Dee a wink. "Bingo! Staring fixedly at the grinning little man she said contemplatively. "That kinky friend of yours, that Malcom Shovel? Malcom Duval? Are you still in filthy touches with him?"

"No, not at all," said Dee-Dee with a theatrical shudder. "Mr. Duval is one of those people who, after having the misfortune of doing it with, not once but stupidly twice, is best forgotten. Why?"

"I was about to ask you the same thing," tittered Maebelle. "Best forgotten? Sounds riveting! If you catch my dirty drift! In answer to *your* question, in case we need some sort of fallback should Peter and Carrots/Corey not wish to toe the Maebelle line." She gave a chortle. "*Now* I remember the dramatic Dee-Dee Malcom Shovel or Duval falling out! What was it you called him? Knightsbridge's answer to The Terminator?"

"Something like that," replied Dee-Dee dismissively.

"As Mother always says, 'sex is emotion in motion', so we'll let sleeping Shovels or Duvals lie," snickered Maebelle. Glancing at her diamond encrusted Cartier watch she said with a cry. "G and T time! See to a couple of mammoth ones, Dee-Dee dear, before we sit down and discuss tonight's plan of action." Giving Dee-Dee a wink as he headed for the telephone box bar she said with a trill. "Don't be at all surprised if Peter, in his new role, joins us for breakfast! Maybe even Corey! Tut-tut, dear! No need to make such a face! Stranger things *have* happened! As you well know I will be in New York for a couple of weeks as from Monday so I would like matters *embryonic* at least. For the moment it's just you and me with a willing accomplice or two pending. Everything crossed, our evil, conniving dinner will see our little irritant fittingly resolved!"

"One mammoth G and T for my gracious schemer," crowed Dee-Dee handing Mabelle a brimming crystal tumbler. "Twinkle, twinkle, super star! *What* a wicked wench you really are!"

"I'll drink to that!" crooned Maebelle. "To Lulu Mayhew, who can forget *The Ides of March* and think of Maebelle in yet another explosive role. The role of Maebelle-cum-Terminator as she most certainly *is* coming back!"

"Me too!" crowed Dee-Dee raising his tumbler. "To Maebelle-cum-Terminator as she most certainly *will* be back!"

"I strongly suggest you take another swallow before you hear what I'm about to say," added Maebelle with a tight smile. "Maybe *two* swallows! To quote Mother again, 'It's not the men in my life that count, it's the life in my men', and while you obviously will never forgive nor forget Malcom Shovel or Duval, give *me* his number and I'll give *him* a call if Corey and the preening Peter prove to be a no-go. To quote dear Mother again. 'Between two evils, I always pick the one I never tried before!'"

*

Making sure Dee-Dee had left on a series of errands and, as an extra precaution, waiting until Trini, the energetic Filipino housemaid was busily hoovering the corridor outside her small office, Maebelle tapped in the telephone number Dee-Dee had reluctantly given to her.

"Of *course*, I remember Duval's bloody number!" he had snapped. "Like Mary Queen of Scots and *Calais*, its forever *staked* through my heart!"

"Mr. Malcolm Duval?" Maebelle crooned making sure she said his correct name. On hearing a growled "Elucidate!" she said graciously. "Good morning, Mr. Duval. The name's Mae Collison. Mr. Donald Donaldson kindly gave me your number seeing you are - and I quote Mr. Donaldson - 'a man of many talents'."

"By *Mr.* Donaldson, I take it you can only mean poncy Dee-Dee shithead *Devereaux* Donaldson," came the sneered reply. Ignoring Maebelle's audible gasp, Malcom Duval added acidly. "If you're the Mae Collison he was always bragging about, then you must also be the Maebelle who prances about showing off what is laughingly described as the latest fashion."

"I am indeed Maebelle the fashion model, but only a very select few know me as the loving Mae Collison," simpered Maebelle.

"Well, as I'm not one of the very select few I'll call you Maebelle. So, what is it you want, *Maebelle*? And what does your reference to me as a man of many talents mean, exactly?"

"A man who can be guaranteed to make a problem go away but in the most discreet of circumstances. At a worthy price, of course."

"As I said earlier. Kindly elucidate. *Maebelle!*"

"I appreciate it's extremely short notice, but you wouldn't happen to be free for dinner this evening, by any chance?"

"And if by any chance I could be?"

"I have two other gentlemen coming along to discuss the annoying matter." Maebelle gave a carefree laugh. "Plus Mr. Dee-Donaldson whom I promise will have been suitably *deodorised* prior to your arrival!"

"Give me the address," grunted Duval, ignoring what Maebelle considered an apt, witty jibe.

"You have a pen?" cooed Maebelle.

"No, I write with a bloody fire extinguisher," sniped Duval.

"How very exhausting!" quipped Maebelle before giving the address.

"One last thing, *Maebelle*," grunted Duval. "As this sounds as if it could turn out to be a waste of my valuable time, on arrival I will need to be handed an envelope containing five hundred pounds cash. If I am not, then I leave!"

"I look forward to see you at eight, Mr. Duval," cooed Maebelle. "Needless to say, it won't be *me* answering the door, but Briggs, my butler." She gave a snigger. "You'll be pleased Briggs will not only relieve you of your coat but also hand you the requested envelope. Toodle-loo, Mr. Duval. The excitement, even if nothing else, mounts!"

*

"I can't believe bloody Malcom Duval will be joining us for dinner," grizzled Dee-Dee on being told the news.

"Aided and abetted by five hundred pounds in crisp readies plus, no doubt, the delicious thought of seeing you again, Dee-Dee dearest," crooned Maebelle, "*despite* Mr. Duval referring to you as Dee-Dee shithead *Devereaux* Donaldson. A subtle term of endearment, perhaps? However, being a superstar of slick repartee, I assured him you'd be suitably deodorised for the occasion."

"Very funny, Maebelle!" hissed Dee-Dee. Scowling at a smirking Maebelle, he said, as if speaking to himself. "I wonder what you'll think of Malc the Bulk?"

"Malc the Bulk?" echoed Maebelle. "Having whetted my voracious appetite; pray explain?"

"For bulk think the Incredible Hulk. For Malc, think of Swedish actors Ola Rapace and Alexander Skarsgård melded into one glorious Swedish meatball!" sniped Dee-Dee. "Added to which not only is Malcom Duval a devastatingly handsome heartbreaker; his spectacular pneumatic drill is also a winner." Dee-Dee gave a snigger, "Despite some of the drill heads used being uber-depraved in the way they're put to use! Need I say more?"

"No, but that doesn't mean I'm stopping you from dashing across to yon duplicitous telephone box and fixing us a large pitcher of restorative martinis!"

FOUR

EAT, DRINK, AND BE MERRY, FOR TOMORROW SOMEONE HAS TO CRY

"Mr. Malcolm Duval," announced Briggs in a sonorous voice as he showed Malcom into the drawing room.

"Mr. Duval" crooned Maebelle, a vision in frothy red tulle with a ruby and diamond feather gracing what she called her "in memory of Ivana Trump" beehive. "How good of you to come!" *Goodness,* she thought. *How astute of Dee-Dee to describe you as a delicious Swedish meatball! Talk about yummy yum!*

"Amazing what five hundred nicker's worth of bait can do," grinned Malcom, patting his breast pocket. "Pleased to meet you, Maebelle. And as I'm sure everyone here is on Christian name terms, please call me Malcom."

"Then Malcom you shall be," said Maebelle graciously. "The gentleman on my right is Peter Proudfoot (she and Dee-Dee had double checked the name on his card), and the gentleman next to him, Corey Marsden. Standing next to the grand piano is my live-in Man Friday, my Jack-of-all-trades, and a former acquaintance of yours, Dee-Dee Donaldson-Devereaux."

"Good evening, gentlemen," said Malcom with a whiter than white smile. "And a special 'hi' to Dee-Dee! You're looking good." He gave a snicker. "It's obvious Maebelle employs a first-rate chef as your former outline - it would be wrong of me to refer to it as a silhouette - is now certainly more Michelin Man than slimline."

"Bitch!" hissed Dee-Dee, loud enough for all to hear. Glowering at Maebelle he said tetchily. "I believe I'm developing one of my irritating migraines, *Miss* Maebelle. Something which always happens when yours truly in under undue stress. So, if you'll excuse me, I'd better go and lie down. Which means I won't be joining you for dinner."

"Go and lie down at your peril!" snapped Maebelle. "As for your sudden migraine? Tommyrot! I appreciate you and Malcom have had your differences, but those differences will have to be forgotten while under my roof! Now, come and shake hands with Malcom" - she gave a titter - "I won't say kiss and make up - so that we can all behave like civilised human beings." Maebelle gave a further titter. "Not that this select little gathering is all *that* civilised! Ha ha!"

A scowling Dee-Dee reluctantly did as he was instructed before moving over to stand next to Maebelle while Briggs diligently served the three men their requested drinks. Turning to face Maebelle, Briggs said solemnly. "Dinner will be served in fifteen minutes, Miss Maebelle, and as the first course is a soufflé, cook has asked that you please be seated before she - as she is prone to say - does her usual magic."

*

"Right," said Maebelle looking at her seated guests in turn. "As none of us really know each other we can skip the small talk and get down to business. Lulu Mayhew, the author. I want her well and truly fucked up. And not only her, but two of her fawning cohorts as well. Once I've finished elaborating on *what* I'd like done, I'll then leave you three to discuss it among yourselves before coming back to me. This is what I'd like you three to do for me . . ."

"Whoa, *Miss* Maebelle, whoa! Hold your horses!" growled Malcom folding his table napkin and placing it neatly on his side plate. "This is where I leave you and your two guests. No offense, gentlemen, but Malcom Marsden does not work - never has - with others so count me out of any further discussions; particularly if such discussions may and mayn't be worthy of *Miss* Maebelle's capricious approval!"

Rising calmly from his chair, Malcom walked toward the door, deftly stepping aside so as to avoid bumping into Briggs carrying a tray of golden soufflés.

Maebelle sat staring open-mouthed at the now empty doorway while Dee-Dee physically slunk down into his chair as if wishing the Aubusson carpet would swallow him up.

Eyeing a dumbfounded Corey and Peter, Maebelle, pulling herself together, said with a hollow laugh. "Well, gentlemen, it looks as if you're on your own. As for you, Dee-Dee dear, may I suggest you take that smug 'I told you so' look of your *very* rotund face before I throw my glass of very expensive Assyrtiko wine over you! Ah! That's much better! Houston may have had a problem but that doesn't mean we have to follow in their tread. In other words, hear me out and then us three can take it from there."

"What about me?" pouted Dee-Dee.

"Well, dear. So long as your promise, on whoever's grave you wish, *not to have*" - Maebelle made several stabbing air quotes - "one of your inconvenient migraine headaches on the night, then yes, you may see yourself as included!"

*

"Is that it?" questioned Corey once Maebelle had delivered her short, prepared speech.

"Yes, that's it for starters," said Mabelle sharply. "Why, did you expect more?"

"Let me simply say, Maebelle, as it's the legendary *you* behind this so-called cold-blooded revenge or feud, I didn't expect your suggestion to be so tame!"

"Tame?" squawked Peter. "I, for one, do not think setting fire to someone's house is tame! It's outrageous!"

"We're not planning on setting fire to the house, Peter, dear," crooned Maebelle. "See it more as a flaming torch tickle!"

"I'm sorry, Miss Maebelle," mumbled Peter, his face reddening, "but I have to agree with Mr. Duval. Therefore, please excuse me as I think it's better if I left you to discuss whatever you feel you have to discuss. Er . . . thank you for dinner. It was . . .er . . . delicious." He gave Maebelle a wry smile. "Pity the evening turned out to be so different to what I was looking forward to. But then, these things happen."

"If you want out, then out you shall be," said Maebelle softly. Giving Peter a gentle smile she added in an undertone. "However, there's no need for you to leave, Peter. Corey, Dee-Dee and I have stacks of time to work on this so why don't we all have another coffee and another brandy and talk about the latest trends and goings on in today's glorious, volatile, tinderbox world."

"Only because you insist, Miss Maebelle."

"I do insist, Peter, just as I insist you stop calling me Miss Maebelle. In fact, I would much prefer it if you addressed me as Mae: my correct name and which only a privileged few are encouraged to call me."

Gotcha! thought Dee-Dee giving Maebelle a discreet wink. *I can hardly wait to see the well and truly stymied you at breakfast! A distinct difference no doubt between tonight's Pete the Treat and tomorrow morning's poor shagged out Pete aka Miss Maebelle's virile treat!*

*

"Right on schedule and in time to join me in a 'job well done' celebratory breakfast Mimosa," crooned Maebelle from where she stood by central island in the stylish Art Deco designed black and white kitchen about to pour herself a glass. Pointing at a second glass she added with a grin. "Your glass awaits you."

Filling the two glasses from a pitcher she was already holding, Maebelle handed a glass to Dee-Dee and said in a syrupy voice. "Not only is Pete the Treat back on board he's taken it upon himself to be the one and only torch bearer and house scorcher!" Maebelle gave a snicker. "Obviously Miss Posy was more cosy, dozy than worldly wisely when it came down to the fascinations and machinations of the Kamasutra! From what I could gather she must have thought even the missionary position a touch too adventurous for her!" She gave another snicker. "I doubt if the now thoroughly initiated will surface for a couple of hours due to an extreme case of serious, sexual exhaustion, or Maebelle SSE as I laughingly call it!"

"Well done, Maebelle!" chortled Dee-Dee. Raising his glass, he added mischievously. "Thank goodness when designers RAD refurbished the duplex they made doubly sure all existing walls, floor and ceiling areas were soundproof. Hence your innocent Dee-Dee, thumb in his equally innocent mouth, having slept undisturbed during the young man's tutelage until his usual seven o'clock wake- up call!"

"Morning everyone!" said Peter brightly from where he stood in the doorway dressed in a pair of underpants later described by Dee-Dee as "something voluminous and vile". Ignoring Maebelle's gasp and Dee-Dee's snickered "walls have ears", he added cheerfully. "Is that a pitcher of something taboo I see before me? If so, the answers yes! I'd adore a glass!"

"Please, take mine while I get myself another," said Maebelle not daring to look at Dee-Dee doing his utmost not to laugh and failing miserably.

"No, Mae precious," replied the grinning graduate. "I can wait until you fetch another glass. What I *can't* wait for is a good morning smackeroo followed by a quick fondle of your delicious bum!"

"Peter!" gasped Maebelle. "Peter! Behave yourself! We're not alone!"

"Oh, don't mind me!" carolled Dee-Dee, doubling up with laughter.

"I don't mind you being there at all, Dee-Dee!" sang Peter. Giving Dee-Dee a playful punch, he added with a leer, "From the many things magical Mae taught me last night, I also learned that when it comes to you, three is no longer a crowd! So, maybe sooner than later, perhaps?"

Dee-Dee, having managed to straighten himself, stood, hands on hips, and said with a cackle. "Oh, Maebelle, what *have* you done? Only a few hours ago you were the one and only Maebelle, fashion model extraordinaire, and now here you are, Eaton Square's answer to Lois Lane along with your very own Superman! Hee hee hee!"

"Oi! Watch your mouth, *tubby*!" snarled the new Peter. "Nobody but nobody, speaks to Miss Mae like that when I'm around!"

"Really, Clark? Not even for a lark?" trilled Dee-Dee followed by a loud "Ow!" on receiving a sharp, sudden slap from a glowering Peter.

"Your Mimosa, Peter dear," crooned Maebelle handing Peter a hastily poured glass, "As for you, Dee-Dee, consider yourself lucky it's still early and you haven't had time to apply your bronzer causing Peter's hand to stick! Now, instead of standing here like The Three Stooges, I suggest we settle ourselves in the breakfast area like the three charming souls we are before dear Briggs appears to see what we'd like for breakfast."

"Briggs is already here, Miss Maebelle," said a sonorous voice from another entrance to the kitchen, "and now the battle of the superheroes appears to be over, I'll be more than happy to come and take your breakfast orders *sans* fruit juice."

As the three sat down for breakfast, a virtually ignored Peter was introduced to yet another side of Maebelle; the sleek, uber-professional side, during which she and Dee-Dee analytically discussed her up and coming engagements of which there were many.

"I've said yes to Paris, Milan, New York and Tokyo," said Dee-Dee matter-of-factly going through a printed list. "And a further yes to Edinburgh, Glasgow along with an assignment at the Royal Albert Dock, Liverpool" - "I Love you! Yeah! Yeah! Yeah!" chanted Maebelle, breaking in. The trendy Beatles' Museum being listed within the impressive building - "I'd stick to modelling if I were you, dear," sniffed Dee-Dee, "plus two further assignments; a show in Zurich and another in Stockholm."

Shuffling the various sheets of paper placed on the table in front of him, Dee-Dee said contemplatively. "Though there's a good deal of travelling involved, apart from the States and Far East, it's all pretty local with no major flights involved. As for *next* year, there're offers from Down-Under which include Sydney, Melbourne and Perth which I need to speak to you about." He gave a snicker. "Whenever I hear the term Down-Under I'm reminded of those wonderful Sergei and Carl the wombat ads on Classic FM!"

"Well, I've certainly enough on my money plate to keep us comfortably roofed for the foreseeable future," crooned Maebelle. "Lucky for us and, regrettably, lucky for Lulu Mayhew as well."

"Why lucky for Lulu Mayhew?" growled Peter, feeling it necessary for the newly crowned king of the castle to reaffirm his macho presence.

"Why lucky?" chorused Maebelle and Dee-Dee in disbelief.

"Are you *totally* stupid or else totally out of touch?" snapped Maebelle.

"What happened? Your mental elevator never managed to reach the top floor?" sniped Dee-Dee.

"H ... hey g ... guys," stammered Peter raising his hands in a placatory gesture. "I was only asking."

"Only asking? Only asking?" chanted Maebelle, her words dripping sarcasm. "Well then, in order to make sure there's a possibility my words *may* have penetrated your thicko skull, I suggest you listen carefully: very, *very* carefully, Peter Proudfoot, as there'll be no such thing as a second chance. Lulu Mayhew is a lucky lady that, due to my endless, professional commitments, it now means I won't be here nor have the time to follow through any planned torching." Glaring at a stunned Peter she added with a hiss. "It's pretty obvious I cannot rely on the likes of you and Corey Humpty Dumpty Marsden when any action may be required, and as my loyal, devoted Dee-Dee will - as per usual - be travelling with me, he will be unable to deal with the matter."

Visibly shaking with anger Maebelle took a deep breath before saying with a tight smile. "Maybe the only outcome of last night's meeting would be for you to meet up with the equally indecisive Corey Marden and the two of you waltz off into a technicolour sunset together!"

Slamming her empty glass down on the table, Maebelle added angrily. "I take it you can see yourself out, Peter Proudfoot, or do I have to summon Briggs so that *he* can show you the exit?"

As a red-faced Peter jumped up from the table and stormed out from the breakfast area, Maebelle turned to a giggling Dee-Dee and said with a smug smile. "No, I didn't think so. Pity, seeing he trained up well; and so quickly!   However, as you and I both know, Dee-Dee, dear, there are plenty more dicks in the sea! Meanwhile, you and I have places to go, assignments to fulfil, photographic shoots to be shot, places to be seen followed by further staggers to the bank. As always, it's up to you and me, kiddo, and long may - ha - we reign!"

"That definitely calls for another Mimosa!" cried Dee-Dee, followed by a warbled "Down-Under, here we come! Model Maebelle and her loyal bum chum!"

"You surely mean another *pitcher* of Mimosas along with a box of Quies ear plugs!" tittered Maebelle, rolling her large, expressive eyes.

DICKENSON AND MARSDEN - ESTATE AGENTS

"A Mr. Peter Proudfoot on the phone for you, Corey," crowed Clarissa, the receptionist. "He says you'll be expecting his call."

Expecting his call? thought Corey with a smirk. *I suppose in a way I was.* "Put him through, Clarissa." He gave a snicker. "But, afore ye do, may I say you sound full of sweetness and light this morning. Got lucky last night, did we?"

If only, thought Clarissa with and inward sigh, before saying in her best come hither voice. "Only *I* know the answer to that, Corey Marsden; thank you very much! So, do I put Mr. Proudfoot on hold, fob him off or put him through?"

"Oh, definitely put him through, Clarissa dear, as I have a feeling what he's about to tell me will - with any luck - make my day!"

After five minutes conversation Corey suggested he and Peter meet for lunch. "Somewhere where we can comfortably talk. May I suggest Marcus at The Berkeley at one? Good. I'll see you there."

GODFREY STREET

"Time for you to grow up and begin to show your true colours, Medora, sweetheart," murmured Lulu staring at the blank computer screen. "Time for you to do something encouragingly nasty to Daddy Gideon or Mummy Eleanora. Maybe both . . ." She began to type; her fingers racing across the keys.

"I'm sorry Gideon," trilled Eleanora, *"but no teddy bears for our little angel. Teddy bears are two a penny and as our little angel is also our priceless,*

special jewel, it's pretty damn obvious - to my uber-active mind, if not yours - that a boring, run-of-the-mill, common *teddy bear will not suffice!"*

"So, what does the light of my adoring heart suggest instead?" questioned Gideon, his blue eyes twinkling and a small smile playing on his manly, oh so kissable lips.

"As an adorable child, your enchanting Eleanora fell -tumbling curls over petit feet - with dear Unka Walt's Jumbo."

"Dumbo, dearest heart. Dumbo!"

"Mumbo, Jumbo, Dumbo, whatever," said Eleanora with a dismissive wave of a heavily bejewelled arm. *"In my nightly prayers to sweet Lord Jesus, I would ask Him to turn my boring teddy* bear *into a wondrous* elephant *bear. Jesus never did, but to sweet, innocent little me, teddy was always a loving elephant; never a boring bear."* She added with a wistful smile. *"A fluffy elephant bear soon to be replaced by a mink-covered elephant bear duly named Elly."*

"Elly?"

"Yes, Gideon dearest. As in Elly the elephant!" Eleanora gave a discreet gulp before continuing. *"After baby cuddles followed by growing up cuddles the name Elly gently morphed into Flip Flap because, as I so rightly pointed out to my bemused parents, elephants have big ears which they enjoy flapping. Hence Flip for one ear and Flap for the other! Darling Flip Flap never left my side until I married you!"*

"Until you found a real man with an elephant trunk of his own to lure you away from Flip Flap, you mean," growled Gideon, flexing his massive thighs and giving a lascivious forward thrust of his bulging crotch."

"Poor Gideon," sighed Lulu on finally leaving the computer. "If you had the remotest idea as to what Medora and Flip Flap the Second have in mind for Daddy Gideon and Mummy Eleanora, you'd be a very shocked pair of parents indeed! Uber-duber-super-wuber shocked in fact! Ha ha! I love it!"

FIVE

THE BERKELEY HOTEL - KNIGHTSBRIDGE

"I suggest we go straight to our table, organise a drink, and order lunch so that we can sit and natter away without being disturbed," said Corey after greeting Peter who had been getting out of a taxi the same as he was.

"Sounds good to me," said Peter raising a hand to shield his eyes from the dazzling glare emitting from the sunlight dancing on Corey's polished pate. *Talk about a fucking glitter ball,* he thought with an inward snigger. *Plus, I can now see why Maebelle and her poison dwarf refer to you as Humpty Dumpty! However, a friend in need is a friend indeed, and hopefully that friend could well be you, Corey Marsden.*

Seated at the table, martinis at hand, wine and lunch orders placed, Peter repeated his opening words to Corey. "Thanks again for agreeing to seeing me, Corey."

"My pleasure, Peter," replied Corey with a bemused smile. "After last night's little debacle with Madam Maebelle Defarge I was more or less expecting a call from you."

Leaning back in his chair, he said with a wry smile. "She talked you into staying the night, didn't she? Oh, no need to look so shocked, Peter. Those who know Mae - Maebelle - and some of us go many years back - are well aware of her many mischievous manoeuvres. As the author Lulu Mayhew once said, Maebelle would make a Black Widow spider's bite more laughable than lethal!"

"Er . . . yes, I did stay the night," said Peter with a gulp.

"And then found yourself callously dismissed after breakfast, no doubt," said Corey taking a sip of his martini. "All in all, a typical replay of Maebelle's 'leave it up to me and Dee-Dee' routine." He shook his gleaming pate. "For an internationally acclaimed super model your naivety at times, Mae Collison, is unbelievable!"

"So, what should I . . . er . . . we . . . do, Corey?"

"Do? We do nothing as far as Maebelle is concerned. We simply leave her and that dreadful Dee-Dee to do their Phileas Fogg *Around the World in Eighty Days* bit and, if she's still hell bent on this childish revenge regarding Lulu Mayhew, we'll take it from there. Meanwhile, I think it would be a good idea if I introduced you to Maebelle's very obvious nemesis."

"You mean Lulu Mayhew?" gasped Peter.

"Who else?" chuckled Corey. "Not that I could truthfully say she sees me as one of her many blue-eyed boys. Ha ha. I'll give her a call later. I know she's always working and can be a bit terse if disturbed."

"Doesn't she have a secretary?"

"Yes, but I also happen to have a private number which she - and only she - answers."

"Gosh! Lulu Mayhew the bestselling author," mused Peter. "Posy will be impressed!"

"Posy? Who's Posy?" quizzed Corey.

"My girlfriend." Peter gave an embarrassed giggle. "At least she was before Maebelle lured me into her evil web. Hopefully, what the eye doesn't see, the heart doesn't grieve over, and Posy will never know about my stupid seduction!"

"Well, rest assured your Posy will never hear anything untoward from yours truly," said Corey reassuringly. "Ah, our first course!" He turned toward the smiling sommelier. "And the very man himself to ensure we enjoy the Sauvignon Blanc he suggested!"

After an agreeable dinner and an equally agreeable two bottles of wine followed by coffee and liqueurs, a relieved Peter returned to the modest Fulham apartment he shared with Posy and literally "filled her in" with a subtly censored version of what he'd been up to.

"So, this Corey whatever thinks the awful woman is more talk than action," murmured Posy as she and Peter lay snuggled up on the sofa following a benign kiss and make up on Peter's return. Reaching for her wine glass, Posy took a sip. "Peter? Is that what he said?"

"Er . . . yes. They go way back and have known each other since they were around nine or ten, so I think he knows what he's talking about."

"Isn't it strange," murmured Posy, "how someone who appears to have so much really has so little. I mean, Maebelle literally has the world at her feet and yet she continues to fret over a childhood slight when she should be counting her blessings! What an ungrateful cow!"

Ungrateful, maybe, but when it comes to making love, Posy dear, she's the ultimate, thought Peter with an inward snicker. *Despite some unexpected enthusiasm during our lovemaking earlier, I may as well have been humping my pillow!*

"Do you know what I really thought when you didn't come home last night," whispered Posy against Peter's hairless chest. "I thought you'd spent the night with her! I can't tell you what a relief it was when you told me you'd spent the night on Algy's sofa."

Little do you know, prying Posy, that Algy called me to warn me you were checking up on me and, being the loyal mate he is, told you I was on the shower and did you want him to ask him to call you back. As expected, you said no. Had you said yes, I would have told you later that I had been far too upset to call you back!

Peter gave a nervous chuckle. "As Algy always says, his sofa is a port in any storm: especially a Posy storm! Ha ha!"

A GEORGIAN TERRACED HOUSE - CANONBURY SQUARE - ISLINGTON - LONDON

"Aha! Madam Circe herself! I have to say I've been wondering when you'd call, Miss - I won't take no for an answer - Maebelle," said Malcom Duval with a chuckle. "Although it *has* taken you three days of deep, darkest deliberation before doing the dastardly deed!"

"Great minds think alike: *Malcom,*" purred Maebelle. "As for the three days, please blame their silence on an always present heavy business schedule as opposed to anything deemed mundane; anything so trite as he who hesitates is lost et cetera! So, down to business. Corey Marsden and Peter Proudfoot are no longer in the portrait which means if you - alone and unfettered - are still prepared to assist me in achieving my goals, I'd be delighted if we could meet before I travel to Paris and Milan next week." She gave a light laugh. "Having learned how *sensitive* you can be - *Malcom* - maybe a teensy-weensy hint of an invitation to lunch as opposed to a *definite* invitation won't be seen as too demanding? And, if my gentle hint doesn't raise Mr. Duval's facial tint, Daphne's, Draycott Avenue tomorrow at one?"

"Daphne's, Draycott Avenue, tomorrow at one," repeated Malcom before hanging up.

"Could lead to a fun game of cat and mouse," muttered Malcom staring at the silent phone.

*

"Could lead to a fun game of cat and louse," snickered Maebelle staring the silent phone.

GODFREY STREET

"I don't wanna puppy! I don't wanna a pony!" shrieked five-year-old Medora as she lay on her back on the sitting room floor, her tiny pink patent diamante buckled shoes thrumming against the Persian carpet. "I wanna pink effalump with a pink how-dee-doo-dah in which pretty Medora can ride!" Taking a deep breath Medora added with a further, frenzied shriek and drumming and thrumming of her tiny heels. "Inside my how-dee-doo-dah pretty Medora will keep a big, nasty stick an' hit anyone who tries to pet my effalump an' tell them to eff-off as you are always saying to each other!"

"Precious wonder, precious heart, no need to speak Daddy Gideon and Mummy Eleanora grown-up upset talk and of course you shall have a Flip Flap like Mummy Eleanora used to have," crowed Eleanora. "I promise!"

Staring down at the smirking little girl, now all sugar and spice as opposed to the earlier doppelganger of Regan, star of The Exorcist, *a scowling Eleanora was tempted to give Medora a hefty kick but poured herself a calming vodka tonic instead, leaving an equally scowling Nanny Mansfield (otherwise known as Jane the Lethal Strain) to deal with the now giggling, triumphant Miss Goody Pink-Shoes.*

DAPHNE'S RESTAURANT - THE NEXT DAY

"Miss Maebelle. Great to see you again," chuckled Malcom - a dashing figure in a navy Brunello Cucinelli blazer, open-neck shirt with a vibrant Romero Britto cravat and matching pocket handkerchief, cream Brioni trousers, and Gucci loafers *sans* socks - reaching for Maebelle's proffered hand. "Now I know what it feels like to visit The Land of a Thousand Stares as everybody - but *everybody* - is looking at us!"

"And no doubt wondering who the handsome gentleman I'm meeting can possibly be," said Maebelle with a dazzling "yes, look all you wish as it really *is* me" smile.

Having been shown to their prime table and champagne cocktails duly ordered, Maebelle wasted no time in getting down to business,

"My two favourite words are carte blanche," she purred. "And if you *do* wish to help me with what I call my LM problem, you will be given carte blanche as far as expenses go in addition, of course, to your basic fee which I'd like you to confirm here and now before we order, so as to avoid another arrogant exit as before."

"Arrogant exit? Miss Maebelle?" chuckled Malcom.

"Maebelle, please," replied Maebelle in a seductive growl.

"Of course! Another arrogant exit, Maebelle? I only *exited* your dinner party because I was given the distinct impression you expected me to work with those two morons and, as I explained, Malcom Duval works alone."

"My apologies for being a touch presumptuous, Malcom *dear*," said Maebelle with another dazzling smile. "So, let's agree your fee, so that we can then go on to utterly spoil ourselves with one of two of Daphne's delicious offerings." She gave a madcap laugh. "In other words, a salad for me and something filling for you!"

"Sounds good to me, Maebelle." Reaching inside his blazer he withdrew a Mont Blanc pen with which he quickly scribbled a figure on the exposed cuff of his shirt.

"Done," said Maebelle giving the amount a desultory glance. "Dee-Dee will have this ready for you to collect later."

"Thank you," said Malcom reaching for a menu, "Now that's done, let's see what your new associate should order so as to seal the deal, as it were!" Giving Maebelle a discreet glance he couldn't help thinking. *I wonder if it's true what they say about you being a very* able *Maebelle; a very able Maebelle who always offers a sample of the star herself as an extra bonus at the end of the day.*

"Penny for them, Malcom," purred Maebelle.

"Oh, they're worth more than a penny, Maebelle, trust me," chuckled Malcom. "So, a plan of campaign regarding your LM problem. Your being abroad as from next should be seen as a bonus along with any further out of the country assignments. As you wish LM no physical harm but an even more terrifying Freddie Kruger type of *Fright Night* instead, this is what I suggest for starters. It's not all that frightening but it should get those worry juices flowing; if not whipped into a frenzy!"

Malcom proceeded to explain what he had in mind for the first of his LM frighteners, his initial suggestion resulting in Maebelle giving a discreet round of applause accompanied by a carolled "Genius! Malcom! Pure genius! And as a possible follow-up?"

"How about this?" chuckled Malcom, followed by what he had in mind for *Fright Night* Two.

"Forget Albert Einstein," crooned Maebelle. "For when it comes to the Twenty First Century's answer to him: you're it!"

GODFREY STREET

"Time for dear sweetness and light darling little Medora to do a 'Topsy' and 'growed' a bit," giggled Lulu as she sat staring at the computer screen. "To date she's been an absolute little horror by putting a couple of Alka-Seltzer tablets in the old-fashioned chamber pot Miss Mansfield insists on keeping underneath her bed - her shrieks were heard as far as the gatehouse - as well as pouring Tate & Lyall's finest into the petrol tank of Daddy Gideon's Ferrari, so let's advance her by a year or two. Shall we make her a tenacious ten, a torrid twelve or, better still, a tricky terrifying thirteen who takes unbelievable umbrage at Mrs Horsfall - no, better change that - Mrs Moorsom, the cook's unintentional decision to place the profiteroles in the *top* compartment pf the fridge freezer and out of dear Medora's reach? Profiteroles adored by Medora and her substitute Flip Flop. Not the elephant as originally demanded but a doting, golden-haired Labrador who happily gambols around the estate with an exuberant Medora astride his back whilst using his ears as reins!"

Lulu gave a giggle. "As Medora so rightly says, *Flip Flop, you may not have large flippy floppy ears and a trunk, but you have a large, fluffy tail and a fuzzy, wuzzy kissy wissy muzzle and, better still, you can sing along with me whenever I decide to sing. Like when Mummy Eleanora plays headboard knock, knock with Daddy Gideon's best friend, Mr. Mimsy Michael Mander, and we really annoy them by singing or hearts out beneath the bedroom window!*

"But enough of the childish stuff! Time for the maddening, mischievous Medora to become the murderous Medora! This must not only be a Medora of sparkling fun; it must be a ruthlessly ambitious Medora capable of the reader positively salivating over the thought of what the new Medora could do next and how she plans to set about it! Take for example Mr. Mimsy Michael who literally *does* end up as a chip off the old block aided and abetted by Flip Flop and teenage tearaway, red-haired Archie Albertson - her best friend next to Flip Flop - and the rumbustious son of Rufus, the woodsman, and owner of an obliging woodchipper."

Lulu couldn't resist a giggle. "Reminds me of a childhood tongue twister, but somewhat altered. The one that goes 'how much wood would a woodchuck chuck, if a woodchuck could chuck wood': my answer being 'as much of mimsy Michael as Archie's dad's woodchipper could!'"

SIX

"PLAGIARIST!" screamed the word sprayed in red paint across a window display of Lulu's latest bestseller in a popular King's Road bookshop. "THIEF!" screamed the word sprayed in red paint across a window display of Lulu's bestseller in a top Knightsbridge departmental store. "UNORIGINAL THIEVING CUNT!" screamed another in a popular somewhat secluded, privately owned bookshop in a discreet, Chelsea side street.

"Someone's done *what*?" exploded Lulu on being told of the rampage by a wide-eyed Maddy Thompson, her long-suffering secretary.

"It's even been on the radio," announced Maddy shakily. "As for yet another shop window in Piccadilly . . . dreadful; quite dreadful!"

"But *who*?" croaked Lulu, almost in tears. "Who and why?" She gave a dismissive shake of her head. "I appreciate Maebelle's a vindictive cow, but she's also a professional and not even she would stoop to something so low and so tacky!"

"Lobie Maseko for you," interrupted Maddy handing over the landline.

"You've obviously heard!" snapped Lulu without any preamble.

"Heard and seen," replied Lobie. "I've just been on to Leo, and he agrees with me. It can only be bloody Mae Collison behind such a puerile, spiteful happening. However, Lulu dear, you can rest assured we won't allow her to get away with this!"

"Are you sure Mae really *is* the one behind this?" said Lulu in a faltering voice. "*Really* sure? One hundred percent sure? After all, there are a good many jealous, grossly vindictive wannabe writers out there who would love to upset and humiliate me!"

"Oh, Leo and I are sure, alright," answered Lobie with a growl. "As I said, Lulu dear, she's not going to get away with this. Not by a long chalk. First, we find the culprit responsible for carrying out her sicko instructions.

Once we've got hold of him, she or them, we'll then deal with Madam Mae-cum-Maebelle and her odious little sidekick; that Dee-Dee Devereaux!" There was a moment's pause. "I take it you're busy for the rest of the day but if you could spare me and Leo a couple of minutes we'll drop by and discuss some plan of action."

"Plan of action?" snapped Lulu. "Surely a plan of *retaliation* would be more in keeping! Call me." Giving Maddy a "what?" type look she added with a hiss. "Lobie Maseko says he'll be calling back and when he does, tell him I'm out. Plan of action? He and Leo Murrain know what they can do with their sodding, ineffectual plan of action. As she's done all her life, Lulu Mayhew will handle this herself and as for you, Mae Collison, a bit of uber-unfriendly advice. Watch your prancing dancing, not all that enhancing, catwalk step!"

"Whatever you say, Lulu," whispered Maddy. "Coffee?"

"Got any arsenic to go with it?" quipped Lulu. "Sorry, Maddy, love; but why is it men always have to be so damn ineffectual?" Staring contemplatively at the young woman she said, as if suddenly seeing some divine light. "Dan Crozier! Do we still have his number?"

"Dan the Man with the impressive hosier? Of *course,* we still have his number!" trilled Maddy. "Spot on, Lulu! Because if anyone can come up with anything solid - I wish! - Dan the Man's the answer! I'll see if I can get hold of him, tout suite!"

A few minutes later Maddy gestured toward Lulu and, covering the mouthpiece, said in a stage whisper. "I've got him and he's all ears! Here!"

Taking the phone from a beaming Maddy, Lulu cried cheerfully. "Dan Crozier! I bet the last person you expected to hear from was maddening Lulu Mayhew. How are you, old friend? Long time no see!"

"Your suggestion, Miss Maddening Mayhew," replied Dan with a warm, deep from the balls chuckle. "How *are* you, dear, apart from being a bestselling author, a popular tv and radio personality among other things?"

"Despite all you say, still your maddening Lulu Mayhew is desperately in need of a solid man of the moment. Hence my calling you!"

Dan Crozier gave another deep, warm chuckle. "As some in the know always say, curiosity didn't quite kill the cat, so, delicious, maddening Mayhew. What's up?"

"You free for lunch?"

"I could be!"

"Godfrey Street, off The King's Road at one o'clock." Lulu gave the number of the house. "See you then, Dan."

"You most certainly will, Lulu, dear. The same good-looking Prince Charming you and your delightful Maddy longed to include in a self-indulgent selfie or two! I look forward to seeing one of my two most favourite 'nay Dan, nay' girls! *Ciao* until we meet for an alternate chow at one!"

"Need I say your sense of tumour remains constant, Dan Crozier!" chortled Lulu. "*Ciao* chow to you too!"

Giving Maddy a thumbs up and a relieved smile, Lulu added cheerfully. "Now if there's one man who can, it's our Dan! So, Maddy dearest, forget the coffee and let's go for a flute of bubbly instead!"

"What do you suggest we give Mr. Crozier for lunch?" asked Maddy as the two sat sipping champagne.

"As he's more of a Christopher Lee lookalike as opposed to a Vincent petrifying Price, something bloody perhaps?" Lulu gave a light laugh. "Please don't suggest a takeaway, Indian, Chinese or pizza as I have a feeling our devious Dan will be expecting something a bit more upmarket! Slices of rare beef and a selection of salads from Fortnum and Mason or else chopped steak from Jago the Butcher for us to make our own steak tartare."

"What if Mr. Transylvania-cum-Mr. Horror doesn't approve of rare beef or steak tartare?" giggled Maddy.

"Tell you what, Maddy. Let's simply make do with a pizza and if Dan the Man doesn't approve; well, tough!"

"Aye, aye! Captain Bligh! Whatever you cry!" tittered Maddy giving Lulu a mock salute and almost spilling her champagne. "Pizzas at dawn and all that blarney!"

"Goodness, Maddy dear! We'll have no alternative but to make you a lie down comedienne if you continue producing witticisms such as that!" said Lulu dryly. "A refill please in preparation for whatever you may come up with next!"

"Oh, forgive me for a sec while I take this," said Maddy with an impish grin as her mobile began to ring. "It's Malky, Malcom, my somewhat persistent suitor. I'll take the call next door."

*

A beaming Dan Crozier arrived at one o'clock on the dot. "I come bearing gifts," he said with an even wider smile (no elongated fangs apparent) on Lulu opening the front door. "A bottle of bubbly, a rather good merlot and two bunches of flowers. Freesias for you, Lulu dear - looking as good if not more lovely than ever - as I know you're a freesia girl, and pink roses for Maddy as I know she always sees me as a rose amongst the thorns! Ha ha!"

"Her thoughts wondering as to who has the bigger prick, no doubt," said Lulu deadpan, reaching for the flowers. "Maddy!" she crooned over her shoulder. "Come and see what goodies Dan *the* most delicious man has brought us! Freesias for me and perky, pink roses for you along with a bottle of bubbly and - I quote - a rather good merlot, which should go well with the exclusive, gourmet type fare we have on the menu today!"

Turning to face Dan, she stood on tiptoe to receive his chaste kiss on her cheek. "Lovely to see you, Dan the Man! We're having drinks in the garden. Ah, Maddy! *There* you are!" she crooned handing the giggling young woman the two bunches of flowers. "Can you find a couple of vases for these *beautiful* flowers, the roses of which - as I said - are for you. Dan, could you be a darling and bring the wine and champers with you. The champers I'll put in the fridge but why don't you open the rather good merlot you so kindly brought and give it a chance to breathe whilst we down a Bloody Mary or three before we eat."

"Sounds good to me," chuckled Dan. "So, lead on Macduffs, one and two!"

*

"Delicious lunch," said Dan with a mischievous grin. Nodding at the pizza crust on his plate he added cheerfully. "A takeaway pizza made even more delicious when downed by a splendid Penfold's merlot!"

"I thought you'd approve," said Lulu with a snort. "Now Dan, to compensate for the pizza, pour yourself a large Courvoisier or, if you'd rather stick to wine or have something else, you only have to ask."

"A large, compensatory Courvoisier will be perfect, thank you," replied Dan with a further fangless smile. "And now, dear Lulu . . . showtime! So, without any further ado, the *real* reason for today's out of the blue in invitation to luncheon!"

Lulu quickly explained the defacing of certain bookshops displaying her bestsellers and why she believed Maebelle was responsible.

"I know it does little to compensate but at least her actions appear to be somewhat petty rather than life threatening, so I wouldn't concern yourself too much about it," said Dan with a reassuring smile. "However, such matters, no matter how trivial, need to be nipped in the bud as it were, so give me a day or two to think about it. What I will need is some sort of schedule as to Maebelle's whereabouts over the coming weeks. You say she's off to gay *Paree* and Milan next week?"

Lulu gave a nod. "Next Wednesday, to be precise."

Raising his brandy snifter Dan said with a chuckle. "Maybe the magnificent Maebelle won't find gay *Paree* to be that gay after all! However, as I said, leave it up to me, Dan, your caring man, and meddling Maebelle will become nothing more than a distant memory."

*

"Rain?" murmured Lulu sleepily. Pulling the duvet over her head she added with a small smile. "As they say, our English weather is more than unpredictable . . . it's totally out of control . . ."

*

"That was your neighbour, Serge Burns, at the door," said an ashen-faced Maddy on stumbling into the kitchen.

"Oh, and good morning to you to, Maddy dearest," crooned Lulu reaching for the jar of Carte Noir instant coffee. She gave a snicker. "A bit early for dear Serge the no urge, isn't it? Please don't tell me it was about poor Maise Brook's television again and he wants us to sign yet another letter of compliant? Well, screw him!"

"No, nothing like that," said Maddy in a choked voice. "It's about the front of the house. Somebody's gone and sprayed the whole of the front with red paint: including your car. Serge says it must have happened in the early hours of this morning as all was fine when he got home at around eleven!"

*

Within an hour of Lulu's sarcastic telephone call to Dan regarding Maebelle's latest "petty as opposed to life threatening" prank, a team of painters arrived to deal with the damage.

"Fortunately, whoever's responsible used an emulsion paint and not an eggshell or gloss, Miss Mayhew," said Louis, the grizzled, grey-headed painter in charge. "Give me and the lads a couple of hours and the front of the house will be as good as new. The same applies to your car." Nodding to where a beaming Serge Burns was happily helping one of his team wash down Lulu's racing green BMW 3, he said with a chuckle. "That Mr Burns seems keen to help. Maybe I should give him a parttime job as a cleaner."

"As long as it's somewhere faraway like Ulaanbaatar in Outer Mongolia, I couldn't agree with you more," sniggered Lulu. "Thanks again, Louis, for coming to the rescue! Now, if you'll excuse me, I need to get back to work."

*

"Damn you, bloody Mae Collison," muttered Lulu through gritted teeth as she sat staring at the blank computer screen. "Damn you!"

Reaching for a much-needed G and T, Lulu took a fortifying sip and said with a twisted smile. "So, big okay then, Madam Maebelle Hell. And whilst you appear to be happily dabbling in red paint, let me assure you, chiller thriller writer Lulu Mayhew much prefers to dabble in the real McCoy! Despite dear Leo and dear Lobie saying they, like Dan, would deal with the situation, I sincerely trust Dan will turn up trumps by beating them to it in his taking the gay out of Mae Collison's to gay *Paree!*"

Taking another sip, Lulu sat quietly for several minutes. "Right," she muttered. "Time again for you, Medora dearest, to help this seething Lulu get rid of some of these irritating frustrations. Time for dear little Medora and friends to calm me down by doing the nastiest of nasties to mimsy Michael!"

Lulu began to type.

"Oh, good morning. Michael," cooed Medora as Michael Mander shuffled into the state-of-the-art kitchenette (gold wall and floor tiles along with a gold-plated kettle, microwave, fridge and sink) serving the main bedroom.

"Jesus Christ! Medora!" squawked Michael, clutching Eleanora's Fendi bathrobe to his scrawny chest. "What are you doing here? Aren't you meant to be at school?" The "you" obviously including Archie sitting on a stool next to the gold-plated countertop while busily chewing on a croissant.

"School holiday," hissed Medora. "But much more important, Daddy Gideon's away on business so why are you here and why are you wearing Mummy Eleanora's bathrobe?"

"Er . . . er . . ."

"Er . . . er?" echoed Medora. "Admit it, Mr. Mimsy Michael, it's simply a case of sucky, yucky, fucky with my rich, yummy, scrummy Mummy than an innocent, cosy sleepover, isn't it?" She gave a Linda Blair like cackle. "More a case of knock, knock, please can I put it in you, Eleanora, darling, than a case of innocent cuddles!"

"You don't know what you're talking about, Medora!" snapped Michael pulling himself and Eleanora's bathrobe together. "Plus, I suggest you show a bit more respect when speaking to your elders!"

"Respect?" yodelled Archie rising from his perch. "If anyone needs to show a bit of respect it's you, you miserable little turd! How dare you speak to Medora like that! How dare you!"

"Whoa! Whoa! Young man!" squawked Michael holding up his trembling hands. "There's no need to lose your temper!"

"No need to lose his temper?" shrieked Medora, her eyes wide. "How dare you speak to Archie like that! Turd? Why, you're nothing more than a pathetic turd-cum-nerd-cum-absurd!"

Storming forward Medora picked up the gold-plated kettle and before Michael could react, swung it sharply against his forehead.

"Oh dear," tittered Medora looking down at Michael sprawled out on the gold tiled floor, a pool of blood forming next to his head. "I know I shouldn't say it, but it seems to me as if mimsy Michael is toast!" Her comment causing the two youngsters to collapse into giggles.

"A truer word was never spoken, fabulous Medora!" gasped Archie in between giggles. Giving the young girl a wink, he added cheerfully. "Just as well I'm built like a brick shit house, so let's get a couple of blankets, wrap him up and pop him down that very convenient rubbish chute next to you. I'll then nip downstairs - hopefully none of the other staff are up yet - and pop him into the boot of Dad's car. He'll be quite safe there for an hour or two and then we can zoom him over to the woodchipper."

"It would have been much more fun to have put him in the chipper while he was still alive," said Medora a touch petulantly. "But then, I suppose wannabe torturers cannot always be choosers! Oh. look at Flip Flop showing us how he also wishes to help in the way he's pulling at one of mimsy Michael's arms!" She gave another giggle. "Just as well he's such a discerning pooch otherwise he'd probably give it a chew! But then, discerning, well-fed pooches - unlike us wannabe torturers - can afford to be choosy!"

Medora, Archie and Flip Flop stood gazing at the scarlet splattered bushes facing the now silent woodchipper.

"All I can say is it looks as if autumn has come early this year and that the autumn colours have never looked prettier" giggled Medora giving Archie a high five and Flip Flop a loving pat on his head. "Now, we'd better get back as I would like to be there when Mummy Eleanora finally wakes up after her *energetic night of knock, knock and discovers that both mimsy Michael and her Fendi dressing gown - one of her favourites - are missing!"*

"Can I also be there?" asked Archie.

"Of course, Archie! You and Flip Flop simply have to be there! After all, Mummy Eleanora does know you were staying over as you and I were going to watch the final episodes of Black Money Love, *and so won't be at all surprised to see you." Medora gave a giggle. "As for the other surprise; watch this space!"*

Much to Medora's annoyance and Archie's disappointment, a decidedly sulky Eleanora made no mention of Michael nor her missing dressing gown.

"A most fitting end for Corey Marsden, when the time comes," mused Lulu, "and a colourful alternative to the scattering of one's ashes. Oh, what a clever author!"

SEVEN

LE BAR - HOTEL GEORGE V - PARIS

"Gosh! We really deserve these!" carolled Maebelle taking a sip of her martini. Giving Dee-Dee a cat that got the cream look she added smugly. "Another triumph, don't you think? The marvellous, magnificent Maebelle, swathed in endless mink aided and abetted by a studded leather bra, pants and thigh-length boots having never looked more desirable, never mind so sublimely kinky!"

"You looked gorgeous; utterly, butterly gorgeous," mumbled Dee-Dee, his mouth stuffed full of olives. He added with a muffled snigger. "Had I been straight I would have been there right on top of gorgeous, sublimely kinky you!"

"Thank God for small mercies and even smaller dicks," chortled Maebelle. Glancing toward the entrance to Le Bar, she added matter-of-factly. "I didn't realise dogs were allowed within these hallowed portals. Present company excluded!"

"They're not," said Dee-Dee, his muffled response interrupted by a piercing scream from Maebelle as the dog in question, a small Jack Russell terrier, now growling and baring its teeth, suddenly dashed forward and bit her on the ankle before turning on its docked tail and dashing from the bar hot on the heels of its dark-clad owner before anybody realised what was happening.

Within seconds the well-trained animal had returned to where its grinning owner stood waiting with an open holdall, jumped in, and within seconds the owner and his tail-wagging accomplice had disappeared among the crowd of people enjoying a stroll along the Champs-Elysées in the evening sunshine.

Back within Le Bar, chaos reigned with a hysterical Maebelle screeching "My leg! My leg! Oh God! Not my leg! Oh God! Will they have to amputate? Oh God!"

Despite Dee-Dee's constant cooing it was nothing more than a tiny nip, and a rapidly summoned doctor verifying the fact, Maebelle continued to wail and rail about the impending loss of her leg and how her career was well and truly finished.

Giving a sigh Dee-Dee beckoned for a waiter and within seconds was holding a large martini for her which she greedily swallowed. The impending amputation apparently forgotten (the nip now covered by an insignificant plaster) she said with a virulent hiss. "You do realise who's responsible for this outrage, don't you?"

"I do indeed," replied Dee-Dee, thankful that Maebelle was back to her usual hedonistic self. "Lulu Mayhew. Who else?"

*

"Although a nip on the ankle instead of a nip in the bud, it certainly had the desired effect," chuckled Dan in a phone call to Lulu. "According to one of the patrons in Le Bar at the time. Maebelle's ensuing performance would have put the likes of Maria Callas to shame. Talk about a diva in feigned distress!"

"I love it! Simply love it!" giggled Lulu. "And the award-winning pooch? How on earth did you find *him*?"

"Pooch's name is Rudi - as in Valentino - and he belongs to a Monsieur Roger Coulon, a friendly thief I know and a great friend. Roger and Rudi are a fantastic duo when it comes diversions and such, which means arranging for Rudi to nip Maebelle in the ankle was a doddle. Or should that be a doggle?"

"Doggle or doddle, you get a hundred and ten out of ten, Dan: as do Rudi and Roger! I suggest endless doggy treats for Rudi from the best pet shop Roger recommends. As for Roger, he will have to wait until I can personally give him the warmest of hugs in lieu of a wicked French kiss! What more can a grateful author say?"

"I am sure Rudi and Roger will be delighted with such rewards," chuckled Dan. "But wait until you hear what I have planned for maddening Maebelle and her tubby sidekick in my next episode of this entertaining saga!"

"You sound just like one of my novels," giggled Lulu. "Just you wait, Dan the Man, until you read my latest, FROM CATWALK TO CATERWAULING. Not that I suspect *anything* would really surprise you!"

"Not even a teenager type kiss when we next meet?"

"You never can tell," giggled Lulu. "For not even *you,* Dan the Man, can tell what goes on inside this febrile mind of mine!"

"Nor you, lovely Lulu, as to what goes on inside this pyretic mind of *mine!*"

"Touché, Dan the Man!"

"Touché, Lulu; woman and writer extraordinaire!" came the chuckled reply as Dan hung up.

PARIS - THE NEXT DAY

"I'm surprised some devious journo hasn't already introduced the new Maebelle to the world," snarled Maebelle glaring at Dee-Dee's reflection in the make-up mirror. "Headlines announcing that Maebelle, the world's most celebrated fashion model is now the new Al Pacino!"

"Maebelle the new Al Pacino?" repeated Dee-Dee with a quizzical raising of a threaded eyebrow.

"If Al Pacino can star in *Scarface, so* why not Maebelle in *Scarred Leg*?"

"For Christ's sake, Maebelle," snapped Dee-Dee. "Enough is enough! You can't even *see* where the wretched dog supposedly bit you!"

Glancing at the giggling make-up girl he added with a hiss. "What's so funny, *chéri*? Care to share the fucking joke with us?"

Her face paling, the girl manged to stammer a garbled "*Pardonne-moi, Monsieur . . . Excuse-moi, Monsieur . . .*" before dashing from the room.

"I'm in serious agony!" gasped Maebelle, determined to have the last word. "Could it be tetanus?"

"No, it's not tetanus, Maebelle, dear! It's more likely to have something to do with those ridiculous shoes you will insist on wearing." Dee-Dee gave a snicker. "Let's face it, darlin'. Yer not exactly Cinderella and those shoes ain't exactly glass slippers!"

"Evil bitch!"

"Takes one to know one, *dearest*! A quickie G and T before one faces the camera? I thought so!"

GODFREY STREET

Smiling to herself, Lulu took a mouthful of gin and tonic and began to type.

"Good morning, Mummy Eleanora dearest," cooed Medora as a red-eyed Eleanora stumbled into the gold kitchenette. "Sleep well?"

"Yes and no," mumbled Eleanora clicking on the gold kettle. "Those wretched owls and their hooting kept me awake!"

"Owls?" carolled Medora. "I didn't hear any owls."

"Well, I did!" snapped Eleanora pouring the boiling water into a gold-plated mug. "Anymore Spanish Inquisition-like questions for ten o'clock on the morning?"

"Only one more, Mummy Eleanora dearest," chirruped Medora. "Is that a new dressing gown? It's much prettier than the one you usually wear."

"Yes, it is," said Eleanora dismissively. "I got tired of the other one and gave it to one of the maids."

Poor, unlucky, maid, thought Medora with an inward snicker. A non-existent dressing gown covered in bloodstains. Only Mummy Eleanora could conjure up such an original gift!

"When does Daddy Gideon get back?"

"Tonight," snapped Eleanora clutching the gold mug to the replacement Dolce and Gabbana dressing gown. "He'll be back tonight in time for the Bartholomew's birthday dinner party." Doing her best not to appear out of sorts, she added brightly. "And what are you up to seeing you said you didn't wish to attend - to quote you - a constipated dinner so-called party with those stuck-up idiots!"

"Archie and I are going to be watching another series on Netflix." Medora gave a giggle. "It's called Let the Right One In, *and hopefully it'll be as good as* Blood Money Black.*"*

Waiting until Eleanora had taken a mouthful of coffee, Medora said in all innocence. "I thought I saw Michael out jogging earlier this morning." Her comment causing Eleanora to choke on her mouthful of coffee.

"Where? Where did you see him?" Eleanora finally managed to splutter.

"Out in the park where I usually take Flip Flop for his early 'do business' walkies," carolled Medora. "Strangely he didn't respond to my called hello and simply continued running as if I wasn't there." She gave a giggle. "I may just as well have been a ghost!"

To Medora's delight Eleanora gave a strangled cry, and, having slammed her coffee mug down on the breakfast counter, staggered out from the kitchenette.

"That's telling her," Medora said with a giggle. Giving Flip Flop's ears s loving rub she couldn't resist a further giggle. "Just wait until she finds one of mimsy Michael's shoes in her shoe cupboard. If that doesn't lead to a further 'knock, knock, who's there -it can't be missing Michael's shoe', then nothing will! What a clever sausage Archie is by suggesting we kept a souvenir or two of mimsy Michael's belongings before popping him into the woodchipper."

Bending to give Flip Flop a kiss on his head she said in a whisper. "I wonder what Mummy Eleanora's maid will think when, in a few months' time, she's asked to bring one, she discovers Mummy Eleanora's missing, bloodstained dressing gown hanging in her fur cupboard? Another spot-on suggestion from Archie was that we collect all of mimsy Michael's belongings from Mummy Eleanora's dressing room so as to give - as Archie said - extra colouring - hee-hee -to mimsy Michael's mysterious disappearance!"

In a later telephone call to Archie, Medora said with a giggle. "I must say I thoroughly enjoyed our little defacing of the local woodland!"

"So did I," chucked Archie.

"Let's not forget Flip Flop," added Medora. "He may not mention it but I'm sure he enjoyed the venture as much as we did." She gave a further giggle. "I could be mistaken, but I am sure I caught him having a discreet taste of what could easily be called our speciality of the day. Our very own Mimsy Michael steak tartare!"

"Oh, what a deliciously wicked Medora you're turning out to be," said Lulu with a giggle. "I thought the scene in Le Bar pretty spectacular, but what Dan has planned for his next bit of mischief-making as *Fright Night* continues to enthral all, is even better! Dastardly Dee-Dee Devereaux thrown overboard when dining on a batteau mouche? Whatever next?"

PARIS - TWO EVENINGS LATER

"Great view - isn't it?" rumbled the bald, Van Diesel lookalike from where he stood on the deck, a few feet away from Dee-Dee, gazing at the illuminated buildings lining the bank as the batteau mouche made its stately way along the Seine.

"It most certainly is," cooed Dee-Dee, an anticipatory tingle running down his spine. *At last, a bald, butch brute with an artistic streak! Who knows what may happen next!* "You here by yourself?"

"*Non*," rumbled the man. Switching back to English he said with an indiscernible accent and a whiter than white smile. "I'm with a couple of friends who appear to be having some sort of disagreement so I thought it best to let them sort it out before I return to the table for what I trust will be a calm and therefore pleasant dinner. You, sir?"

"Oh, I'm here on my ownsome, lonesome," said Dee-Dee with a Bardot like pout. "My er . . . partner having decided to have a contemplative evening alone."

"Girlfriend?"

"Er . . . in a way I suppose she is," tittered Dee-Dee. "Girlfriend, boyfriend, who cares?"

"Hopefully, for your sake, someone does," replied the man turning to face Dee-Dee.

Before Dee-Dee could respond the towering Van Diesel lookalike grabbed hold of the lapels to his jacket and, without any apparent effort, nonchalantly tossed the startled little man overboard. His flailing form crashing into the wake of the batteau mouche as it continued its stately way along the Seine.

Despite being overweight and not at all athletically inclined, Dee-Dee was an accomplished swimmer. Treading water and shouting for help, he started to swim and within minutes managed to reach the riverbank where a curious crowd along with a couple of gendarmes were watching and waiting.

Helping a spluttering Dee-Dee from the water, he quickly assured the concerned gendarmes that he was unhurt before explaining how he was attacked and agreeing with the gendarmes that they get their colleagues to board the batteau mouche at its next stop and arrest the "mad, wild man" who had suddenly attacked him for no apparent reason.

On boarding the batteau much at the next stop, the gendarmes were unable to find a man answering to Dee-Dee's description.

As Dan later explained to Lulu. "It didn't take Henri, my contact, more than a few seconds to don a wig, stick on a false moustache once he'd dealt with Devereaux, and return to the table where Marie and Bernard, two more of the team were waiting. Within seconds the three were chatting away as they tucked into dinner. Like the other diners, they were briefly questioned by the gendarmes if they had seen a man answering Dee-Dee's description and, like the other diners, were unable to help."

A SUITE - HOTEL GEORGE V - PARIS

"Someone did *what?*" shrieked Maebelle after a crumpled, decidedly worse for wear (but dry) Dee-Dee was finally allowed to return to the hotel and explain the reason for his lateness and his bedraggled appearance.

Trying to make light of the situation Dee-Dee - having mixed both himself and Maebelle an extra-large martini - said airily. "The rather dishy Van Diesel lookalike obviously found me too hot to contemplate - or handle - and in a moment of utter frustration decided to throw me overboard prior to my Garbo-like dinner!"

"Garbo-like dinner?" interrupted Maebelle. "For fuck's sake, Dee-Dee Devereaux, stop talking in riddles and be sensible for once in your sordid, little life!"

"Garbo-like - I vanna be alone - me, on my ownsome, lonesome, solo dinner is what I meant, *Maebelle* dearest," pouted Dee-Dee.

"Forget your ridiculous I vanna be alone dinner as it's blatantly obvious this is another vile plot carried out on behalf of that odious Mayhew creature," snapped Maebelle. "First of all, she has me viciously attacked by a wild, out of control Rottweiler in Le Bar . . ."

"Jack Russell, Maebelle! Not a Rottweiler!" Dee-Dee gave a snigger. "There's a notable difference."

"Attacked by a rabid dog and now you're thrown from a speeding dinner boat into The Seine by an equally out of control madman! Whatever next?" Maebelle reached for her mobile. "I know it's late but bloody Malcom Duval had better pull his sodding finger out - while he still *has* a finger! - and *do* something!"

"Maebelle?" questioned Malcom on answering. "It's a bit late for you to be calling. Is everything okay?"

"No, Malcom. Everything is *not* okay!" Spitting out the latest drama involving "poor, innocent Dee-Dee" she ended the tirade by saying in a no-nonsense voice. "Forget anything to do with red paint. I want action, not some flaky, shaky 'oh dear, what can the *splatter* be' ineffective happenings!"

"Your word is my demand, Maebelle, dear," replied Malcom silkily. "And I can assure you what will happen to Lulu Mayhew in a couple of days' time will happily put your seething mind to rest!"

"For your miserable sake I certainly hope so," snapped Maebelle, terminating the call.

Staring at Dee-Dee who was well into his second "I'm so traumatised" martini, she said in a disbelieving voice. "He assures me Lulu Mayhew's next fright will be a winner but, in retrospect, you were right in ditching Mr. Malcom Duval! Again, in retrospect, maybe Corey Marsden and Peter Proudfoot aren't such a pair of blithering arseholes after all!"

Glancing at her vintage Cartier wristwatch she said with a mutter. "Sod this." Holding out her empty glass for a refill she reached for the mobile with her free hand and tapped in the contact number.

"Corey?" she crooned on hearing his sleepy "hello?". "It's Maebelle calling from Paris. I realise it's late and I apologise for waking you, but I need to see you and Peter Proudfoot *immediately* on my - our - return from Milan next Tuesday. Cancel any plans the two of you may have so that the two of you can join me and Dee-Dee at Eaton Square for a working dinner."

Maebelle took a deep breath. "Now, a further apology. I apologise for being a touch strong when we last spoke but I'm a great believe in letting bygones be bygones" - *So why the longstanding bitterness against Lulu Mayhew?* thought Corey - "and I trust you feel the same way."

"Oh, I most certainly do, Maebelle," yawned Corey, his face breaking into a "I knew it! I just knew it!" smile. "I too am a great believer in letting bygones be bygones, and I can guarantee Peter and I will be with you next Tuesday. Shall we say eight o'clock?"

"Perfect," purred Maebelle. "We look forward to seeing the two of you." Her words followed by a definitive click.

Now wide awake, Corey promptly telephoned Peter and gave him the good news. "It looks as if Malcom bloody Duval has landed himself firmly in the shit," he announced with a chortle. "In other words, you and I are back in business!"

*

Malcom Duval sat staring at the silent mobile on his desk. "Fuck you, Maebelle," he muttered, reaching for the brandy snifter. "Fuck you and your sicko desire for any more devious happenings involving Lulu Mayhew whom one can only admire despite all your ranting and raving. The good thing is that me and the team are paid up to date which means I - we - will no longer be carrying out any further assignments of your tawdry, tacky behalf."

Taking a satisfying swallow of brandy, he added with a hollow chuckle. "As for the next scheduled *Fright Night,* this is now cancelled." Malcom gave another chuckle. "Just as well as I couldn't quite envisage poor Lulu Mayhew with a shaved-head and pussy, her body covered in red paint reminiscent of a gold-painted Shirley Eaton in *Goldfinger*!"

Taking a further sip, he said with a growl. "Time for a change of scenery Duval. Time to do another Amerigo Vespucci and head for the liberating U. S. of A. What's more, I'll fly direct to sunny California where I'll be able to catch-up with several equally inclined chums. Maybe I'll even give distant cousin Belinda a call as it can do no harm in saying hi. Not only is Belinda the greatest of fun, she's also a top lawyer who always wins!"

Giving a further chuckle, Malcom burst into a loud off-key rendering of his own version of *San Francisco Here I Come.* Namely, "San *Fag Crisco*, here I come, not that I'm all that keen on bum!"

Adding a further generous dollop of brandy to the empty snifter, he murmured contemplatively. "However. before I board my broomstick maybe a little 'take that, bitch!' gesture to a certain lady who thinks she's the fashion world's answer to Venus Di Milo and Helen of Troy combined. *What* a good idea! Meanwhile I'll give Maddy a quick call as she's always good for a shoulder to whinge on!"

GODFREY STREET

"Tell me! Tell me!" cried Lulu. "Did the dreaded Dee-Dee end up as The Seine's answer to Esther Williams or not?"

"He most certainly did," laughed Dan. "Though, according to Henri, Dee-Dee Donaldson-cum-Devereaux proved himself to be more of a Mark Spitz than a floundering fish. To quote Henri. 'Little bastard proved himself to be quite a swimmer and made the riverbank in gold medal time!'" He gave another laugh. "An extra bit of good news is that Malcom Duval - Maebelle's so-called hitman - is no longer in her good books. I need to make a few more calls to see exactly what's going on. If this *is* the case, it could mean that any other irritating ploys concerning you could be on hold indefinitely. But, as I said, let me make a few calls and get back to you."

"Dan, not only are you an absolute star; you're an absolute darling as well!" Lulu gave a giggle. "Let me assure you that if Medora ever met you, she'd literally flip flop!"

"I can hardly wait to hear what dear, innocent Medora, Archie and Flip Flop get up to next," chuckled Dan.

"Nor can I," giggled Lulu. "Lunch tomorrow, here at one?"

"Already in my mental diary," chuckled Dan. "See you then, Princess Pen!"

"Princess Pen?" giggled Lulu looking at the silent mobile in her hand. "Why, Dan the Man; not only are you a one hundred percent *real* man, but a flatterer and a romantic to boot. I like it! I like it!"

*

"According to hearsay Maebelle's latest tantrums are even more outrageous than before," announced Dan as he and Lulu sat having a glass of wine. "To the extent that she's now doing a Madonna and demanding full-time bodyguards for herself *and* Devereaux!"

"It gets better by the minute," giggled Lulu. "So, what gave you in mind for her next fright night?"

"For her next fright night?" chuckled Dan. "People say it takes two to tango whereas *I* say it also takes two to *tangle.* I adore teasing you, Lulu dear, so - as *you* are prone to say - watch this space!"

EIGHT

AN ELEGANT DUPLEX APARTMENT OVERLOOKING EATON SQUARE - BELGRAVIA

"Thank *God* that little jaunt's finally over," muttered Maebelle as Briggs and a maid collected Dee-Dee's one Gucci suitcase and her seven Louis Vuitton cases before carrying them upstairs. "Time for a much-needed drink, Dee-Dee, so, back to your labours pronto, and mix a *gallon* of lethal martinis! It may not be what the doctor ordered regarding my damaged leg. But who gives a damn!"

"Your legs have never looked more striking, Maebelle dear," said Dee-Dee over his shoulder from where he stood by the red telephone box doing Maebelle's bidding. "Apart from a touch of make up on your *one* ankle - and which only you and I know about – nobody's noticed anything untoward."

"Well, I most certainly do - mentally!" sniped Maebelle. "What time did you say Marsden and Proudfoot would be here?"

"Six o'clock," said Dee-Dee handing Maebelle her demanded drink. He nodded toward his mobile on the bar counter. "And as we know from Mr. Duval's no punches spared text, he's no longer interested in - I quote - 'our puerile shenanigans'."

"Malcom Duval?" repeated Maebelle. Taking a long sip of her martini, she added drily. "Never heard of him."

Unfortunately, I have a feeling you - we - will be hearing from him again sooner than later, thought Dee-Dee, a distinct shiver running down his spine. *Mr. Duval, like yourself, is another person who does not forgive nor forget.*

"Dee-Dee?" said Maebelle snapping her fingers. "Dee-Dee?"

"Oh! Sorry Maebelle," came the hasty reply. "I agree with you. Malcom Duval? Never heard of him!"

GODFREY STREET - THREE DAYS LATER

"Lulu, dear, the car's here," chirruped Maddy on answering the intercom.

"On my way!" called Lulu reaching her Lulu Guinness clutch bag. "Still no sign of Dan?"

"No, but he did say he'd see you there if he couldn't get here in time to escort you!"

"So, he did!" carolled Lulu on joining Maddy in the lobby. "How do I look?"

"Like a bestselling author *should* look!" crowed Maddy. "A million euros!"

"Liar! See you later, dear."

GLADORA FINE ART - MAYFAIR

"Glorious paintings, Daphne dear," crooned Lulu with an inward shudder. "Rather like the artist," she added, giving Daphne Dimbleby, the reason for the event, a chaste kiss on the cheek.

"Flatterer!" cackled Daphne, a Madge Simpson lookalike, but a lookalike with green and purple streaked hair. "Your dishy but decidedly spooky-looking guest arrived a few minutes ago and is in the next room no doubt subtly seducing a group of wannabe vampirettes!"

"Vampirettes?" giggled Lulu.

"Well, he does look like one of those glorious, elongated Count Draculas one sees in those vampire movies, dear," cackled Daphne. Narrowing her green and purple shadowed eyes she leaned forward as if examining Lulu's elegant neck. "Not that I can see any fang marks! Haw-haw!"

"Oh, Daphne! You're such a tease!" crooned Lulu, thinking; *Stupid cow!* "Forgive me while I go and see what my midnight muse is up to!"

"Miss Mayhew? Miss Lulu Mayhew the author?" said a pleasant, tenor voice.

"Yes, the last time I checked that was definitely me," replied Lulu with a light laugh. The response being one of her favourite comebacks.

"Delighted to meet you, Miss Mayhew," said the man with a warm smile. "I've read both you books, and I have to say I can hardly wait to read your next one."

"All good things come to those who wait," crowed Lulu, craning her neck in an attempt to spot Dan among the animated crowd. She gave an embarrassed start. "Oh, please forgive me. I didn't mean to appear rude. I was simply trying to spot someone who's already arrived."

"Lucky someone," smiled the man proffering his hand. "With luck we'll meet again."

"Please," said Lulu, remembering she was speaking to a potential buyer as well as a fan. "Let me go and find my friend and then we'll come and say hello properly." She added coquettishly. "Your name, kind sir?"

"Malcom. Malcom Duval," replied Malcom with a "gotcha!" smile.

"As I said, we'll see you in a minute, Malcom," smiled Lulu giving a twiddle of her fingers as she walked away.

Making her way through the animated throng into the second half of the gallery Lulu eventually spotted Dan towering above an admiring group of Daphne's so-called vampirettes. "Ah! There you are!" she crooned, her voice causing part of the group to spin round, their coos of admiration changing to cries of "it's Lulu Mayhew, the author", "I *loved* your book!" along with the dreaded "May I have your autograph?".

"It's usually the gentleman who rescues the damsel in distress," chuckled Dan once he and Lulu had managed to extricate themselves from the excited group, "not the other way round." Giving Lulu a light kiss on the cheek, he said in a conspiratorial whisper. "You look lovelier than ever, and do we really need to stay? I'm sure Troy and Tamara are already at the restaurant."

"Yes, Dan," giggled Lulu. "See it as your lost chivalry being given a chance to redeem itself! Now, there's someone we should go and say hello to as I was a touch rude to him due to my lecherous lust in finding you! So, come along."

"Malcom, I'm back," she crooned giving Malcom a tap on the shoulder.

"Oh, so you are," beamed Malcom who had been chatting to the garrulous Daphne. Proffering his hand toward Dan who hesitantly reached out and gave it a desultory shake, Malcom said, not missing a beat. "And you, good sir, must be the mysterious gentleman this lovely lady was looking for."

"Just *look* at the two of them Lulu dear," crowed Daphne. "A true portrait of *Beauty and The Beast*!" Putting her hands to her face she added with an anguished cry. "Oh my God! Forgive me as I didn't mean to sound so rude..."

"Please," smiled Dan. "It happens all the time. People thinking I'm a doppelganger for Dracula, just as I'm sure people think this gentleman a doppelganger for some glamorous movie star!"

"Thank you, kind sir; thank you!" gushed a red-faced Daphne. "Now, if you" excuse me, I've other souls to greet and paintings to sell. Ha ha! So, see you when I see you!"

"She looks exactly like one of her er . . . *vibrant* paintings," chuckled Malcom. "Maybe I'll bid for her later when the auction starts!"

"Not only a movie star lookalike but a *rich* movie star lookalike," quipped Dan. "So, Malcom; apart from wanting to bid for a walking, talking painting of the artist herself, may I ask what kind of business you're in?"

"Tobacco," replied Malcom without hesitation. "I own several tobacco farms in Zimbabwe, the former Southern Rhodesia, and, despite the political problems out there, the farms still manage to generate a comfortable business which, through various channels, allows me to keep a Swiss bank account well fed!"

"You sound more alluring by the minute!" chortled Lulu, instantly aware of the growing animosity between the two men. Taking hold of Dan by the arm, she said brightly. "Interesting talking to you, Malcom, but Dan and I have a dinner to attend so, enjoy the rest of your evening." She gave a giggle. "Have fun hanging Daphne!"

"Have fun hanging Daphne?" muttered Malcom watching as the two walked away. "I'll have more fun hanging fashionista Maebelle out to dry! As for you, Lulu Mayhew, you obviously have not the slightest iota that I fully intend having you as my assistant hangman."

*

"You didn't like him, did you?" said Lulu as the chauffeur driven limousine sped its way along Sloane Street en route to The Ivy Chelsea Garden where they were meeting friends for dinner.

"It's not a case of me not liking him, Lulu. It's a case of me recognising his name from somewhere. A name associated with something decidedly unsavoury. I can't quite put my finger on it but what I *do* know is that it's something not quite right.

Staring at the glossy, passing shops, Dan gave a start. "Got it! Malcom bloody Duval is currently involved with none other than your nemesis. Maebelle!"

"Involved with Maebelle?" gasped Lulu. "How on earth do you know that?"

"The Dan Crozier grapevine!" replied Dan, his face grim." He slapped his knee. "I *knew* it! I just *knew* there was something off about the guy and I very much doubt his being at the gallery this evening was by chance." (At this stage Dan's "grapevine" was apparently unaware of Malcom's falling out with Maebelle.)

"Jesus Christ!" exclaimed Dan as the limousine drew to a halt outside the restaurant. "Could you hold the fort for a minute or two with Troy and Tamara, Lulu dear, as I need to make a couple of urgent calls!" He gave a snort. "You may think you're the king of the bloody castle, Malcom Duval, but may I remind you, at times castle can be adapted to rhyme with arsehole!"

"Sorry about that," said Dan cheerfully on joining Lulu, Tamara and Troy at the bar. Smiling at Lulu he said matter-of-factly. "As expected, James confirmed what I was thinking. Castle King is to be avoided at all costs. I see you three have ordered a bottle of bubbly. However, after what James told me, I deserve a large whisky!"

AN ELEGANT DUPLEX APARTMENT OVERLOOKING EATON SQUARE - THE SAME EVENING

"I've said what I had to say," said Maebelle with a tight smile; a smile which a sniggering Peter would later describe to Posy as "a rictus of saccharine menace. "So, gentlemen, are you in or out?"

"Count me as most definitely in!" enthused Corey. "After what happened to poor Dee-Dee over in Paris, how could you expect me *not* to be in!"

"I agree with Corey," said Peter firmly. He gave a snigger. "It's time we put red paint to bed and come up with something more compelling." Seeing an opening for moving to top of the class and becoming teacher Maebelle's pet, he added solemnly. "So, how about this."

Peter began to elaborate on what he had in mind, and, to his growing satisfaction, he found Maebelle, Dee-Dee and Corey absorbing his every word; their expressions changing from their former scepticism to ones of admiration.

"And you really believe you - we - could get away with such a manoeuvre?" asked Maebelle in a sultry voice.

"Get away with it?" chortled Peter. "See it as already done!" *And if this doesn't make Posy eat her cutting words then I'm Popeye the Sailor man,* he thought with an inward chuckle.

"I think Peter's plan deserves a toast in something more than mere champagne, so why not champagne cocktails all round. Dee-Dee dear, could you do the honours." Maebelle turned to where Peter sat, a self-important smile on his face. "I owe you a big, personal thank you, Peter dear," she purred. "I take it you will be staying for breakfast." Said as a statement, not a question.

*

Anticipating a major showdown with Posy on his return to the Fulham flat a few minutes before noon the next day, Peter nervously reached for the note he found resting against the kettle on the kitchen counter. Giving a loud gulp, he unfolded the sheet of paper, his nervous expression quickly changing to one of relief.

You and Algy's sofa are certainly getting to know each other, he read. *Out and about. Pilates et cetera plus lunch with les girls. Love you. Back around six. You owe me a spoiling dinner. xx. Posy.*

"Thank Christ for small mercies," muttered Peter delving into the fridge for a can of restorative Coca-Cola. "Now I can have at least two more showers - maybe even go for a sauna - before Madam returns for - when it comes to sniffing the slightest hint of an alien perfume - Posy would put a sniffer dog to shame!" He gave a chuckle. "I have no idea what perfume Maebelle prefers, but instead of dabbing a touch on her wrists and behind ears as I understand most women do, I swear she bathes in the fucking stiff!"

Taking a further sip from the can, Peter said softly. "Do I tell Posy of what I suggested Corey and I do in order to win Maebelle's approval? I don't see why not as she's bound to put two and two together when she sees or hears about it on the news. As I keep saying to myself, once Posy realises that I'm the instigator, the *brains* behind the disaster, she will see me in a new light. She'll see me as Peter Proudfoot, man or the moment, instead of Peter Proudfoot, an everyday fellow."

MEGAN'S BY THE GREEN RESTAURANT - PARSONS GREEN - FULHAM

"My God, Peter," whispered Posy, her eyes wide, as she sat staring at Peter across the table. "And you really think - no, make that sincerely *believe*

- you and bumbling Corey Marsden will get away with it? I mean, Peter darling, it's not only explosive; it's a Hiroshima wipe out!"

"Glad you approve," said Peter smugly, "Another bottle of wine to wish us well?"

*

"Blithering idiot," murmured Posy studying her reflection in the mirror as she touched up her lips. Having announced the need to "visit the little girls' room" she had left a decidedly drunken Peter in order to calm down, gather her thoughts together and work out what to do next.

"I *know* he spent the night with that odious woman," hissed Posy, "and as for that ridiculous plan of his, surely Peter must realise the next port of call for him - and that equally idiotic Corey - can only be a bloody prison cell! Obviously, there won't be the slightest hint of anyone else's involvement, meaning that posturing monstrosity and her ghastly sidekick get away scot-free."

Reaching for her clutch bag Posy added sadly. "Surely Peter must have some inkling as to the damage his infatuation with Maebelle is doing to our relationship? Doesn't he realise my true feelings for him? For the loveable idiot he is?" Giving her reflection a grimace, she added spikily. "As Dolly Parton so rightly sang. *Stand By Your Man,* and that's exactly what I'm going to do! Forget pistols or fisticuffs at dawn, Madam Maebelle, for, as far as I'm concerned, you're about find yourself and your loathsome little sidekick crawling into a vibrant and highly spectacular sunset!"

NINE

GODFREY STREET - THREE DAYS LATER

"Good morning, Miss Mayhew. It's Marie Jennings, the secretary at Gladora Fine Art."

"Good morning, Marie," replied Lulu raising a quizzical eyebrow. "How may I help you?"

"I'm calling because we've received an envelope here at the gallery marked for your attention and asking us to forward it to you. Are you quite happy for me to do this?" Marie gave a light laugh. "I'm asking because there are so many odd people around, such as stalkers, perverts" - she gave a further laugh - "or even serial killers, so one can never be too careful."

"Instead of forwarding it to me, Marie, please open it," said Lulu. She gave a snicker. "At least I'll have a bona fide witness if it's anything threatening!"

"I'm sure it's only a fan letter," said Marie. "Please hold on while I try to find my elusive paper knife!" Lulu could hear Marie's whispered, "Now where did I put the bloody thing," followed by sounds of shuffling and finally, a cheerful "Here goes, Miss Mayhew."

"*Dear Miss Mayhew,*" read Marie. "*Simply a brief note to say how much I enjoyed meeting you at the opening of Daphne Dimbleby's exhibition the other evening before your companion whisked you away! If, by any chance you would care to meet for lunch within the next day or two, please let me know. I'm a great fan of Bellamy's in Bruton Place which I find chic and discreet as well as serving the most delicious food. If you do care to meet, my telephone number and email address can be seen at the bottom of the page. Kind regards. Malcom Duval.*"

"What a charming note, Miss Mayhew," giggled Marie. "I wish somebody would go to such trouble at having a note like that forwarded to me!"

"I'm sure you receive endless such notes, Marie dear," said Lulu silkily. "Now, if you could kindly give me Mr. Duval's telephone number and email address, I can take it from there."

"Malcom Duval," murmured Lulu on hanging up. "Interesting. And as I'm a firm believer in 'do it now' and 'there's no time like present', let's do exactly that!"

Lulu's email to Malcom was succinct. "*I would have loved to join you at Bellamy's, but unfortunately my Rottweiler of a publisher is hounding me regarding the latest Lulu Mathew. Maybe in a couple of weeks' time? My apologies. Lulu.*" "Pity," she murmured pressing send. "Could have been fun,"

A few minutes later her main line started to ring.

"That certainly won't be Duval seeing he doesn't have any of my numbers." muttered Lulu reaching for the phone. "And it won't be Dan, Leo or Lobie as they always come through on my private line, so let's see who this is. Hello," she added crisply. "How may I help you?"

"Is that Lulu Mayhew?" asked a tremulous voice.

"No, it's Zasu Pitts, Miss Mayhew's secretary," replied Lulu glibly. "Miss Mayhew won't be until later. May I take a message?"

"Er . . . yes please, if you would be so kind. My name is Posy Webber and I need to speak to Miss Mayhew urgently. In fact, please tell Miss Mayhew it's serious, extremely serious, and could she please call me back on the number I'm about to give you. Miss Mayhew must please, *please* call me, no matter what the time. I repeat, it's most urgent. In fact, I'm prepared to say it's a matter of life and death."

Before a somewhat flabbergasted Lulu could respond, the line went dead.

Lulu spun round in her chair to speak to Maddy who had just entered the room carrying two mugs of coffee. "I've just had *the* most extraordinary call from a Posy Webber saying she needed to talk to me urgently about a life and death matter and would I call her back!"

"Call her back? But you were just talking to her," replied Maddy placing one of the mugs on Lulu's desk while taking a sip from the other.

"I was, but as you well know I hate taking blind calls, so I said I was you whilst referring to myself as Zasu Pitts - sorry! - and I would have you ask me to call her back." Lulu added a touch nervously. "I wonder what the hell she meant by a life and death matter."

"Did she leave a number?"

"Of course."

"So, let *me* call her back and say I'm you responding to her urgent call."

"Here," said Lulu handing Maddy a post-it note.

"Let's see *exactly* what Miss Posy Webber has got to say for herself," murmured Maddy tapping in the number. "Miss Webber? Lulu Mayhew calling regarding your rather strange message. Would you care to explain?"

"Oh, Miss Mayhew. Thank *God* you called," replied Posy with a sob. "I'd much prefer to talk to you face to face. Is there any chance we could this morning as what I have to tell you is extremely serious."

"If what you wish to tell me is so serious, Miss Webber, I suggest you tell me here and now," said Maddy sharply. "Otherwise, I'm hanging up. If you *don't* tell me and if you call again, I have your number which can easily be traced and have you up for harassment!"

There was a stunned silence followed by a series of sobs and gulps before Posy managed to speak. "It concerns my boyfriend, Peter Proudfoot and a colleague of his, Corey Marsden, Miss Mayhew, and the fashion model, Maebelle. To cut to the chase, Miss Mayhew, they are planning for you to have a serious, even fatal, motor accident whilst travelling to Bristol next Wednesday for a book signing. They have plans for someone to shoot out the tyres to your limousine on its approach to the Clifton Suspension Bridge, resulting in the vehicle possibly ending up in the River Avon!"

Maddy sat staring at Lulu as if transfixed before saying calmly. "Miss Webber, I'm going to put our ensuing conversation on speaker phone as well as record it. Now, and for the record, could you please repeat what you just said, Miss Webber? Miss Webber? Miss Webber, are you still there?"

Maddy gave Lulu a panicky look. "Miss Webber? Miss Webber would you please answer me!" Her frantic question answered by a distinct click.

"It sounds as if she just hung up" said Maddy in disbelief. "Here, let me try her again on another phone." Punching in the number, Maddy listed for a moment. Looking at Lulu she said with a shake of her head. "Now I'm getting an engaged signal. She sounded in such a state it wouldn't surprise me if she's gone and dropped the wretched phone."

"No doubt, if she's genuine, she'll call back," said Lulu in a no-nonsense voice.

After ten minutes silence Lulu said to Maddy. "I have a nasty feeling about this. See if you can find an address for this Posy Webber. Once we've got that and as Dan appears to have done one of his regular disappearing acts, I'll have Lobie get one of his cronies to go round to wherever it is and check if she's okay. Better still. I'll get whoever it is to bring her back here."

*

"Silly, disloyal girl," said Peter with a grimace as he stood looking at Posy's silent, crumpled form lying on the kitchen floor, a growing pool of blood forming next to her head. "What a pity you couldn't be more like Maebelle. Not only is she a wildcat in bed but when it comes to the admiration stakes, nobody but nobody, can hold a candle to the amazing Maebelle!"

Placing a bloody hammer on the kitchen counter he added softly. "You should have checked that I had definitely left for my meeting with Corey before you decided to call bloody Lulu Mayhew and double-cross us." Reaching for his mobile he called Corey and explained what had happened.

"I'll get someone round there right away," snapped Corey. He gave a snigger. "Just as well she was at your flat and not at her place, for you can bet your bottom dollar, bloody Mayhew will have someone round there to check on her before you can say Jack Robinson farted! Wait there for the guys to arrive. Meanwhile, I'll ring Maebelle and bring her up to date."

Hanging up Corey immediately called Maebelle. On hearing Dee-Dee's camp "Good morning from the world's most glittering catwalk. The imitable Dee-Dee Devereaux, Miss Maebelle's *Manneken* Friday speaking!" he said without any preamble. "Dee-Dee, it's Corey Marsden and I'm calling about something which Miss Maebelle needs to hear, as there's been a major hitch in our plan involving Lulu Mayhew's anticipated swan dive into the River Avon next week!"

"Miss Maebelle's sitting across from me. Let me give her the phone."

"What is it?" snapped Maebelle. "I heard you say something about next week and the River Avon?"

"Before I give you any details, Miss Maebelle, let me say that young Peter Proudfoot has now proven his loyalty a hundredfold," said Corey before going on to explain how Peter happened to overhear Posy Webber's telephone conversation with Lulu and his reaction to her duplicity.

"So, the Janus-faced cow is dead, is she?" hissed Maebelle."

"Dead as a doornail, Miss Maebelle.

"And you've already made arrangements for getting rid of the body?"

"All done, Miss Maebelle."

"Please ask Peter to call round to the apartment as soon as he is able," said Maebelle without hesitation. "That young man certainly deserves a bonus. As for Lulu Mayhew, we'll have to think again. No doubt she will be travelling to some other promotional event sooner than later."

Maebelle gave Dee-Dee a glare. "Care to share what you find so funny, Mr. Devereaux?"

"But of course, Maebelle dear," tittered Dee-Dee. "Here I am thinking I was a *wow* between the sheets but obviously there's nobody who can beat the acrobatic, conniving, calculating fashionista Maebelle; femme fatale extraordinaire!"

"You know what, Dee-Dee Devereaux," said Maebelle with a rare, genuine smile. "There are times when I actually like you; like now! So, come here, little man, and let your momentarily misguided Maebelle give you a big sloppy kiss!"

"A big sloppy kiss? No thank you," tittered Dee-Dee. "How about I mix a large jug of vicious Bloody Marys instead?"

"A *much* better idea," crooned Maebelle. "Not only a plump and - at times - an irritating little person, but a clever little person as well!"

GODFREY STREET

"As for bloody Mae Collison - excuse me - *Maebelle* and her Mr. Fixit's plan for me to end up in the River Avon, they'll have to think again," crooned Lulu. "What's more, let me assure you, *Maebelle,* this time you've gone too far. So far, in fact, that you're about to topple off the bloody catwalk!"

She turned to where Leo, Lobie and Maddy sat facing her (Dan still out of the picture). "It's time to teach that bitch and her fat little accomplice another lesson, only this time a lesson that will be taken seriously. So, my friends, off with the dunce caps and on with some highly intelligent thinking caps!" Lulu gave a giggle. "I think I may just include my imaginary Medora's Flip Flop as he does appear to be a pooch extraordinaire. So much so that even I, his creator, am stunned at times by what Flip Flop ends up doing!" Eyeing a bemused Lobie she added with a laugh. "As I just said, Flip Flop's a highly intelligent pooch belonging to deliciously wicked little Medora Maddox, *the* leading characters in my next book."

Eyeing Lulu, a grinning Lobie said in feigned disbelief. "Unless I'm mistaken, little Medora's imaginary Flop - therefore *my* imaginary Flip Flop as well - has just suggested in tail thumping morse code what we should do with Maebelle. While the dreadful Dee-Dee Devereaux took an assisted dive into The Seine, and you were supposed to match this by taking your own, spectacular nosedive into the River Avon, the brilliant Flip Flop has suggested Maebelle take a high dive into the Thames instead! However, not a run-of-the-mill high dive, but a special high dive when she's doing a photoshoot in Canary Wharf next week."

"Doing a photoshoot in Canary Wharf next week?" echoed Lulu. "What's that supposed to mean?"

"Thanks to the internet I was able to check on Maebelle's forthcoming assignments. Next week she'll be shooting an advert for a new soft drink fittingly titled *SKY HIGH,* and what better place to shoot this than Canary Wharf: London's answer to Manhattan."

"Sorry, but I still don't follow," said Lulu. "How does a high dive come into it?"

"A turn of phrase, nothing more," replied Lobie. "However, thanks to clever Flip Flop, I should have said a *dunk* in the Thames. The dunk, all thanks to a *hunk,* who will be waiting in the wings to do exactly that."

"A dunk and a hunk?" said Lulu a touch irritably. "I still don't get what you're trying to say."

Lobie gave a grin. "What Flip Flop and I are trying to say is I've a friend who used to work in a circus under the name of Larry the Lasso. Not only is Larry an expert with a lasso, he's also an expert with motorbikes and taking part in riding The Wall of Death in between lassoing scantily clad ladies! What Flip Flop thumped is that Larry, riding a motorbike and closely followed by a colleague on *his* motorbike, suddenly appears as Maebelle is being filmed seated at a table with a glass and a bottle of *HIGH DIVE* prominently displayed. Within a flash Larry then lassos her and within seconds she's caught by the second biker before she can hit the ground. The two roar up to the actual river where Larry takes over and throws Miss Maebelle in. And if *that* doesn't give her a taste of her own. medicine, I'll eat my very expensive Fedora!"

Lobie gave a chuckle. "The humiliation of such an undignified happening being recorded plus a sharp reminder of whatever happens to bloody Dee-Dee Devereaux could also happen to her, should make the two them think again. As Dan so rightly said; watch this space!"

"And the inspiration behind all that was my imaginary, darling Flip Flop?" chortled Lulu.

"One hundred percent your contagious, imaginary Flip Flop!" chuckled Lobie. "That's exactly what he thumped out in his very own and highly exclusive tail wagging morse code!"

"Clever, *clever* Flip Flop!" crooned Lulu.

"You don't have to ask," grinned Maddy. "Imaginary doggy treats and genuine champers coming up!"

CANARY WHARF - THE FOLLOWING WEDNESDAY

Maebelle, dressed in a fluorescent orange trouser suit with a matching turban and spiky shoes to match the glass of *SKY HIGH* along with the relevant bottle sitting on the table in front of her, sat smiling at the camera. About to say - "Where better a place to enjoy a delicious glass of *SKY HIGH* than sitting here surrounded by the skyscrapers of Canary Wharf" - she was interrupted by the angry roar of two powerful motorbikes and their masked riders racing toward the set. Within the blink of an eye, the camera crew and others watched in disbelief as a shrieking Maebelle appeared to shoot into the air before being caught by the second biker. The onlookers' looks of disbelief changing to looks of incredulity as the two bikers, skidded to a halt at the water's edge, the first biker taking hold of a shrieking, wildly kicking Maebelle, before releasing her from the lasso and throwing her into the marina.

"Bloody Hell! I trust you managed to catch all that?" cried Les Pilkington, the director, to one of the camera crew.

"Perfectly, Les," grinned the cameraman. "And let me tell you, Les, the shots I manged to take are nothing less than bloody *Oscar* worthy money shots!"

As Les was talking to the cameraman a concerned crew member, fully dressed, dived, fully into the frothing water and within seconds, helped by other members, managed to drag a hysterical Maebelle back to safety and set her down on the paving stones.

"Talk about endless fucking Oscar worthy money shots," muttered the cameraman as he kept snapping away as a bedraggled, sopping wet, wailing Maebelle was helped to her feet. "Thanks, Miss Maybelle. The pics I've been lucky enough to take today will be a great help toward the purchase of a villa on Majorca along with the small bar I plan to buy."

GODFREY STREET

"I caught something about it on the news," crooned Lulu on taking Lobie's call. "Minutes later Maddy and I sat and watched a news update regarding an incident at Canary Wharf." She gave a giggle. "I have to say Maebelle did *not* look her best! In fact, on seeing a closeup of her tearful, muddy face, poor, startled face I am sure, had our imaginary Flip Flop been watching with us, he would have given a few, cheerful barks as if to say. 'Who's a clever dog, then?"

*

"Who was that at the door?" asked Lulu glancing up from her computer as a smiling Maddy entered the room. "We weren't expecting anyone, were we?"

"It's Lobie Maseko accompanied by a gentleman he'd like you to meet," said Maddy doing her best to keep a straight face.

"Who?" snapped Lulu, eyeing Maddy suspiciously.

"Best you come and see for yourself," snickered Maddy, "I have to say he's *very* good-looking!"

"Humph," muttered Lulu as she got up in order to meet Lobie and the mysterious good-looking gentleman waiting upstairs.

"And who is this good-looking gentleman?" crooned Lulu on spotting the large golden retriever - Lulu was convinced the animal, his large furry tail softly thumping against the carpet, was smiling at her - standing next to a grinning Lobie.

"Miss Lulu Mayhew, I'd like you to meet the former Mr. Taurus, renamed a few hours ago as Mr. Flip Flop. Mr. Flip Flop has been residing at the Battersea Cats and Dogs Home and is now looking forward - with Miss Lulu Mayhew's blessing, of course - to taking up permanent residence here, at Godfrey Street."

"Well, Mr. Lobie Maseko, all Miss Lulu Mayhew can say is how on earth could she resist such an offer?"

Falling to her knees Lulu stretched out her arms and said with a cry. "Welcome to Godfrey Street and your new home, Flip Flop!"

On hearing Lulu's passionate cry Taurus, now Flip Flop, gave an excited bark as he bounded across to the kneeling Lulu and, on being gathered up in her arms, smothered her face with seemingly endless licks.

"Wow!" exclaimed Lobie. "If that isn't an ardent example of love at first sight, then I'm a white man!"

Not only did Lobie arrive with Flip Flop in tow, but with a generous supply of doggy treats and a large packet of goodies from Wyndhams, the butchers, along with a cooler bag holding two bottles of chilled Dom Perignon.

As Lulu, Maddy and Lobie, duly armed with flutes of celebratory champagne sat watching Flip Flop contentedly chewing on a juicy bone, Lulu turned to Lobie and said mischievously. "Dear Lobie, I wonder if you're thinking what I'm thinking?

"From the few excerpts you've given me to read regarding the further exploits of the wily Miss Medora Maddox," replied Lobie, a whiter that white smile lighting up his dark, handsome face. "Maybe a mishap or two involving a few more of Maebelle's associates as friends she has not. Unless that dreadful Devereaux can be seen as one."

"I can see my position as a bestselling author easily usurped by a certain Lobie Maseko, a new bestselling author," chortled Lulu. "So, new bestselling author, tell me what I had in mind?"

Giving Maddy a conspiratorial smile, Lulu said proudly. "Magnificent Maddy has once again proved herself invaluable when it comes to digging up information of all sorts and has already come up with a couple of names. Maddy?"

"First on my list are a couple on a par with Maebelle when it comes to ostentation and posturing," announced Maddy looking at her notepad.

"God! What a terrifying thought!" interrupted Lobie. "Anyone I may have been unfortunate enough to have already met?"

"I very much doubt it," said Maddy crisply, "Their names are Chuck and Tita McBain. Chuck McBain's president of a major accountancy firm: his other claim to fame being he once danced with Diana, Princess of Wales. As for Tita, his wife, a wannabe interior designer - she was once a Twiggy lookalike before she morphed into The Michelin *Woman* - her claim to fame being she knows *everyone* worth knowing!" She gave a snicker. "As some bright wag put it, instead of cornflakes for breakfast she enjoys a bowl of cut up pages taken from a copy of Debrett's! I assume Chuck McBain advises Maebelle on her finances while Tita supplies the feel-good factor."

"Anyone else?" asked Lobie.

"I have two more couple down as definite, and three more listed should we need them."

"So," said Lobie turning to face Lulu. "What does darling Medora have in mind for Mr. and Mrs McBain?"

"You mean what do Medora, Archie and Flip Flop have in mind for Mr. and Mrs McBain," giggled Lulu. "Seeing Mr, McBain loves nothing more than roaring round and showing off in his open Porsche and Mrs McBain is the ultimate snob and Everest social climber-cum-mountaineer; how about this!"

"Unbelievable," chuckled Lobie after listening to what Lulu had in mind for the McBains. Eyeing Lulu, he added matter-of-factly. "Any news on Dan the Man?"

"Dear Dan has done what he usually does and seems to have disappeared. No doubt he'll reappear when least expected." Lulu gave a giggle. "As he glibly says, he may mysteriously disappear now and then, but Dan the Man will never, ever go down the pan! His words, not mine!"

*

As if psychic, Lulu received brief text from Dan two days later.

"Not quite Nobel prize worthy, is it?" chortled Maddy handing Lulu's mobile back to her. "*Sincerest apologies for sudden departure Princess Pen. In States for another week or two. Will explain all on return. Dan the - at times - invisible man.*"

"At times the invisible man?" snorted Lulu. "More like Baroness Orczy's *The Scarlet Pimpernel*. Lulu Mayhew version. We seek him here, we seek him there, we abandoned souls seek him everywhere. Is he alive and kicking or down the pan? That oh so elusive, Dan the Man!"

TEN

"BIZARRE ATTACK ON POWER COUPLE" heralded one tabloid. "SWEET AND SOUR!" shrieked another.

"I take it our latest 'touché Maebelle' meets with your approval?" chuckled Lobie in his regular early morning call.

"Medora, Archie and Flip Flop could not be more thrilled, nor I," replied a delighted Lulu. "So, dearest Lobie, tell me *exactly* what happened as those various news reports aren't all that informative."

"Easy-peasy, to use one of Medora's favourite sayings," laughed Lobie. "All went smoothly; even though I still have a pallet containing several cans of syrup residing in my garage! But, to put it in a nutshell, we simply carried out what you suggested. Slick and I have been keeping an eye on the two McBains and their movements. Knowing McBain would be attending some business dinner last night and knowing he was a strong supporter of the don't drink and drive brigade, he'd obviously arranged alternative transport.

"Once he'd left, we had no problem in getting hold of Mrs McBain, chloroforming her, gagging her and stripping her naked before tying her up and placing her in the open Porsche. We then filled the interior of the Porsche up to seat level with syrup." He gave a snort. "Once the syrup had reached seat level, we went on to scatter a sack full of cut-up pages of Debrett's over her. This done, armed with a flagon of brandy-enhanced coffee and sandwiches, we made ourselves comfortable in a nearby car and waited for hubby's return" Lobie gave a further chuckle. "To say McBain almost had a heart attack on finding his beloved Porsche partly filled with syrup and his naked wife seated inside and covered with a type of strange confetti, would be putting it mildly. But, as Slick so rightly said, his apoplectic reaction on seeing the damage to his beloved Porsche was far greater than his reaction on seeing his naked, paper strewn wife!"

"Brilliant, Lobie! Brilliant!" laughed Lulu. "I'm looking at my very own Flip Flop and from the morse thumping of his tail he's saying - and quite rightly too - 'I told you what a clever dog I am, didn't I?'" She gave another laugh. "I'd love to be a fly on the wall in Maebelle's apartment this morning!"

AN ELEGANT DUPLEX APARTMENT OVERLOOKING EATON SQUARE - BELGRAVIA

"Have you seen this?" screeched Maebelle slamming a copy of one of the lesser tabloids down on the breakfast table. Maebelle insisting on having all the dailies delivered "just in case".

"Give me a chance, Maebelle dear," replied Dee-Dee, theatrically stifling a yawn. "Your delightful Dee-Dee Devereaux is still in the process of emerging from his not at all required beauty sleep!"

"Look at these headlines!" shrieked Maebelle, banging her fist on one of the crumpled pages. "It's pretty bloody obvious Lulu Mayhew's behind this! No matter what you may think!"

"Behind *what?*" echoed Dee-Dee hastily smoothing one of the crumpled pages, "Oh my God!" He added with a trill. "Sweet and sour"? I love it! Absolutely love it!"

"Love it?" shrieked Maebelle. "Have you finally lost what was left of your former puerile mind? How *dare* you laugh at me!" Sweeping the crumpled papers to the floor she raised her fist à la Scarlet O'Hara in *Gone with the Wind* and said with a strangled cry. "This is war, Lulu Mayhew! Open war between Maebelle, fashion model extraordinaire, and Lulu Mayhew, bestselling author of trash!"

"Hold on, Maebelle," said Dee-Dee. "Hold on and think very carefully. In all seriousness, can you honestly say Lulu Mayhew is behind this? Let's face it, and you've said it yourself, those pretentious McBains should be renamed the mountaineering *McPains*, what with their never-ending social climbing and showing off!"

"That's beside the point!" shrilled Maebelle. "Who else would have the imagination to think up something like this? Answer: only a twenty-second-rate writer of trashy novels! That's who!" Giving Dee-Dee a glare, she said coldly and calmly. "Now, Mr. Devereaux, I suggest you go and pack a bag as I have no wish to set eyes on you for at least a week; if not longer. Furthermore, I do not need you here when I meet up with Peter and Corey.

Both of whom I will be telephoning once your grotesque little form is out of my sight!"

"Bitch! Ungrateful, uncomprehending, unrealistic bitch!" spat Dee-Dee storming into his private suite (the original staff quarters). "This time Madam Mae Maebelle Collison, you've gone a step too far! If you want a war, forget tame Lulu Mayhew and think uber-dangerous Dee-Dee Devereaux, because whatever peace treaty you have the audacity to even think exists between you and him is no longer! I'm sick and tired of your childish, temper tantrums, sick and tired of mollycoddling you. In fact, I'm sick and tired of the whole Maebelle scenario. So, as from this very second, Dee-Dee Devereaux is now your arch enemy: your number one enemy! And once I've packed a few belongings it'll be a replay of Pontius Pilate plus!"

Still muttering to himself Dee-Dee quickly tossed a selection of clothing into a suitcase along with a bag of toiletries. Within minutes of his upset with Maebelle he entered the kitchen and, on seeing Mrs Edwards busy preparing breakfast, said breezily. "Mrs Edwards, please inform Miss Maebelle I have left, and, unlike Arnold Schwarzenegger, I won't be back!"

Staring wide-eyed as Dee-Dee exited the kitchen, the non-plussed woman called out in her broad Yorkshire accent. "Will do, Mr. Dee-Dee!" Returning to her task she said with a snigger. "Unlike Arnold Schwarzenegger? Pull the other one, Mr. Dee-Dee. You're no more like that Big Arnie than I'm another Marilyn Monroe!"

Hailing a cab Dee-Dee clambered in, hauling the suitcase after him. (He refused to place this next to the driver as he was convinced the driver would expect an additional tip!).

"Chelsea Harbour Hotel, please," he crooned. "And please, cabbie, no cheerful chitchat as I'm not in the mood!"

"Okay, guv! No chitchat, cheerful or otherwise," replied the burly taxi driver eyeing Dee-Dee in the rearview mirror. "Christ!" he muttered to himself. "Which fuckin' Christmas tree did you just fall from? An', if the missus was 'ere, she'd soon tell you pink on the fuller figure is not at all flatterin'! Not fuckin' flatterin' at all!"

Arriving at the elegant hotel situated next door to the world-renowned Chelsea Harbour Design Centre, Dee-Dee checked into a suite. On being shown to the suite, he graciously gave the startled porter a fifty pence coin, rang room service and ordered a sandwich along with a celebratory bottle of Dom Perignon before unpacking.

Minutes later a waiter arrived with a trolley bearing the requested sandwich and an ice bucket with the requested champagne. As with the porter, Dee-Dee graciously handed the taken aback man a fifty pence piece followed by a cooed "Please make sure you close the door after you!"

Armed with a flute of champagne and a mouthful of smoked salmon sandwich, Dee-Dee made himself comfortable in an armchair. Checking his mobile for what he termed one of his "you never know" numbers, he reached for the room telephone and asked the hotel switchboard to put him through to the selected number,

On hearing Lobie's mellifluous "Good morning. Lobie Maseko speaking," Dee-Dee said with a trill. "Good morning Lobie Maseko. *Dee-Dee Devereaux* speaking! And before you keel over in surprise, please do your best to remain upright because what I have to say - bateau mouche or no bateau mouche! - will, without doubt, vigorously tickle your delectable fancy!"

"I can assure you, Mr. Devereaux, it takes more than an unexpected phone call to cause me to keel over or tickle my delectable fancy," said Lobie silkily. (Had Dee-Dee been able to see Lobie he would have seen a man rigid with shock, but still able to start recording the ensuing conversation.) "Therefore, please continue with this amazing revelation of yours. Better still, where are you and why don't we meet so you can reveal all face to face?"

"I'm now staying at The Chelsea Harbour Hotel so why not come here." Dee-Dee gave a titter. "I'll make sure I'm decent!"

"If that's the case, I've no need to rush," said Lobie smoothly. "I'll meet you in the bar at noon."

*

"Maddy Thompson, Miss Mayhew's secretary speaking. How may I help you?" carolled Maddy.

"Maddy, it's Lobie; Lobie Maseko. Is Lulu about?"

"She's busy working on her new book, Lobie, and I've been given strict instructions she's not to be disturbed."

"I appreciate she's working on a new novel, but I really do need to speak to her." Lobie added wryly. "You'll probably find it hard to believe but I've just had none other than Dee-Dee Devereaux call me!"

"Dee-Dee Devereaux? Bloody hell!" exclaimed Maddy; her former business-like manner instantly forgotten. "That *is* a surprise. Hold on while I connect you."

"Maddy says Dee-Dee *Devereaux* called you?" said Lulu without preamble on taking Lobie's call. "What the *fuck* was he on about?"

"I'm not too sure. Lulu, but I'm meeting him at noon at The Chelsea Harbour Hotel where he told me he's now staying as opposed to Eaton Square. Obviously, there's been some serious trouble on the old home front." There was a moment's silence before Lobie said with a chuckle. "Are you thinking what I'm thinking?"

"Yes! I'll see you there at noon. Talk about the plot thickening: even Medora would be impressed!"

THE CHELSEA HARBOUR HOTEL - RIVERSIDE BAR

"Aha! *There* he is! Mr. Maseko, the man himself!" carolled Dee-Dee as Lobie entered the bar. "I'm about to submerge myself in a large martini; would you care for the same or something else?"

"Thank you, I'll settle for a glass of white wine," said Lobie proffering his hand. About to do the same, Dee-Dee - still seated - froze at the sight of Lulu entering the bar a few steps behind his guest.

"What the fuck is she doing here?" he said in an audible hiss.

"She, like Lobie, is here to find out what you're up to Mr. Devereaux," said Lulu with a tight smile on joining Lobie. "According to Mr. Maseko, you've deserted the hallowed portals of Eaton Square or were you - I'm being tactful here - asked to leave? Before you answer," continued Lulu, her voice dripping with sarcasm, "can we please cut all this surname crap. You know me as Lulu and Mr. Maseko as Lobie just as we know you - albeit a plus or minus - as Dee-Dee! Therefore, *Dee-Dee,* please explain to Lulu and Lobie the reason behind this clandestine meeting."

"It'll be my pleasure, but not before you tell me what you'd like to drink; *Lulu,*" pouted Dee-Dee. "I'm having a martini whilst Mr. Maseko - oops! *Excuse-moi* - Lobie, is having a glass of white wine."

"I'll have the same," purred Lulu making herself comfortable on a chair facing him. "So, Dee-Dee, *dear.* Reveal all."

"If only," tittered Dee-Dee giving Lobie a coquettish look.

"Sorry, Dee-Dee," said Lulu spikily. "When it comes to cricket and a sticky wicket, the dishy, sex-on-legs Lobie does *not* bat for your team so, instead of fantasising, please tell us what exactly is going on."

"Drinkies first," tittered Dee-Dee. "Dirt second! As Her Maj used to say!"

Having ordered a bottle of Sauvignon Blanc for his two guests, Dee-Dee went on to explain his earlier disagreement with Maebelle.

"I can't see why she still harbours this extraordinary grudge against you, Lulu, but she does," said Dee-Dee solemnly. "I can only apologise for *my* part in those ridiculous pranks, and I can assure you they were all Maebelle's doing with me as a not all that willing participant." He gave a titter. "I *loved* your latest tit for tat. Talk about a toffee-nosed toffee apple and a sugar-coated Porsche! Wunderbar!"

"Anything else we should know about?" said Lobie in a strictly business voice.

"Oh, she's definitely gunning for Lulu, but as to what she plans to do next, I honestly have no idea," replied Dee-Dee. "All I know is that a Malcom Duval is no longer in the picture having been replaced by Corey Marsden, whom you know, and her current toyboy, a Peter Proudfoot." He added mischievously. "I take it you two have something else planned should she and her cowardly cohorts come up with some other outlandish ploy."

"I'm sure if Lobie and I can't think of anything equally outlandish, the imitable Flip Flop will," sniggered Lulu.

"Flip Flop?" repeated Dee-Dee.

"My super dog and Lobie's psychic comrade in *harms*," said Lulu with a giggle. "And I can assure you, Dee-Dee, anything Maebelle plans to do in her ridiculous *Maebelle of La Mancha* quest won't hold a candle to what Flip Flop has tucked away in that glorious, furry, golden head of his!"

"Maebelle of La Mancha quest?" questioned Dee-Dee about to take a sip.

"Chasing windmills," snickered Lulu. "Not only is the ridiculous woman beyond redemption; judging from Lobie's expression, she's about to become victim of another mind boggling happening!"

"What Lulu's saying is that Flip Flop and I have a psychic connection," added Lobie deadpan. "Meaning he and I mentally flip flop ideas between ourselves!"

"Please tell me you're having me on," trilled Dee-Dee beckoning a nearby waiter in order to ask for another martini. "Better make that another two! Large," he muttered. "And please hurry."

"Having you on?" repeated Lobie. "Not at all. In fact, Flip Flop has just sent a message saying that as you're here with us, perhaps you may be a touch irked - his woofs, not mine - to hear Corey Marsden and the latest toyboy are not only your replacements they're about to move into your former flatlet within Maebelle's Eaton Square apartment."

Unable to work out if this was all pure fabrication on Lobie's part, Lulu said with a start. "Good Heavens! It sounds as is if I too am getting some sort of message through the ether!" She gave a mischievous snicker. "Poor Dee-Dee! I sincerely trust that the pink suit you're wearing is not the only item of clothing you manage to bring with you!"

"Ha! He's back to messaging me." Stifling a grin Lobie said in a sonorous voice. "According to Flip Flop, wicked Corey appears to be hellbent on taking whatever you *didn't* take, straight to the nearest Oxfam outlet!"

"Oh no!" cried Dee-Dee. "Not my gold lamé jacket! Not my leopard print velvet onesie! Not my diamante-encrusted jockstraps!"

"Your *what*?" chorused Lulu and Lobie.

"Gotcha!" crowed a gleeful Dee-Dee. "That'll teach you to tell porkies about your mysterious Flip Flop!" Glancing at his gold Piaget wristwatch he said nonchalantly. "I take it you *will* be joining *moi* for a spot of lunch. Sadly, not even the most illustrious pooches are allowed into the restaurant which means I am unable to extend my invitation to your supernatural Flip Flop!"

"Let's just keep it to a drink," said Lobie. "Now, why don't you tell us why we're here and, should we be at all interested, tell us exactly what you have in mind?"

"Think Peter Proudfoot," announced Dee-Dee having taken an impressive swallow of one of the replacement martinis. "As Maebelle's current between the sheets flavour of the month, he's therefore a sort of Achilles' heel. Destroy him and who knows, maybe it could lead to a chink in her self-inflated armour."

"I don't like the sound of destroy him," grunted Lobie. "Mayhem, yes; but murder? A definite no-no." He glanced toward Lulu. "Agreed?"

"Oh, yes. I most definitely agree with you, Lobie," replied Lulu with a nod. "Murder is one hundred percent out!" She gave an inward snigger. *If Medora and Archie could hear me, they'd accuse me of being a total wuss!* She gave Lobie a conspiratorial smile. "Any further psychic suggestions from Flip Flop?"

"A highly reflective one, in fact," chuckled Lobie, playing along. Turning to face Dee-Dee he said with a whiter than white smile. "I take it you know the whereabouts of Maebelle's hairdresser?"

"Her hairdresser?" exclaimed Dee-Dee. "Of course. Why?"

"Did you ever see a seventies British horror film named *Theatre of Blood*?" asked Lobie matter-of-factly.

"*Theatre of Blood*? No, I don't think so," replied Dee-Dee in a puzzled voice.

"It was one of those endless horror films churned out at the time. *Theatre of Blood* starred the imitable Vincent Price," explained Lobie. "In the film he played a frustrated, failed actor who decides to take revenge against all those - or so he claimed – who thwarted what should have been a glittering career. Among the many colourful, characters he attacks is a Miss Chloe Moon, played by Price's wife, Coral Browne. Poor Miss Moon finds herself roasted under a hairdryer by the wily Vincent P posing as a hairdresser!"

"So, what are you suggesting?" squawked Dee-Dee.

"What *Flip Flop's* suggesting is that we do something similar. But, instead of roasting Maebelle, we supposedly roast her hairdresser under his very own dryer! To make a valid point, a CD of *Theatre of Blood* addressed to Maebelle will be attached to her hairdresser's smock!"

"You mean put him under the hairdryer instead of Maebelle?" said Dee-Dee wiggling with fiendish delight.

"Yes. Flip Flop suggests we snatch him from his flat - we'll have to find out the address - chloroform him, return him to the salon where we will sit him in a chair, shave his head, singe the bits taken, randomly stick the singed bits back, give him a further heady whiff of chloroform and leave him there until he's found by the cleaner or a member of his staff!"

"And that's it?" said Dee-Dee as if still waiting for the punchline.

"That's it," said Lobie.

"And you truly think Maebelle will be able to put two and two together? I very much doubt it!" sniped Dee-Dee. "Knowing her, she'll see it as some silly prank carried out by other members of his staff. A silly prank from which he'd soon recover!"

"So, what do *you* suggest, Mr. Clever Clogs?" snapped Lulu.

"Instead of *Theatre of Blood* why not another film?" said Dee-Dee ignoring Lulu's sarcastic reprimand." Giving a loud whoop, he added with a clicking of his fingers. "Think *The Godfather*! Where, Instead of Maebelle finding a horse's head in her bed, she wakes up to find the head of some anonymous young swain! The head of a shop mannequin, obviously. That should be enough to give her the screaming heebie-jeebies!" Dee-Dee gave a further snicker. "Particularly if the artistically blood smeared head is discovered lying between her and Proudfoot when they deign to wake up! It'll take some planning" - delving into an inside pocket his jacket he triumphantly produced a keyring - "I still have the keys to the apartment, plus I know the code for the alarm. And before you ask, being Maebelle, she's so sure of her invincibility that she'll never think of changing it despite the constant turnover of staff."

Taking a sip of the second martini, he added in a perfect imitation of Maebelle's imperious voice. "Dee-Dee Devereaux? Never heard of him!"

"After that little dissertation I am sure Lulu - like myself - would be delighted to join you for lunch," chucked Lobie giving Lulu a knowing wink.

*

Dee-Dee called Lulu two days later. "I've got the head and some stage blood," he crowed. "So, when can I see you and the luscious Lobie?"

"You can see me and the luscious Mr. Lobie Maseko anytime," snickered Lulu. "However, you'd best be warned, Dee-Dee dear, that nobody - even as unique as Dee-Dee Devereaux - will ever come between him and his adoring Flip Flop!"

"Not even if I ask nicely on all fours?" tittered Dee-Dee.

"*Especially* if it's *you* on all fours asking ever so nicely!" giggled Lulu, hanging up.

ELEVEN

GODFREY STREET

"She likes to be in bed by midnight," said Dee-Dee with a sniff. "So, allowing for Mr. Proudfoot to earn his keep, it'll be at least a good hour and a half before it would be safe to enter the master bedroom."

"An hour and a half?" sniggered Lulu. "Poor Peter Proudfoot! He'll be shagged out before he reaches twenty-one!"

"The sooner we plant the head, the better," said Lobie. "So, how about this coming Friday; if the coast is clear?" Giving the two a whiter than white smile he added mischievously. "I appreciate it's not Friday the thirteenth, but I'll have to suffice."

"As long as they're in residence, so to speak," muttered Dee-Dee. "Tell you what, why don't I ring Mrs Edwards the cook on Friday morning with some cock and bull story about one of her recipes? She knows I was particularly fond of her beef goulash, so she'll gladly give it to me. An added plus is that she always had a sympathetic ear after one of Maebelle's inevitable scenes."

Putting on a Yorkshire accent, Dee-Dee said, shaking his head. "Poor Mr. Dee-Dee! Miss Maebelle's been saying such terrible, terrible things about you!" He added seriously. "I'll casually ask what she'll be giving them for dinner and if her response confirms that they're staying in, then it's full steam ahead!"

"I have to say you're getting pretty good at all this," chucked Lobie.

"I am, aren't I?" replied Dee-Dee smugly. "What's more, you and Lulu will soon realise that Dee-Dee Devereaux, super sleuth, is just one example of my endless, extraordinary, hidden talents!"

*

An excited Dee-Dee telephoned Lobie. Friday, mid-morning. "As expected, dear Mrs E couldn't have been more helpful. Yes, Madam Elizabeth Bathory Defarge and her substitute vibrator will be dining at home this evening, Therefor I suggest we meet as discussed outside St. Michael's, Chester Square, at one a.m. From there it's an easy trot round to Eaton Square." He added camply. "I've just given the head - sadly not *given* head - a few daubs of blood, and, though I say it myself, Mr. Head has never looked better-cum-bloodier!"

ST. MICHAEL'S CHURCH - CHESTER SQUARE - LATE FRIDAY

"I see we're both early," whispered Lobie as he slipped into the passenger seat of Dee-Dee's rented car. Glancing over his shoulder he said with a soft chuckle. "I take it our friend, Mr. Head, is ready and waiting inside the holdall back there."

"Why not introduce yourself," chirruped Dee-Dee. "Introduce your dashing self and wish him all the best for his assignment!"

"Why not?" chuckled Lobie, leaning over and unzipping the holdall. "Wow!" he exclaimed on seeing the handsome, blood smeared head. "I'm impressed! Let me assure you, Dee-Dee, if I woke up and found that gruesome guy in my bed, I'd do more than freak out! I'd have a bloody heart attack! Okay. Enough of this nervous chatter. You ready?"

"As ready as I'll ever be," replied Dee-Dee shakily. "Lead on, MacLobie! The sooner we transplant Mr. Head - ha ha! - and get the hell out of Maebelle's apartment, the better!"

*

"So far, so good," whispered Dee-Dee as he and Lobie made their way stealthily up the staircase to the bedroom floor. Pausing outside the door to the master bedroom, Dee-Dee said with a soft snicker. "Someone's certainly snoring! It's either an exhausted Proudfoot or an overly self-satisfied Maebelle!" Eyeing the partly open door, he added with a further whisper. "How considerate of them to leave the door ajar. Plus, they left one of the side lamps on."

Lobie and Dee-Dee cautiously approached the vast, elaborately draped bed where the outlines of a gently snoring Maebelle and a loudly snoring Peter could be seen: the two conveniently lying apart. Without any hesitation, Lobie proceeded to carefully pull down the bedclothes while keeping a watchful eye on the snoring couple. On seeing his nod, Dee-Dee carefully placed the head between the two, level with their thighs. His move leading to Lobie gently pulling the bedclothes back as before.

Five minutes later the two were once again outside St. Michael's.

"Well done, Dee-Dee," said Lobie in a relieved voice. "Talk about a tense few minutes!"

"Tense, but brilliantly rewarding," tittered Dee-Dee. "Oh, Lobie! What I wouldn't give to be there when they wake up!"

"Likewise," laughed Lobie. "However, I'm sure hearing about it won't be a letdown. In fact, hearing Maebelle's version of what happened will surely be even more scary than the real happening!"

"You're right, there, my friend," chortled Dee-Dee. "For when it comes to colouring a happening, dear Maebelle makes glorious technicolour look washed out!"

"Something I didn't expect," snorted Lobie.

"What? Finding a *snoring* beauty instead of a sleeping beauty?" interrupted Dee-Dee. He gave a giggle. "Who said the camera never lies!"

"Touché!" chuckled Lobie. "Now, let's get back to Godfrey Street where Lulu, Flip Flop and a couple of large restorative-cum-celebratory drinks are eagerly waiting to hear how we got in with our salute to *The Godfather.*"

AN ELEGANT DUPLEX APARTMENT OVERLOOKING EATON SQUARE

Maebelle's scream as she sleepily reached down to fondle Peter's guaranteed early morning reveille call and found herself fondling a bloodstained head instead, ended up with a startled Peter hurling himself out of the bed and ending up on his backside on the thick pile carpet: his own terrified shrieks rivalling Maebelle's ongoing screams.

On realising it was a dummy's head and not the real McCoy, Peter spent the next five minutes urging Maebelle to calm down and, despite it being early, insisted on pouring each of them a pacifying, early morning brandy.

"That venomous bitch!" hissed Maebelle, having finally pulled herself together. "Who on *earth* could she have coerced into carrying out such a grotesque assignment?"

"It's pretty bloody obvious!" snorted Peter, still shaking after seeing the head and having to deal with Maebelle and her hysterical reaction. "Bloody Dee-Dee Devereaux, that's who! Not only must he still have a set of keys to the apartment; he also knows the alarm code. No doubt he was helped by either Lobie Maseko or Leo Murrain!" Unable to help himself, he said with a hollow laugh. "You have to hand it to them for originality if nothing else."

"I'm so pleased you find it so amusing," snapped Maebelle. "And, unlike you, Peter Proudfoot, what happened remains strictly in my bedroom. In other words, not a murmur to anyone. As far as I'm concerned, it was simply a quiet, uneventful evening spent at home."

"Whatever you say, Maebelle," muttered Peter. Giving Maebelle a sidelong glance, he added tremulously. "When you said unlike you, Peter Proudfoot, what happened remains strictly in my bedroom, what did you mean?"

"Precisely what I said," replied Maebelle airily. "You are no longer an accessory in my bedroom, my apartment or my life. Therefore, without any further ado, I would like you to get dressed and leave before I find it necessary to call the police and have them escort you from the premises."

"Leave? Call the police? Buy *why,* Maebelle?" responded a bewildered Peter with an anguished cry.

"See it as nothing more than Peter Proudfoot is no longer wanted on the voyage," said Maebelle with a tight smile. "Now, I'll leave you to get dressed as I need to make a phone call or two. I trust one of my calls won't have to be to the police?"

TWO DAYS LATER

"There's still nothing in any of the papers or anything on the telly about our latest deed," said Lulu in her regular early morning catch-up with Lobie.

"Yes, so I gather," replied Lobie. "Dee-Dee having been on the blower a few minutes ago." He gave a sigh. "Something's not right, Lulu. And God only knows what Maebelle's up to next!"

"Whatever she's up to, it'll be to my detriment; that's for sure," murmured Lulu. "Anyway. If you hear anything, please be sure to call me."

"You don't have to ask, Lulu," replied Lobie in a hurt voice.

"Sorry, Lobie dear. I didn't mean to sound ungrateful. Take care and we'll speak later."

AN ELEGANT DUPLEX APARTMENT OVERLOOKING EATON SQUARE

"You are so kind as so generous to give me a rare interview," gushed Martha "The Quill" Watson, a doppelganger for Two Ton Tessie O'Shea and feature writer for *NOW & HOW!* magazine. Placing her notebook and pen into her copious Chloé Marcie tote bag, she added coyly. "Now, if darling Claus and Marcus, his assistant can take a few photographs . . ."

"But of *course*," crooned Maebelle with one of her dazzling "aren't I simply gorgeous" smiles. Leaning forward she added conspiratorially. "And please, *dear* Martha, whatever do, make sure you keep your darling promise and lead with my words of wisdom."

"On my Boy Scout and Girl Guide's honour!" nodded Martha, her endless chins wobbling in confirmation. Turning to face the two men standing next their equipment, she added with a gurgle. "Time to earn your keep, boysie boos! Ready when you are!"

Jesus! thought Maebelle. *And here I was thinking bloody Dee-Dee was camp!*

GODFREY STREET

"You've got to hand it to her," giggled Lulu as she and Maddy sat having breakfast. "The woman must have the balls of a dinosaur - I take it male dinosaurs did have balls - for not only does she look a zillion euros in the photograph; nothing, but nothing can compete with her opening lines. Here, I'll read it to you again. But in *my* dulcet tones as I could never mimic a banshee in agony, no matter how hard I tried."

Clearing her throat, Lulu began to read. *"As my dearly departed grandmother so wisely told me: 'Those who can, do, and those who can't, leech'. In today's world, the bitter jealousy and the envy which prevails against those who do succeed, is rife: culminating in all kinds of unparalleled strife. How right dear Grandmother was! However, and, despite the recent, unpleasant happenings in my otherwise glittering, glamorous life, I will continue to overcome such strife and continue with my glorious, glittering, privileged, professional life."*

"As you so aptly said," chortled Maddy, "the balls of a dinosaur! Hold on a sec whilst I take this." Giving Lulu a wink, Maddy reached for the landline. "Good morning!" she carolled. "Maddy Thompson speaking on behalf of Lulu Mayhew. How may I help you?"

"Maddy, it's Lobie calling on a borrowed phone! I like your polite response when answering the landline." He gave a chuckle. "I take it you've both seen today's popular rag?"

"We're both sitting here having literally picked ourselves from the floor where we've been rolling about with laughter!" replied Maddy with a titter. "I take it you'd like a word. Here she is!"

"Lobie!" crooned Lulu. "Heavenly, isn't it? No matter what we think - never mind what Medora, Archie or Flip Flop's imaginary doppelganger think - the woman is bloody unbelievable, isn't she?"

"That she is," chuckled Lobie. "Not only is she unbelievable, she's also unputdownable and therefore unstoppable!"

"Leave it to Medora and me," chuckled Lulu. "Medora, I'm sure, will have something delicious up her Mango sleeve. I only need to find out what this is! You and Leo free for a drink this evening?"

"We're both free and, in fact, I was also ringing to suggest you join us for dinner and a catch-up."

"Why not?" crooned Lulu. "Come here for a drink beforehand."

"Will do! We thought *Scalini,* if you're in a pasta mood."

"I'm immediately in a pasta mood when anyone mentions *Scalini,*" giggled Lulu. "See you around seven."

"Perfect - or, better still - *perfetto,*" chuckled Lobie. "See you at seven."

*

"So, Medora, let's see what mischief you're up to today," murmured Lulu eyeing the blank computer screen. "And as it's another 'teach them a lesson' time; how about this." Lulu began to type.

"*Hot on the heels of the dreaded McPains,*" tittered Medora, "*must surely be Hector the Hideous and Hilda the Horrendous Young. Hector being a doctor and Hilda, a potter of little note.*"

"*Obviously she'll be clay in our hands.*" sniggered Archie. But, what about him?"

"*What about him?*" giggled Medora. "*Whilst people usually cry 'is there a doctor in the house?' Why don't we cry: Is it true? Did the doctor and his wife each really swallow a mouse? The answer is yes, and I'm not joking. Their strange little act leading to a great deal of choking!*"

Lulu glanced at the screen. "Love you. Medora," she murmured. "I'll quickly forward a copy of Medora's latest prank to Lobie and Leo so that we can discuss what *we* plan to do with Madam Maebelle sooner than Clive Cordell's suggested later." She gave a giggle. "Hopefully the thought of swallowing a couple of mice won't put the two Ls off their dinner!"

*

"Great thinking, Lulu," grinned Leo reaching for his drink. "Only you could think up the likes of Doctor Hector and pottering Hilda Young choking on a mouse!" He gave a chuckle. "Unlike another doctor we know who no doubt prefers to choke on something else!"

"How is dear Dr Clive Cordell?" asked Lulu deadpan. "I take it he and Andy McCulloch aka Robert Apps are still living happily in conjugal bliss in that palace on Cheyne Walk?"

Noting the two men's startled expressions, Lulu said cheerfully. "I do my homework and no, I'm not jealous of Robert Apps' success despite, whenever I hear his name mentioned, I inwardly turn *Fifty Shades of Green.* Joke, gentlemen! Joke! I'm actually quite a fan!"

"Thank Christ for that," muttered Lobie, "Phew!" he added, wiping his forehead with the back of his hand in feigned relief. Flashing Lulu a whiter than white smile; he added mischievously. "And Just as well seeing Leo and I bumped into the two of them a couple of evening's ago and . . ."

"And?" interrupted Lulu. "Go on; out with it!"

"We invited them to dinner. Dinner tonight, to be exact!"

"Invited them for dinner?" said Lulu in a parody of Edith Evans' famous "A *handbag?*" Giving the two a grin, she added with a chortle. "A literary mouse as well as a doctor in the house? No doubt you'll have an ambulance nearby in readiness for whatever happens next!"

"Two ambulances, in fact," snorted Leo. "One for Clive and Andy; the other for me and Lobie. And in case you think you'd been forgotten, there'll be a hired Roller on standby to bring you back to Godfrey Street!"

"Such meticulous planning deserves another drink afore we go," chortled Lulu. "Lobie, would you do the honours as I do believe Miss Mayhew could be having a mild attack of the vapours!"

*

"The famous Robert Apps in person!" crooned Lulu giving the smiling Jude Law lookalike a firm handshake.

"Likewise, the famous Lulu Mayhew in person," smiled Andy. "Clive never stops talking about you and, like him, I've enjoyed your books and look forward to reading the next one."

"Why, thank you, kind sir," replied Lulu with a camp fluttering of her eyelashes. "Praise from such a dashing, *handsome* author is praise indeed!"

"Okay! Enough of the camp sparring," said Lobie cutting in. "We're here for a 'getting to know you' dinner: not an 'anything you can do I can do better' one!"

"Touché, my lovable Lobie," sniggered Lulu giving the beaming waiter a smile as he pulled out her chair. Murmuring *"Grazie,"* as she took her place opposite a wary looking Lobie. Glancing round the busy restaurant and the well-heeled diners, Lulu added with a further smile. "I absolutely adore *Scalini's* and can truthfully say that out of London's amazing restaurants, it remains a firm favourite."

"Clive and I are also great fans," said Andy in a rich baritone. "We adore anything Italian and, to prove a point, have recently purchased a somewhat dilapidated but glorious fifteenth century villa in Liguria; high up in the Cinque Terra east of Portofino." Giving Lulu a warm smile he added, eyes twinkling. "Once we've finished with the refurbishment, Clive and I trust - along with Leo and the dashing Lobie, of course - you'll be one of our first guests."

"I've mentally just booked my flight to Genoa," laughed Lulu. "I've never visited Liguria but having read - and reread several times - Jess Walter's wonderful *Beautiful Ruins,* I'm already a fan."

"You won't be disappointed, Lulu," said Clive cutting in. "Before we'd even clambered out of the car, we'd fallen in love with the place. The villa sits on a set on a series of four impressive arches; hence its name, Villa *Degli Archi.*" He gave a proud smile. "It's fabulous."

Halfway through dinner Lobie looked at Clive and said casually. "Any news of the Maebelle front?"

"Apart from the fact she's now heavily in cahoots with Corey Marsden and Peter Proudfoot's replacement, a guy named Monty Livingston who, according to hearsay, makes a pneumatic drill appear a very poor second!" replied Clive waspishly.

"I've been reading about her latest misadventures," said Andy. "To say they're highly entertaining wouldn't be doing them justice." Giving Lulu a smile, he added mischievously. "I have to say they sound remarkably like something a typical Lulu Mathew character would dream up!"

Giving Lobie a quick "can we trust these two?" and getting a discreet nod in response, Lulu took a deep breath and said matter-of-factly. "You could be right Andy. However, I can assure you it's purely coincidental despite similar Madam Arcati happenings occurring in my latest."

"Yes, I'm sure it's all coincidental," chuckled Clive. "So, come on Lulu, reveal all! I take it the latest Lulu Mayhew comes complete with an *unhappy* ending?"

"Don't spoil it for everyone else!" chortled Lulu. "However, to see if you're another Madam Arcati yourself, you'll simply have to wait until the book is out."

"Spoil sport," chuckled Clive. "However - and I mean it - if Andy and I can be of any assistance in, say, bringing a Lulu Mayhew plot or two to life - we've already discussed this between ourselves - you only have to ask."

"Strange you should say that?" replied Lulu giving Leo and Lobie a "here goes" glance. "Medora Maddox, the lethal teenage heroine in my latest, is about to carry out a further 'that'll teach you' mission." She gave a snicker. "Imagine if what I'm about to tell you really happened! In other words; fact instead of fiction."

"Maebelle, you mean?" interrupted Clive.

"You said it; not me," giggled Lulu.

"Sorry, I didn't mean to interrupt," said Clive on receiving a discreet nudge from Andy. "You were saying?"

"Medora, who makes Hilaire Belloc's *Matilda* look like a Botticelli angel, decides it's time another dubious couple I have had the misfortune of having had dealings with within in the past. Their names are Robert and Jacqueline Swallow - renamed Roger and Norma Walton in the book - and again, friends of Medora's parents - who get a taste of their own bitter medicine." Lulu gave a giggle. "Robert Swallow's all-consuming hobby is Carriage Driving - no doubt he sees himself as a reincarnated Prince Phillip - meaning he's a keen participant in every available Carriage Driving competition, whilst Norma is an avid gardener: so much so she's even created her very own Poison Garden, inspired by the Alnwick Poison Garden adjacent to Alnwick Castle in Northumberland. And this, my friends is what dear, scheming Medora suggests."

*

"Talk about a pair of show-offs," snorted Medora. *"Wretched Roger - I like that - never stops bragging about his latest win and how he plans to come first again at the next event in which he'll be participating, whilst nauseating Norma - again like wretched Roger - keeps going on about her flowering poison garden; a challenge to the one at Alnwick."*

"With that dreadful head yellow hair, she looks exactly like a laburnum bush," snickered Archie. *"One of the deadliest of plants. So, what are you suggesting?"*

"It's got be something to do with carriages and gardens," replied Medora. *Gently fondling Flip Flop's ears, she gave a giggle. "Goodness! I'm getting serious vibes, Archie, delicious, deadly serious vibes from my darling Flip Flop here. Oh, along with a hint of a song!"*

"Hint of a song? What song?"

"That song from Oklahoma! *Something about a carriage . . ."*

"You mean The Surrey with The Fringe on Top?*"*

"That's the one! So, as Flip Flop so brilliantly suggests, why not simply change the title to The Slurry with The Fringe on Top? *That's it! That's it! We turn one of Roger's prized carriages into a veritable* slurry pit *with Roger as a naked, unwilling passenger along with the naked, gardening mad Norma as the other unwilling passenger as the smelly, slurry-filled carriage heads its way in direction of the local village market! And if that doesn't poison the two of them, then happily the vile fumes emanating from the* Slurry with The Fringe on Top will *do their damnedest to make sure the Swallows never show their ugly faces at another competition, local market or village fete - pun not intended - ever again!"*

TWELVE

A WEEK LATER

"I've had a couple of guys suss out the Swallow's place outside Hardwick, a small village near Henley," announced Lobie in his daily catch-up call with Lulu. "Apparently the property is quite something and, get this, the place is called *Manoir Nous Sommes Les Meilleurs* despite being set in the English countryside!" He gave a chuckle. "And if that isn't a touch arrogant, once again I'll be chewing on that much-chewed fedora!"

"Unless my French is even worse than I believe that translates as Manor We're the Tops," sniggered Lulu. "And please, no need to munch on that poor fedora! So, as I take it, you're not munching, what next?"

"We thought next Wednesday, around midnight," replied Lobie. "Thursday is market day in Hardwick, which means a naked Robert and Norma gracing a carriage filled with slurry as it oozes its way along the High Street could be quite a showstopper!"

"Sounds good Lobie, but a major question. How on earth will it be possible to have those two handling the horses, never mind them being naked?"

"It's all arranged. Sid, the guy whose been sussing out the place, will be sitting between the tightly bound couple and holding the reins."

"Sitting in between the two and holding the reins?" exclaimed Lulu. "Is he mad?"

"Not mad but probably getting there!" chuckled Lobie. "To add a further touch of disbelief to the joyride, Sid will be wearing a frogman's outfit, complete with goggles and an oxygen tank." He gave a snigger. "I don't know about the flippers! Sid has a bone to pick with Robert Swallow; something to do with a rigged race which saw Sid lose a substantial amount of money." There was a pause before Lobie added with a further chuckle. "I take it you'll be joining Leo and me at the Thursday market for a looksee?"

"As sure as God made little green apples," chortled Lulu. "Accompanied by Maddy and Flip Flop! Need it be said that Flip Flop simple adores anything to do with markets. In other words: food! However, let's not forget Maebelle. Come what *Mae*, another unpleasant happening shouldn't be on hold for ever as I'm sure the same doesn't apply to her. God knows what *she'll* have planned for her next revengeful act." She gave a snicker. "So, why not another quick 'in and out' with something inspired by what we have planned for the Swallows?"

"You mean another quick in and out for me and Dee-Dee?" chuckled Lobie.

"Yes, indeed. Let me think about it and I'll get back to you. However, Lobie, if truth be known, I still don't fully trust the fickle Dee-Dee. Worms turn, and when it comes to one of the wriggliest, he most certainly tops the bill. At the moment he and Maebelle are at daggers drawn, but what's to stop him suddenly returning his little dagger back to its scabbard?"

"Hopefully, he won't," murmured Lobie.

"You said it, Lobie; not I." replied Lulu sardonically before terminating the call.

To Lulu's surprise Lobie called back within the hour.

"I didn't want to say anything until I knew for certain," he said cheerfully. "But I've just head confirmation that Maebelle is the celebrity guest who will be opening the next Carriage Driving competition near to Henley in three weeks' time! So why not delay our Slurry with a Fringe on Top until then? If that's okay with you, of course."

"Okay with me?" carolled Lulu. "Why, Lobie, dearest Lobie, you've just made my day!"

There was a moment's pause before Lobie said tentatively. "I know it was less than an hour ago, but have you had a chance to think of our latest in and out?"

"I have, and you coming up with this change in plan adds an extra zip to what I had in mind! This can now take place after our newly located audacious, aromatic surrey episode. In other words, a quick in and out to Maebelle's apartment, as before, in order to top up all those window boxes she's so proud of, with a liberal coating of slurry." Lulu gave a giggle. "That should get right up her nose!"

"Take it as done, Lulu, Medora Mayhew," chuckled Lobie. "Meanwhile, I'll ask Sid to have one of his guys keep an eye on Dee-Dee and, should he appear to do anything suspicious, to let me know."

*

"A major change of venue for you, Medora," murmured Lulu and she began to make a few changes to the previous day's writing. The words local market or village fete replaced by the words nearby Carriage Driving competition.

The three weeks seemed to fly by with Lulu busy totally absorbed in her new book and Leo and Lobie occupied with day to day running of their own businesses.

"Leo and I will call by Godfrey *Strasse* around ten tomorrow to collect the lovely you, Maddy and Flip Flop for the show to end all shows," chuckled Lobie in a telephone call the previous evening.

"We'll be ready and waiting, along with a delicious picnic hamper," replied Lulu with a light laugh.

"Just as *we'll* be along with a well-stocked cooler containing champagne and white wine," chuckled Lobie. "Until tomorrow then. *Ciao* and pow! Wow!"

CARRIAGE DRIVING COMPETITON - OXFORDSHIRE - THE NEXT DAY

"That was Sid on the blower," said Lobie glancing up from his mobile. "So far, so good. Robert and Norma Swallow were rudely woken from their beauty sleep by Sid and his band of merry men around six a.m. The team having already dealt with Robert's favourite carriage." He gave a chuckle. "How they carted - ha! - the slurry from wherever to there, I don't think we really need to know." Lobie glanced at his Rolex. "If all goes as scheduled, our alternate version of *The Four Horsemen of The Apocalypse* - read Robert, Norma, Sid and *The Slurry with The Fringe on Top* - should be making themselves known round about now." Lobie added with a whoop. "Judging from the distressed, ripple effect taking place among the onlookers, judges et cetera, our four horsemen are definitely making sure they're the centre of everyone's attention!"

"Good God!" exploded one gentleman onlooker. "What in God's name is *that*?" His words directed at the open carriage slowly passing by; a tightly bound, stark naked, slurry smeared Robert and Norma seated on either side of the driver clad in a frogman's outfit; complete with goggles and breathing apparatus.

More gasps and indignant cries followed along with shocked exclamations of "It can't be!" "What's that dreadful smell?" to the more explicit "Jesus Christ! The carriage looks - and smells - as if the bloody thing's filled with shit!" and finally, a disbelieving "Good God! It's Robert and Norma Swallow starkers and smeared in what can only be shit!"

Before anyone had a chance to react, Sid jerked the reins resulting in the two horses and carriage racing off to a discreet, nearby smallholding where two of Sid's colleague were waiting. Within minutes a distressed Robert and Norma found themselves briskly hosed down - along with the carriage - before handed towels with which to dry themselves before getting dressed in the clothes they had been wearing earlier.

"You've no doubt upset today's event," sniggered Sid no longer wearing his frogman's suit but dressed in jeans, T-shirt while still wearing a mask. "But if you take a left at the gate, you'll soon find yourselves back at the competition grounds." He added cynically. "Sorry about the carriage not being a hundred percent dry but better to arrive smelling of detergent as opposed to good old slurry. Enjoy explaining all - if you can - when you get there!"

*

To Lulu's annoyance, one of the organisers managed to contact the driver bringing Maebelle and her replacement for Peter Proudfoot to the event. Having been told by the incensed man to stop the limousine and give his mobile to Maebelle so that he, the organiser, could explain what had happened, Maebelle, having listened to what had occurred, ended the call by saying crisply. "Thank you for letting me know. Mr. Livingston, my manager, and I will now return to London. However, you will appreciate I expect my fee paid in full; despite what you call 'an unforeseen happening'."

Handing the mobile back to the driver. "As you may have gathered, today's event has been cancelled so turn where you can and take us back to Eaton Square."

Leaning back against the plush rear seat Maebelle said with a growl. "I am not happy with this; not happy at all! That spluttering individual on the phone and his lot blaming today's disruption on some minor group of activists or rival competitors, but to me it stinks - and I use the word deliberately - of Lulu Mayhew and her little band of miscreants! A hint of things to come."

"I think you could be overreacting, Mabelle," said Montgomery (Monty) Livingston, a young Errol Flynn lookalike, a touch nervously. "Forgetting any activists for the moment, when it comes to rivals in any form of competition, it's not unusual for the most unlikely and the most unpleasant things to happen."

On seeing Maebelle's furious expression following his comment, Monty said hastily. "However, you could be right. So, I'll make doubly sure to keep my eyes open."

A LAVISH DUPLEX APARTMENT OVERLOOKING EATON SQUARE - TWO DAYS LATER

"What on *earth* is that atrocious smell?" questioned Maebelle on entering the breakfast room, her elegant nostrils flaring as she took another distinctive sniff. "It smells like a bloody third world outhouse in here!"

"Tell me about it," said Monty, visibly gagging. "What's more, I'm pretty certain it's coming from the open window. Hold on while I have a quick look at the gardens below."

"Shit!" he exclaimed on peering out of the window. "It's the bloody window box! It looks as if it's been filled full of shit! *Liquid* shit! In fact, it looks as if *all* the window boxes on this level have been topped up with the same." Pulling himself back from the window, Monty said nervously. "I don't know about upstairs but give me a sec while I go and check."

GODFREY STREET

"Despite your misgivings regarding Dee-Dee, he's certainly turned up trumps - *yet again* - when it came to dealing with Maebelle's window boxes the other night," said Lobie a touch pointedly in his daily catch-up call with Lulu. "Okay, Leo and Sid were there to help carry the jerrycans filled with slurry, but again, it's all thanks to Dee-Dee having a key and knowing the alarm code that we were able to sneak in and out without disturbing Madam Deadly Nightshade and her latest, no doubt thoroughly exhausted pogo stick! Okay, we didn't dare deal with the window boxes to the master bedroom, but they were the only window boxes left unsullied." About to add a witty "Or should that be un-slurryed?" thought it better not to risk it,

"I know you keep on insisting Dee-Dee Devereaux is now one of us," sniped Lulu, "but I still don't trust him." She added laconically. "So, what happens now?"

"We wait and see what Maebelle comes up with next but, as Clive so aptly said" - Lobie gave a snort - "or should that be *Apps*-ly? - best we leave it alone and if Maebelle *does* come up with something, then, and only then, do we act."

"You sound exactly like some second-rate wannabe guru, if you don't me saying so," snickered Lulu. "And as Medora, Archie and Flip Flop are being doubly demanding at the moment, then yes, let's take a break." Lulu proceeded to blow a stream of kisses down the phone followed by a cheerful. "Love you, Lobie Maseko! Speak to you tomorrow!"

"Let sleeping bitches lie?" mused Lulu as she placed herself in front of the computer. Giving a dozing Flip Flop alongside her chair a gentle pat, she added with a wry chuckle. "No way, José! Instead, I'll be joining Medora, Archie and a yowling Flip Flop as they energetically murder the old Crickets' song of *That'll Be The Day*! So, my comrades in harms, let's see what we can come up with next? I hate to admit it, but I'm running out of tacky blasts from my glorious past - the exception being Corey Marsden - so, if Leo and Lobie wish to sit on their expensively clad butts, so be it. But - ha! - the zillion euro question. Why should I? I appreciate Clive Cordell is a no-no, but I wonder if I could cajole my rival scribe, Mr. Robert Apps, into giving a helping hand. Only one way to find out."

Smiling to herself, Lulu reached for the phone. "I'll first of all check with the hospital that Clive is on duty before I give Andy aka Robert a call and suggest we have a quiet 'don't tell anyone else' lunch a.s.a.p. If he agrees, then it's up to me and Medora! So, hospital first, and, if the coast is clear, Mr. Chiller Thriller himself!"

Five minutes later Lulu tapped in Clive and Andy's number. On hearing a deep, resonant, cheerful "Elucidate!" she replied with an equally cheerful. "Lulu Mayhew elucidating! I assume I am speaking to Andy McCulloch, aka the amazing Mr. Robert Apps?"

"Lulu Mayhew!" exclaimed Andy. "This *is* a surprise! Clive's not here. He's at the hospital if its him you're after."

"Actually Andy, it's you I'm after. Does that surprise you?"

"Yes and no, Lulu. Yes, if you're about to ask for a contact or such; and no, if it's something else entirely. If it's something else entirely, feel free to prattle on."

"I'll happily prattle on," laughed Lulu, "bur preferably over a lunch à deux. You free anytime this week? Today perhaps?"

"Today would be ideal as I have a meeting with - shall I say a source - at Claridge's at noon - but should be through by one-thirty at the latest. So, somewhere near there if possible."

"Totally possible! Are you partial to Cecconi's?"

"Extremely partial," chuckled Andy, "I'll see you there at one and, if I happen to be a few minutes late, please forgive me in advance!"

"Oh, I'll forgive you alright," murmured Lulu as she hung up. "But will you forgive me?"

CECCONI'S RESTAURANT - MAYFAIR

"Hi!" grinned Andy on approaching the table. "Only three minutes late so I trust I'm still in your *very good* books! Ha ha!"

"How could I ever say otherwise," replied Lulu with a warm smile. "I'm having a glass of Pinot, but please order whatever you prefer."

"A glass of Pinot sounds perfect." Reaching inside briefcase he'd been carrying, Andy pulled out a hardback book. "The latest Robert Apps. Hot from the press!"

"Why, thank you Andy," crooned Lulu. "I really appreciate that." Eyeing the vibrant cover, she flicked the book open. "Signed as well! This certainly deserves a peck on the cheek!"

Leaning forward she gave Andy a light kiss on the cheek before summoning a nearby waiter and ordering a bottle of Pinot Grigio.

"So, Miss Lulu Mayhew," said Andy having taken an appreciative swallow of wine, "cards on the table. I take it this clandestine meeting of the Titans can only have something to do with the wretched Maebelle, fashion model extraordinaire. Don't look so surprised, Clive obviously keeps me firmly up to date as to what's going on, which means I'm well aware of the goings on regarding that ridiculous grudge the woman continues to hold against you." He gave a warm laugh. "I would go as far as to say the happening at the Carriage Driving competition the other day surpasses something even Robert Apps could come up with!"

"Really?" murmured Lulu. Reaching for her wine glass she took a reassuring sip before saying contemplatively. "Do *you*, personally, ever get the feeling there's someone in your life, an irritating someone, who needs some sort of payback?"

"On a daily basis," replied Andy. "And I'm not talking about my publisher but Joe Public in general. It's jarring Joe who's the true Svengali - the inspiration - behind most of my grisly plots."

"Bingo!" said Lulu with a cat that got the cream smile. "You've gone and confirmed what I hoped you would say so now, the really serious question. Instead of simply writing about them, have you ever considered putting your darkest thoughts into practise? Making fiction become a reality?"

"Constantly," replied Andy matter-of-factly.

"Perhaps my fictional Medora could be a perfect partner for your newest character," added Lulu equally as blandly. "I'm thinking Nathan Leopold and Richard Loeb and their murder of young Bobby Franks in Chicago back in the roaring twenties."

"In other words, a *Leonora* and Loeb of the twenty-first twenties," chuckled Andy. "This Mr. Loeb having nothing to do with *your* Mr, Lobie, of course."

Lulu sat playing with the stem of her wine glass, her gaze holding Andy's penetrating gaze. Clearing her throat, she added cryptically. "Those two would have gotten away if clumsy Nathan hadn't dropped his spectacles. Can you believe it? After all their careful planning can you believe that he'd go and do something as careless as that?"

"Yes, I can," replied Andy. "Both were caught up in the heady euphoria of the moment and, remembering their youthful arrogance - Leopold being nineteen and Loeb eighteen - Nathan most probably was unaware he could have lost his specs close to where they'd concealed Bobby's acid splattered body in a convenient culvert."

"A steadfast, reassuring factor is that neither the wicked Leonora nor her accomplice, the young Loeb, are no longer in their teens nor do they wear glasses," giggled Lulu.

"Meaning they shouldn't get caught and therefore have no need for a substitute Clarence Darrow," chuckled Andy."

"Would the fictional teenage Loeb have a substitute Bobby Franks in mind?" questioned Lulu.

"He does indeed, and, for Leonora's information, his name is Paul McDowell; otherwise known as McDowell the Foul. Blessed with movie star looks, he's a keen darts, player, a keen cyclist, a much sought after music teacher plus leader of the local church choir with a penchant for ripping off elderly, rich widows. An aunt of mine having been one of his victims. Aunt

Enid is now vegetating in a care home." Andy gave a hollow chuckle. "And it's not only elderly rich widows he has an eye on, but some of his more pliant pupils as well!"

"Sorry to hear about your aunt," said Lulu dismissively. "However, this Mr. Paul McDowell sounds as if he could almost be a character in one of your novels. Not only a lothario-cum- gold digger but a bit of a paedo to boot?" She gave giggle. "Need I say *this* Leonora likes the sound of him and, dare she also say it's like music to her ears? But please, unlike Nathan and Richard, not a chisel but something a touch more glamorous!"

"Leonora's on!" replied Andy with a grin. "So, when do they - we - start?"

"Over desert would be as good a time as any," giggled Lulu. "Let's order. I'll be finishing with a horrific, calorific, delicious tiramisu!"

"To accompany you with something equally calorific and sweet - could that be strychnine sweet? - I'll have chocolate fondant with caramel ice cream."

*

Andy telephoned Lulu minutes before she and Maddy were about to have dinner.

"I'll keep it short and sweet," he said without any preamble. "How about if Leonora and Loeb treat the Foul McDowell to the following."

THIRTEEN

A MEWS HOUSE - CLABON MEWS - KNIGHTSBRIDGE

Paul McDowell, a thirty something tall, thin figure sporting a Salvador Dali moustache and Elvis Presley sideburns and described by some of his more erudite pupils as a randy, rancid tapeworm, replaced the receiver and said smugly to himself. "Well done, Paulie boy! Another old trout well and truly hooked before her swim by date! Hence methinks a celebratory toast would not go amiss! Ha ha!"

Walking through to the state-of-the-art kitchen, he opened the fridge and took out a half-full bottle of Sauvignon Blanc. "Not quite the merry Widow Clicquot but it will have to do; my recurring mantra being waste not, want not."

Reaching for a wine glass, he poured the wine and, raising the glass in a toast, said mockingly. "Here's to you and your present millions, Mrs Catherine Fortescue: part of which will soon be mine." Paul gave a snigger. "Now I've got the old cow salivating for a further dose of the McDowell loving charm, I'll leave it until later before I call Granny Midas and suggest a romantic dinner at The Ritz as opposed to somewhere that's 'in'. Yours truly being a firm believer that somewhere tried and true will always come through!"

GODFREY STREET

Inspired by Andy's input, Lulu wasted no time in making sure Medora would be similarly inspired.

"Archie, it's Medora. I've just had Jennifer Griffiths on the phone; she's a friend from school. Poor girl was in tears due to what she described as a disgusting suggestion from Mr. Tickner, the music teacher, having asked her to stay on for a few minutes after a lesson."

Medora couldn't resist a derogative snigger. "To quote Jennifer, Mr. Tickner supposedly said to her that not only would he like to tinkle her keys he'd also like to tickle her fancy!"

"Tinkle her keys and tickle her fancy?" snorted Archie. "Doesn't sound all that disgusting to me. Jennifer Griffiths, you said. You've mentioned her before and, if I remember correctly, you describe her as someone who would make a warthog look attractive!"

"Moi?" giggled Medora. "Surely you don't think your devoted Medora could ever be so unkind no matter how justified the description?"

"No, I'd never," chortled Archie. He gave a snigger. "However, it does sound as if Mr. Tickner needs more than his eyes tested plus a lesson in manners. You said he was a music teacher?"

"I did."

"Well then, let's think up something tuneful for a different sort of music lesson."

"I'd already donned my colourful thinking cap before calling you," replied Medora. She gave a giggle. "It appears Mr. Tickner seems to think himself a second Andrea Bocelli and prides himself singing solo in the local church choir. Like Bocelli, he sings tenor but what's to stop us from making him sing castrati?"

"A bit late for that if they've already dropped!" guffawed Archie. "But why not? We can then send them back to him anonymously along with a recording of Barbra Streisand singing The Way We Were *in her distinctive mezzo soprano instead of Bocelli's bollocking tenor!"*

*

Lulu's cautious "Is the coast clear?" was met by Andy' cheerful, "As clear as the Sahara sky!"

"As clear as the Sahara sky?" repeated Lulu. "That's a first." *Good Hades, if such turns of phrase make you a multi-million selling author, maybe I should take a leaf from, your book and, instead of writing what I deem something worthwhile, simply go for the dregs,* she thought sarcastically. Resisting the temptation to repeat what she was thinking, Lulu said in a strictly "Okay, let's get down to business type voice." "I thought maybe you'd like to hear the update on Medora and Archie's latest 'teach them a lesson' stratagem. I can either read this to you now, or else email it through. Your call."

"Oh, please read it," enthused Andy. "Far more enthralling to hear it coming from the author's lips than making do with a dreary email." He gave a chuckle. "Not that I'm implying an email from the brilliant Lulu Mayhew would ever be deary! Ha ha!"

Bloody Hell! thought Lulu with an inward snicker. *I said it before, and I'll say it again. A million plus books? Talk about a topsy-turvy world!*

"Right, here goes," said Lulu as she began to read in her best Moira Stewart voice.

"That's great, Lulu," announced Andy a few minutes later. "Really great. Getting down to brass tacks (*Another ten out of ten for originality,* thought Lulu a touch spitefully), I know for sure Clive is a no-go, and how sure are you that your Lobie and Leo would go for something that hasn't affected you personally?"

"My thoughts exactly, Andy," murmured Lulu. "I too have a very strong feeling they would both balk at the idea. Which means I can't really approach Sid or any of his sidekicks either as it would get straight back to Lobie."

"Hmm. I see what you mean," said Andy. "I know it sounds odd, but what about asking the very in between in-betweener?"

"Very in between in-betweener?" echoed Lulu.

"That Dee-Dee Devereaux person. Who, as we both know from recent experience, that when it comes to loyalty, *his* idea of loyalty is as fickle as the English weather."

Another ten out of ten for originality, thought Lulu with a further inward snicker. "Dee-Dee Devereaux," she murmured. "Now there's a thought."

"Any chance we could meet up with him?"

"There's every chance," chortled Lulu. "Knowing Mr. Janus Face Dee-Dee Devereaux, he'll jump to it if it's guaranteed to upset someone, no matter who the someone is! He thrives on such merry japes. The more merrily mischievous, the better!"

"Any chance of calling him today?"

"Not only a chance. I'll give him a call as soon as we finish talking. If I do manage to get hold of him, I'll say that we would like to meet up with him to discuss a private and what could be decidedly lucrative matter. Mr. Devereaux's hero worship for Mr. Midas is said to almost rival his unrivalled self-esteem! If I *do* get hold of him and he agrees to meet up today if possible; Scalini's at one? Lunch, of course, is on you!"

"Isn't it always," chuckled Andy before hanging up.

Andy was about to pour himself a coffee when Lulu called back.

"The things we have to suffer in bringing the three mischiefs together," carolled Lulu. "And yes, Mr. Devereaux would be delighted to meet us for lunch today."

Brilliant," said Andy. "No questions?"

"Not a question as to why I suggested lunch, meaning I didn't have to win him over with any hints of possible mystery, murder or mayhem! However, instead of an immediate yes, I was subjected to a very roundabout yes. In the form of a rhyme no less!"

"Go on," chuckled Andy.

"Mr. Devereaux's idea of a yes being a yodelled - and I repeat verbatim:

'Caviar from the virgin

The virgin sturgeon is a very fine fish.

The virgin sturgeon needs no urgin'

That's why caviar is my dish.

I gave caviar to my boyfriend - he was a virgin tried and true -

Now my boyfriend needs no urgin'

There's nuthin; he won't do!'

His little rhyme followed by a trilled 'What time and where?'"

"Christ," muttered Andy.

"No, caviar," giggled Lulu.

"Take it as done," chuckled Andy,

A POPULAR CAVIAR BAR - PICCADILLY

"Well, this *is* a surprise!" cooed Dee-Dee in approaching the banquette where Lulu and Andy were seated; the two having arrived half an hour earlier to discuss their strategy in order, as Lulu laughingly put it. "In order "to discuss the utterly, cuttingly seduction of the dreaded - but vital - Mr. Devereaux!"

"Lovely to see you, Dee-Dee!" crooned Lulu proffering her cheek for a kiss. "Love the suit. Lavender, is it?"

"Lavender's blue, dilly, dilly, to go with the address, dilly, dilly!" carolled Dee-Dee seating himself opposite the two. "Deliciously complimented by my saffron cravat and matching pocket kerchief! *N'est-ce pas*?"

"Delightfully so," giggled Lulu. "I don't think you've met Andy McCulloch before?"

"No, we haven't met," trilled Dee-Dee, "but I do know his alter ego is Robert Apps, the author, whose books - like *yours*, darling Lulu - I absolutely *adore!*" He added slyly. "Is this what this impromptu little gathering, akin to Willie S's three witches is all about? You and Mr. McCulloch-cum-Apps working together on a book inspired - I use the term lightly - by the likes of a monstrous Maebelle?"

"Goodness!" exclaimed Lulu. "Not only a symphony of colour but a mind reader to boot for that's exactly what Andy and I have been discussing."

*

During the half hour prior to Dee-Dee's arrival Andy had agreed to baiting him with what he no doubt would put forward himself.

"Anything to do regarding the downfall of Maebelle is something he'll go for at Olympic gold medal speed," said Lulu firmly. "Particularly after his dismissal!"

"Talking of collaborating on a book, maybe we should seriously think about it," mused Andy. "Many of today's writers are doing just that. I mean, if James Patterson can write a book in collaboration with Dolly Parton; need I say more?"

"Hmm," murmured Lulu, her lips twitching. "I've never been called a Dolly Parton lookalike before but do go on."

*

Dee-Dee glanced briefly round the busy restaurant before saying mischievously. "I take it my little rhyme had something to do with the apt selection of our luncheon venue?"

"It did indeed," replied Andy with a grin. "So, beluga caviar for starters, or even as a main course and dessert course if so wish. We're sharing a bottle of Dom Perignon. Care to join us?"

"Yes, please," crowed Dee-Dee followed by a gleeful. "Yum, yum, what a lucky tum. Plus, I'll do as you so expansively and *expensively* suggested, admirable Mr. Andy. When we order, I'll begin with beluga followed by sevruga and finish up with the ossetra."

Ignoring Lulu's and Andy's startled looks, Dee-Dee happily accepted a flute of champagne from the bemused wine waiter. True to form he showed no reaction as Lulu ordered a modest seafood salad and Andy the grilled turbot.

Eyeing Lulu and Andy, Dee-Dee took a swallow of champagne before saying in a no-nonsense manner. "Right, you two, before we tuck in; out with it! Why am I here and what do you want from me? As those who know so wisely say, there is no such thing as a free lunch."

"Andy, why don't you explain to Dee-Dee what we gave in mind," said Lulu without hesitation. "After all, Paul McDowell is your chimera, so to speak."

"That he is," replied Andy with a thin smile. Looking directly at Dee-Dee he asked offhandedly. "Dee-Dee, have you ever sung in a choir?"

"Sung in a choir?" trilled Dee-Dee. "Good Hades, yes! I'm an accomplished tenor and an active member of the local church choir, *despite* other members' often unkind comments regarding my sometimes off-key *Do. Re. Mi. Sol. Fart. Si. Do!*"

"Bloody Hell," muttered Lulu.

"How convenient," said Andy with a smile. "Because this is what Lulu and I have in mind and where we think you could prove yourself not only to be a sensation, but a singing, swinging sensation as well!"

"Goodness," cackled Dee-Dee. "I wonder if they do caviar doggy bags here, as I have a distinct feeling that I could be asking for at least four on leaving!"

Dee-Dee, his face devoid of any expression, sat listening to what Andy had to say about Paul McDowell. At Andy's "so, we would appreciate your help; in other words, would you be interested or not?" he said with a grin. "Of course, I'm interested: but on one mega condition,"

"And that is?" replied Andy warily.

"You mentioned that Mr. Foul McDowell sports a splendid Salvador Dali moustache so, in addition to your *castrati*, I insist that I'm allowed to *castrati* his moustache and keep it for my next slumber number."

"Slumber number?" giggled Lulu.

"For stuffing a pillow!" trilled Dee-Dee. "Need I say it'll make a pleasant contrast to the usual pubic hairs I always ask for!"

"Jesus, Dee-Dee Devereaux," chortled Lulu. "At times you really are too much!"

"Of course, you can have Foul McDowell's tash," chuckled Andy. "And, if you really *are* a fan, maybe I'll let you have a tuft or two of Robert Apps's pubic hair as an extra thank you for your help!"

"I can hardly wait to rest my weary head on my newest pubic-pillow," trilled Dee-Dee. "Now, where's that first course as I really *do* need a caviar kick!"

*

"Truthfully, what do you think?" asked Lulu and she and Andy stood outside waiting to hail a passing taxi.

"What do I truthfully think?" replied Andy. "I think Dee-Dee Devereaux could be our answer to a host of intrigues." He gave a chuckle. "Whereas the majority may see him as a dizzy, over-the-top, highly camp queen, to me it's nothing more than a cover-up. Beneath that relentless, *Priscilla, Queen of the Desert,* performance there lurks a ruthless persona. An embittered little man who, at the end of whatever the day, will not be taking any prisoners."

Andy gave a further chuckle. "Before he asked for Foul McDowell's moustache, I actually thought he'd be asking for his dick or his tongue!"

"Saved by a taxi!" carolled Lulu hailing an approaching taxi with a glowing FOR HIRE sign.

Clambering into the cab, they made themselves before continuing their conversation regarding Dee-Dee.

"My next question . . ."

"And mine as well," interjected Lulu. "He obviously isn't going to let Maebelle get away with her recent behaviour, and God only knows what's fermenting in that coiffed head of his when it comes to making Maebelle rue his dismissal day!" She added pensively. "As Lobie and Leo - Clive doesn't even enter the equation - weren't at all eager to participate in any other happenings to do with Maebelle, and Lobie sticking to his guns by saying, in no uncertain terms. 'No more horseheads for me and Leo; enough is enough'."

 "You don't suppose . . ." said Andy tentatively.

"I *do* suppose!" chortled Lulu. "My only concern being that there may not be enough caviar in the Caspian Sea to keep Mr. Greedy guts Devereaux interested! However, we can but try. Despite his condescending 'Give me a day or two to think about any probable pillow filler as I'm on an away day to Brighton tomorrow. I'm lunching with an old friend whom I wittily refer to as Brighton Belle due to his extensive collection of toy trains and skill at dealing with troublesome points. Hee-hee!'"

She paused to take a breath before continuing in a parody of Dee-Dee's affected voice. "Who knows, I may even come back to you with a yes, as the thought of being tickled by Foul McDowell's moustache and Andy's tantalising tufts does appeal somewhat. But, as I said, I'll have to think about your suggestion; my priority being what else I can do to upset the monstrous Maebelle. In other words, Lulu, dear; you and Andy will have to simply wait and see'."

*

Lulu was sitting at computer, chuckling to herself as Medora and Archie began to put into practice the luring of Foul McDowell - now known as Feely Macavity - to a nondescript caravan site where he would be given, to quote Andy - "A singing lesson with a difference" - when the landline rang.

"Maddy Thompson, Miss Lulu Mayhew's secretary, how may I help you?" she purred on answering.

"*Per-lease*, Miss Maddy Thompson Lulu Mayhew," carolled Dee-Dee. "If you're going to be playing silly buggers with your callers at least try to disguise your everyday vocal cords!"

"Apologies, Dee-Dee," said Lulu a touch sarcastically. "Not all my callers are blessed with such acute hearing akin to that of a bat or greater wax moth! I take it you're calling to tell me it's a resounding yes to our suggestion."

"I'm actually calling to tell you my answer's a resounding no," trilled Dee-Dee.

"No?" gasped Lulu. "Why a resounding no?"

"Because Foul McDowell's moustache and a few testosterone-infused pubic-tufts from Andy-cum-Robert will still require a bit more extra spicing," said Dee-Dee teasingly. "No, Lulu! Please don't interrupt but hear me out! I've spoken to Brighton Belle - correct name Benedict James Bogart - who could be interested but on one major condition."

"And that was?" replied Lulu querulously; her temper rising.

"Whilst I would have been happy with a reward of the afore mentioned moustache, and several tantalising tufts should I help you; Brighton Belle is far more demanding. Hence me saying no."

"His one condition Dee-Dee! Damnit!" snapped Lulu.

"Easy-peasy, Lulu dearest," tittered Dee-Dee, revelling in Lulu's obvious reaction. "Brighton Belle would need a complete Hornby 'Master Cutler' train set plus five thousand pounds cash to cover what he described as advance ticket sales."

"Please tell Mr. Brighton Belle his advance ticket sales are guaranteed, along with the desired 'Master Cutler' train set. Where are you?"

"Still in Brighton playing choo-choo trains with Belle. Why?"

"Whilst you give Mr. Bogart the good news, I'll call Andy and give *him* the good news. Are you on your mobile?"

"No, I'm on a landline."

"Give me the number and I'll call you back. Dee-Dee, you're a star! Oh, say hi to Brighton Belle for me. I look forward to meeting him!"

On calling Dee-Dee back, it was arranged that Lulu, Andy, Maddy, Dee-Dee and Ben Bogart, aka Brighton Belle, would meet up at Godfrey Street at eleven o'clock the following day.

A MEWS HOUSE - CLABON MEWS - KNIGHTSBRIDGE

"Is that the charming Senora Fortescue?" questioned Paul in what he considered a seductive Latino growl.

"This is she," replied octogenarian Catherine Fortescue with a coy giggle. "May I ask who's calling?"

"Senor Don Juan," said Paul smoothly. "Otherwise known as the Seducer of Seville!"

"Oh Paul!" giggled Catherine. "You are *such* a tease!"

"A seductive tease who would be honoured if you would care to dine with him this evening," continued Paul in his normal tenor. "Deeply honoured."

"This evening?" repeated Catherine. "Oh Paul," - she gave another giggle - "Or should that be *Don* Paul? Hee-hee. I can't tonight as it's a bridge night. As is tomorrow, and I could never let the girls down. But it would be lovely if we could have dinner the evening after."

Bloody two evenings' time? thought Paul irritably. *Damn these women and their bloody bridge!* He gave an inward snigger. *Rather like me with my passion for darts. Show me a dartboard and I'm hooked! Hence me having several darted - ha ha! - around the house. Not only here in my study, but in the entrance hall and kitchen as well. Michael van Gerwen, eat your Dutch heart out!*

Slipping back into Don Juan mode he said glibly. "Although the evening after tomorrow seems an eternity away, Senora Catherine, I will sadly, yet patiently wait, until I arrive in my chariot of desire and sweep you away to The Ritz for and elegant dinner à deux."

"The Ritz? My favourite!" squeaked Catherine. She added coquettishly. "And at what time will Don Paul be arriving in his chariot?"

"We'll dine at nine, Senora Catherine, so I will call by the house (an impressive mansion in the exclusive Boltons) at eight o'clock. I trust the elegant Senora Catherine will be entertaining me with the latest gossip and a flute or two before we venture forth?"

"Oh Don - I mean Paul - of course this wicked Senora will!" giggled Catherine. "At times like this I could easily forsake a bridge night but, as I said, I simply cannot disappoint Hortensia Higginbottom and other friends. So, until Thursday, Paul dear."

"Until Thursday, Catherine, *dear,*" replied Paul in a resigned voice. "I shall be counting the minutes."

Replacing the receiver, Paul took a sip of his whisky soda before saying to Bollocks, a large, neutered tom cat asleep on a chair opposite. "Well Bolly, it looks as if we may have another sugar mummy within the next week or so. And, despite Mrs Catherine Fortescue resembling a bleached ostrich well beyond its sell-by date, what she's worth makes her - momentarily that is - look like a veritable Helen of Troy!"

GODFREY STREET

"Good morning, lovely Lulu!" carolled Dee-Dee - resplendent in tones of yellow - as he followed Maddy into the sitting room; a towering figure in his wake. "Allow me to introduce Mr. Ben Bogart aka Mr. Brighton Belle!"

"Goodness!" exclaimed Lulu reaching for Ben's proffered ham-like hand. "Forget the Flying Scotsman for, when compared to you, Mr. Brighton Belle, even Union Pacific's Big Boy would look a toy train! Delighted to meet you! Maddy, my Girl Friday, you've already met." She added graciously. "Please take a seat. Tea? Coffee? Something stronger?"

"I'll settle for coffee, thank you; black, with six sugars," rumbled Ben as he lowered himself cautiously onto a sofa. His massive frame topped by a face Lulu would later describe as "a face that could rival that of Pre-Raphaelite painter Henry Wallis's supine Thomas Chatterton's peaceful visage instead of the anticipated Boris Karloff or Fred West."

"I've explained to Ben what you and Andy have in mind," chirruped Dee-Dee. "Talking of which, where *is* the charming Mr. McCulloch? I take it he will be joining us?"

"Talk of the devil," murmured Maddy on hearing the melodic chiming of the front doorbell. "I'll go and let him in."

Further introductions made, the four sat studying each other while Maddy, perched on a nearby stool, sat posed to take notes.

Giving Lulu an encouraging smile, Andy said cheerfully. "Lulu, I suggest you take over and explain exactly what your Medora and Archie have in mind. Aided and abetted by Flip Flop, of course."

After Lulu had finished speaking, Maddy, without asking, exited the room, returning with a tray bearing an ice bucket containing two bottles of Veuve Clicquot and five champagne flutes.

"Allow me," said Andy taking hold of the tray while Maddy opened the distinctive Tommy Parzinger cocktail cabinet so he could set down the tray. Glancing toward Lulu, he added mischievously. "Congratulations on your splendid résumé. I'm quite sure not even Robert Apps could have come up with what you so aptly described as 'musical mayhem in high C with Foul McDowell coming to earth with a bass clef of a surprise!'" He nodded at Ben. "Two weeks today, you reckon?"

"Two weeks today," rumbled Ben. "As soon as I get back to Brighton, I'll begin to put everything in motion."

"I take you mean *locomotion*?" camped Dee-Dee. Clapping hands, he added gleefully. "If this is what magical Medora and admirable Archie can do with the Fowl McDowell, imagine what they could do with Maebelle! But first things first. Apart from the fact she's always on my agile mind, I too have a contribution: a highly unpleasant man named Giles Blundy who happens to be another teacher. A maths teacher at my old school. A maths teacher whose idea of geometry included a great deal of" - he made finger quotes - "pupil juxta-positioning. Need I say more?"

FOURTEEN

AN ELEGANT DUPLEX APARTMENT OVERLOOKING EATON SQUARE

"Corey, its Maebelle. I need to see you tout suite! I also need to introduce you to my new Man Friday; a divine piece of swashbuckling manhood - ha! - named Monty Livingston." She added smugly. "As I told a very jealous Babs Browning, he not only *looks* like a young Errol Flynn he embellishes the legend!"

"Bully for you, Maebelle," hissed Corey. "What happened to Peter Proudfoot?"

"Please don't play the innocent with me, Corey Marsden, as you know, full well, Proudfoot - like his predecessor, the inadequate Malcom Duval - was given the heave-ho. But, getting back to you meeting Monty; is there a chance you could drop by for a drink this evening, around sixish?"

"In other words, be here this evening at six or else!" quipped Corey. "Why the rush?"

"Monty and I are off to New York tomorrow which means I would like to get one or two matters put into motion whilst we're away. Plus, it would be pleasant to see you again." There was a moment's pause before Maebelle said snidely. "I understand Lulu Mayhew and Clive Cordell's Andy McCulloch are now bosom buddies."

"Yes, so I heard," replied Corey. "Word has it they may even be collaborating on a book."

"Where did you hear that?" snapped Maebelle.

"From the man himself," said Corey smugly. "I spotted Clive Cordell and Andy - aka Robert Apps - at Mona Lotts's drinks do the other evening. They were talking to that dreadful magazine editor, Portia Pettigrew, about books in general when McCulloch came up with little gem." He added casually. "How did you hear about it?"

"From Monty. You may not have known it but he, too, was at Mona Lotts's do the other evening."

"Ah yes! The dashing lothario who had all the ladies buzzing around him like bees around the proverbial honey pot! A young Errol Flynn lookalike you say." Corey gave a snigger. "From what I heard, not only with the looks of a young Errol Flynn but a young Errol Flynn combined with a *bit* of Monty *Python,* if you catch my drift. Ha ha!"

"Very amusing, Corey dear. So, until we see you at six."

"Yes, see you at six!"

GODFREY STREET - A FEW HOURS LATER

"Don't you and Lobie ever worry about the police when it comes to these ongoing incidents between you and Maebelle?" quizzed Maddy as the two sat enjoying their G and Ts after an intensive morning's work on Lulu's latest.

"Not really," said Lulu reaching for a cheese straw. "For example; according to one of the organisers at The Carriage Driving Competition the culprits responsible were none other than a group of do-gooders with some inane grudge against exploiting horses for entertainment; rather like those against hunting." She gave a giggle. "In fact, the do-gooders are a marvellous excuse for anything untoward these days. Another example was the painting of this house red. At the end of the day, it was conveniently assumed that the culprits were simply a few do-gooders who objected to the context of my books."

"Let's drink to all those beneficial do-gooders," chortled Maddy raising her glass. "Long may they continue to do good by condemning even the most innocent of normal, everyday happenings!"

AN ELEGANT DUPLEX APARTMENT OVERLOOKING EATON SQUARE

"That must be Corey," on hearing a brisk knocking on the front door. "The wretched porter must have let him in. Why he can't call on the intercom like everyone else, I'll never know."

On hearing Corey's cheerful greeting to Briggs who must have let him in, she added with a hiss. "Remember what I told you!"

"Yes; at virtual gunpoint," replied Monty with a show of perfect whither than white teeth. "No need to have butterflies, Maebelle dear, seeing I have been practising my lines!"

"Corey dear," crooned Maebelle as Corey entered the elegant drawing room. "It's lovely to see you again." She gave a girlish giggle. "Why, I'd almost forgotten what the handsome you looked like! You handsome devil, you!"

"Darling Maebelle," replied Corey with a laugh. "Whereas *you* may have almost forgotten what *I* look like, it's impossible to forget what *you* look like seeing you're never off the cover of endless magazines! Why, I could swear I saw at least six of you smiling at me as I walked past the newsstand at Sloane Square station!"

"Flatterer!" crowed a delighted Maebelle. She gestured toward Monty standing a few steps behind her. "Allow me to introduce you to my new manager, Monty Livingston. Monty, meet Corey Marsden."

"Hi!" said Corey. He added playfully. "Despite Maebelle having introduced us, forgive me if I use what I had been planning to say. Namely, 'Mr. Livingston, I assume? Ha ha!"

"*Dr* Livingstone, I *presume,* Corey, dear," snapped Maebelle. "If you *are* going to use famous quotes, make sure they're correct!"

"Corey, Corey Marsden," said Corey ignoring Maebelle as he reached for Monty's proffered hand.

"Great to meet you Corey," replied Monty. Giving Maebelle a discreet wink, he said mischievously. "Has anybody ever told you that you have a double? A double who is also called Corey. An American actor name Corey Stoll?"

"Endlessly," chuckled Corey. Eyeing Monty he said with a faux smile. "Apparently what you say can work both ways. Has anybody ever told you that you're the spitting image of Errol Flynn? A *young* Errol Flynn as seen in *The Adventures of Robin Hood*?"

"Endlessly!" laughed Monty. "With emphasis on the young, of course! Ha ha!"

"As Snow White's wicked stepmother allegedly said, *mirror, mirror, on the wall, who's the fairest of them all,*" said Maebelle cutting in. "So, if you two Narcissi have finished *stroking* each other's egos, may I suggest Monty/Errol sees to my drink and sees to whatever Corey Stoll wishes to drink, so that we can then sit down, catch-up and, who knows, perhaps even get down to discussing my latest idea for upsetting a certain irritating bone of ongoing contention."

SPECTACULAR 17ᵗʰ CENTURY HOUSE - CHEYNE WALK - CHELSEA

"Right, Andy! Herewith endeth the bullshit! What exactly are you and Lulu - Madam Mischief Mayhew - up to? Okay, okay, you say you're thinking of collaborating on a book, but forget the fiction and give me the facts! In other words, what the hell are the two of you up to?"

Andy sat looking at Clive across the breakfast table. Taking a sip of coffee, he set down his cup and said quietly. "Okay, Clive. And because I love you more than life itself; herewith the whole truth and nothing but the truth. Firstly, may I suggest a drop of brandy in our coffees as I have a feeling you - not so much me - are going to need."

Having topped up their coffees with a generous amount of brandy. Andy sat back and, having encouraged Clive to take a fortifying sip, he went on to explain what he and Lulu had in mind for Paul McDowell.

"Castrate him?" shouted Clive. "Are you mad? The pair of you have no idea what something like that would involve! Do you now wish to add the term murderer to your present bestselling author?"

"Whoa! Hold it right there!" snapped Andy. "Surely a simple, uncomplicated snip and a drop or two of disinfectant shouldn't be that difficult?"

"Difficult?" yelled Clive. "You have the temerity to think cutting off someone's balls isn't dangerous, never mind difficult? Or perhaps you and bloody Lulu think matters of surgical skill and the term hygiene are not appliable? Without these, what you're suggesting could be disastrous! And as I already said, plain bloody murder!"

Glaring at Clive, Andy said sarcastically. "Assuming my passionate lover has no wish to see me in my new role as a murderer as opposed to a bestselling author, perhaps he could suggest an alternative for this wannabe Fred West and his wannabe Lulu, Rosemary?"

Ignoring Andy's cutting response, Clive poured himself another cup of coffee along with a hefty dollop of brandy. Taking a swallow, he sat staring at a scowling Andy before saying. "Seeing I have no say in the matter and seeing I love you dearly, the thought of you and Lulu - along with this Mr. Brighton Belle - getting into trouble is too much for you doctor lover to bear. Therefore, I have no alternative but to assist you three in turning Lulu's Mr.

Tickner into eunuch seeing he's beyond becoming a castrato. So, tell me more."

"Thank Christ for that, and a million thanks, Clive," said Andy in a relieved voice. "As for your valid concerns regarding hygiene et cetera: the planned snipping will take place in a private abortion clinic, somewhere in Pimlico, owned by a friend of the mysterious Brighton Belle." He couldn't resist a chuckle. "The woman who owns the clinic has the somewhat unfortunate name of Miss Bea Gotts. Or, as Dee-Dee Devereaux wittily said. Miss Best-Be-Forgotten!"

"Very amusing, Andy, but please remember that I am not happy at all about any of this," muttered Clive. "Christ! Is that the time," he snapped glancing at wristwatch. "Bugger, I'm going to be late."

Springing from his chair, he grabbed his briefcase, gave Andy a quick peck on his forehead and left.

"Well, that went better than expected," murmured Andy as he poured himself a fresh cup of coffee. "Lulu and the others will be pleased. I only hope - for all our sakes - Clive doesn't get cold feet and, like the good Catholic boy he was, gets the ultimate urge and feels he has to confess his sins to a convenient boy in blue!"

Minutes later when giving Lulu the good news, her reaction was similar. "God help us if he suddenly goes all Hippocratic oath on us and feels he has to confess of his wrongdoing," she sniped. "But then, as his lover is a highly *imaginative* novelist, maybe he can assure this reader that there will be a happy ending to this snippy tale!"

GODFREY STREET - THREE DAYS LATER

"Good morning, Lulu, it's Ben; Brighton Ben calling."

"Good morning, Ben; I was just thinking of you," carolled Lulu. "Any news?"

"Yes; some very good news in fact." said Ben cheerfully. "One of my many London contacts is a lady named Inga Stafford. Inga is a close friend and currently employed as a companion to a rich old dowager, named of Maureen Moran who, surprise, surprise, is an avid bridge player and close friend of a Catherine Fortescue who, surprise, surprise, is presently being escorted here, there, and everywhere, by a certain Mr. Paul McDowell!"

"All this in three days, Ben? You're a star!"

"It gets better," chuckled Ben. "According to Inga, Mrs Fortescue has been making enquiries about various Italian sports cars, so it looks as if Mr. McDowell, is, without doubt, flavour of the month. And, before you ask, Mrs Fortescue is away for a few days as from next Tuesday which means McDowell should be spending one or two evenings at his house in Clabon Mews or else, out on the prowl for another moneyed old biddy!"

"So, sometime next week?"

"Sometime next week. I'll alert Andy so that he can organise Clive, plus I'll also alert Bea Gotts, the woman who owns that very private abortion clinic."

"Goodness, Ben," giggled Lulu, "I can already see another Master Cutler trainset puffing its way to Brighton!" After they had stopped laughing Lulu said matter-of-factly. "Will you be helping with the actual er . . . bodysnatching, or will someone else be handling this?"

"It'll be me and a mate," said Ben. "Dee-Dee, as expected, wanted to come along but I said a firm no."

"Good," said Lulu. "Not that you, saying a definite no, will stop him from plaguing you again!"

"The answer will still be no," chuckled Ben. "Final question, Lulu. What do you want done with McDowell's er . . . trophies?"

"Done with them?" squawked Lulu. "Jesus, Ben: just bin them! I really don't wish to know!""

CLABON MEWS - A WEEK LATER

"What the fuck . . ." murmured Paul on hearing the distinct buzzing of the laser alarm on the bedside table. "Jesus," he hissed, tossing aside the duvet. "Someone's obviously just entered via the bloody basement door!" Staring at the adjoining security camera, he added tersely. "Three of the fuckers not wearing masks so they obviously mean serious business. Okay, idiots! Touché!"

Wearing nothing but the shorts he slept in, Paul crept out from the bedroom and began to make his way quietly down the thickly carpeted stairs.

Whoever it is must still be in the basement entrance leading to the kitchen, he thought with a twisted smile. *Okay, Mr. Burglar or burglars, you may not know it, but you're in for a very unpleasant surprise!*

One hearing whispering coming from the pitch-black kitchen - *No torch?* thought Paul. *Even better!* - he made his way toward the archway leading to the kitchen where, on entering, he reached across to the container where the darts serving the kitchen dartboard were kept. Taking a handful of darts, Paul reached over toward the main switch and rheostat serving a battery of spotlights. Shielding his eyes as he turned the rheostat to full Paull yelled an ear-splitting "Stay where you are!" as he flicked the switch.

Visibly startled at the sound of Paul's voice and temporarily blinded by the bright lights, Ben, another man, and the insistent Dee-Dee, stood blinking rapidly while staring and trying to focus as to which direction Paul's yelled command had come from.

"Take that, you bastards!" shouted Paul as he began throwing darts at the three bewildered figures; his action followed by a shrieked "My eye! My eye!" as a dart pierced Dee-Dee's right eyeball and a further gurgled cry as a dart caught Ben in the throat. Luckily for the man accompanying Ben and Dee, the dart aimed for his head landed in the hand with which he was shielding his eyes from the glare.

"Almost three bull's-eyes," whooped Paul. "Now, my shocked and suitably subdued gentlemen, one of you had better explain why you're here as I don't think stealing from me was on your agenda. If what you tell me satisfies my curiosity, you can then pick up your unconscious King Harold - did none of you idiots realise you were in Clabon Mews; not bloody Hastings? - and get the hell out of here as I think King Harold is in desperate need of a hospital. If your explanation is *not* satisfactory, I will call the police - you illegally entering my house is all on camera - and as I am a kindly soul as well as an expert dart player, I will also call an ambulance. The choice is yours."

Ben, having removed the dart from Dee-Dee's eye and the dart from own throat, stood glaring at Paul, his face contorted with a mix of pain and anger. "Okay, okay," he rasped, clutching his throat. "Hear me out!"

Ben quickly explained how an anonymous caller, claiming to be a friend of one elderly woman conned by Paul, had offered the three of them a substantial sum to come along and teach him a lesson. As previously agreed with Lulu and Andy, no correct names were to be given should anything go wrong.

"To me, it looks as it's you three idiots who have been taught a lesson," chuckled Paul, "Now, pick up King Harold here and fuck off before I change my mind and call the police!"

Watching as Ben and the other man helped an unconscious Dee-Dee up the stairs leading from the basement and out of sight, Paul closed and relocked the basement door and reset the alarm (only connected to the master bedroom) before re-entering the kitchen. Turning on the work top lights, he then switched off the ceiling lights before pouring himself a large brandy.

"So, one of the old girls wanted revenge, did she?" he muttered. "Bullshit! Or, after tonight's little happening; bull's-eye!" Taking a satisfying swallow, he said to the dimly lit room. "Catherine Fortescue, you may not know it, but tonight is your lucky night for, as far as Paul McDowell is concerned, you no longer exist. It's obviously time to let sleeping old girls lie for a couple of months or more. In other words - for the time being, that is - it's out with the old and in with the nubile!"

Paul gave a chuckle. "Out with the old and in with the nubile? Ha ha! Good one, Paul! Let's drink to that!"

Taking another hefty swallow and murmured philosophically. "Pity about the Alfa Romeo sport. Just a well I tend to cycle when visiting locally. Otherwise, like the BMW old Babs Watson gave me and which I promptly sold, it would have made a cheerful addition to my bank account."

GODFREY STREET - THE NEXT DAY

"He *what*?" shrieked Lulu. "He attacked you with *darts* and Dee-Dee is in hospital having lost an *eye*! For God's sake, Ben. You assured me - us - your plan was foolproof! Does Andy know about this?"

"He's not answering the landline nor his mobile," said Ben wearily. Gently touching the dressing on his throat, he added sarcastically. "*Dr Cordell*, of course, is also unobtainable." He gave a growl. "I've left several messages for McCulloch. Perhaps you could give him a try."

"Obviously, Ben. Obviously. But poor Dee-Dee. Which hospital is he in?"

Ben mentioned a name. "However. he told the doctor and the nurse in charge he had no wish to speak to the police - the dart hitting his eye being an accident - and he wished to be discharged as soon as possible. It wouldn't surprise me if he's not already back at his flat. I have tried calling the number several times but keep getting the bloody answering machine."

"Let me try," murmured Lulu. "Hang up and I'll call you back." Using the landline, she punched in Dee-Dee's number.

"Dee-Dee!" she exclaimed on hearing a snapped "What?" "It's Lulu! Ben's just been telling me what happened. I'm so, so sorry."

"Not as sorry as I am, Miss Lulu bloody Mayhew," hissed Dee-Dee. "And, in best Chaucerian speak, kindly fuck off and please, *please,* never, ever, contact yours one hundred percent *untruly,* ever again!"

Lulu gave a jump as Dee-Dee slammed down the phone.

"Dee-Dee obviously isn't in the best of spirits," chortled Maddy from where she was sitting. "Was it something to do with what Ben going on about earlier? Something about an eye?"

"Yes. When they broke into bloody McDowell's house last night, he attacked them by throwing darts of all things, one of which got poor Dee-Dee in the eye."

"God, no!" whimpered Maddy, her hands flying to her face. "Poor Dee-Dee. No wonder Ben's upset, but not as upset as Dee-Dee from what I managed to overhear."

"You must have also heard how, as far as he's concerned, I no longer exist," replied Lulu dryly.

"Oh, we all know Dee-Dee," said Maddy with faux cheerfulness. "Give it a day or two and you'll be back to being the best of friends."

"Somehow I don't think so," murmured Lulu. "We'll simply have to wait and see. However, I won't be holding my breath."

"Er . . . will all this unexpected upheaval alter Medora's plans regarding the dubious Mr. Tickner?"

"No, not at all, and why should it, seeing Lulu Mayhew wites fiction, not fact," snickered Lulu. Giving a sigh, she reached for the landline. "I'll try Andy once more and then leave it. It'll be interesting to hear his thoughts on the matter. With luck Ben may have managed to get hold of him since we spoke." Punching in Andy's private number, she gave a shrug. "One can but try."

"Andy?" exclaimed Lulu on hearing Andy's grunted "Andy McCulloch speaking, Keep it short." "Andy, it's me, Lulu. Did Brighton Ben get hold of you?"

"Yes, Lulu, he did," growled Andy. "What's more, I'm surprised he hasn't called *you* back after our somewhat heated conversation."

"Somewhat heated conversation?" repeated Lulu. "Care to explain?"

"There's nothing *to* explain, Lulu. However, since we last spoke, I've had a change of mind. There will be no collaboration with you over any book plus Clive and I have no with to see you, Lobie Maseko or Leo Murrain again. So, goodbye, Lulu Mayhew. Goodbye and good luck."

"What the *hell* is going on?" cried Lulu staring at the silent phone in her hand. "First Dee-Dee, and now, Andy!" She turned to face an equally bewildered Maddy. "What, and more importantly, why?"

"Maybelle," whispered Maddy, her eyes widening.

"No," whispered Lulu with growing horror. "Not Maybelle. Paul Mc Dowell."

Several hours later, with Dee-Dee and Andy's unexpected reactions to what Lulu nonchalantly dubbed "the McDowell saga" cast aside, Lulu sat down in front of the computer and began to type. "So be it," she muttered. "Farewell fleeting Leonora and piss off slimeball Andy aka Robert Apps. As if I care seeing loyal Medora's still here!"

*

"*Archie, I have to say I'm not all that enamoured with our plan regarding Mr. Tickner. It's far too complicated,*" *said Medora with a frown.* "*This means Flip Flop and I have been thinking. Instead of turning him into a would have been castrato, why not do something almost as effective?*"

"*I think cutting off someone's balls would be more than effective,*" *snorted Archie.* "*It'd be fucking horrendous!*"

"*Despite me being a gorgeous young thing - your words, not mine - I can somehow appreciate the sordid fact,*" *giggled Medora.* "*However, and suitably inspired by Dee-Dee's little mishap, imagine if Mr. Tickner was no longer able to* read *music one hundred percent.*"

"*What do you mean?*"

"*He needs two hands to play the piano and two eyes to read the music. No, I'm not suggesting we cut off one of his hands, but what if we damaged one of his eyes? Someone being careless with a catapult, perhaps?*"

Archie gave a snicker. "*I used to be a wiz with my catapult, if you remember. Like the time you dared me to shoot out the blue light outside the local police station, being one of them!*"

"*So, there's your answer! Poor Mr. Tickner, alone on his bicycle on another old or young girlie hunt, when bam! He's suddenly hit in the eye by a stone or marble from some errant catapult!*"

"Brilliant! Medora! Bloody brilliant!" crowed Archie. "An eye for the girls but in a sicko way!"

FIFTEEN

"Hmm," murmured Dee-Dee eyeing his reflection in the bathroom mirror. "I appreciate it will be at least another six weeks before I can be fitted with my glass eye, but I have to say yon temporary eyepatch is somewhat appealing." He added with a snicker. "Johnny Depp aka Jack Sparrow, eat your dastardly doubloon of a heart out!"

Giving his reflection a further appreciative glance, Dee-Dee, said with a growl. "As for you, Miss Lulu Mayhew and Mr. Andy McCulloch, what I have in mind for the two of you would make the dreaded Davy Jones look a charmer! It won't happen just yet, but when it does, it'll even make walking the plank seem a doddle!"

Reaching for the large glass of vodka and orange juice resting on the vanity top, he took a long sip while staring contemplatively at himself. "No, not bad; not bad at all; but maybe a little something to give it that extra bit of oomph? After all, if - as Messrs. Gilbert and Sullivan randy gondolier so lewdly warbled - one can have a *pair* of sparkling eyes; why not a sparkling eyepatch?"

Exiting the bathroom, Dee-Dee sashayed his way through to the guest bedroom and opened one of the cupboards where he stored the Christmas decorations.

"Just what my eyepatch needs," he snickered reaching for a partly filled packet of glitter. "And while a sprinkle of golden glitter should so the trick, why not, to truly set it off, a pound coin in lieu of a wannabe iris! As *very* Long John Silver could have said. 'Thar's gold in them thar eyeball, me hearties!'"

Reaching for his mobile, Dee-Dee tapped in a number. "Peter, Peter, people eater!" he carolled on the call being answered. "It's Dee-Dee! Your new, one-eyed avenger!"

"Dee-Dee!" yodelled Peter. "I've been waiting for you to call! How are you getting along?"

"Getting used to keeping my one eye on the ball. Meaning this one-eyed avenger - Diana Rigg eat your Emma *Peeling* out - is simmering gently," chortled Dee-Dee. "You still game for what I suggested when I spoke to you last week?"

"Still game?" exclaimed Peter. "I'm champing at the bit! So much so I may need a new set of molars!"

"Goody good," carolled Dee-Dee. "The Ivy Chelsea Garden at one? I'll call and make a reservation."

"I'll be there . . . disguises or no disguises?"

"No, no disguises. Hopefully some gossipy member of London's social grapevine will see us together and spread the bad news accordingly! Until then, toodle-oo, Pete the Treat!"

THE IVY CHELSEA GARDEN

"Dee-Dee! Great to see you!" cried Peter giving the beaming little man a hug. Taking in Dee-Dee's azure blue linen suit, pink shirt, vibrant Romero Britto cravat and, glancing downwards, his pink suede loafers, he added cheerfully. "A rival to Mr, Gainsborough's *Blue Boy.* As for the glittering eyepatch with its glittering eye; Cyclops would be green with envy!"

"Thank you, Peter, *dear,*" purred Dee-Dee. "And look at you! A total harmer-charmer in your navy blazer and cords and, unless my *eye* deceives me, a goatee but no moustache."

"It's my unicorn look," chortled Peter. "An inverted horn as it were!"

"Not quite a horn of plenty," tittered Dee-Dee. "However, from what I remember about the mannequin's head saga, your other horn of plenty remains firmly tucked away down south!"

"Thank Christ you haven't changed, despite all that's happened," grinned Peter as the maître led them to the table.

"Eye not quite right," hissed Dee-Dee. "Looking suitably stunned is none other than Leo Murrain with some vacuous bimbo."

"If you look, eyes - oops! *Eye* left," hissed Peter, not to be outdone. "It's Agatha Christie herself with the conjoined Maddy Thompson. To say they look completely gobsmacked is putting it mildly!"

Making himself comfortable, Dee-Dee said with a smile. "Pity they don't do an Ebola cocktail here as I'd simply *love* to send a couple to each of their tables. Never mind. Meanwhile, I'm going to have a champagne cocktail. You?"

"A champagne cocktail sounds just the thing," said Peter. Reaching for Dee-Dee's arm he added softly. "I could be wrong, but it looks as if Mayhew and Thompson are leaving." Pulling at the lapel to his blazer, he gave an exaggerated sniff. "I'm sure I used a deodorant this morning."

"As did I!" trilled Dee-Dee. "An application of Clinique for Men each day can sadly - at times - keep the most virile of raunchy wolves at bay!" He nodded to where Leo and his lady friend were sitting. "Obviously Mr. Murrain and Miss Barbie are beyond the olfactory zone. In other words, ignore them and let's get down to discussing what we're here to discuss." Dee-Dee added sotto voce. "With all the chatter going on, nobody can hear us so, who do we destroy first. Maebelle or the wretched Foul McDowell?"

"I suggest we deal with McDowell first," said Peter. "And may I say, Dee-Dee, you're quite remarkable in the way you've adapted to life in general following your unfortunate accident."

"It wasn't a fucking accident, Peter Proudfoot!" snarled Dee-Dee. "It was fucking deliberate! However, I agree with you, McDowell first, and then Maebelle." He gave a snort. "Once Maebelle hears of McDowell's misfortune, she'll realise there's no escape and she could be next. And though ladies are said to glow, fashion icon Maebelle will be sweating like a drove of pigs when she realises tomorrow *is* another day!"

"Apparently she's been in New York for a" - Peter made finger quotes - "*Skyscrapers and Drapers* fashion shoot, so it's just as well we agree on McDowell being first in our 'that'll teach you' queue." Peter gave a twisted smile. "Any suggestions?"

"An eye for an eye is far too obvious," mused Dee-Dee. "As would be the removal of a hand - piano keys - or even a foot - foot pedals. However, if one is the keyword; one what?"

"One . . ." pondered Peter.

"Yes, one, and a very telling one at that," replied Dee-Dee.

"I think I've got it!" said Peter excitedly. Cupping a hand to his mouth, he added furtively. "Not only is McDowell an accomplished darts player and music teacher, he's also a keen cyclist despite being the on and off owner of the occasional expensive car."

"So?"

"So, how about a bicycle ride with a difference? How if we arrange for the following to take place when least expected."

Dee-Dee sat listening his one eye widening. *"Brillante,* Peter," he whispered. *"Brillante."*

*

A week later, Paul, on this way to choir practice, began to pedal energetically uphill seconds before he reached the summit and started to freewheel on the downward slope toward the local church. Whistling cheerfully as he gathered speed, his whistling came to an abrupt stop as his bicycle appeared to do a sudden cartwheel. A horrified Paul found himself thrown into the air before landing face down on the tarmac where he lay bleeding and groaning before two alarmed members of the choir, about to enter the church, rushed over to check on him.

None of the members paid any attention to the bicycle lying on the grass verge nearby: a broken branch wedged between the spokes of the front wheel. On the bicycle being righted and placed against the fence bordering the road, nobody noticed the piece of branch as it dropped onto the grass, nor a similar piece lying in the road.

"Nice shot, though I say it myself," muttered the hooded figure as he walked nonchalantly from the scene; a small crossbow neatly hidden beneath the raincoat he was carrying.

*

Paul's facial injuries were formidable: a broken jaw, broken cheekbones, a broken nose and most of the flesh to his face scraped away. He began to weep on being informed by one of the doctors in attendance that it would require several operations and skin grafts before his reconstructed face would bear any resemblance to its former self.

In between his endless recriminations regarding the incident, Paul refused to accept it as being an unfortunate accident.

"I keep telling you idiots it was no bloody accident!" he yelled at anyone - police or otherwise - who contradicted him. "Just as I tell you, here and now, come hell or high water, I'll eventually find out who was responsible! I'll find out who turned me from a George Clooney lookalike into a doppelganger for bloody Quasimodo and, when I do, they'll rue the day they were fucking born."

*

"I said it before, and I'll say I again," carolled Dee-Dee. "*Brillante,* Peter. Abso-fucking-lutely *brillante*! A zillion out of ten for coming up with your suggestion of one fucked up face, along with a trillion bull's-eyes for your reincarnated Robin Hood! I bet, when she hears about this little happening, Madam Maebelle will be needing more than a run-of-the-mill incontinence pad! She'll need a bloody Hoover Dam!"

*

"I'm dreading our return to London," murmured Maebelle gazing at a dozing Monty sitting opposite her in the dimly lit First Class cabin. "Not that he seems to care. Bloody idiot! Oh, my requested glass of champagne, how lovely. Thank you," she purred, glancing up at the smiling flight attendant. "I simply *love* your new uniforms!" She gave a tinkly laugh, followed by a typical million euro-cum-million-dollar model Maebelle smile. "Maybe I should show it to the world in my next show!"

"Oh, Miss Maebelle!" exclaimed the young woman looking suitably flustered. "Would you really?"

"You never know," replied Maebelle with a further smile.

Staring at the excited woman as she made her way along the aisle, she said with a soft growl. "Idiot girl! As if Maebelle would ever allow herself to be seen in any sort of uniform: no matter what the altitude!"

Turning her attention back to one of the day's English newspapers she had been given (the papers having been put on another plane earlier before its flight to New York in time for any return flights to London), she gave a slight on spotting a small article headed *Popular Teacher in Unfortunate Accident.*

"Good God," she muttered. "Could this be the notorious Paul McDowell we all know about? The Paul McDowell who makes Porfirio Rubirosa look a mere novice? Please don't tell me this has something to do with McDowell having to defend himself against three burglars the other week. His form of defence being a series of well-aimed darts!"

Her comment followed by a crash as she dropped the crystal champagne flute. Clutching her elegant throat, Maebelle said in a hoarse whisper. "No, it can't be! But then, it can only be! Dee-Dee Devereaux going around telling everybody his eye was seriously damaged by an errant champagne cork! What if it wasn't? What if it was something personal, something between him and Paul McDowell? What if? What bloody if?" she added with a loud cry, her mini outburst causing several of her fellow passengers to glance irritably in her direction.

"Oh, my God! Monty! Monty!" she hissed reaching over and slapping his hand. "Monty! Wake up, damn you! Wake up!"

"Wha . . .? Back in Old Blighty already?" said Monty with a yawn.

"No, you idiot!" hissed Maebelle. "We're not back in Old bloody Blighty, but I have a strong feeling we'll soon be landing up to our *eyeballs* in a mega load of shit!"

AN ELEGANT DUPLEX APARTMENT OVERLOOKING EATON SQUARE

"At least we weren't targeted with some *mis*-guided missile on our way into town," quipped Monty handing Maebelle a large G and T. "Aw, c'mon, Maebelle, honey," he added in a James Stewart twang. "Just because some bloody nondescript music teacher decides to do a loop the loop on his way to an ecclesiastical choir practice and seriously damages himself, doesn't mean it was deliberate!"

"No?" shrilled Maebelle. "Just as a carriage filled with shit and its owners covered in shit was an everyday occurrence: wasn't deliberate? You have a very short memory, Montgomery Livingston! And what about the window boxes? Never mind the mannequin's head in my very bed! Pure, pure, Devereaux! God *knows* what he'll conjure up next!"

"*Montgomery* Livingston?" repeated Monty with a grin. "My, you *have* gotten your pantyhose in a twist! Look, if it helps put your mind at rest and apart from the live-in staff and me being here, there's still plenty of room for another person, so why not have a full-time bodyguard on site? Come to think of it, I know the very person. An ex-army chum of mine name of Bradford Rillington-Hale. I'll check with Rill - that's what he calls himself - and see what he's up to."

"Not another Errol Flynn lookalike, I trust?" said Maebelle, her perfect lips twitching.

"No, not another me lookalike," chuckled Monty. "Rather more of a Woody Allen lookalike but looks can be deceiving. Rill's an expert in hand-to-hand combat, has a collection of different coloured belts in karate, and is believed to have topped at least a dozen troublesome souls; if not more."

"Interesting," pouted Maebelle. Reaching for her drink she added mischievously. "Hopefully, for your sake, Monty dear, I don't slip into Mia Farrow mode and go all gooey over Woody Rilly!"

"I somehow doubt it," sniggered Monty. "According to a certain shower peeper I know, when it comes to Rill getting a woody, it's not all that goody! Ha ha!"

"Talking of which, how is *your* woody goody feeling?" said Maebelle with a lascivious smile.

"He's not suffering from jetlag, if that's what you're inferring, *Miss* Maebelle," grinned Monty. "Therefore, why not leave your drink and let's celebrate our safe return in our own, if not unique, uber-enjoyable way!"

"What a splendid idea, *Woody*!" simpered Maebelle. "I take it you'll be my charabanc to yon bedchamber?"

"Your charabanc of fire *and* desire, my lovely Maebelle!" yodelled Monty hefting Maebelle out of her chair and embracing her within his hefty arms.

GODFREY STREET

"Unbelievable, totally unbelievable," muttered Lulu as she and Maddy sat with their respective mugs of coffee; one fortified with a dollop of brandy, the other with a dollop of Drambuie. She gave a giggle. "A glittering eyepatch with an appliqued pound coin in lieu of an iris? As I said, unbe-bloody-believable, and, I have to admit, utterly original and utterly fabulous!" She gave another giggle. "Dare I use it in my book? Maybe Medora and Archie's next victim can be some flamboyant East End hoodlum sporting such an eyepatch?"

"Why not?" carolled Maddy. "After all, . . ."

"It *is* fiction!" they crooned in unison.

"What would you call him? This one=eyed hoodlum," tittered Maddy, reaching for her coffee.

"Something with a touch of the exotic," replied Lulu. Glancing at Flip Flop asleep next to the sofa she said brightly. "How about Flippy Foxton, or, better still, Flip the Zip, a mean hand with a whip?"

"How about you put Flippy Foxton or Flip the Zip on a *very* back burner and think again," said Maddy in a no-nonsense voice. Taking a further sip of coffee, she said matter-of-factly. "A glittering wicked one-eyed wonder such as Dee-Dee Devereaux deserves something really out of the mundane; something serious OTT!"

"You're absolutely right!" crooned Lulu. "So, with Flip Flop's inspiration firmly repositioned on the back burner, why not christen the devious, kaleidoscopic Dee-Dee with the sing-song name of Aye! Aye! Golden Eye!"

"Aye! Aye! Golden Eye?" crowed Maddy. "I love it!" She gave a grin. "Cue for a song, *n'est-ce pas?*"

"Definitely a cue for a song!" cried Lulu as the two young women put down their coffee mugs and, springing to their feet, began dancing round the kitchen chanting "Aye! Aye! Golden Eye! Aye! Aye! Golden Eye!" Their cheerful chanting soon joined by a yowling, howling wide awake, enthusiastic Flip Flop leaping about on his hind legs.

As the two, still giggling, collapsed onto the sofa, Lulu, giving Flip Flop a loving pat, turned to Maddy and said breathlessly. "On second thoughts, Aye! Aye! Golden Eye is far too original and far too exciting to end up a mere happening in *FROM CATWALK TO CATERWAULING,* so why not save him for another book?" She gave a giggle. "Why don't I make Aye! Aye! Golden Eye a private detective, but a detective with a difference: a detective with a penchant for saying: 'Not only gold with methods bold, but a success story as yet untold'!"

"Do it!" cried Maddy excitedly. "Exit Robert Apps! Come in Aye! Aye! Golden Eye! A stellar fella if ever there was!"

"Do I make him a gorgeous Adonis-cum-Mr. Universe lookalike or a nerdish shrimp who looks as if he couldn't say boo to a goose? Pun *not* intended!"

"Oh, he's got to be gorgeous, uber-vain, and swings both ways. But without a hint of Dee-Dee Devereaux, looks wise!" enthused Maddy, "Uber-gorgeous in fact, seeing Detective Aye! Aye! Golden Eye is in competition against such a splendiferous eyepatch!"

"An Ola Rapace lookalike? A George Clooney lookalike? Or, to really get my readers salivating, a dishy Michael Fassbender lookalike?" giggled Lulu.

"Oh, definitely mind-blowing Michael!" tittered Maddy. "Like any lovelorn soul will surely agree, there is nobody, but nobody, as gorgeous as he!"

"Give me a few more weeks with Medora and Archie and then we can welcome Aye! Aye! Golden Eye, with open arms!" said Lulu.

"Medora, Archie, and Flip Flop will no doubt be somewhat miffed with the arrival of the eye-popping Aye! Aye! Golden Eye," chortled Maddy.

"However, as *their* tome, i.e., *CATWALK TO CATERWAULING,* will, without a doubt, become another Lulu Mayhew bestseller; what will they have to be miffed about? Ha ha!"

"A book without a Flip Flop? Not on your nellie!" cried Lulu. "I don't wish to appear a touch predictable but surely nobody will be at all surprised to discover that Eye! Eye! Golden Eye's faithful companion is a handsome golden cocker spaniel who just happens to be named Clip Clop?" She gave a chortle. "And, if you can't put two and two together, Maddy dearest, then you certainly - unlike clever *moi* - deserve a follow-up G and T!"

"Silly me," tittered Maddy. "Why should they be surprised seeing Flip Flop, like his creator, remains invincible!"

SIX WEEKS LATER

"Oh Archie! Oh Archie!" wailed Medora over the telephone as she stood looking at Flip Flop gazing adoringly up at her, his tail wagging furiously akin to a flag caught up in a playful breeze. She added with an ear-splitting screech. "Didn't I tell you we should have dumped Mummy Eleanora and Daddy Gideon into your dad's woodchip machine - or farmer Donald's piggery - instead of burying them in the wretched orchard?"

(Three years ago, when the devious deed took place, Medora had pooh-poohed Archie's tongue-in-cheek suggestion they weigh down the two bodies with gold bars taken from Gideon's private vault and dump them in a distant reservoir.

"What? And deliberately drown part of my inheritance?" quipped Medora. "No way, José! We'll simply bury them somewhere in the grounds." She gave a snicker. "Bury them in some old sacking instead of the gold-plated him and her coffins as stipulated in dear Daddy Gideon's Will!")

"Er . . . why? What's happened??" stammered Archie.

"What's happened?" replied Medora with - if possible - an even louder screech. "What's happened is that Flip Flop must have gone back to the burial spot, had a good sniff round and decided to do a seven dwarfs and dig, dig, bloody dig! Hence him proudly presenting me with either Daddy Gideon's or Mummy Eleanora's thigh bone! That's what's happened!"

THE END

"Thank goodness for that," muttered Lulu swallowing the remains of her G and T. "Give me a day or two and then I can get to work on *AYE! AYE! GOLDEN EYE!* Where - as with the reincarnated, reinvented Flip Flop - the dreadful Maebelle will also be reappearing: this time in the sinuous form of Cymbeline; a steamy songstress with vampiric tendencies!" She gave a giggle. "With Cymbeline being a neuter-general name, the world is steamy Cymbeline's oyster: until she swallows a bad one!"

SIXTEEN

AN ELEGANT DUPLEX OVERLOOKING EATON SQUARE

"Whilst I appreciate the fact we arrived back the day before yesterday, I've said it before and I'll say it again, thank *God* that little foray to an extremely faraway Down-Under is over," crooned Maebelle as she and Monty sat drinking a couple of extra-large "thank God we're back" martinis. She gave a snort. "Not that the length of the flight seemed to bother you seeing your snored most of the way back; whereas I, despite my exhausting photographic schedule, remained alert and as a result I - much against my will, I hasten to add - was *forced* into to reading Mayhew's latest, devoted tribute to trash seeing there was nothing else apart from a selection of magazines."

Raising his glass, Monty said with a chuckle. "I can appreciate all those endless changes and all the posing must be exhausting, but I can assure you, having you play - whenever your hands were free - ha! - on my always willing to please didgeridoo, was equally - if not a touch more - exhausting!"

"Exhausting or not, I'm sure you'll agree your irresistible Maebelle is an accomplished didgeridoo player!"

"Gold medal, worthy!" chuckled Monty. Topping up their martinis, he added matter-of-factly. "Out of interest, what did you think of her book? I can't quite remember the title. Something t do with the Catskill Mountains or something like that."

"Nice try, Montgomery!" snapped Maebelle. "You know damn well it is *nothing* like that, and it's pretty, damn obvious *FROM CATWALK TO CATERWAULING* smacks of me! However, there's nothing I can do about it as" - she made finger quotes which, while holding her martini and not spilling a drop, was somewhat of an achievement - "all names, locations et cetera are imaginary and any reference to actual people is purely accidental!"

"You're absolutely right, there's nothing we can do," said Monty contemplatively. "However, that doesn't mean we should allow her to get away with it."

"It doesn't?" squawked Maebelle.

"It doesn't, and she won't," replied Monty. "So, why not sit and calmy enjoy your martini and forget about Lulu Mayhew for the time being. Let her revel in the success of her latest book - unfortunately it's already a bestseller - and while she's attending book signings or giving interviews, she'll know, in her heart, something unpleasant is just waiting to happen."

"Promise?" said Maebelle with a smile that would have made Lucretia Borgia look a mere amateur.

"I promise, and it will," said Monty firmly. He gave a chuckle. "I know we've just come off a major flight, but what would you say to a mini flight in a private jet somewhere not too far for a romantic, digeridoo-type dinner?"

"A mini flight in a private jet somewhere for a romantic, digeridoo-type dinner?" crooned Maebelle. "Where to and where?"

"Paris. The Tour d'Argent," replied Monty with a grin.

"You're on!!" yodelled Maebelle. "Hopefully I can find some suitable little numero to wear!"

*

"*FROM CATWALK TO CATERWAULING* is literally flying off the shelves," announced Maddy. "So, it goes without saying that your presence at tonight's charity dinner is sure to win over even more fans."

"Hopefully," giggled Lulu. "Though I have to admit what I'm helping so save - some rare species of a multi-coloured toad found only in the Amazon or something like that - is a toad I've never heard of. Unless of course by toad they mean a multi-coloured scumbag or heel! I have a list of those!"

"Goodness!" tittered Maddy. "What if they decide to present you with one as a thank you?"

"If he's the real McCoy, okay. If he looks like any of the toads on my list; forget it!" replied Lulu with a grin. "Talking of toads, any news of Dee-Dee Devereaux, a one-eyed toady if ever there was, who, like the dreaded Maebelle, has become suspiciously quiet."

"Maebelle, I know, has been on some fashion gig in Australia," said Maddy. "As for Dee-Dee Devereaux, we both know that he's been seen out and about with one of Maebelle's endless exes - that rather dishy

Neanderthal, Peter Proudfoot." She gave a snicker. "From what I hear, it almost is."

"No wonder Dee-Dee Devereaux looked so smug when we spotted the two of them at The Chelsea Ivy Garden the other day," giggled Lulu. "And not only smug but footloose as well: if you catch my drift!"

"Drift well and truly caught!" tittered Maddy. "Oh Lulu, you can be *so* wicked at times."

"Only at times? Goodness, maybe Aye! Aye! will be able to give me a much needed, shot in the arm!" giggled Lulu. "Continuing with our what who's up to what today, any news on Doctor Kildare and his bedtime story?"

"Nothing. And nothing new about Corey Marsden either. In fact, all are suspiciously quiet on all fronts."

"So, it seems," mused Lulu. "The million-dollar-cum-euro question being but, for how long?" Gulping the rest of her coffee, she added, all business, "Right! Time to go and say good morning to the unconquerable Detective Aye! Aye! and see what *he's* up to today!" She gave a giggle. "Maybe today could be the day he meets Cymbeline, the sly, sexy, singing siren. I can hardly wait!"

"Neither can I. Or should that be Aye! Aye!?" tittered Maddy. "Call me, if you need me. Meanwhile I'll be working my way through all that stack of fan mail which could easily make Santa look a poor second!"

On entering her office, Lulu made herself a cup of instant coffee with a smidgen of brandy before settling down in front of the computer. Looking at the collection of post-it notes she'd brought with her, she said with a murmur. "Talk about midnight and three a.m., thoughts. I like my note regarding Cymbeline - read Maebelle - 'she claimed she was in her early thirties, give or *fake*' - and, what about this one regarding Aye! Aye!? 'A detective who is late is a detective who is not there'. Or better still. 'I'll put a fucking torpedo under his waterline!' But first, a description of my mighty hero."

Lulu began to type.

PI Aye! Aye! Golden Eye! A doppelganger for Irish actor Michael Fassbender despite sporting and eyepatch of lacquered brass, a head of stormy, black waves and a pair of unruly sideburns reminiscent of two over-the-top caterpillars, sat eyeing (literally) the note sitting pride of place on his desk. Namely, centralised and not to be ignored, as was Eye! Eye's usual early morning wont.

(Before continuing, and before the anyone asks, our hero's somewhat unusual Christian names came into being all thanks to his mother, a devout fan of Ian Fleming. For the record, Aye! Eye! Golden Eye's full name was the tongue-twisting Aye! Aye! Golden Eye, Warren-Fitzpatrick.)

"Delilah!" he called out in his deep, spine-tingling voice. "This cry for help from some wannabe desperado named Egbert Underwood II. Did he say what it was about?"

"Obviously I asked," chirruped Delilah Temple, a bubbly Debbie Reynolds type as she danced into Aye! Aye's Mies van der Rhoe inspired office, "but he totally ignored me despite me repeating myself several times." She gave a titter. "I must have sounded exactly like one of my grandfather's old seventy-eight records whenever they got stuck! However, I have to say he did sound very out of sorts. Out of sorts but still a charmer."

"After such a colourful rendition, Delilah," said Aye! Aye! slipping off his red, white and azure blue striped jacket, "and as your good - or bad antennae - are usually one hundred and ten spot on, I have no alternative but to speak to Mr. Mystery Man."

He handed Delilah the post-it note. "Being a top, top, detective extraordinaire, it's obvious to me that Mr. Egbert Underwood, has somehow managed to tickle your endlessly tickled fancy, so I suggest you get him on the line then ask him to hold while you put him through. Then you do your best RADA bit, saying 'Oh, he's now on another call!' and then, with your usual Mata Hari, Theda Bara skills, you ask him to hold on whilst you chat him up and see if you can glean anything useful. After a few minutes you then say, suitably frustrated, it would probably be better if you got me to call him back, promising to make sure you won't allow me to take another call until he's spoken to the elusive me!"

"Aye! Aye! Aye! Aye!" tittered Delilah, "I'll do my usual scissors job and, if he's scissorable enough, I'll then report straight back to you as if on winged heels!"

"Scissorable enough?" repeated Aye! Aye! "I take it such a word can only be found in the CONCISE DELILAH TEMPLE DICTIONARY."

"Where else?" chirruped Delilah heading for the door. "To quote the not so effervescent Big Arnie. 'I'll be back!' But before I call him back, I'll see what I can find out about Mr. Underwood on the internet. Oh, before you ask, Clip Clop and Hoppy are out jogging, or, in Hoppy's case: hopping."

Clip Clop, a handsome golden cocker spaniel being Aye! Aye's! four-legged super sleuth and Hoppy Hickey, his one-legged assistant.

'Got to keep it in the family,' Eye! Eye! would chortle when explaining Hoppy's gleaming prosthetic leg with its matching shoe of the day. Hoppy, a twenty-something Disney Prince Charming lookalike, would insist on Mr. Wonky Was (his name for his replacement leg) wearing the same shoe as Mr. Still Here. The mystery of Hoppy's missing leg remained just that: a mystery. Need it be said that Clip Clop - much to Hoppy's feigned chagrin - took great tail wagging delight in occasionally hiding Hoppy's matching shoe of the day.

"When they get back, please tell Hoppy to pop into my office as I need an update on Miss Meadows and her missing Tommy."

"Knowing Miss Misery Meadows, I take the only Tommy in her life must be a cat, and a neutered one at that!" trilled Delilah on dancing out.

Five minutes the was a brief knock before Delilah popped her head round the door and said chirpily. "As prophesied, he called again, and now is more than likely champing at the bit, while awaiting your call. But, before you do, a quick resumé on Mr. Underwood. It's the same old story; money and it's supposed glory not always that hunky dory. Mr. Underwood is worth a cool two billion plus and recently remarried - for the sixth time - a sultry chanteuse with the stage name of Cymbeline. Need I say more?"

"No," chuckled Aye! Aye! "Let's call Senor Desperado as it is well-nigh obvious - as your ever active antennae tell you – that the cause for his distress can only be the sultry Miss Cymbeline. QED!"

"Will do!" trilled Delilah. "But afore I do, and in preparation for your verbal tussle with Senor Desperado, may I suggest the aid of a teeny-weensy vodkatini?"

"Yet another fine example of your ever active antennae," replied Aye! Aye! with a dazzling whiter than white and one gold capped tooth smile. "A vodkatini sounds just the ticket. Make it a large one!"

"Having a large one being your prerogative," snickered Delilah with a toss of her blue and purple-streaked topknot.

Aye! Aye! had barely settled in his Herman Miller Executive chair, a copy of the latest HOT FROM gossip magazine on the desk, when Delilah, giving a quick knock. reappeared and said breathlessly. "I, literally - just called Mr. Underwood on his mobile, and not only did he pick up on the first ring, but the wretched man is waiting downstairs in reception!"

"Zeus!" exclaimed Aye! Aye! "He must be desperate! I take it Miss Spendthrift asked him to wait?"

"She did, as well as saying in a whisper that could have been heard in Tokyo, he looks as if he has an army of angry red ants in his pants!"

"A surefire assumption that the singing Cymbeline must be looking for a replacement anthill," chuckled Aye! Aye! "Well, let's not prolong the poor man's agony. Ask Miss Spendthrift to send him up: in the nicest, possible way, that is!"

*

"Mr, Underwood, sir," announced Delilah, barely suppressing a giggle as she ushered a tubby little Mr. Magoo lookalike into what she referred to as the golden inner sanctum.

"Mr. Underwood," schmoozed Aye! Aye! rising to his size fifteen feet. "This is a surprise as I was just about to call you." Proffering a beringed hand he added mano to mano. "Aye! Aye! Golden Eye! PI Extraordinaire. Delighted to meet you." He gestured to one of the Herman Miller chairs facing his Parzinger desk. "Pray, have a seat. I was about to partake in the uninhibited pleasure of a mid-morning vodkatini contrary to a de rigueur coffee. Miss Temple, may I add, being a mixologist extraordinaire! Goes with the territory one could say!! Ha ha!"

"A vodkatini could not be more perspicacious," fluted Egbert Underwood, his fleshy lower lip trembling. "In fact, a second waiting in the wings, wouldn't go amiss!"

I could take to this little fellow, thought Aye! Aye! Despite the usual, boring tale of woe tale of woe he's about to spin.

*

Armed with their vodkatinis the two men sat looking at each other, Delilah having left them alone but not before a tittered: "Don't worry about refills as I'll be back!" on closing the door behind her.

"Mr. Underwood . . ." - "Eggy, please" - "Er . . . Eggy, and please call me Aye! Aye! Let's not beat about the hedgerows. I can see you're a tad distraught so, without any further ado, I suggest you spill the Heinz."

"Heinz?"

"Beans."

"It concerns my wife, wife number six, a ravishing chanteuse with the stage name of Cymbeline," whispered Eggy. Pausing to take a reassuring *swallow of his vodkatini, he added with a wail. "I believe she's hired a hitman to kill me!"*

About to ask Eggy how he knew of Cymbeline's wicked ploy the office door opened and a panting Clip Clop padded in. (Wily Clip Clop skilled at opening a lever handle by standing on his hind legs and grabbing hold of the handle in his jaws.)

"Clip Clop!" exclaimed Aye! Aye! "Surely you know it's extremely rude not to knock before entering a room?"

Staring at the buoyant, tail wagging golden spaniel, a disconcerted Eggy said a touch waspishly. "As I was saying, PI Aye! Aye! before this unexpected intrusion, I believe my wife has hired a hitman to kill me."

"So, you said: twice," replied Aye! Aye! glancing up at Eggy while fondling a now drooling Clip Clop's floppy ears. "What a wicked woman your Cymbeline must be. Order a hitman to kill you? Trust me, Eggy, such a thing will never do!"

Reaching across his desk for the intercom Aye! Aye! said in a no-nonsense voice. "Delilah, please ask Hoppy to come to my office tout suite as there's a change in strategies: a wandering tomcat having been usurped by a hired, no doubt hunky, hitman!"

"Yes, Maddy?" said Lulu glancing up on Maddy entering the office.

"Lobie and Leo have arrived and are now upstairs in the sitting room, drinks in hand, awaiting the arrival of Godfrey Street's answer to the Queen of Sheba," chortled Maddy. She gestured toward the computer. "How's it coming along?"

"Brilliantly!" crooned Lulu. "I'm hopelessly in love with PI Aye! Aye! Clip Clop, his wannabe Flip Flop, and Aye! Aye's! assistant, the one-legged, hunky, Hoppy! Mwah! Mwah" *Mwah*! Give me a minute whilst I go and powder the Mayhew nose and then I'll join you!"

She gave a giggle. "Needless to say. Aye! Aye! Clip Clop and hunky Hoppy have caused their mischievous muse to do a total turnabout! Why let sleeping Maebelles lie when one such creature could be the inspiration behind another case for the intrepid PI Aye! Aye! Golden Eye!"

*

"Good mid-morning!" crowed Lulu on entering the sitting room. "And how are London's answer to Heckle and Jekyll this merry morn?" Reaching for the G and T handed to her by the ever-attentive Maddy, she added crisply. "You two look a touch put out. Anything I should know about or is Chelsea destined *not* to win on Sunday?"

Taking a hefty swallow of his drink, Lobie gave a grimace and said sonorously. "While we were waiting for you to finish doing whatever it is ladies do prior to making an appearance, Maddy was generous enough to talk freely about your latest novel based on a colourful PI inspired by Dee-Dee Devereaux and a sultry songstress inspired - surprise, surprise - by none other than the wild Maebelle."

"Oh, she did, did she?" sniped Lulu. giving Maddy a glare. "So much for any conversation between me and my *loyal* secretary being confidential." Taking a sip of her G and T, she added with a purr. "Had you arrived a tad later no doubt she also would have been able to tell you how Maebelle - oops! Cymbeline - wishing to get rid of her wealthy hubby - finds the sublime answer in the form of one Simon Strudel; a mercenary known for his vivid imagination when it comes to helping people leave our planet in a totally foolproof way! Unfortunately, *because* of your arrival, dear Maddy missed out on being told what witty scenario I had in mind for Cymbeline-cum-Maebelle. A scenario which - should Maebelle ever read the book and puts two and two together - could see her getting her exclusive Ann Summers' knickers in a twist!"

"For Chrissake, Lulu!" erupted Lobie. "Forget bloody Maebelle! And when I say forget her and her ridiculous vendetta against you, which, if truth be known, appears to have now become *your* vendetta against her! Enough is enough! What's more, Leo and I have decided we will no longer be involved in any of your ridiculous scenarios hinting of things to come in order - hopefully - to upset the poor woman. As I said, enough is enough!"

"Really?" crooned Lulu.

"Yes, really," replied Lobie. "As from now!"

"Well then, *gentlemen,*" said Lulu with a tight smile. "I suggest you *don't* finish your drinks but get to your clumsy trotters and get the *fuck* out of my house."

Spinning her head à la Linda Blair in *The Exorcist.* Lulu sat staring at Maddy for a moment before saying with a sibilant hiss. "As for you, Madeleine Thompson, you have an hour in which to pack your bags and leave. Regarding any money you think you may be owed; speak to my accountant." She gave a derisive snort. "Unlike the Janus-faced you, Lulu Mayhew will *not* quibble over what pittance you claim you're owed."

"Jesus! Lulu!" roared Lobie springing to his feet. "Get a grip! Okay, Leo and I will leave but you can't do this to Maddy. Not only does she put up with all your paranoia and me, me, me shit, she's a vital cog in your writing wheel and when it comes to loyalty . . ." Lobie paused for a second before saying as if wishing to lighten the mood. "When it comes to loyally, it's a neck and neck finish between Maddy and Flip Flop!"

"How dare you compare *anyone* to the incomparable Flip Flop!" shrieked Lulu. "Out! Out! Damn the two of you! As for you, *loyal* Maddy Thompson, simply leave the house keys on the hall console when *you* leave!"

Glaring at the three as they exited the room, Lulu reached for her drink, took a gulp, and said in her best "Mummy loves you" voice to Flip Flop who had been sitting on his haunches, ears twitching as he watched the ensuing drama. "It's now just you and me, Flip Flop. But as they say, best things come in threes, therefore listen closely to your adoring Mummy Lulu as she makes this decidedly unexpected, surprise, surprise call."

Reaching for her mobile she tapped in a saved number. "Benedict?" she crooned. "The one and only Brighton Bell Benedict? Surprise! Surprise! For 'tis *moi*! The one and only Lulu Mayhew speaking! I trust you can tear yourself away from your trains and give me a second of your timetable or two?"

*

As Lulu began speaking to Ben, Lobie, Leo and Maddy were standing outside the front door conferring among themselves,

"Pay no attention to her, Maddy," said Lobie placatingly. "She doesn't mean it."

"Oh, yes she does!" snapped Maddy. "It's been brewing for some time. There have been numerous similar outbursts recently but not quite as spectacular as today's. Plus, when checking her day to day writing her increasing, pent up anger against the world in general has become glaringly obvious! All I can say is that she and Maebelle have inadvertently switched roles with Lulu becoming the villain of the piece and Maebelle the victim!" She gave a hollow chuckle. "God only knows what she has in mind for poor Cymbeline!"

"So, you're taking your dismissal as gospel? You're really quitting?"

"So much so that, apart from a few personal items, I've had my suitcase packed and ready for at least five weeks," replied Maddy resignedly. "However, I can assure you if ever the word relief was spelled out in lights on Broadway or Piccadilly Circus; today's the day!"

SEVENTEEN

"Hold on, Lulu. while I instruct the driver of the Master Cutler to make an unscheduled stop," rumbled Ben. "Hold on."

An unscheduled stop? thought Lulu with a snicker. *What is it they say about men being boys when it comes to their toys?*

"The Master Cutler is now waiting patiently in between stations," announced Ben into the phone. "As you say, Lulu, this *is* a surprise. According to Dee-Dee I was never to call you again. So, being a good Brighton boy, I haven't."

"I never said such a thing!" snapped Lulu. "If the truth be told, when I called Dee-Dee to sympathise and say how appalled I was to hear about him losing an eye, he told me he never wished to speak to *me* again. Your name was never mentioned."

"That's ridiculous, Lullu," grunted Ben. "It wasn't your fault we were waylaid by a champion darts player! If anyone should be in purdah, it's that bloody McDowell character!"

"Don't tell me you haven't been told what happened to him?"

"Dee-Dee did mention something about him being involved in some sort of accident."

"Some sort of accident?" echoed Lulu. "As a result of this 'some sort of accident', McDowell is presently in the process of getting a new face! Surely someone must have brought you up to date?"

"Well, all I'm prepared to say is a new face compared to his former arrogant one can only be an improvement," chuckled Ben. "From what I managed to glimpse before he started throwing those bloody darts; his face certainly needed a refit! But enough of the small talk. How can I help you, Lulu, as it's pretty obvious you're not calling in order to invite me to lunch or dinner."

"Tut-tut, Ben," chided Lulu. "You know you're always welcome here at any time. However, as you're not the easily hoodwinked type, I'll be straight with you. I have an irritating problem - more of an irritating itch - which needs to be well and truly scratched."

"Interesting," mused Ben. "And may I ask the identity of this irritating itch which needs to be well and truly scratched?"

"His name is Andy McCulloch, also known as Robert Apps, the author."

"And why, may I ask, does Mr. Apps require a severe scratching?"

"Because he let me down regarding a mutual project and Lulu Mayhew does not do let down!"

"Wasn't this McCulloch or Apps character the reason behind the attack on McDowell?"

"He was, taking priority over another irritation; a highly successful fashion model named Maebelle."

"Of course! The notorious Maebelle. Well, Lulu, you're in luck as Brighton Bell Bogart *is* at a bit of a loose end as we speak and if another train is in the offing, he wouldn't say no to giving a certain Miss Lulu Mayhew a helping hand in scratching her irritating itch!"

"An itch which could easily turn into a nasty rash if not dealt with sooner than later: if you catch my Atlantic Drift," giggled Lulu. "As for another train; easy-peasy. So, puffer Ben, when do you think your loose end could fit me into its timetable and travel up to London for a sort it all out lunch?"

"How about Friday at twelve?"

"Friday, here at Godfrey Street around twelve would be perfect! Any preference for a before lunch drink?

"I'm going through a pastis phase at the moment."

"Pasis it is! Maybe part of a Harlow stinger?" tittered Lulu. "I make a mean Harlow stinger!"

"Even better," rumbled Ben. "Jazzy Jean dressed in white crème de menthe, cognac and a splash of pastis representing her blonde tresses will certainly hit the spot!"

"One Harlow stinger coming up," giggled Lulu. "Another question. Do your tastebuds have an affiliation with lobster?"

"A very strong affiliation!" chuckled Ben.

"Goody! Hopefully sex-on-legs Rex at The Chelsea Fishmonger will have a couple just waiting to be whisked away and hopefully our meeting will be on a par with our delicious lunch," giggled Lulu.

"Oh, it will," rumbled Ben. "See it as a wondrous soothing balm which, if applied correctly, will get rid of that nasty itch in no time! Until Friday, then."

"Until Friday," said Lulu with a triumphant smile as she put down the phone. Glancing at a dozing Flip Flop, she added cheerfully. "And whilst we're lunching on delicious lobster, my darling Flip Flop, *you* shall be gnawing on a delicious beef marrow bone courtesy of Wyndham's the Butcher!"

*

"Welcome, Benedict!" crooned Lulu on opening the front door. "Oh!" she exclaimed on being handed a large bunch or red roses. "Red roses! My favourite!"

"Need I say I did not forget the handsome gentleman next to you," rumbled Ben with a grin. Before stooping to give Flip Flop a hearty pat he handed Lulu a neat package adorned with a bright red bow and said with a chuckle. "I didn't know what to get for Mr. Golden Boy so I lake it a box of doggy chews, or 'The Original Treat Box' according to the label, is in order?"

"Oh!" exclaimed Lulu for a second time as she took hold of the package. "Oh! Flip Flop simply *adores* doggy treats!" she cooed. (*Christ, dear! No need to overdo it with the ohs!* thought Ben waspishly.) "Now, instead of standing chatting on the doorstep like two old biddies in *Coronation Street,* come in and let me offer you a lethal Harlow stinger or two. Then, and only then, will you be in a suitable frame of mind to hear about my irritating itch, and *my* suggestion as to how we scratch it!"

Lulu gave a giggle. "I trust your response will be more that of *The Ice Man* than that of a Tommy Noonan!"

"Tommy Noonan?"

"The nerdish gent who played opposite Marilyn Monroe in *The Seven Year Itch.*"

"But, of course," rumbled Ben. "Silly Benedict!"

Armed with their respective stingers, Lulu said, without any preamble. "Ever been to Italy, Ben?"

"Italy? Yes, several times. When I say several times, I mean I've done the usual touristy bit: namely Rome, Venice and Florence."

"Well, if you're seriously interested in helping me scratch, you could find yourself visiting a place east of Portofino. By place, I mean a somewhat splendid eighteen century villa - or about to be, according to a source - belonging to a Dr Clive Cordell and his partner, a Mr. Andy McCulloch: also known as Robert Apps, the author."

"Aha! With Mr. Apps, as opposed to simple Mr. McCulloch, being the itch that requires a severe scratching."

"You forgot to use the word irritating," responded Lulu with a thin smile. "And no, not only Mr. Apps, as I'd like the villa totally scratched as well, making it more Pompei AD79 than *Architectural Digest* 2023 in appearance!" She added sarcastically. "Dr Clive Cordell is far too negative a soul to deserve such a spectacular send off, so best to scratch when he is not in residence. Leave him be as he'll no doubt dissolve into deepest mourning." Glancing at a bemused Ben, she said with a giggle. "I wonder if he'll set a new trend whereby doctors will be seen wearing *black* surgical coats instead of their usual white!"

"You never know," replied Ben deadpan.

"Apps is now spending a great deal of time there whilst supervising the ongoing refurbishment and working on his new novel. He's presently here in London but should be returning to their villa, Villa Casa Degli Archi, for the whole of November. A fine time for hatching your scratching!" Lulu gave a further giggle. "Remember, remember, the fifth of November. Gunpowder, treason and plot! Therefore, a lethal *mis*guided rocket - read missile - of sorts wouldn't be totally out of order. Need I say more, or shall we adjourn to the dining room in order to attack those beckoning lobsters?"

"Why not?" chuckled Ben. "Far better to be beckoned by a lobster than a prawn!"

"Care to explain?" quipped Lulu.

"Explain?"

"Your preference for a lobster as opposed to a prawn," giggled Lulu.

"Maybe I'm a closet size queen," chuckled Ben.

"Aren't we all," snickered Lulu. "We're lunching in the kitchen so down Miss Harlow and follow me."

AN ELEGANT DUPLEX APARTMENT OVERLOOKING EATON SQUARE

"Oh my God! Oh my *God*!" shrieked Maebelle. "Oh my God!"

"Jesus! Maebelle!" shouted Monty on bursting into the study. "What the fuck's going on? What's happened? Are you okay?"

"Oh my *God*! Monty!" shrilled Maebelle clutching him to her elegant frame. "That was lousy Lionel, Lionel Labanter, my agent, on the phone, with *the* most sensational news!" Stepping back and still holding hands, she gave Monty one of her famous zillion-watt smiles and said, enunciating each word. "I. Have. Just. Been. Offered. A. Leading. Role. In. The. Film. Adaptation of Robert App's bestseller. *High Jinks in High C*!"

"From model to movie star!" exclaimed Monty giving Maebelle a hug. "*Brava*! My love! *Brava*!"

"Oh my God! Oh my God!" shrilled Maebelle. "Imagine Oscar night! Imagine the applause . . ."

"I'm sure it will be thunderous, Maebelle dear," said Monty with a smile. "However, and not wishing to steal your thunder, what happens next? When do you er . . . start filming et cetera, et cetera?"

"Lionel tells me I have to be in Los Angeles, week after next - in anticipation of me saying yes he's already started a magical juggling around with my various commitments - but, prior to that I have just confirmed a meeting with him and a representative from Bromeando Films tomorrow at eleven." Putting her hands to her face à la Edvard Munch's *The Scream,* she added with a wail. "Oh my God! Oh my God! What does a potential award-winning actor wear for such a vital meeting?"

"So, it's off to L.A. week after next, huh?" said Monty with a grimace. "I take it you'll be met, and suitably feted, once you set foot on Californian soil."

"Once *I* set foot on Californian soil?" repeated Maebelle. "Once *we* set foot on Californian soil, you mean." Putting a finger to Monty's lips she added with a purr. "Surely you didn't expect me to accept their offer unless my business partner and inverted - sometimes perverted - commas, personal partner would be joining me?"

"You actually said that?"

"I certainly did," pouted Maebelle. "To more or less quote Lionel, he told Bromeando Films unless they agreed to you being part of the deal, there would be no deal!" She gave a snicker. "Not that I totally believe him for it sounds too good to be true!"

"And they agreed to whatever he *did* say?"

"Of course, they agreed, *Montgomery*!" snapped Maebelle. "After all, there's never been a movie made starring the legendary Maebelle before."

"With more to follow, I'm sure," said Monty, his sculpted lips twitching. "Well, my darling, this calls for a celebratory flute of bubbly and, if you're not too up in the air about it all, maybe a further 'well done you' celebration back on bedroom earth!"

"What a *bon* idea!" trilled Maebelle. "An undress rehearsal as it were for Oscars' night!"

*

"Penny for them, Maebelle, dear," said Monty as they sat having a further flute of champagne each following a frenzied, yowling celebration on the study floor.

"I can't believe what I'm about to say, Monty, but wouldn't it be wonderful if Dee-Dee was here to celebrate my good news?"

"Dee-Dee Devereaux, here with us?" said Monty with disbelief. "Great Scott, Maebelle! What's caused this mega turnabout?" He gave a chuckle. "Can it be that Madam Maebelle, feline model extraordinaire is, in some incongruous way, *mellowing*?" He gave a hoot of laughter. "Mellowing Maebelle? I have to say I like the sound of it!"

"You know what, Monty dear? So do I," purred Mabelle reaching for the phone. "And before we have a change of mind, let's give him a call." Without hesitating she tapped in Dee-Dee's number with a mauve painted nail. "It's ringing," she announced in a stage whisper.

"If you're hunky, over six-foot tall, eye-poppingly well-endowed and stunningly good-looking; please leave a message. If not, simply hang-up and do not call this number again," crooned a familiar voice.

"Dee-Dee Devereaux, you never change! 'Tis Maebelle calling, along with a white silk Givenchy scarf in lieu of a mere white flag of truce. As you well-know, I am almost six-foot tall in stilettos, strikingly good-looking but when it comes to well-endowed; forget it! Call me or ignore me! The decision is yours!"

"Maebelle?" squawked Dee-Dee on answering. "Maddening Maebelle waving a white flag? Are you sure it isn't a wicked, blinding puce? Darling one, how *are* you? Please don't tell me that having successfully destroyed all those bowing before you, there's no one left apart from the lowly likes of the scintillating, sex-bomb Dee-Dee Devereaux!"

"I can assure you the flag is as white as the driven snow. Dee-Dee dear, and I am happy to say there are still oodles of lesser mortals left to annoy and destroy but, as I said to Montgomery Livingston, my resident *beau* and

188

arrow - a typical Dee-Dee Devereau pun, *n'est-ce pas*? - there is only one Dee-Dee Devereaux and I feel it's time the two of you - in other words, the three of us - should meet."

"As you well know I only meet in extravagant havens," trilled Dee-Dee, "and if you're free around sixish. you could find me artistically draped across their uber-lengthy banquette in my latest extravaganza: namely the Snuggery champagne bar in Claridge's!" He gave a titter. "Despite your so-called flag of truce, I shall be wearing a rhine-encrusted suit of armour with a gold-plated helmet and visor close at hand, and a jewel-encrusted Fabergé dagger on the table in front of me; just in case!"

"You mean one of your usual 'I don't wish to be recognised' get-ups?" giggled Maebelle. "We look forward to seeing you."

"Hold on! Madam! Hold on!" carolled Dee-Dee. "This *beau* with what can only be a *flaming* arrow. Merely good-looking or a Clooney-cum-Rapace-cum-Fassbender-cum-Pitt good-looking?"

"Think of a well hung, young Errol Flynn on a *very* good-looking day!" crooned Maebelle.

"Taxi!" yodelled Dee-Dee into the phone. "Taxi!"

THE SNUGGERY BAR - CLARIDGE'S

"Darling Dee-Dee!" crooned Maebelle on entering the elegant bar. Aware of the looks and discreet nudges of the other customers she added gaily. "People on seeing twinkling you must think they've turned on the Christmas lights early this year!" She gave a madcap laugh. "Dazzling, darling! Utterly dazzling! Love the lilac sequin jacket, darling! So . . . so . . . so . . . well, so *lilac*! As for the rhinestone eyepatch . . . *tres, tres* eye-catching!"

"And you don't look too past tense yourself, Maebelle dearest," pouted Dee-Dee as he languidly rose to his feet. "A symphony in Death Row black." He nodded toward a bemused Monty. "And this splendid example of macho manhood is, I take it, Mr. Montgomery Livingston. The latest man of many men." Said as a statement and not a question.

"You are *so* predictable!" shrilled Maebelle as she sank elegantly onto a chair. "And yes, this is Monty and, as I told you, another Errol the Peril with *all* the legendary accoutrements!"

"He also speaks," interrupted Monty a touch sharply. Hands held firmly to his sides, he said with a thin smile. "Maebelle has told me a great deal about you, Dee-Dee - I take it I may call you Dee-Dee?"

"You just have; twice," tittered Dee-Dee. "So, yes, you may."

"Thank you. As I was about to say, Maebelle has told me a great deal about you, *Dee-Dee,* and my first impression on seeing the colourful you, in person, is how spot on she was/is with her description."

Get you and your anaconda cock! thought Dee-Dee with an instant loathing. *No attraction here, fatal or otherwise and, if my well-attuned sixth sense tells me right, you, Mr, Livingston are a snake in the grass - forget any arse - and not to be trusted!*

"Champers for everyone?" he crooned, summoning the hovering waiter. "And as this little gathering - *sans* any cauldron - is destined to be a success, maybe dinner afterwards? On me of course!"

"Let's wait and see, shall we?" purred Maebelle. "As the saying goes, 'slowly, slowly catchy monkey! And yes, champers would be divine!"

"I take it you're not suggesting your witty, erudite, elegant technicoloured host is in any way related to a *monkey*!" trilled Dee-Dee.

"Not even a brass one, I can assure you," chucked Monty as he sat down on a chair next to Maebelle.

"Witty as well as pretty," crowed Dee-Dee mentally rubbing his hands with glee. "Where *do* you find them, Maebelle dearest! Oh, what I wouldn't do for a sneaky peek inside that little black book of yours! Aha! Saved by Monsieur Jeeves accompanied by Monsieur Bolinger! A far better alternative to that dreary old bell! Hee-hee!" His comment resulting in Monty giving Maebelle a look of disbelief.

Fully aware of the brief exchange, Dee-Dee thought mischievously. *Devereaux, you evil ageless queen, control yourself!*

Accepting a flute of champagne from the waiter, he raised the flute in the form of a toast. "To old friends, and when I say it is utterly, butterly, fabulous to see you again, dear, *dear* Maebelle, your Dee-Dee truly means it!" Taking a further sip. He added mischievously. "Maebelle dear, I recognise that Hiroshima about to burst expression. So, let it out and tell Dee-Dee all!"

"The magnificent Maebelle is about to become an even more magnificent movie star!" crooned Maebelle, her loud announcement causing a combination of curious and a few irritated looks. "Forget ghastly Gloria reminiscing in that decaying hacienda on that much abused boulevard as it will now be me, Maebelle, toast of *all* the boulevards!" Flashing Dee-Dee a zillion-watt smile, she proceeded to tell him her exciting news. Not giving him the chance to offer his congratulations, she added airily. "Darling, dearest, Dee-Dee; as you're such a *brilliant* brain when it comes to fashion, why not accompany Monty and the gorgeous *moi* to L.A. for the duration of the shoot? Better still, I *insist* that you accompany me in the enviable role of my personal fashion consultant!"

"Why, Miss Maebelle," crowed Dee-Dee in feigned disbelief. Fluttering his eyelashes, he put a finger to his chin and fluted, à la Balance Dubois. "Ah tho-ought you'd nevah ask!" Giving a giggle, he added with a cry. "An' my answer to yah winsome lil' question is a loud yais!"

*

"I'm curious, Maebelle," said Monty in the taxi taking them back to Eaton Square. "Despite the ups and downs in his technicoloured life, Dee-Dee Devereaux never seems to be wanting" - he gave a chuckle - "for anything. I take it there must be some sort of a private income or some weirdo of a sugar daddy!"

"Ever heard of Donaldson Diapers?" tittered Mabelle. "Every time a used diaper is discarded, Dee-Dee Devereaux receives another type of little deposit!"

"Jesus!" said Monty! "Donaldson Diapers? It's no wonder why he changed his surname! Ha ha!"

EIGHTEEN

AN ELEGANT TOWN HOUSE - NOB HILL - SAN FRANCISCO

"Good evening, Renata," grinned Todd Steman, a blond Ben Affleck lookalike, on greeting Renata Bonifacio, his hostess. "And thank you for also inviting my house guest," he added, glancing over her shoulder. "I take it he's already arrived?"

"About ten minutes ago," simpered Renata Bonifacio, an elegant Claudette Colbert lookalike, "and, like you, Todd, a total charmer!"

"Good evening, Mrs Bonifacio," said a voice behind Todd. "Malcom Duval." Stepping up next to Todd, Malcom proffered his hand and said smoothly. "How very kind of you to invite a total stranger to your daughter's twenty-first birthday celebration."

"My pleasure," replied Renata offering a limp hand in return. "Mr. Bonifacio tells me it's your first visit to our city, so welcome. Welcome to San Francisco! Now come and meet Tinkerbel, my daughter, and then I'll leave you and Todd, Mr. Steman, to circulate."

Tinkerbel? thought Malcom with an inward snigger. *Who next? Captain bloody Hook?*

Giving Malcom a flutter of her heavily mascaraed lashes, Renata added coquettishly. "People tell me that my darling Tinkerbel and I could easily pass for twins. Me? Twenty-one?" She gave a tinkly laugh, "Aren't people naughty!"

Jesus! thought Malcom. *Not another bloody Maebelle. Talk about out of the fucking frying pan and into the fire!*

"People can also be correct, Mrs Bonifacio," replied Malcom with a faux smile.

"Renata, please."

"People can also be correct when making comparisons, *Renata*," said Malcom silkily. "I look forward to meeting your twin sister!"

"Oh, you English!" tittered Renata giving Malcom a playful punch on the arm. "Follow me!"

*

"Her twin sister?" muttered Malcom to a sniggering Todd after Renata had introduced him to the gangling, giggling Tinkerbel, before leaving the two men to circulate. "As a certain English advert keeps reminding all and sundry, she should have gone to Specsavers!"

He glanced round the vast, over-decorated room and the animated well-dressed guests. "As I was warned, a blend of Versailles meets *Architectural Digest.* Papa Bonifacio must be loaded."

"Triple loaded," sniggered Todd. "And then some."

"The guy standing over there talking an elderly couple."

"You mean the tall guy who looks like that Dracula fella? That Christopher Lee or whatever his name is or was?" Todd glanced at his watch and said with a grin, "Whichever one he is, he's early as it's only just gone eight, and nowhere near midnight!" He gave Malcom a grin. "His name's Dan Crozier, someone else over from London and who also happens to be staying with me. Why, ring any bells?"

A clanging of bells would be more appropriate, thought Malcom, his pulse racing. *What the fuck is bloody Crozier doing here in San Franciso, and how the fuck will he react on spotting me standing here with you?*

"It looks as it you're about to find out seeing Count Dracula has obviously spotted you and is now floating toward us, his fangs well and truly on display!" added Todd with a giggle.

"Well, if it isn't Dan Crozier, aka Dan the Man, in the flesh," grinned Malcom proffering his hand. "Malcom Duval. You may remember me." Turning to face Todd he said cheerfully. "The last time I saw this reprobate was back in London."

"As you can obviously see, I'm here now," grunted Dan, ignoring Malcom's proffered hand. "As for the term friend. A bit inappropriate I would have thought seeing how your *close* friend in London, model Maebelle, is no close friend of my closest friend in London, namely Lulu Mayhew, the writer. In fact, it's common knowledge that they dislike each other intensely."

Glancing at an open-mouthed Todd, Dan said through clenched teeth. "Enjoy the party, Todd. I'll see you back at the apartment; if not later, then at breakfast."

"Jesus! Crozier!" snapped Malcom. "A bit of an overreaction, don't you think? I realise it was you who instructed your Lulu Mayhew not to have anything to do with me because of my relationship with Maebelle and, as you're now being openly aggressive toward me, maybe you'd care to explain why?"

"Explain?" echoed Dan. "There's nothing to explain. Unless you care to explain the graffiti on a selection of bookshop windows and the vandalising of a certain house on Godfrey Street, Chelsea, by painting the whole front red."

"I have no idea what you're talking about," said Malcom smoothy. "As for Lulu Mayhew, I was given to understand *she* was the writer of ridiculous fiction; not you."

"Bastard!" roared Dan throwing a hefty punch which landed with a resounding crunch on Malcom's nose.

"My noth! My noth!" gasped Malcom clutching his bleeding face.

"Dan! Dan!" yelled Todd. "What the fuck's wrong with you?"

"Get those bastards out of here!" bellowed a red-faced Pedro Bonifacio as he and two of his bodyguards stormed over to where the three men were standing. Giving Todd an angry shove, he added with a yell. "That includes you. Todd Steman! How *dare* you insult me and my wife by bringing such trash into our home! Out! Out!"

Eyeing the two bodyguards holding Dan in a vice-like grasp he said sharply. "Throw him out onto the street. As for our former friend here, a severe kick or two in the arse will suffice. Now, *go*, Goddamnit! Go!"

*

"Fuck! Fuck! What's the *matter* with the two of you?" shouted Todd, brushing his trousers having stumbled and fallen onto his knees after being literally thrown out of the house. Glaring angrily at Dan and Malcom who stood glaring at each other, he said with a virulent hiss. "As for you, Dan, I strongly suggest you find yourself a hotel for tonight, as I certainly have no wish to see you back at the apartment. Furthermore, the keys please. I'll get Jodie to pack up any luggage you have in readiness for you to collect some time tomorrow. You have Jodie's mobile number so simply let her know when."

Taking a deep breath. He turned to face Malcom. "As for *you*, Mr. Duval, I don't wish to know you and hopefully, ever have the misfortune of meeting you again! What's more, you two arseholes should consider yourselves bloody lucky Pedro - Mr. Bonifacio - didn't call the cops!"

Dan stood staring back at Todd. "Okay, okay," said in a placatory voice, "However, I refuse to apologise for my behaviour, so, no apologies and no excuses given. I'll do as you say, I'll find a hotel - just as well I always carry my wallet with me - and call Jodie in the morning before I come round to collect my passport and any luggage. I shall also wite an apology to your friends." Gazing at an embarrassed Todd, he added softly. "Meanwhile, Todd, you'd do well to remember that there are always *two* sides to every story."

Not bothering to acknowledge a scowling Malcom still holding his bleeding nose, Dan turned on his heels and lumbered away.

An hour later, having checked into a modest hotel near to Todd's apartment, a resigned Dan sent Lulu a text message.

San Fran done and dusted in more ways than one. Back in London late tomorrow or day after. Dinner Scalini's? Will confirm on arrival. XXX. Avenging Angel Dan the Man.

SCALINI RESTAURANT- WALTON STREET

Apologies for not meeting last night, but the flight was delayed and when I did arrive, yours truly was totally knackered," beamed Dan on greeting Lulu. "However, here we are with you looking truly wunderbar, as always!"

"I thought *I* was supposed to be the writer of fantastic fiction," giggled Lulu, making finger quotes. "But look at you, Dan the Man, not only the usual dashing, handsome, smouldering, conniving, smiling, cadaver I know and adore, but a gloriously wicked one with a hint of a suntan! What? No more curfews?" She added with a gentle smile. "You have been missed."

"You too, Princess Pen," replied Dan (Lulu could swear that she caught a glimpse of a tear). "But, before we both burst into song about how wunderbar we are, yon ice bucket contains a bottle of your favourite Pinot Grigio; unless you'd prefer something else to start with."

"A glass of Pinot - dare I say it? - would be wunderbar!"

The two sat in silence while the smiling waiter poured a glass of wine for Lulu and topped up Dan's glass. Nodding a smiling "enjoy" he placed the bottle back in the ice bucket and left.

"So," said Lulu, "tell me about this unexpected meeting with Duval in San Francisco. A cocktail party, you said." She gave a loud, unladylike snort. "Pity it wasn't in some dark alley. Is that the reason for your sudden return? Afraid, perhaps, what you might do to him if you ran into him again?"

"Well, Princess Pen," replied Dan with a grin. "I *did* break his nose!"

"You did what?" shrieked Lulu, much to the consternation of the nearby tables. "Oh, Dan the Man! I do love you! Tell me! Tell me!"

Dan quickly regaled Lulu with what he laughingly described as a minor contretemps at the Bonifacio's cocktail party. "As a result, and having completed what I was doing over there, I felt it time for me to leave. So, here I am, back in Old Blighty with a cleanish slate; my discreet assignment in San Francisco successfully completed." He gave Lulu a knowing look. "Talking of which, what's the latest with the ongoing Maebelle saga?"

"Oh, the usual with Madam Maebelle revelling in her unwavering role as Madam unchallenged She Bitch Itch," said Lulu blithely.

"She Bitch Itch?" chuckled Dan. "Is that grammatically correct or is it what you writers refer to as poetic licence?"

"Who cares?" trilled Lulu. "She-bitch, total bitch, bitch itch or supreme bitch, they all apply!" Taking a sip of wine, she paused for a moment before leaning across the table and saying in a conspiratorial whisper. "Rumour has it that she and a certain objet d'art are back to being the closet of bosom buddies once more."

"*By* objet d'art you can only be referring to the dreaded Dee-Dee Devereaux."

"Who else? According to my spies - you're not the only one with sources extraordinaire - the three of them were seen huddled together in Claridge's the other day."

"Three of them?"

"The third one being a Montgomery Livingston, Peter Proudfoot's virile replacement."

"Until the next poor sod," said Dan with a grin.

"Poor sod indeed," snickered Lulu. Looking at Dan she said matter-of-factly. "You do know Dee-Dee lost an eye."

"Yes; and taking it in his stride - or mince - whatever you prefer."

"Well, one of the other men with him on the night of his unfortunate accident; a Mr. Benedict Bogart . . ."

"Are you referring to a Ben Bogart also known as Brighton Ben?" exclaimed Dan.

"The very one! A lovely man with a fetish for toy trains," giggled Lulu. "I even gave him a locomotive to remember me by!"

"Talk about a blast from the past!" chuckled Dan. "Great guy. One of the best." He did a double take. "Jesus! Are you saying Ben was involved."

"He was. Allow me to explain."

Lulu gave a brief recap on the events leading up to the planned attack on Paul McDowell, writer Robert Apps's bone of contention, and what happened on the night. "There's more to tell," said Lulu. "Andy McCulloch - the *real* Robert Apps - Robert Apps being his pseudonym - and I were collaborating on a book, but he no longer wishes to have anything to do with innocent *moi* after what happened. As for Dee-Dee; when I called him to say how sorry I was about his hideous accident, I too was given short shrift and, like Apps - read McCulloch - cast into the wilderness." She gave a snicker. "Talk about a Chinese puzzle!"

"I take it you and Ben still friends."

"Most certainly. What's more he's up in London the day after tomorrow so, why don't we three get together as I'm sure Ben would love to see you."

"And me him," laughed Dan. "Okay, it's a date!"

"Goody good!" cried Lulu. "First of all, let's order, and then I can happily fill you in on what Ben and I have in mind for the come-uppance of Mr. Apps!" Giving Dan a coquettish smile she added perkily. "Oh, Dan, *excusez moi*, and let me rephrase that! I'll give you the gist of what Ben and I have in mind, and when we meet, *you*, Ben and I can discuss it further."

"From the sound of it I'm already part of the team," said Dan with a broad grin.

"You've always been part of the team, Dan. Even during one of your unexpected and never explained absences!"

"Glad to hear it," said Dan with a warm (no fangs) smile. "Now, bring me up to date what you two have in your mischievous minds for Mr. Apps. In other words, what exactly have you got up your scheming sleeves for the poor sod!"

"Ben agrees with me that what we have planned come strictly under the term fixable damage, whilst any *physical* - read personal - damage is strictly to be avoided," continued Lulu. "Again, what we have in mind will *not* take place whilst Apps is *at* the villa, but on a Saturday when he always accompanies Isidoro, the cook, to the local market. Something he apparently enjoys. Clive Cordell is due at the villa in a few weeks' time, so he won't be there either. We believe a few blown-out doors and windows should do the trick and get him seriously worried. There's a giant rocket, aptly named Notorious, so a couple of these should do the trick!"

"And you have this all planned?"

"Down to the minutest detail, thanks to an Italian contact of Ben's, an old roue who insists on calling himself Zorro - which as you know is Spanish – despite him being more *Italiano* than pasta! Signor Zorro has been a genius in organising all." Lulu gave a light laugh. "Obviously *molto lire* have changed hands. It all takes place this coming Saturday - not quite Guy Fawkes night - but then wannabe Guy Fawkes's cannot be choosers!"

VILLA CASA DEGLI ARCHI - LIGURIA - ITALY

"Even the bestselling Robert Apps cannot find the words to express his delight at your unexpected arrival here last night," said Andy with a warm smile. "So, come along and see what has happened since you were last here. I appreciate you saw the finished dining room plus the master bedroom, but I saved the main salon for this morning."

Flinging open the carved, double doors he cried a cheerful "Ta da!" followed by an anxious. "What do think?"

"It's fabulous, Andy! Absolutely fabulous!" enthused Clive eyeing the room decorated in tones of terracotta, ivory, blue and yellow. "It's *La Dolce Vita, magnifico* and *brillante* rolled into one." He gave a chuckle. "My speaka-da-lingo is getting better, *non credi*?"

"As you say, *magnifico*," chuckled Andy,

"I heartily approve of the two Salvador Dali inspired sofas in the form of Mae West's lips," chortled Clive. "Which of sofas is me and which one is you?"

"I thought we were a couple of hearty, healthy homosexuals; not a pair of pouting drag queens," chuckled Andy. He nodded toward a tall, metallic sculpture standing in front of the French doors opening onto a terrace. "The dieted gent over there is Alberto. Though not a work by the great Alberto Giacometti himself, I found this eye-catching double while trolling round one of the many flea markets in Genoa. I have no idea who the sculptor is, or was, but I tell anyone who asks that it's by Giacometti." He gave a further chuckle. "Needless to say, they take my word for it, and are suitably impressed!"

"Who wouldn't be on viewing such a splendid, *magnifico* room," replied Clive.

"So, how about some *magnifico* home-produced vino to celebrate your approval of the grand salon!"

"Home produced?"

"It's a present from Carlo, the head honcho of the local village." Andy gave a chuckle. "Be warned. Being of literary mind I've christened the six bottles Carlo's Kerosene. See what you think when you try it. If you find it a touch too" - he made air quotes with his fingers - "keroseney, there's a generous supply of Pinot Grigio on hand."

Andy led Clive through to the-state-of-the-art *cucina* where he took two unlabelled bottles from the large Bertazzoni fridge.

"I usually accompany Isidoro to the market on a Saturday, but he's trotted off on his ownsome this merry morning with strict instructions to see if he can find any truffles in order to make your favourite *Tagliatelle al Tartufo* for dinner this evening."

Pouring a glass from the innocent-looking bottle, he handed the glass to Clive and said with a grin. "Have a taste and tell me what you honestly think."

"Wow!" gasped Clive on taking a sip. "I can now see what those American Indians meant by firewater!" He added with a mischievous smile. "To quote a certain Oliver Twist. 'Please sir, I want some more'."

"More?" bellowed Andy in a fearsome parody of Mr. Bumble the beadle. "Of course, you may have some more, lad!"

Topping up Clive's glass he then poured a glass for himself. Raising his glass in the form of a toast, Andy said with a gentle smile. "Here's to us, and here's to Villa Degli Archi and many more fabulous years together."

The words were barely out of his mouth when there was a loud explosion and flashing of light as a giant Notorious rocket burst through the kitchen window resulting in Andy and Clive throwing themselves onto the floor.

"What the fuck?" cried Andy covering his head with his hands. "Jesus" he yelled on hearing a second explosion from somewhere else inside the villa. Slowly pulling himself to his feet, he quickly glanced round the kitchen which, apart from the broken window and the remains of the rocket sparking weakly where it lay, nothing appeared to have been damaged. "Clive?" he called out nervously. "Clive? You okay?"

"Shaken as well as stirred but okay. Apart from a ringing in my ears, I'm fine," replied Clive shakily. "I'm over by the fridge. Jesus! Is that a fucking *rocket* on the floor?"

"It is, and it sounds as if one also went off in one of the other rooms! What the fuck was that all about? Fucking Guy Fawkes type rockets? Jesus!"

GODFREY STREET - LATER THE SAME DAY

"Lulu, Ben, simply to tell you I've just had a triumphant Signor Zorro on the blower telling me in his best pidgin English, 'za eagles zay land boom, boom, no?'. He then went on to say that *both* McCulloch and Cordell were in the villa at the time . . ."

"Jesus Christ!" cried Lulu. "What the hell were the hell were the two of them doing there? Apps was meant to be at the market whilst Clive Cordell supposedly here in London!"

"I know, I know, but - apart from getting one helluva fright - neither were hurt."

"Pity," sniggered Lulu. "However, and with a slight alteration to the words of Celeste's and Frankie's song from *High Society* - Who wants to be a *murderer*? *I don't*! - well done, Ben. It'll be interesting to see what happens next: particularly in the Maebelle camp! That's if Andy McCulloch does make a fuss of the incident. Which, having gotten to know him, I somehow doubt it!"

"So, what now?" asked Ben with an audible yawn. "Another fanciful plan for adding a worry line to Maebelle's flawless forehead?"

"Why not?" trilled Lulu, not rising to bait. "And, instead of *one* worry line, why not make it two!"

VILLA CASA DEGLI ARCHI - LATER THE SAME DAY

"One of Carlo's endless nephews claims to have seen two strangers in the vicinity of the main gate around the time of our unexpected visitors," announced Andy as he and Clive sat enjoying a pre-dinner martini on the pool terrace. "He told Carlo both were carrying what looked to be gun cases; in other words, those two bloody rockets."

"We both know who's responsible for this morning's little upset, don't we," said Clive matter-of-factly.

"Damn right, we do," growled Andy. "Bloody Lulu Mayhew and her rotten lot!" He added with a derisive snort. "Like the puerile plots of her novels, the butler *did* do it! Well, Miss Mayhew, you may not realise it, but you are about to write a definite *The End* to your final trite, trashy novels!"

"I'll drink to that!" enthused Clive. "Lulu Mayhew being a prime example of you sow what you reap!" He gave a snicker. "Knowing the unfortunate demise of certain characters in your books, Andy, love, all I can say is God help her and God help her hangers on!"

NINETEEN

AN APARTMENT IN THE CASTRO - SAN FRANCISCO

"Who the fuck can that be calling so early," muttered Todd about to step into the shower. "Okay, fucking okay, I'm coming, damn you," he grizzled leaving the bathroom and reaching for the intercom in the adjoining bedroom. "I'm here," he snapped. "Who is this so bloody early on a Saturday?"

"Todd Steman?" said a clipped voice.

"Maybe, maybe not, despite the fact you must have pressed the button with his name on it," replied Todd, his voice dripping with sarcasm. "Who's trying to find him?"

"It's Maclom Duval, we met the other night. I need to speak with Dan Crozier, I know you told him to go to a hotel but maybe you relented and he's back there with you."

Jesus, bloody Malcom Duval whose nose Dan broke the other night, and who I told I never wanted to see again, thought Todd, his face paling. "Er . . . as you said, I told him to find a hotel and collect any luggage et cetera later before returning to London or wherever," he croaked.

"He was planning on returning to London?" snapped the voice.

"Er . . . I believe so," stammered Todd. Adlibbing. he said with a laugh. "Or it could easily have been New York and *then* on to London, But that's Dan! Here, there, and everywhere!"

"I take it you have his London address and phone number." Said as a statement and not as a question.

"Look er . . . Mr. Duval, I don't know what the other night's minor fracas was about, but Dan Crozier and I are no longer on speaking terms, so . . ."

"So, *what*? Mr. Steman."

There was a prolonged silence broken only by the static of the intercom, before Malcom said smoothly. "Apart from our *minor* fracas as you so blithely put it Mr. Todd, I take it you *do* remember Mr. Crozier just happened to break my nose."

There was a further crackling of static before Malcolm continued in the same smooth manner. "For your sake, Mr. Steman, and further to your reluctance to give me the information I require, you'd better pray I find Mr. Crozier's current address and phone number in London otherwise you can expect a more persuasive visit from a colleague of mine. Good day to you, *Mr, Steman.*"

"Jesus," muttered Todd, visibly shaking with fright. "Jesus, Dan, what the *hell* is going on between the two of you?"

Checking the front door was doubly locked, bolted with the security chain in place, Todd hurried through toe the kitchen where he quickly poured himself a large vodka on the rocks. Reaching for the landline he shakily pinched in the most recent London number he had for Dan, only to get a recorded message to say the number was no longer in service.

"Shit," he groaned. "Shit! Shit! *Shit*! Think, Steman, Think! Aha! I'm sure if I call Lulu Mayhew, that writer friend of his, she'll be able to pass on a message or, better still, get Dan to call me. I know we had a falling out, but this Duval character sounds as if he's seriously out to get Dan. I know it's none of my business, but Dan is - or was - a friend so the least I can do is warn him. Once I have done so, it'll be a simple case of doing a PP (Pontious Pilate) and forget about him."

Todd took another hefty swig of vodka. "Now, all I have to do is find the wretched woman's number."

Setting aside his drink, he began scrambling through what he described as his "odds and sods" kitchen drawer. Discarding several notes and business cards he said with a small triumphant cry. "Bingo! It's early afternoon over there so, with luck, she'll be there working on her latest."

Todd tapped in the number which, after several rings, the call went to voice mail. Once the message ended, Todd said crisply. "Good morning - or afternoon - Miss Mayhew. This is Todd Steman calling from San Francisco with an urgent message for Mr. Dan Crozier should you see him. Please inform Mr, Crozier that a certain Mr. Malcom Duval is trying to get hold of him. Er . . . Mr, Duval did not sound at all friendly: in fact, quite the opposite. If needs be, Dan can call me. I am in and out so, if he doesn't get hold of me, can he please leave a message and I'll call him back pronto."

Todd was about to hang up when a woman's voice said breathlessly. "Hello? Lulu Mayhew here! I literally was coming through the front door when I heard my private line ringing. Sorry, you were saying?"

Todd repeated the gist of his message.

"Well, Mr. Steman, I'm sorry but I can't help you," replied Lulu briskly. Her mind racing, she said with a light laugh. "If Dan is back in London, he certainly hasn't tried to contact me. Have you tried telephoning him?"

"Obviously, Miss Mayhew," said Todd a touch sharply, "but the number I have is no longer available. Here, let me give it to you."

"That's the same number I have," tut-tutted Lulu. "Oh dear. All I can do, should Dan contact *me*, is pass on your message and ask him to call you as soon as possible. I take it he has your number there in San Francisco?"

"Yes, he does, Miss Mayhew," muttered Todd. "Thank you, Miss Mayhew. Fingers crossed Dan will call you. Goodbye."

*

Putting down the phone, Lulu turned to Dan who had arrived a few minutes earlier having been invited to stay for a few days and said with a grin. "Your friend Mr. Steman calling from San Francisco. He sounds in a right old state saying the dubious Malcom Duval is trying to find out where you are."

"The plot thickens," chuckled Dan. "Rather like his nose." Fondling a blissful, visibly drooling Flip Flop's furry ears, he said with a grin. "I take it there's a new novel in the Mayhew pipeline?"

"Yes, indeed," carolled Lulu. "A new novel featuring a one-eyed detective wittily named Aye! Aye! Golden Eye! who simply *had* to sport a brass eyepatch, aided and abetted by his one-legged partner, aptly named Hoppy Hickey. Naturally, Aye! Aye! Golden Eye! is the proud owner of super dog Clip Clop, a gold cocker spaniel. Shall I continue?"

"Good God no!" replied Dan in feigned horror. "It's already too much for a simple hitman to digest so, let's say I look forward to buying a copy hot from the press."

"At least I have a guarantee of *one* sale," chortled Lulu. "Aha, that could be Ben," she said, reaching for the phone. "Ben? Please tell me this is a happy chappie call and not a I told you so type call."

"Definitely a happy chappie type call regarding *Bella Italia*," chuckled Ben. "An unexpected bonus being that both Apps *and* Cordell were in the villa at the time of Signor Rocketman's unexpected visit! Uh-uh, before you even ask, no one was injured: unless you call being covered in dust and a severe ringing in the ears injured."

He gave a further chuckle. "Apparently Apps's immediate reaction was to put the blame on some local, delinquent youths, which means the local police will not be looking into the matter." Ben added sonorously. "Meanwhile, he was also overheard saying to Cordell that he knew exactly who was responsible for the so-called attack. So, Lulu luv, I'd keep looking over those pretty shoulders of yours, if I were you."

"Will do, Ben, and thanks for the update," crooned Lulu. "Tell you what, Dan Crozier is here with me as we speak - maybe I should invite him to move in as a temporary bodyguard - and, if it's a bright, sunny day, why don't we drive down to Brighton tomorrow and take you to out lunch." She gave a giggle. "Even if tomorrow turns out to be a dull, miserable day."

"Why not? Drop by for a drink beforehand and then we can go on from there." Ben gave a snigger. "In the meantime, it'll give me a chance to check out *the* most expensive restaurant in the vicinity as you're paying."

"So, not your favourite Wheelers then?"

"Wheelers is no longer, I'm afraid, hence a bit of the Sherlock Holmes with *The Good Food Guide.* See you *domani.*"

Having sent Dan upstairs to unpack - Lulu having insisted he stay in Godfrey Street for as long as he wanted or needed to - before going out, accompanied by Flip Flop, to Chelsea Green in order to visit "Sex on Legs, Rex," the cheerful fishmonger and various other shops.

After an hour Lulu returned to her office where, booting up the computer, she yodelled a cheerful "Time to let loose the dogs of war followed by a murmured. "Oh, P.I. Aye! Aye! Are we going to have fun today!"

Settling down in front of the computer, Lulu began to type.

*

"To quote baldy Brynner, star of The King and I, 'It's a puzzlement', said Aye! Aye! Golden Eye! tapping his gleaming, brass eye-patch. 'Two anonymous skyrockets fired through the downstairs windows of The Manor House, thus upsetting the elderly Countess Codswallop and her dinner guest, young Donkey Dean, the local blacksmith's son, known for his remarkable skills with his anvil. What a conundrum!"

"Perhaps the culprit could be Miss Trixie Tittle, Donkey Dean's on and off girlfriend," suggested Hoppy. "Apparently Miss Trixie is no pixie in the jealousy

stakes!" He gave a throaty chuckle. "Not that I'm one to pay too much attention to local tittle-tattle!"

"No, not Miss Trixie Tittle-Tattle - I mean Miss Trixie Tittle," boomed Aye! Aye! striking a Napoleonic pose (one hand tucked into the top of his saffron yellow and purple stripe waistcoat). "Unless my brilliant grey matter deceives me, I would say The Countess did it!"

"The Countess Codswallop herself?" echoed Hoppy, his bloodshot eyes widening. Adopting a flamenco dancer's pose in competition to Aye! Aye!'s Napoleonic one, he sang, with a click of his fingers. 'No way! Jose! No way! I say!" followed by a spluttering fit of coughing.

Leaning against a convenient door jamb, he managed to rasp. "That ancient relic's old enough to be Methuselah's great, great grandmother. Plus, she hobbles along aided and abetted by a pair of ebony canes with carved skulls as handgrips."

"Smoke and mirrors, my dear Hoppy Hickey, smoke and mirrors," rumbled Aye! Aye! He gave a sardonic chuckle. "Please don't tell me your seriously believe Donkey Dean was there because of his skill at conversation, eh? Clue number one; he has no conversation. Clue number two; despite Donkey Dean possessing a very impressive, personal walking stick, you are obviously unaware of the fact that when The Countess believes she is alone and unobserved in the sanctity of her bedchamber, she is known to dance a mean Charlston in front of a row of mirrors!"

"I still think the butler did it," rasped Hoppy with a sulky pout.

"No, you're wrong, totally wrong," said Aye! Aye! in a no-nonsense rumble. Giving Hoppy a tut-tut, silly you, smile you, he added with a smirk. "The Countess did it. She did it, knowing that the blame would be put on Miss Trixie Tittle, resulting in an embarrassed Donkey Dean having to compensate for his conniving girlfriend's misdemeanour by subjecting The Countess to endless renditions of his very own Anvil Chorus!"

EXECUTIVE OFFICES - BROMEANDO FILMS - LOS ANGELES - TWO WEEKS LATER

"Welcome to Los Angeles, Miz Maebelle," schmoozed Sylvester Steinberg, a polished, Uriah Heep lookalike (known in certain circles as Sylvia Slimeberg) proffering a limp, manicured hand toward a graciously smiling Maebelle as she, Monty, and Dee-Dee were shown into his over decorated office (later described by a giggling Dee-Dee as "Louis X1V OD'ing on heroin plus!") by a secretary more Mr. Universe than Playmate of the Month. "Welcome Mr. Livingston - your photograph doesn't do you justice! Ha ha! and, I assume, Mr. Devereaux. Ha ha *ha*! Please take a seat over there in what I call the conversation area, though at times it has been referred to as Sylvester's *slaughter* area! Ha ha ha! Champagne for everyone?"

"Champagne would be lovely," crooned Maebelle.

"And so, say all of us!" trilled Dee-Dee.

His beady, black eyes firmly fixed on Dee-Dee, Sylvester said in a curt aside to the hovering Mr. Universe. "Samson, would you do the honours."

Turning his attention back to the now seated Maebelle, Sylvester said in a no-nonsense voice. "As requested, a script was sent to Mr. Devereaux and, as expected, he could find no fault with your compelling role."

"I found it to be perfect, Mr. Steinberg!" crowed Dee-Dee eyeing Sylvester's python print onsie with open envy. "What's more - that's if I'm allowed too, of course - I can't wait to be on set and seeing those magic words morph into a galaxy of big screen characters under your expert direction!"

"Sylvester, please. And that applies to all of us! As they so wisely say: No formality ensures Bromeando immortality! Ha ha!"

Ignoring the ensuing, hollow laughs coming from Maebelle and Monty, Sylvester gave Dee-Dee a lecherous smile and said in a soft, come-hither voice. "Thank you for your kind words, *Dee-Dee.* However, I still feel the script could well do with the inclusion of an additional character. A brief, yet colourful appearance which would give an obvious winner that unexpected, little zip! That extra little *snort,* if you dig!"

"Forgive me, Sylvester!" trilled Dee. "But I don't quite *dig* your dig. I may be a petite soul, but it doesn't mean that I'm akin to one of Snow White's seven: if *you* dig? In other words, please explain."

"What I'm *saying,* and what I need you to *do*, Dee-Dee, is meld yourself, your very own, sparkling personality, into the movie. I'm a firm believer in the word stimulate, Dee-Dee, and that's exactly what you will do by making a shot-in-the-arm appearance in Bromeando Films' forthcoming, award winning, *Hight Jinks in High C!*"

"You mean you want Dee-Dee Devereaux to appear in *my* film?" hissed an outraged Maebelle, doing her utmost not to shriek or scream.

"I don't *want,* Maybelle," replied Sylvester deadpan. "You may not know it, but I, the one and only Sylvester Steinberg has just introduced a soupçon of genius into the film in which you are also appearing. The soupçon being a character based on your delightful friend supposedly here as an advisor to what you wear: the colourful, charismatic Mr. Dee-Dee Devereaux appearing in *High Jinks in High C!* as the mischievous ... er ... the mischievous *Titus Testis*! Any further questions?"

A PRIVATE BUNGALOW - BEVERLY HILLS HOTEL

"Well, that certainly came as a *bit* of surprise," grimaced Maebelle tossing her Louis Vuitton handbag onto a nearby sofa. "Dee-Dee Devereaux a potential movie star? Whatever next!"

"Aw, c'mon Maebelle," trilled Dee-Dee. "There's no need to get your Janet Reger's in a twist. As Sylvester Steinberg said, it's merely a bit part - in other words, a walk-on part - and *nothing* that could possibly detract from the glamorous *vous!*"

"Hmm," grunted Maebelle. "As they say, one'll simply have to wait and see."

"Well, I think it's a great idea," cut-in Monty. "Keeping it in the family, so to speak."

"Some family," snickered Dee-Dee.

"I heard that, Dee-Dee Devereaux!" snapped Maebelle. Turning to Monty she said with a saccharine smile. "A large vodkatini, please, Montgomery, seeing I most certainly need - no, better still - *deserve* one!"

"You still on for an amble along Rodeo Drive later?" said Monty diplomatically as he quickly prepared the requested drink and handed it over.

"Only if you insist," pouted Maebelle reaching for the proffered vodkatini. "Ah, bliss," she purred on taking a sip. Glancing up at Monty she said sarcastically. "I've never understood the fuss made over Rodeo Drive. To me, it doesn't compare to Bond Street, plus all the buildings are so flat!"

"As long as their contents aren't flat, why complain," chortled Dee-Dee.

"You know what, Dee-Dee Devereaux," sniped Maebelle. "I think it would be an excellent idea if you took your smug, irritating little self to your own bungalow and treated yourself to a soul-searching ponder or nap. Or, better still, take a loooong underwater dip in the hotel pool."

"Two - no, make that three - utterly, butterly, brilliant ideas," tittered Dee-Dee springing to his feet. With a twiddle of his fingers, he added a cheery "See you later, Dee-Dee hater!" and sashayed out from room.

"God, he can be *so* annoying," hissed Maebelle holding out her glass for a refill. Fluttering her eyelashes at a bemused Monty, she said in a little girl voice. "Do you think he could really steal my thunder in the film?"

"Never!" came the emphatic reply. "Mark my words, Maebelle. It was pretty obvious - to me, anyway - that drooling Steinberg is only trying to get into Dee-Dee's pants and, once he's accomplished that little nasty, I doubt if anyone in the audience will even catch a glimpse of his latest lust!"

"You really think so?"

"Maebelle, darling. I *know* so." Blowing her a kiss, Monty said cheerfully. "Why else do you think you're the one being interviewed live on a major TV channel tomorrow? A major happening not even mentioned by the predatory Mr. Steinberg to the preening, posturing Mr. Devereaux!"

"You're absolutely right. He didn't, did he? Oh, I can't wait to see that wannabe Norma Desmond's reaction once he realises that he's the one who has been left high and dry on the boulevard's grass verge! So, in order to celebrate, why not that proposed stroll down flat Rodeo Drive as suggested!"

A STYLISH APARTMENT - RUSSIAN HILL - SAN FRANCISCO - THE NEXT DAY

"Sorry for springing myself upon you like this," said Malcom for the umpteenth time as he and his cousin Belinda Maddox, sat having breakfast in the sun-filled kitchen, "but the thought of another night spent in a somewhat seedy hotel was not exactly seductive." He gave Belinda, an elegant Catherine Deneuve lookalike, a playful grin. "*Capiche*?"

"*Capiche* recurring," replied Belinda with a throaty laugh. "It's lovely to see you and, as long as you don't mind sharing the apartment with Maestro, feel free to stay for a week or two. I say a week or two, simply because after a couple of weeks - no matter *how* charming they are - guests begin to take their toll!"

"How could one not be flattered at being asked to share an apartment with you *and* the magnificent Maestro," laughed Malcom giving the large ginger tomcat in question an affectionate stroke. "Jesus!" he added with a grin. "When Maestro purrs, he certainly purrs!"

"And when Maestro yowls, he certainly yowls," chortled Belinda, pouring herself another cup of coffee. Eyeing Malcom across the breakfast table she said matter-of-factly. "Any plans for today?"

"Even if I said I was seeing a man about a dog, I'd telling you an outrageous porky pie," replied Malcom with a chuckle. "And no, I've no immediate plans apart from inviting you to an extravagant lunch if you're free, that is."

"Lunch would have been lovely, but today is a no-no, I'm afraid. In fact, I'm lunching with a client, a dreadful woman who wishes to talk about her impending divorce; her fifth, would you believe."

"That's the price you pay for being a hight successful lawyer known for your unfailing skill at getting the best settlements for those damsels and dowagers in distress!" said Malcom with a rakish grin. He glanced at the small television unit on a nearby counter. "Hold on a sec. Did you happen to catch what the newsreader just said?"

"I wasn't really paying attention seeing we busy talking," said Belinda. "Something about an exclusive interview, live from L.A. with some fashion model over here making a film. The interview taking place after the midday news."

"The name of the model: did you happen to catch it?" said Malcom a touch sharply.

"As I just said, Malcom, *dear*," replied Belinda, equally as sharply. "I was listening to you prattling on and not really paying attention to the bloody television. But if you *must* know, my beady, always active, lawyer mind *did* catch the interviewee's name. It was Maebelle, the famous English model."

"Bloody hell," muttered Malcom.

Raising a well-shaped eyebrow Belinda said with a snicker. "Don't tell me you know her. Better still, please don't tell me she's one of your many, global conquests!"

"Not quite," chuckled Malcom, his mind racing. *Bloody Maebelle over here and in L.A., no less. There must be a God!*

"Malcom?" said Belinda. She gave a light, sardonic laugh. "From the deafening silence following my innocent question, it's pretty damn obvious you *do* know her more than a nonchalant 'not quite.' So, what's she like? From what one can glean from the papers and various magazines she gives the impression of being a bit of a diva."

"A bit of a diva!" snorted Malcom. "Make that more of a furious feline on a very hot, tin roof!"

"A furious feline on a very hot, tin roof?" chortled Belinda. "Oh. Malcom, Tennessee Williams would have been so proud had he been around to hear you using his title in vain!" Glancing at her vintage Cartier wristwatch she said brightly, "Sadly I must leave you to your reminiscing and, no doubt, watching the interview with the felicitous Maebelle."

"Wha . . .? Ah yes, the interview," murmured Malcom. Giving Belinda a smile he said cheerfully. "As you cannot manage lunch, how about dinner at a restaurant of your choice?"

"Dinner I can do," replied Belinda. "I'll call you later with a time and the name of the restaurant. No, enough of the waffle. I'll see you at Trader Vic's at seven-thirty. I'll have Zara, my secretary, make the reservation."

"I'll see you there at seven-thirty. In the meantime, as you Americans always say, have a nice day!"

*

Five minutes prior to midday, Malcom poured himself a large glass of California chardonnay before placing the bottle on a table next to a large Chesterfield sofa in what Belinda airily described as "the rumpus, bump-us room". The sofa and several chairs facing a giant television. Making himself comfortable, Malcom reached for the remote control and onto the relevant channel.

Within seconds the large screen filled with a picture of a sleek, South American gentleman who introduced himself as Luis Robledo, introducer of the stars.

Giving the camera a dazzling smile, Luis said in a deep, honeyed voice. "My guest today is a lady whom I am sure you will all recognise, so, without any further, I take great pleasure in welcoming the one and only Maebelle, British fashion icon extraordinaire!"

His smirking introduction followed by wild applause, cheers and a few valiant wolf whistles as the camera switched to a serenely smiling Maebelle sitting next to him. The applause increasing in volume as Maebelle, dressed in a sapphire blue trouser suite, her elegant feet sporting strappy, diamante stiletto sandals, her dark hair piled high the form of a beehive and studded with diamond and sapphire pins; the pièce de résistance being a diamond and sapphire choker which Luis assured the cheering audience "was worth several kings' ransoms", acknowledged the enthusiastic audience with a regal wave.

"Wow!" chuckled Malcom, taking a hefty sip of wine. "I have to say it, Maebelle, you look fan-fucking-tastic! Now let's hear the never heard before gems you're about to share with us today!"

Thanking Maebelle for being a guest on his "ardently viewed show", Luis went onto say yet again what a pleasure it was to have her on his show before expressing his surprise she was in Los Angeles to make a *film* and not for some extravagant fashion show or fashion shoot.

Without hesitation, Maebelle, eyes and teeth flashing, went on to describe her leading role (the term "leading role" being repeated ad infinitum throughout the interview) in "darling Sylvester Steinberg's exciting chiller thriller, *High Jinks in High C!*"

"And this is your first professional acting role," schmoozed Luis, his eyes widening as if Maebelle had announced she was a frustrated baseball player at heart.

"My dear Luis, my whole *career* as a top fashion model has been a professional acting role," replied Maebelle with a zillion watt smile and a toss of her sparkling head. "In fact, you can easily say it's been a professional act from cradle to today's much sought after Maebelle! For not only do I owe it to my myriad of fans; I owe it to myself!"

"If only they knew," grouched Malcom turning off the television. "However, talk about a rancid blessing in disguise. Unfortunately for you, dear Maebelle, instead of San Franscisco here I come, it's now a case of Los Angeles here I come. Robledo did manage to mention Dee-Dee Devereaux, but you soon put a stop to that! I therefore assume the two of you must have kissed and made up and he's over here with you." He gave a chuckle. "It gets better by the minute, Talk about a *double* rollover! Ha ha!"

A PRIVATE BUNGALOW - BEVERLY HILLS HOTEL

"Bitch! Selfish bitch!" hissed Dee-Dee turning off the television. "Not only did I barely get a mention, thanks to narcissistic Maebelle and that fawning Montgomery, which means slimy Sylvester will now have to do something mega for *moi* to make up for that little fracas! Otherwise, Dee-Dee Devereaux simply vanishes!"

Striking a pose à la The Prince of Darkness, he added dramatically. "Stardom be damned!"

Little did Dee-Dee realise the validation of his prophecy.

TWENTY

GODFREY STREET

"I thought this might tickle your fickle fancy," rumbled Dan handing Lulu his mobile. "Some interview I spotted involving your favourite femme fatale now very alive and high kicking in L.A., City of Angels!"

"Give me! Give me!" camped Lulu, snatching the phone from Dan. "Oh. My. God," she growled on viewing the clip. "Norma Desmond, eat your heart out! I've heard of arrogance, but this takes the term to a new high." She gave a snicker. "Interesting to note that when the man interviewing her -who is he, by the way? - attempted to talk about Dee-Dee - he must be over there as well - she simply slapped him down!"

"I'm sure you can't wait to see the film," said Dan with a grin.

"Maybe it'll be one of those 3D efforts," sniped Lulu. "Deathly, disastrous and subsequently ditched!"

"It's obvious I'm speaking to a devoted fan," chuckled Dan.

"Jesus, Dan!" snapped Lulu. "Talk about being blessed! Every time something untoward happens to the bloody woman, something good comes along and she comes up reeking of Chanel No 5!"

"As I've said time and time again, Lulu: forget about bloody Maebelle. You've so much on your own plate and when push comes to shove all she is - you've said it yourself - is an irritating itch. Therefore, why not pretend she's a mosquito and all you're having to deal with is a mere mosquito bite!"

"Yes, a fever carrying female *Anopheles* mosquito," quipped Lulu. "Next thing will be poor me suffering from an agonising case of malaria!"

"There are other things scarier than malaria," sniggered Dan. "So, consider yourself lucky." He nodded at his mobile still in her hand. "From what we just saw, what's the bet that Dee-Dee's already busy plotting something decidedly unpleasant against Maebelle after her blatant dismissal of him whenever Mr. Sleek mentioned his name." He gave a chuckle.

"Knowing Dee-Dee, it'll be more of a rabid dog type bite than a mere mosquito bite!"

"Fingers crossed, oh Danny boy," sang Lulu. "Fingers very crossed!" She gave a giggle. "Or, better still, down on your knees and pray, or - as it involves Dee-Dee - down on your knees and blow!"

"Good one, Lulu!" guffawed Dan, wiping away his tears of laughter. "Now, as a well-known writer of crime, what do *you* imagine Dee-Dee would consider a suitable compensation for Maebelle's deliberate and very public slight against him?"

"One of the worst things he could do is make her repeatedly forget her lines whilst filming," giggled Lulu. "If that were to happen, the mind boggles! Which gives me an idea. They say time heals many wounds whereas *I* say Maebelle's outrageous behaviour would require an *ocean* of time. And as Pacific Time is approximately eight hours behind Greenwich Mean Time this means the time in L.A. must be . . ."

"Please don't tell me?" rumbled Dan.

"Why not?" carolled Lulu. "I've done worse!"

BROMEANDO FILMS - SYLVESTER STEINBERG'S OSTENTATIOUS OFFICE - EARLIER

"I'm furious, Sylvester! Simply furious," shrilled Dee-Dee as he stood glaring at the smirking director. "How could you allow that . . . that *gorgon* to appear on national television and simply override that idiot of an interviewer every time he mentioned me!"

"Dee-Dee, Dee-Dee, *per*-lease," schmoozed Sylvester. "Surely, you of all people, should realise that I cannot be held responsible for what comes out of a person's mouth" - he gave a lewd snigger - "but, as you well know, I happily accept responsibility for what I *put* in a person's mouth!"

"It's not fucking funny, Sylvester!" shrieked Dee-Dee slamming his fist onto Sylvester's supposed antique desk, "You *promised* me star billing next to bloody Maebelle, yet here I am with no billing: not even a filling!"

"So," said Sylvester, spreading his scrawny arms wide. "Remember one major thing, my little friend, I am the director of the movie, and I am also responsible for what ends up on the cutting room floor." Giving Dee-Dee a gold capped, lecherous grin, he added smugly. "Something which you too have been doing Dee-Dee; but in the nicest, profitable way! Something I trust you will continue to do, albeit on the cutting room floor, this very office floor and certainly my king size bed as opposed to my bedroom floor. A privilege which your avaricious Maebelle will never share!"

"You mean . . .?

"I mean," leered Sylvester rising from his supposed antique desk chair, "my office floor, sitting room floor, kitchen floor or *any* floor - we'll spare the bedroom floor as the bed is a surefire winner in the bounce and comfort stakes - are at your command whenever there's an upset due to a Maebelle demand!"

"If that's the case," said Dee-Dee with a playful pout, moue and finally, a grin. "Why not a bit off office floor time before you take me out for a very expensive late lunch!"

A PRIVATE BUNGALOW - BEVERLY HILLS HOTEL

"Lulu bloody Mayhew?" exclaimed Dee-Dee on seeing the name of the caller. "Talk about it never shits but it stifles! Miss *Mayhew*!" he crowed on answering. "What a displeasure! At least you won't be able to drop poison into my shell-like via a transatlantic phone call!"

"Dee-Dee, *darling*!" cried Lulu. "As acerbic and as affectionate as ever! I rang to sweetly say how much I *loved* your non-appearance on Luis Robledo's television *chat* show! Talk about an accolade!"

"Bitch!" hissed Dee-Dee, his cherubic face breaking into a delighted grin. Giving a chortle he said, tongue in cheek. "I was brilliant, don't you think? *So* brilliant, that you simply *had* to call to see what I had in mind as a thank you for darling, generous Maebelle."

"You obviously haven't lost the ability of reading minds through the ether," giggled Lulu. "Tell me, have they actually started filming this impending catastrophe of hers and yours?"

"There's a general meeting at the studios next week where we will be introduced to the rest of cast and crew," carolled Dee-Dee, "which means we get to meet Baz Malone, current heartthrob and the film's leading man." He gave a snicker. "The studio's PR department are vigorously trying to sell Malone by saying he's the new Burt Lancaster though, judging from his photographs. I consider him more of a *burk* than a Burt! However, the poor guy does have my deepest sympathy seeing he will have to repeatedly kiss Madam Maebelle on camera! In answer to your question, we begin rehearsals next week with the actual filming beginning the week after." There a pause before Dee-Dee said with a titter. "More breaking news is that salivating Sylvester Steinberg has insisted on *moi* making a cameo appearance in the film; prepare to meet the charming, alarming Titus Testis."

Ignoring Lulu's stunned silence, Dee-Dee said a touch waspishly. "After that *very* brief answer to your question regarding the starting date we start filming, may, may I ask why the sudden interest?"

"Because, as a writer of fiction which, at times, can turn out to be fact, how about this as a thank you for the loyal, loving 'I always think of others' Maebelle, movie goddess in waiting, with more such enchanting episodes to follow."

"Lulu, loveliest Lulu, in preparation for what you're about to tell your born-again loving swain, could you hold on for a sec whilst I pour myself a Hoover Dam size vodka!"

Several minutes later Dee-Dee, having listened to what Lulu suggested he should do, said with a titter. "How could I have ever doubted you, utterly butterly, gorgeously smutterly Lulu Mayhew! With my imaginary sleuth fedora now on my handsome head and my poison pen well and truly poised! Not only give a clue as to what you have in mind but, better still, reveal all!"

MAIN REHEARSAL ROOM - BROMEANDO FILM STUDIOS

"Having once again introduced you all to each other," announced Sylvester to the assembled cast, "today I will be working with Maebelle and Baz on scene three, page twenty. Therefore, I would like the rest of you to follow Herod, the assistant director to room two, where he will go through your lines with you, offer suggestions and answer any questions."

Turning his attention to Maebelle dressed in what she considered her rehearsal outfit (a leopard pattern jumpsuit and faux snakeskin boots) and a laconic Baz Malone slouched against the doorpost while busily probing his mouth with a toothpick, Sylvester said briskly. "Having been informed that we would be rehearsing this particular scene today, I take it you both know your lines."

"Yeah, I know my effing lines," mumbled Baz. "Why, did you expect me to come here today unprepared?"

"No, of course not, Baz," replied Sylvester tightly. "After all, you *are* the ultimate professional."

"To quote you, like Baz, I too, being the ultimate professional, also know my lines," said Maebelle with a strychnine smile. "So, shall we begin."

"Good," grunted Sylvester giving Maebelle a curious "Where the fuck did Lionel Labanter find you?" type of look. "Now, this is a very important scene as it sets the tone for the whole movie; the two of you having a heart-to-heart discussion in a restaurant. So, Maebelle, sit yourself down next to the table over there and you. Baz, on the chair facing her. Perfect! Now, when I say action, please start. Remember, this is literally a read through, and I will be making improvements as we go along."

Improvements as we go along? thought Maebelle, giving Sylvester an indignant look. *Since when does Maebelle, fashion model extraordinaire, need any improving?*

"Action!" cried Sylvester.

"Jessica," drawled Baz in what he assumed to be a European accent, "we have to talk as I can no longer hide my feelings from you."

"Not surprising," crooned Maebelle slipping into the role of Jessica, "seeing your brainbox would make a pinhead look like a second Mount Everest. *Arsehole!*"

"Er . . . what did you just say? What did you just call me?" snapped Baz, his eyes narrowing.

"I didn't *say* or call you anything, Baz Malone. I was merely repeating the script."

"What script?" said Sylvester. "It doesn't say anything like you've just said in the director's script."

"Nor mine," sniped Baz.

"I simply acted out the words I learned from the script I was given," said Mabelle haughtily. "And if you'll give me a moment to get the copy from my handbag, I'll happily show you."

"I believe you, Maebelle dear," said Sylvester diplomatically. "However, let's have another little look, shall we?"

Having fetched her copy Maebelle nonchalantly tossed it over.

"So kind," muttered Sylvester reaching down to pick up the script from the floor. Skipping the scene in question he began flicking through the follow-on pages. "This can't be right," he murmured. "This can't be right."

Looking at Maebelle and at a bored Baz back to his manipulations with a toothpick, Sylvester said nervously. "I'm going to read another couple of lines from page twenty-seven in the director's copy and, I would appreciate it if you, Maebelle, give me your comeback line."

"*Niente problema,*" crooned Maebelle.

"Right," said Sylvester, "Here goes. 'Do you remember that moonlight night at the harbour; the magical, moonlight night we first met?'"

"How could I forget it," trilled Maebelle. "You may think of yourself as God's gift to women, my friend, but, if the truth be known, *all* the women *I* know, refer to you as leader of the halitosis choir! So, if you're thinking of kissing me: forget it!"

"Enough! Enough!" yelled Sylvester. "What you're saying is *not* in the original script! What you're saying is something else entirely. Where the *hell* did your script come from?"

"Your office, Sylvester, where else?" said Maebelle with a grimace. "If you ask me, it's someone out to sabotage our film. Someone with an obvious grudge against you, me or the studio!" Mascaraed eyes narrowing, she added with a virulent hiss. "Is Dee-Dee Devereaux here today?"

"He was certainly here for the general meeting, so I take it he is now in the meeting with Herod and the others," replied Sylvester barely acknowledging Maebelle's question, his mind focussed on the bastardised script.

This, with one or two changes, easily turn out to be the comedy hit of the year! he thought with an inward snigger. *The greatest screen comedy since* Auntie Mame!

"Sylvester! Did you hear what I said?" snapped Maebelle.

"No, Maebelle, I-did-not-hear-what-you-said-as-I-was-busy-reading-this-very-amusing-script," replied Sylvester through gritted teeth.

"What I said is perhaps a little tête-à-tête between Mr. Devereaux, you, and *moi,* wouldn't do any harm."

"Why a meeting with Devereaux?" replied Sylvester, returning his attention to Maebelle's copy of the script.

"Because, Sylvester, this brutally *murdered* script simply shrieks Dee-Dee Deveaux!"

"Are you implying Dee-Dee is responsible for the rewrite?"

"I am indeed. In fact, I *know* he's the guilty party!"

"And *what* a party!" yodelled Sylvester. "See if you can set up a meeting with the uber-talented and uber-delicious Dee-Dee this afternoon. Now, you and Baz will have to excuse me as I need to speak to those who rule, without delay!"

Clutching Maebelle's copy of the script, a grinning Sylvester pulled on his jacket and raced from the rehearsal room.

OFFICE OF OSCAR DE SADE - HEAD OF DROMEANDO FILMS

"So, Sidney, whaddya think?" grunted Oscar de Sade, a giant bear of a man sporting a vibrant ginger toupee which bore little resemblance to his bushy ginger and grey freckled sideburns, walrus moustache and Mel Gibson chin puff.

"Whadda I fink?" lisped Sidney Salamander, a doppelganger for Charles Dickens' Fagin and Oscar's unparalleled financial advisor. "I fink it fuckin' brilliant! Dat's whadda I fink! Dis studio needs da shot in the jugular an' Syl's idea, dis rewrite of da present script iss - as I jes said - fuckin' brilliant!"

"What about Robert Apps, the author?" asked Sylvester, barely able to contain his excitement.

"Whaddaboutim?" snapped Sidney, his question followed by a rancid belch. "The studio bought da rights to hiss book. He getta da credit *an'* da cash! End of story!"

"If you say so, Sidney," interrupted Oscar. "Dat's - that's good to know."

Sidney turned his attention to Sylvester. "Dis Devereaux guy, you say he not only rewrote dis piece of da script, but he iss also in da movie?"

"Yes, he has a small bit part," interrupted Oscar.

"Small bitty part, eh?" grinned Sidney, followed by another loud, aromatic belch. "Dat must be a surefire fuckin' first for you den, Osc! Ha ha ha!"

"I would appreciate it if we could get back to the reason for this impromptu meeting; this *vital* meeting," growled Oscar, giving Sidney a glare. "I say we keep the title; the words high jinks meaning exactly what it conveys."

He glanced at Sylvester. "Any idea where we might find Devereaux?"

"He should be in one of the rehearsal rooms with Herod," replied Sylvester.

"Great," grunted Oscar reaching for one of the many phones littering his desk. "Mildred!" he snapped. "Get me Herod Basin. He's taking a rehearsal, so you'll find him in one of the rehearsal rooms. Ask him to find someone called" - he gave Sylvester another glance - "what's this Devereaux guy's full name?"

"Dee-Dee Devereaux," said Sylvester in a stage whisper.

"As him to find a guy named Dee-Dee Devereaux and get someone to bring him to my office right away!"

*

An hour later Dee-Dee, in addition to a bigger part in *High Jinks in High C!* had been elevated to the incomparable role of scriptwriter and a guarantee that his name would appearing again in the credits; first in the role of the flamboyant Titus Testis and secondly as script writer.

*

Congratulating Dee-Dee in a whispered "Well done, my little passionflower" followed by a discreet French kiss, a glowing Sylvester returned to the set where he handed out hastily printed photocopies of Maebelle's sabotaged script, wittily referred to as "da script dat launched da thousand quips" by a grinning Sidney.

Addressing the reassembled cast and crew Sylvester said cheerfully. "As you will see, there's been a major change to the scripts first handed out, so please return your original copies as the ones now in your possession are the ones we will be working with. This means some of you all have a lot of work to do learning your new lines" - he gave a chuckle - "but I can assure you that it'll be worth it,"

Turning to face the two glowering leads he said in a no-nonsense voice. "Maebelle and Baz, we'll continue working on your scene with you, Maebelle, repeating the lines you have learned, and you. Baz, the lines *you* have learned as these have now been approved by the powers that be." Clapping hands, he added briskly. "Right! Let's get started as we've already wasted enough time!"

"I take it, seeing you were summoned to the lion's den, you're the little genius responsible for those wicked amendments to my copy of the script," hissed Maebelle having made sure she and Dee-Dee were not overheard.

"Who else?" cooed Dee-Dee with a smug smile. "Not only will the new version with an uber-witty Maebelle see you recognised as not only a glamorous model but as a brilliant, glamorous comedienne as well! In other words, your ever-growing success and my about to be success, going hand in hand!"

"But not quite in the hand-to-hand manner practiced by you and Sylvester," replied Maebelle with a mascaraed wink.

"Nicely-Nicely Johnson may have sung *Sit Down You're Rockin' the Boat* in the original *Guys and Dolls,* whereas in *my* updated version it's a case of *Lie Down Unless You Prefer to Choke!*" replied Dee-Dee with giggle.

"Touché! Dee-Dee. Dear," crooned Maebelle. "Now, you'll have to excuse me as my gracious presence is required on set." About to walk away, she turned and said conspiratorially. "Your thoughts on Baz Malone?"

"I much prefer not to even *think* of Mr. Malone," snickered Dee-Dee, "as you will find out when you eventually get to one of the later scenes in your delicious, devilish, Devereaux-doctored script!"

"A teensy-weensy hint to help make my day?"

"Poor Baz," tittered Dee-Dee. "Talk about a fade out!"

A STYLISH APARTMENT - RUSSIAN HILL - SAN FRANCISCO - TWO DAYS LATER

"It gets better by the minute," giggled Belinda handing Malcom her mobile showing the latest updates on what she called her favourite "gossip and soon forgotten fuck ups" column. "Take a look. According to Tallulah Thesaurus, gossip columnist extraordinary, there's been a major rewrite to the film in which your present affliction, that Maebelle, is meant to be filming. Plus, another name you enjoy hawking over, Dee-Dee Devereaux, already appearing in the film - you'll have a field day hawking over this - has been put in charge of the rewrite!"

Malcom sat staring at the mobile in his hand, his handsome face darkening. "Oooookay," he muttered through gritted teeth. "Oooookay. I know I keep putting off my destructive descent on L.A. but from what you've just shown me, another week or two's delay won't do any harm." He gave a derisive snort. "It will, in fact, give those little seeds of undiluted terror not only time to germinate, but time to grow and then positively and horrendously flower!"

TWENTY-ONE

GODFREY STREET

"I have Mr. Underwood on the line," cooed Deliliah. *"Do I tell him to get lost or is he found?"*

"Found!" replied PI Aye! Aye! Golden Eye! *"Best put the old sod through otherwise we'll only be subjected to another of his tiresome, vituperative outbursts!"*

"Putting him through, lucky you!" trilled Delilah.

"Good morning to you, Eggy!" said Aye! Aye! smoothly. *"I take it - seeing you're speaking to me in person - that all is well in the world of Egbert Underwood?"*

"For the moment," grizzled Egbert. *"Meanwhile, do you have an update as to the whereabouts of my Lucretia Borgia of a wife?"*

"We do indeed," crooned Aye! Aye! *"At present Madam Cymbeline is appearing in cabaret at Diva's Dive, an upmarket nightclub in Las Vegas."*

"Oh? She is?" replied Egbert, unable to contain his surprise at Aye! Aye!'s crisp answer.

"As for Rev the Revolver, the supposed hitman," continued Aye! Aye!, *"he's currently on an assignment in faraway Haiti."*

"Oh," said Egbert. *"Oh, really?"*

"Yes, really," snickered Aye! Aye!

"In other words, there's no need for me to keep looking over my shoulder?"

"That's correct, Eggy. There's no need to keep doing a Jessie.' His witty comeback a reference to another songstress, the fluting Jessie Matthews, famous for her cheerful rendition of* Over My Shoulder.

"Doing a Jessie?" questioned Egbert.

"Yes, a Jessie Matthews as opposed to a Jesse James," sniggered Aye! Aye! wiping away his ensuing tears of laughter. "Admit it, Eggy, when it comes to wondrous wit, PI Aye! Aye! Golden Eye! has no equal!

"So, I'm safe for time being with Cymbeline away in The States and Rev the Revolver up to no good in Haiti?"

"Condom safe!" said Aye! Aye! cheerfully, hastily removing the phone from his ear as Egbert suddenly gave out a shout. His unexpected reaction followed by several thumps and sounds of energetic chopping before someone gently replaced the receiver.

"Great Scott! Clip Clop!" exclaimed Aye! Aye! "I do believe Mr. Egbert Underwood may have just come a cropper at the hand of some unexpected chopper!"

*

"Judging from both your expressions I take it it's been a good working day," said Lobie with a chuckle.

"It certainly has," replied Lulu with a giggle. "However, the reason for Flip Flop's self-satisfied expression is all due to a quick 'walkies' to the Green where - needless to say - he was presented with a delicious bone by the always-spoiling-him Sex-on-Legs Rex who, despite being the fishmonger, seems to always have a bone - and not a *fishbone*! Nota bene - tucked away for Flip Then, to top it all, an equally delicious choccy treat by Paul, at The Pie Man!"

"Lucky Flip Flop is all I can say," grinned Lobie giving Flip Flop a loving pat. He nodded toward Lulu's desk. "Am I allowed to know the latest regarding PI Aye! Aye! Anything vital to report?"

"Oodles!" chortled Lulu. "Seconds before you arrived, PI Aye! Aye! Golden Eye! was in the middle of a phone call with the irritating Mr. Egbert Underwood when irritating Eggy was cut-off - literally - mid whinge by none other than Christian, the very *un*-Christian chopper! A gory scene described by PI Aye! Aye! as 'a gourmet offering of Eggy steak tartare'!"

"You certainly know how to get one's gore-buds going! I can't wait," laughed Lobie. He took a sip of coffee. "Talking of gore-buds, I hate to admit it, but one has to admire Maebelle and the dreaded Dee-Dee. Dee-Dee especially. Talk about a human tapeworm determined to get inside the mind of anyone he sets *his* beady mind on! E.g., that Sylvester Steinberg, the director! According to rumour and all thanks to him, the manipulative, manoeuvring Dee-Dee is in the process of rewriting most of Apps's original script which will see Bette Davis's *Baby Jane* a sweet, gurgling infant compared to Maebelle's Jessica."

He added cynically. "Apps must be pretty pissed-off, but what do you expect when you sell yourself to the highest bidder! What's more, knowing Maebelle and Dee-Dee, it wouldn't surprise me if, aided and abetted by the studio, they didn't turn *High Jinks in High C!* into a bloody musical!"

"But those two couldn't hit a high note, no matter how hard they tried!" scoffed Lulu. "And if they *did* appear in a musical version of the film, my immediate reaction would make a visit to the vomitorium in ancient Rome look a mere puddle. However, stranger things have happened."

She gave a pout. "Knowing those two they'd somehow manage by doing as Rex Harrison did as Professor Higgins in *My Fair Lady.* They'll *speak* their songs instead of singing them; the end result being a standing ovation!"

"I know, I know," chuckled Lobie. "I keep thinking of your latest, reinvented Maebelle, that poor Cymbeline . . .'"

"Poor Cymbeline and her new prissy comrade-in-harms, you mean," tittered Lulu. "Poseidon the painter" - she twinkled finger quotes - "a *struggling* artist from hell. An artist who does *not* live in a garret but in a mansion that makes Mara Largo look like a mere cottage. Pun intended! Oh, if only it could happen to Madam Maebelle as fact and not fiction." She added sourly. "However, knowing *her* luck she could very well find some local blinkered swain just rolling in it, as well as with her, but with an eventual ghastly ending just waiting to happen on the rose-tinted horizon! Oh, and before I forget, Dan sends his regards. He's gone and gotten himself involved in one of his typical 'here today, gone tomorrow' do-gooder parables again, and is now in capricious Cape Town sorting out some distraught friend."

"I wondered why he wasn't here but didn't wish to pry," muttered Lobie.

"Dear Lobie, tactful as always," tittered Lulu. "But then again, what does one expect from Dan the almost Invisible Man!"

BROMEANDO FILM STUDIOS - A PRIVATE BUNGALOW

"It's a good thing I don't suffer from writer's cramp," crooned Dee-Dee as he and Sylvester sat altering the seemingly endless pages in front of them. "Even though I say it myself, this rewritten scene between Jessica and Baz's surly Count Belmondo is quite something."

"As is this scene I'm checking where you and he meet for the first time," snickered Sylvester selecting a page. "When I first read what you'd written, poor, startled Danny the gofer, had to help me up from the floor as I literally fell off my chair I was laughing so much!" He gave a cackle. "This is the part that really cracks me up!

"Belmondo: 'Who are you and what are doing loitering outside my lady friend's establishment?' Titus: 'Lady friend's establishment? I never realised that pre-evolution whatevers even *knew* about such tantalising creatures. Don't you lot get your kicks by messing about with microbes and such?' Belmondo: 'If, by messing about also means your nose, then yes, I am that very pre-evolution whatever.' Belmondo raises his fist as if to strike Titus. Titus: 'Pray, do, you pre-evolution piece of fossilised doo-doo! Talk about a *sedimental* hard-on!'"

"How about this one between me, as Titus, and Jessica," carolled Dee-Dee. "The scene in which she and Titus go skinny dipping and she catches a glimpse of the Titus torpedo."

Speaking in falsetto Dee-Dee added. "Jessica: 'Is that a dagger I see before me?'" Titus: 'Not quite a dagger, but it'll sure make you stagger!' Jessica: 'Make me stagger?' She gives a high-pitched laugh. 'It takes more than a mere dew drop to make this singing sensation stagger!' Titus. Sulkily. 'You don't know what you're missing, Jessica.' Jessica gives another high-pitched laugh. Jessica: 'You mean I can't *see* what I'm supposed to be missing, Titus, dearest! C'mon! I'll race you back to where we left our clothes before this freezing water takes a final toll on the Titus ding-a-ling!'"

Sylvester blew Dee-Dee a kiss. "Thank goodness that doesn't apply to Titus Testis in real life!"

"Oh, no?" giggled Dee-Dee with a Cheshire Cat smile.

"Definitely an oh, no," replied Sylvester with a lecherous leer. "My precious Dee-Dee having a willy much more *exceedy* than needy! As I keep telling you, when I was first introduced to your splendid, travelling companion, my immediate thought was 'goodness, young man, you must have been front of the queue when they were handing the best of the willies out!'"

GODFREY STREET

"Talk about a rebound I did *not* expect," snapped Lulu, eyeing Leo and Lobie who had joined her for their usual catch-up drink and dinner, "was dear Dee-Dee's doctored script becoming the actual script for Steinberg's film with Robert Apps's original script, storyline whatever, well and truly binned!" She added wryly. "It's pretty, damn obvious I made a gross error with my suggestion that Maebelle, aka the revamped, reborn Jessica, being a bitchier pain in the butt. Instead, it appears I've turned her into a bloody heroine; a wise-cracking Auntie Mame of the put-down!"

"We can't all be perfect, Lulu, dear," snorted Leo.

"Oh, fuck off, Leo, *dear*," chided Lulu, "you know what I mean." Taking a sip of her G and T, she_added with sigh. "It's now a conundrum as to what Aye! Aye! will be doing next."

"Can't he go show up in Vegas?" suggested Lobie.

"No, he can't, seeing there's no valid reason for him to visit glittering Las Vegas," murmured Lulu. "Added to which he takes it upon himself and Clip Clop to walk the Blue Trail, the scenic, coastal between Riomaggiore and Monterosso in the Cinque Terre, Italy, seeing they both deserve a holiday of sorts."

"Meaning?" questioned Lobie.

"*Esattamente,*" said Lulu with a giggle. "Naturally, he and Clip Clop just happen to bump into two, elegant, confirmed bachelors who own a sumptuous villa in the area. Two gentlemen *aptly* named Bobby Brewer and Jonno Collins. The initials B and C giving a hint of things to happen."

"You never stop, do you?" said Leo admiringly.

"How could I *ever* stop?" giggled Lulu. "Not only do I speak to you two lovable rogues on a daily basis I also converse, plot and ponder with my fictional fiends and characters on a daily basis as well. Some know-it-alls say that being a writer is lonely, but I strongly disagree. When one is dealing with the likes of a Cymbeline or an Eye! Eye! Golden Eye, how on *earth* could one ever be at a loose end or alone! However, getting back to Maebelle, I'm loath to admit it, but I have a nasty feeling that wretched film will be a box office sensation."

She gave a grimace. "When gambler Sky Masterson sang *Luck Be a Lady* in the movie, *Guys and Dolls,* he could have easily been referring to the likes of Maebelle who, let's face it - and I'm sorry to have to say it - appears to be Lady Luck personified! Grrr!"

"Do you think she'll make another film?" asked Leo.

"Oh, yes, many, many more," said Lulu dryly. "So many, in fact, the film industry will find itself running out of fucking celluloid!"

EXECUTIVE CAFETERIA - BROMEANDO FILMS

"Dee-Dee, darling!" crooned Maebelle. "When you have a minute!"

"For you, Janus Jessica Maebelle, I have more than a minute, I have a minute and thirty seconds: *as from now*!" carolled Dee-Dee as Maebelle sat herself elegantly at the table where he was sitting nursing a large coffee. "So, spout, before I start to pout!"

"Oscar de Sade's party tonight," crooned Maebelle without any further preamble. "I'm at sixes and sevens as to what I, as the star, should wear." Placing her hand on his, she added coquettishly. "As you've been doing such wonders, not only with that oh, so deliciously, wicked script and my even more delicious character, but with my wardrobe as well, I really would *treasure* a teensy-weensy bit of help in my choosing something with which to positively *Sten gun* the hardboiled locals!"

"Sten gun the hardboiled locals?" tittered Dee-Dee. "My dear Maebelle; you don't need an outfit of my choosing to help you do that: your mere presence being ammunition enough!"

"You are so *sweet*!" purred Maebelle, forfeiting Dee-Dee the satisfaction of a typical Maebelle reaction to his snide comeback. "So, come on; pretty please!" She added with a mascaraed wink. "I'm sure you're planning on something out of this world, something utterly scrumptious, and, as the saying could also go, *two* scrumptious outfits are better than one!"

"I know *just* the outfit for you!" carolled Dee-Dee, wriggling with fiendish glee. "It's the cocktail dress you'll be wearing in one of your forthcoming scenes. The scene in which you attack Baz Belmondo with a stiletto heel.! The mauve, pink and gold tiger print, strapless, backless cocktail dress set off with aforesaid gold stilettos! A major plus is that nobody apart from you, the wondrous *moi*, and the wardrobe personnel have seen the stunning ensemble!"

"Dee-Dee, you're a positive genius!" carolled Maebelle. "I knew, I just *knew* I could rely on you to advise timid me!" There was a brief pause before she added a touch tentatively. "May I ask what *you*, Dee-Dee dearest, will be wearing?"

"Why, a matching mauve, pink and gold velvet tiger skin print onesie, what else?" crowed Dee-Dee.

"What else?" said Maebelle faintly. "How silly of me even bothering to ask."

PANTALONES SABELOTODO - THE DE SADE MANSION - BEVERELY HILLS

"Good evening, Miss Maebelle, you are looking doubly lovely this evening," beamed Oscar De Sade taking hold of Maebelle's graciously proffered hand and giving it a sloppy, wet kiss. Turning to the small, over decorated Christmas tree (human version) standing next to him, he added proudly. "This lovely lady next to me is Ophelia, Mrs De Sade, my very lovely wife."

"A pleasure to meet you, Mrs De Sade," purred Maebelle, quickly taking in the ostentatious gilded, moulded, heavily swathed reception room visible behind the smug couple. "And thank you for inviting me to your beautiful home. A fairy tale castle come true!"

"Thank you dear," whistled Ophelia De Sade, her tight, painted lips barely moving. "Please call me Ophelia."

"Thank you, Ophelia," smiled Maebelle. "May I also say you must know a *very* adventurous interior decorator!"

"I do," replied Ophelia, in a tight-lipped whistle as if repeating a hallowed, wedding vow. "His name is Caspar Cruet, and, as you so rightly say, he's made our home a fairy tale castle come true."

A fairy tale castle come true, thought Maebelle wryly. *How remiss of me not to realise one of the Brothers very Grimm was a frustrated interior desecrator! As for you, Ophelia De Sade, judging from the number of facelifts you've had, your* exterior *decorator, i.e., your plastic surgeon, would make a weightlifter jealous!*

"Miss Maebelle? Miss Maebelle? are you okay?" grunted Oscar giving Maebelle a curious look.

"What? Er . . . yes, I'm fine, thank you. Oscar," stammered Maebelle.

"Then perhaps you could kindly move along as we have other guests to greet!"

"Oh, of course! Silly me. It's just that I'm so stunned, so *mesmerised* by your beautiful home that I was literally struck dumb! Ha ha!"

Just as I am by that gorgeous, gangling Gary Cooper lookalike standing over there, thought Maebelle with an inward giggle. *Beware Mr. Gangly with must surely be an uber-impressive dangly, you're now well and truly in my predatory sights!*

"I love your dress, Maebelle," whistled Ophelia, coming to Oscar's rescue. her painted lips barely moving in her mask-like face, "So unusual. So *brave.* It's how I imagine a decorated crosswalk would look like. A *sparkling* decorated cross walk to be exact!"

"How imaginative of you, Ophelia! *Soo* uplifting!" cooed Maebelle. "Strange you should say that as *your* charming outfit and jewelled accessories remind *me* of a colourful mosaic: an ancient *Roman* mosaic! Now, knowing which side my Ryvita is buttered, I'd best do as dear Oscar suggested and not *hold-you-up* any longer!"

"What a dreadful woman!" whistle Ophelia in a tight-lipped aside to Oscar.

"She may be a dreadful woman," grunted Oscar, "but that dreadful woman is going to be paying for that island you want in the Caribbean; so be nice!"

"Be nice, Oscar?" whistled Ophelia, her tight lips doing their imitable version of a miniature lambada. "If it helps toward our dream Caribbean-island, not only will I be *nice* to the over-decorated, over-dressed monster, I'll be *extra* nice! I will even . . ." Her whistled response cut short by Oscar's expansive cry. "The genius little man himself! Welcome, Dee-Dee! Welcome to our home! This charming lady next to me is Ophelia, my very lovely wife. Ophelia, this is Dee-Dee Devereaux, the genius behind my new movie!"

"Good evening, Dee-Dee," whistled Ophelia through her lambada dancing lips. "I'm delighted to finally meet Oscar's man of the moment! Darling Oscar never stops talking about you and what a *saviour* you have been: what a saviour you *are!*"

"All part of such an esteemed job plus role, Mrs De Sade," replied Dee-Dee with faux modesty - "Ophelia, please!" - "All part of such an esteemed job plus role, *Ophelia.* Er . . . has er . . . anyone seen Miss Maebelle? Or perhaps she's yet to arrive."

"Oh, she's definitely arrived," whistled Ophelia. She gave a grimace which could have been a smile or a moue of disapproval. "You can't miss her! Simply lookout for a whirling, twirling, sparkling crosswalk and that'll be her!"

A whirling, twirling, sparkling pedestrian crossing? thought Dee-Dee, barely able to suppress his giggles. *I would have thought* that *coming from a titchy, bitchy over decorated, over jewelled, artificial miniature Christmas tree is a bit rich; but there you are!*

"And may I say, Dee-Dee, what a pleasure it is to see such a handsome young man wearing formal black tie instead of some bizarre outfit which calls itself trendy."

"Thank you, Ophelia. Yes, I much prefer the traditional, the tried and true, the *smart*," carolled Dee-Dee. "I can never understand why any man, young or old, would wish to parade about in outfits better suited to the likes of Gary Glitter or Liberace!"

"My thoughts *exactly*!" sniped Ophelia. "And, talking of stopping the traffic, your lady friend approaches. I'll leave you to compliment her on her fancy-dress costume while I go and talk to our more soberly attired other guests."

"Cow!" giggled Dee-Dee as Ophelia stalked off. Turning to greet Maebelle he said with a puckish grin. "Your new friend, Ophelia, who irrefutably has no intention of drowning, simply *loves* your dress!"

"You *Janus*!" hissed Maebelle on approaching. "You set me up, didn't you?"

"Set you up?" exclaimed Dee-Dee. "That's bullshit with a capital B, Maebelle! Everyone, but *everyone,* is talking about you and your out-of-this-world cocktail dress! Had *I* appeared in a matching onesie, everyone would have ended up talking about the dashing Dee-Dee Devereaux and *not* Bromeando's newest star!"

"Oh?" said Maebelle almost skidding to a stop. "Oh? I hadn't thought of that." Giving Dee-Dee a sharp look she said matter-of-factly. "You could be right, but knowing you as I do, there's always a hidden sting in the tail or a knife in one's back!"

"If you look at the lineup of photographers waiting to get a photo of you, perhaps you'll discard your earlier words of wisdom and think again; *dear*," snickered Dee-Dee. "Now, watch this."

Turning to face the group of photographers, Dee-Dee carolled cheerfully. "Here she is, gentlemen. The one and only Maebelle. Having already conquered today's fashion world, tomorrow will see her as the superstar of the film world! However, tonight is *your* night as she poses for you in a special outfit to mark the occasion. A glorious cocktail dress that would have even made the great Elsa Schiaparelli a tad *vert*!"

"Elsa Shrapnel? Who the fuck is she?" called out one of the photographers, a burly Burt Reynolds lookalike.

"Why ask about Madam *Shrapnel*, when you have - but only for a moment before she's whisked away - the gorgeous Maebelle here in front of you," carolled Dee-Dee. He gave the grinning photographer a mischievous wink. "Unless you'd prefer to photograph *moi*, Dee-Dee Devereaux, script writer and actor supreme!"

"Well said," called another photographer. "So, Mr. Dee-Dee Devereaux, script writer supreme, if you wouldn't mind moving for - as I'm sure my colleagues will agree - we'd be happier photographing Maebelle!"

"Your wish is my command, gentlemen," yodelled Dee-Dee. "Miss Maebelle is all yours!"

"You're almost forgiven, but not quite," murmured Maebelle as Dee-Dee started to saunter away.

"I'll be totally forgiven when you see yourself spread across the papers on the morrow!" tittered Dee-Dee as he surreptitiously slipped his business card into the proffered hand of the grinning Burt Reynolds lookalike preparing to take a closeup of the graciously smiling Maebelle. His quick-silver gesture followed by a reciprocal wink from the so-called Burt and a firm thumbs up.

"Hopefully yon subtle slipping of my calling to Mr. Burt Reynolds the Second will lead to some sort of *Deliverance* before the night is out!" chortled Dee-Dee to himself. He gave a titter. "The planned assignation having nothing to do with *High Jinks in High C!* as I'm pretty sure the old boy would balk at the idea of this yet to be made Dee-Dee masterpiece. Anticipated title: *Buggery in the Bungalow*!"

*

"I've been watching you all evening," murmured the Gary Cooper lookalike in a rumbled aside having snuck up, unnoticed, to where Maebelle was standing studying what Oscar De Sade claimed to be "a genuine pricey Picasso". "Allow me to introduce myself, Preston Pulmonary. Unlike the majority of people here tonight, I am not in the movie business but a struggling artist who, thanks to a convenient inheritance, is not exactly starving nor living in a garret!"

Maebelle, her mind going into overdrive, said with a purr. "A struggling but not a starving artist having to make do with a garret thanks to a convenient inheritance? How *very* convenient for you, Mr. Pulmonary."

"Preston, please!"

Then I insist you call me Maebelle! And, as I was saying, how very convenient for you to have an inheritance to help cover your living costs plus, I take it, vitals such a paints, canvasses and paintbrushes."

"Yes, it is," rumbled Preston Pulmonary unfazed by the bitchy innuendo. Giving Maebelle a penetrating "I know you're thinking what I'm thinking" look, he added is a seductive whisper. "And if it's not beneath Oscar De Sade's newest star to accept an invitation to view my make do garret later, tomorrow or whenever it suits?"

I take it that invitation also includes a viewing of your personal paintbrush, thought Maebelle mischievously.

About to reply with some witty quip, Maebelle gave a start. "I knew I'd seen you before. In fact, you were in the papers just the other day. You're *the* Preston Pulmonary, heir of The Pulmonary Pet Foods empire."

"Guilty as charged," rumbled Preston. "Heir today, heir tomorrow, and heir for several decades still to come!"

"When you *put* it like that, how could Oscar De Sade's newest star *not* accept your kind invitation. However, there is a complication, but complications need not necessarily *be* complications, need they?" crooned Maebelle. "Take Mr. and Mrs De Sade for example. They're always entertaining and I'm told an invitation to their spectacular Las Vegas abode is not to be missed!"

"My thoughts exactly, Maebelle," murmured Preston. Reaching for Maebelle's hand he gave it a light kiss. "And while everyone will be thinking *Viva Las Vegas* you and I could be enjoying our very own *Viva La Malibu!*"

TWENTY-TWO

VILLA CASA DEGLI ARCHI

"It'll be interesting to see how much Bromeando Films finally fuck up my original novel," chuckled Andy as he and Clive sat enjoying breakfast on the pool terrace, "and now they've got bloody Pinocchio Devereaux poisoning the script, God only knows!"

"Pinocchio Devereaux? Why Pinocchio?" snorted Clive.

"Because the only thing long in that little bastard's life is his distorted nose, nothing else," sniggered Andy. "Lulu Mayhew has the audacity to call it fiction, but when it comes down to the likes of Dee-Dee Devereaux, it's all balderdash and bullshit!"

"But think of the money, honey!" chortled Clive.

"You're right about that, lover! After what Oscar De Sade paid me, as far as my bank manager and I are concerned, they can use my original work for toilet paper!"

"Spoken like a true, avaricious soul, Andy dearest," snickered Clive. "Hence my never-ending worship of your hirsute bod!" He took a sip of coffee. "Any new ideas regarding payback for Miss Mayhew's challenge to Mr. Stephenson's inspired rockets?"

"Not at the moment. As the saying goes; 'slowly; slowly, catchee monkey'. Only, this time I won't be catchee-ing a monkey, I'll be catchee-ing a couple of *very* surprised arseholes instead!"

BROMEANDO FILM STUDIOS

"That's it, folks!" carolled Sylvester à la Bugs Bunny. Clapping hands, he added cheerfully. "It's a wrap! Thank you all!" Turning to a graciously smiling Maebelle and smugly smiling Dee-Dee he said with a faux smile. "And an extra thank you to our charming guests, Maebelle and Dee-Dee. Two remarkable people and - dare I say it - *High Jinks in High C's* very own Bobbsey Twins! Ha! Ha!"

"I take it I don't count?" growled Baz Malone from where he stood next to one of the crew.

"Ah, Baz," crooned Sylvester unfazed. "No need to jump the gun, pull the trigger, whatever, as I was just coming to you!" Giving Baz a nicotine-stained smile he added mischievously. "Plus, a special thank you to big Baz Malone; an alluring Don Juan character if ever there was!"

"Aw, shucks, Syl," drawled Baz, his handsome face breaking into a whiter than white smile he said laconically. "A Don Juan character you said? I like it, though, if the truth be known, Miss Maebelle would make any self-respecting Don Juan run for the hills! As for that posturing, ode to a pansy, Dee-Dee Devereaux, not even Hannibal's army - if they were around today - could satisfy him." He gave a derisive snigger. "The saddest thing for me is, having allowed myself to appear in this catastrophe of a film, I too am nothing more than a Don Juan character with no self-respect!"

Giving a stunned, Sylvester, Maebelle and Dee-Dee a vigorous V sign, Baz turned on his heels and walked away from the set while merrily whistling *Take My Hand, I'm a Stanger in Paradise.*

A PRIVATE BUNGALOW - BEVERLY HILLS HOTEL

"Talk about a self-destructive huffer-puffer!" giggled Dee-Dee as he and cameraman Boysie Barstow - the Burt Reynolds lookalike - lay on the king size bed sipping pina coladas (dubbed penis hard-onners by Dee-Dee). "For once Maebelle, Sylvester Steinberg, and even yours truly, were at a loss for words!"

"All I can say - and I speak for the rest of the crew," rumbled Boysie, "it's a pity the arrogant arsehole didn't leave sooner. Lucky for him you'd finished filming when you did otherwise you can bet your bottom dollar, me, and some of the other camera guys would have taught him a lesson or two in manners." Giving Dee-Dee a bear-like hug, he added contemplatively. "As for his rudeness to all of you - you especially, my little English acorn; unbelievable."

"I trust your referral to me as your little English acorn has nothing to do with my personal acorn," quipped Dee-Dee, burying his face in Bosie's hairy chest and feigning embarrassment.

Boysie gave out a deep, rumbling, laugh. "As you English are so fond of saying, out of little acorns great oak trees grow. And even though your personal acorn isn't exactly an oak, it's a very spry and active sapling!" He gave another, rumbling laugh. "Talking of little saplings that grow, I'm famished, so how about I take you out for dinner at a favourite restaurant of mine and maybe even introduce you to a couple of friends. There's no need to make a reservation as they're used to me turning up unannounced."

"Out to dinner? Yes, please. As for meeting of your friends, that has to be a no-no, I'm afraid," simpered Dee-Dee. "Tomorrow is an uber-busy for Maebelle and *moi*. Maybe another time."

"Whatever you say, Dee-Dee," replied Boysie a touch sharply. "C'mon then. Get your glad rags together. As I said, I'm famished."

"Will do," trilled Dee-Dee leaping from the bed. "But before I do anything else I must make a quick call to Maebelle. and, as its business, I'll quickly pop outside."

"Try not to be too long as I really am starving! Ha ha!"

"Ta!"

Out on the terrace and making doubly sure he was out of earshot, Dee-Dee tapped in Sylvester's number. "Syl," he whispered on the call being answered, "anything on this Barstow creep?"

"Yes," said Sylvester. "He's to be avoided like the plague. However, forgetting *that* bit of info; any luck in getting the info *I* asked for?"

"But, of course," trilled Dee-Dee. "As you well know, when it comes to pillow squawk, I'm no bumbler-mumbler! He's invited me to dinner plus he wanted me to meet a couple of his friends later."

"Get out of your dinner engagement and come here instead," snapped Sylvester. "As I just said, Boysie Barstow's to be avoided at all costs. It takes a lot to shock me but what I was told about your new, bestest friend, stunned even this worldly-wise, steadfast friend! This weary man of the world! So, Dee-Dee, get rid of him and I'll see you when I see you!"

"Aye! Aye! sir," carolled Dee-Dee. "A cancelling I shall go!"

*

Half-an-hour later an irate Boysie contacted Malcom Duval. "The little shit stood me up," he snarled. "He was on the phone minutes before we were about to leave - he *claimed* he was on the phone to that bloody Maebelle woman, but I somehow doubt it - plus he refused to confirm any future arrangements saying he'd be too busy working with fucking Steinberg on some new project."

He gave a derogative laugh. "However, as you anticipated, he did ask if I had a shady contact or two in L.A. who could help sort out a tiresome problem - that Montgomery creep, no doubt - so I gave him yours as you suggested."

"Well done," chuckled Malcom. "Thanks, Boysie. It can't have been much fun seducing Mr. Devereaux but you did it! Now, as you're at a loose end, how about you have dinner with me: The Palm at eight?"

"See you then!" laughed Boysie before terminating the call.

*

"So, tell me more about the mysterious Mr. Barstow," trilled Dee-Dee taking a sip of wine.

"As I said, a guy to be avoided like the proverbial plague," replied Sylvester. "Apparently, he's often referred to as the man of a hundred faces: his latest face being that of a photographer. However, his appearance at the De Sade's party remains a mystery seeing nobody in PR has any idea as to who could have invited him. Did he mention any particular paper - or magazine - to you?" Sylvester couldn't resist a snigger. "Or was one far too busy playing with his flashbulb."

"Very funny. Very droll, Sylvester, *dear*. You know better than that, seeing the only bulb I've enjoyed playing with - read planting - belongs to a certain, very direct, director!" carolled Dee-Dee.

"A most flattering and direct answer, if I may say so," said Sylvester, visibly preening.

"And, before you ask, yes; I did manage to get a contact number for him: two in fact," said Dee-Dee delving into the inside pocket of his pink Ralph Lauren blazer and pulling out a folded piece of paper.

"Here they are." He gave a snicker. "It'll be interesting to see who answers when you call either of them."

"Something I'll leave until the morning," replied Sylvester. He added, with lewd chuckle. "My next move has nothing to do with Mr. Barstow but a *lot* to do with the charming young man sitting so prettily opposite me!"

"Need this pretty young man say he has no intention of complaining," trilled Dee-Dee proffering his empty wine glass. "And, if I may have a top-up, I'll certainly drink to that!"

AN OVERTLY OSTENTATIOUS MANSION - PARADISE COVE BLUFFS - MALIBU

"That's exactly what my unique vocal cords needed," purred Maebelle giving Preston Pulmonary (she would later describe him to Dee-Dee as a decidedly *un*gifted painter along with all things else, especially his paintbrush) a coquettish look. "As I always say, there is nothing to equal a soothing swallow of eager, escaping spermatozoa to lubricate their glorious sound waves!"

"If you can wait for an hour or so, I'll be more than happy to help you make *waves* again," schmoozed Preston. "But, for the moment, I have to admit that the Pulmonary pistol has run out of ammunition!"

"Not being a greedy, wanton woman and knowin' I'll soon be gettin'," replied Maebelle in her best Mae West drawl, "this pistol suckin' woman is happy to wait! And, if the waitin' includes a flute of champagne, then the happier this waitin', *wantin'* woman will be!" Said with a straight face despite knowing a perplexed Monty was waiting for her back at the hotel.

"God! I simply *love* the way you British speak," schmoozed Preston with a lovesick smile.

"The way we Brits talk?" replied Maebelle feigning a hurt voice. "*That,* may I remind you, Preston Pulmonary, that was me in *Mae West* mode and *not* a tribute to Anna Neagle or that jarring Julie who *should* have danced all night!"

"Whoever you are, to me you're always perfect, Maebelle," schmoozed Preston. His diplomatic response accompanied by a suggestive wink and a sly, licking of his chapped lips. "Now, if I have any strength left, let's see if I can manage to summon Samson and have him bring us a bottle of the Widow and a couple of flutes."

"You don't mind this Samson seeing us in bed together?" said Maebelle, a touch alarmed in case the potential bringer of cheer was a gossip.

"I can assure you Samson has seen the *world* at play, Maebelle, dearest, and when it comes to turning a blind eye, Samson is an expert."

Reaching for the house phone on the Parzinger table next to the bed, Preston tapped the relevant button. On hearing a high-pitched "How may I aspire to your latest desire, sire?", Preston asked for an iced bottle of Veuve Clicquot champagne and two chilled flutes to be brought up to the master bedroom suite.

If that's your idea of a Samson, I hope to God you don't see me as your Delilah, thought Maebelle with an inward snicker as a Puck-like figure, dressed in a pink T-shirt, pink Bermuda shorts and sporting a pair pink Crocs skipped into the room: a gold tray, made in the shape of a palm leaf, bearing the requested items.

"Good morning, Mr. Preston!" sang the little man placing the tray on a nearby gilded console table with a flourish. "Good morning, Mr. Preston and Mr. Preston's latest notch of the night, behold your get your tousled-heads-together champers!" Eyeing Preston he added in a further singsong voice. "Breakfast will be served by the pool in thirty minutes precisely. I take it croissants with caviar followed my scrambled eggs with shavings pf white truffles will suffice. If not, why not, then take it up with Hamstrung Harriet the cook and not this poor, overworked Samson." Giving Preston a puckish smile, Samson turned on his Crocs and wafted out.

"Is he for real?" whispered Maebelle.

"Oh, Samson's real alright," replied Preston as he poured them each a flute. He gave a Vincent Price type chuckle. "Wait until you actually *meet* Madam Hamstrung Harriet the cook; a presence not easy to forget. Among others caring for my simple well-being are Nelson the Column, the head gardener: never mind Horatio Hornblower, the general handyman and Fenella Fly-by-night, the kennel maid. Tubby the Turbo, my chauffeur, you met last night."

Perhaps this wasn't such a good idea after all, thought Maebelle reaching for the proffered flute. *Thank* God *Montgomery thinks that I'm away in Vegas with Mr. and Mrs De Sade! I should never have agreed to come to this tribute to Pompeii with its triple dose of another Dee-Dee, a doppelganger for Lulu interfering Mayhew and a stud who turns out to be more of a Herman Munster than a Gary Cooper. Added to which do I, the one and only Maebelle, need to demean my elegant self with the likes of this ongoing cartoon set in a mishmash of Versailles-cum-Taj Mahal-cum-Pompeii when I have Monty and a perfect fuck-pad waiting for me back at the hotel.*

Placing her champagne flute firmly back on the tray Maebelle gave a startled Preston a scathing look and said haughtily. "Enough is enough! Now, if you'll excuse me, I need to get dressed. Whilst I'm getting dressed, please inform your *tuba* of a chauffeur that I require his services in order to drive me back to the Bevereley Hills Hotel: tout suite!" Maebelle raised a hand. "No, Preston Pulmonary, not another word unless you wish to be the cause of a *pulmonary* embolism!"

*

"Monty! Oh, Monty, dear; I'm back! A day early!" crooned Maebelle on entering the bungalow. "Elvis may have crooned *Viva! Las Vegas!* but that's one ditty your lovely Maebelle will not be shouting to the skies! Monty? I can hear whispering coming from the second bedroom. Who the *fuck* is in there with you?"

Striding toward the closed door, Maebelle began banging on the door. "What's going on Montgomery! Open the door, damn you! Open the door!"

Opening the door for a mere fraction, a glowering Monty said angrily. "What the fuck, Maebelle, you weren't due back until tomorrow!"

"Well, I'm back," snarled Maebelle, "and I'd like to know who the hell you have cowering back there!"

"I am not cowering," said a calm female voice, "and, furthermore, who the fuck are you? Bitch."

"Who the fuck am I? Bitch?" shrieked Maebelle flinging herself against the door; Her furious response sending Monty stumbling backwards and ending up on the floor at the feet of a partly dressed Barbie lookalike. "I just happen to be the one and only Maebelle, superstar of Oscar De Sade's latest box office hit, *that's* who I am! Not some peroxided slut having it off in *my* private bungalow with *what* was supposed to be *my* lover!"

"Your *lover*!" exploded Monty, back on his feet. "So, who or what, pray tell, is Mr. Preston bloody Pulmonary?"

"Pres . . . Preston Pul . . . monary?" stammered Maebelle. "I have no idea who or what you're talking about. More to the point, who is *she*?" The latter said with a dramatic pointing of a finger.

"*She* is Miss Coral Cartagena, and *she* just happens to be a financier with Betram, Hookum and Billingsgate, financial advisors unsurpassed. Anything else, before I get dressed and go, Miss Future Superstar? Such as a course in manners or, better still, you can have him along with a cheerful 'up yours'," said the young woman with a tight smile on reaching for her jacket and handbag lying on a nearby chair. Giving a startled Maebelle and an embarrassed Monty a cursory nod, Coral Cartagena pushed past Maebelle and exited the cottage.

"You lowlife! You bastard! You double crossing piece of shit!" screeched Maebelle raising her hand as if about to give Monty a resounding slap: her action thwarted by Monty grabbing her by the wrist.

"Now you listen to me, Madam Maebelle," he said through gritted teeth. "Don't you think it somewhat strange that while you were in Las Vegas with Oscar and Ophelia De Sade, their virtual doubles were sitting three tables way from me at *Spago's* last night."

"Impossible!" snapped Maebelle. "We were all in Vegas!"

"You're not on a make-believe film set now, Maebelle," sniped Monty. "Next time you decide to let your desire for a fuck get the better of you, you should at least check out your alibis before spouting them! But enough of any recriminations, Enjoy the rest of your bed hopping stay; I'm out of here!"

"What about your things, your clothes? What about me? What about *us*?" shrilled Maebelle.

"Clothes I can buy," snorted Monty, "As for *us*? What *us*? Us, to you, is simply a word and what's more, I am quite sure you will have no trouble in finding another gullible *us* during the remainder of your stay. Now, if you don't mind, I'd appreciate some privacy while having a shit, shower and shave before getting dressed."

He gave a chuckle. "Being a good Boy Scout and therefore always prepared, I keep my passport, credit cards et cetera locked in a spare briefcase. Therefore, as I have no wish to bid you *adieux* before I leave, this, my dear Maebelle, is goodbye!" Before Maebelle could respond Monty closed the door.

Literally spitting with rage, Maebelle, about to hammer and the door, managed to retrain herself. "No," she hissed. "No, I won't give him the satisfaction. Give me a moment to get my act together and then I'll pop over and see darling Dee-Dee for, no matter what happens, Montgomery Livingston is not going to get away with this!"

She gave a light laugh. "As dearest Dee-Dee always says, better to be safe than sorry, I'd best give *him a* ring before I invade his *gîte* in case he's otherwise engaged."

"You're back!" exclaimed Dee-Dee on answering.

"Yes, dearest, I am and what's more I need to talk to you. tout suite! Are you in the murky middle of something or are you sulking solo!"

"Definitely sulking solo, so come and join me for a late breakfast and reveal all." Switching into thirties gangster mode he added with a camp snarl. "Da whole sordid troot an' nuttin' but da troot as anything else would be unacceptable!"

TWENTY-THREE

DEE-DEE DEVEREAUX'S BUNGALOW - BEVERLY HILLS HOTEL

"So, another lust hits the dust," trilled Dee-Dee having listened wide-eyed to Maebelle's latest drama. "What's that? Stud number three within the last year or so?"

"Who's counting," came the breezy reply. "Could be three or even four if one takes into account the likes of Miles the smiles Saunders, Peter Proudfoot, Montgomery Livingston, Malcom Duval or Preston Pulmonary: who knows or cares."

Maebelle added with a mischievous smile. "I have to say I was surprised - and highly relieved - to find you home alone. I would have imagined you'd be either with Sylvester or else assisting your favourite cameraman polish his lens yet here you are, in all your Gucci glory!"

"According to caring Sylvester, Mr. Cameraman - aka Boysie Barstow - is to be avoided at all costs," replied Dee-Dee curtly. "Apparently, he not only plays at being gay when the mood suits him, he's heavily involved in all sorts of unsavoury delights such as drugs, money laundering, extortion, pimping, people trafficking. You name it, he's into it!"

"At least we have each other," said Maebelle softly: her unexpected, almost gentle reply seeing Dee-Dee blinking in astonishment.

"We have?"

"Yes, Dee-Dee, dearest, we most certainly do. When all is said and done, we're like two peas in a pod. We've been through a lot together with even more trials and tribulations to come. What I'm trying to say, Dee-Dee, dear, I'll be watching your back and hopefully you, mine."

"Consider it done!" carolled Dee-Dee. "Now, how about we order a late breakfast to celebrate our new-found tryst - or should that be brunch? Why don't I order a bottle or three of champers along with a basket of brioches and croissants, fresh fruit and eggs benedict."

"As long as my croissant is a croissant-*neuf* I couldn't think of anything more delicious!" crooned Maebelle. Her witty comeback accompanied by a typical Maebelle thousand-watt smile.

"Make that *deux*!" trilled Dee-Dee reaching for the house phone.

Replacing the receiver Dee-Dee said crisply. "Tell me honestly, Maebelle, Is this ongoing feud with Lulu Mayhew really worth ii?"

"It may surprise you, Dee-Dee, dearest, but I've been asking myself the very same question. And you know what, it's not! Look at the two of us here in glittering L.A., me having made what can only be my Oscar-winning film debut and you having written your first screenplay. A screenplay which the other Oscar - ha! - and everyone else involved assures me is going to be another winner! So, who needs Lulu Mayhew whose only achievements are a couple of rather tacky novels. None of which have proved themselves to be film worthy, nota bene!"

"You're one hundred percent correct, Maebelle, dear - ah! breakfast-cum-brunch has arrived - so let's drink a champagne toast to what we have agreed; a toast to no more Lulu Mayhew madness. In other words, let's simply forget her. Her and the others!"

"Others?"

"The likes of Robert Apps, Malcom Duval and any of the other scalps festooning your Ferragamo belt! Forget them as well for they, like that nasty Rumpelstiltskin, will continue to angrily stamp their clumsy feet before finally spinning and digging themselves into deepest oblivion!"

Dee-Dee and Maebelle sat in a companiable silence sipping their champagne as the waiter deftly set up the table leaving two chafing dishes and the champagne bucket on a nearside console. Murmuring a barely audible "thank you; enjoy" as he pocketed the five-dollar bill, the waiter gave the pair a brief smile and left.

As if synchronised, Maebelle and Dee-Dee sat staring at each other before bursting into fits of laughter.

"Maybe not just yet!" giggled Dee-Dee.

"Maybe not just yet!" trilled Maebelle.

"In fact, not at all just yet," they cried in unison, clinking flutes.

"Okay," said a grinning Dee-Dee, "now that's decided, who first, Mayhew or Montgomery Livingston?"

"Neither of those two reprobates," crooned Maebelle. "If anybody, I'd say Duval and Apps."

"Only one way to resolve that little conundrum," tittered Dee-Dee fumbling inside a trouser pocket and producing a pound coin, "and that's to toss for it. Heads for Mayhew or Montgomery: tails for Duval or Apps." With a flourish, Dee-Dee spun the coin.

"Tails!" crooned Maebelle.

"Tails it is!" crowed Dee-Dee eyeing the coin as it settled on the table.

"Right, Mr. Scriptwriter," crooned Maebelle. "Start scripting!"

VILLA CASA DEGLI ARCHI

"It's all falling into place," announced Andy as he and Clive sat having breakfast on the pool terrace. "Shakespeare may have written in his *King John,* one should fight fire with fire, but how about we fight Lulu Mayhew and her little army of thugs *not* with fire . . . wait for it" - Andy reached for his note pad lying on the table - "but how about this?"

"This?" echoed Clive.

"Yes, this," said Andy swivelling the pad so that Clive could read what he had written. "Have a look."

"Okay, let's have a dekko at your suggested this," chortled Clive quickly scanning the page. "Bloody hell, McCulloch," he said glancing up at a bemused Andy. "I knew you were an acclaimed writer of fiction, but this takes your writing to the elevated status of pure genius!"

"I take it you approve?" chuckled Andy.

"Approve? I most *heartily* approve, endorse, rubber-stamp or whatever you wish me to say," laughed Clive. "As I just said, it's pure bloody genius!"

DEE-DEE DEVEREAUX'S BUNGALOW - BEVERLY HILLS HOTEL - THREE DAYS LATER

A smug Dee-Dee reached for the house phone. "Maebelle precious, sweetheart, strychnine sweet, sugar plum or anything else that tickles your world-famous fancy," he carolled. "As discussed, I've been seriously scripting so, if you'd care to join London's elegant answer to Truman Capote for an inspirational breakfast, why not traipse across to Bungalow Guillotine in, say, half-an-hour?"

"It's that good, is it?" crooned Maebelle.

"Good?" exclaimed Dee-Dee. "Good doesn't come into it, Maebelle dear! As I said, in half-an-hour you could be meeting not only London's answer to Truman Capote; but London's answer to a combination of Mr. Breakfast at Tiffany's, Lawrence Sanders, Noël Coward. Down-Under's glorious Gary Disher and even more of such exalted calibre! So, squeeze into your corset, paint your face and do whatever else you need to do and sashay your million-dollar butt over here where my *all* will be revealed!"

Half-an-hour later, on the dot, Maebelle knocked on Dee-Dee's door.

"Goodness!" trilled Dee-Dee on letting her in. "Maybe they should rename you Maebelle Greenwich Mean Time; although Maebelle Cuckoo Clock would be prettier!"

"I could have been early," crooned Maebelle over her shoulder as she sailed into the sitting room, "but I didn't want to disappoint sadistic you, knowing that you wished me to arrive simply *bursting* with anticipation! Which I am!"

"Goody! Now, let me fix you a Mimosa whilst you feast your fevered eyes on what I've suggested we do with the dreaded Duval or the appalling Apps."

"Gimme! Gimme!" crooned Maebelle reaching for the proffered pages.

"Now, read them like a good little Lucrezia, and I'll be back in a jiff."

"Oh-my-God!" gasped Maebelle. "Oh-my-God!"

"Nasty, aren't I?" tittered Dee-Dee handing Maebelle her drink.

"Nasty?" You're more than nasty, Dee-Dee dear; this is both brilliantly nasty *and* brilliantly wicked with a capital neon-lit red N and W!"

"I'll certainly drink to that!" trilled Dee-Dee, sinking onto a nearby chair.

"Malcom Duval toeless in San Fag Crisco and Robert Apps toeless in *Bella Italia*? I love it! Simply love it!"

"I have to admit I was a tad inspired by ridiculous Robert's *The Omnipotent,* but then, didn't Nero inspire home fires burning à la Ivor Novello? So, as I said to myself; why not?"

"Why not?" crooned Maebelle. "But a teensy-weensy suggestion. Instead of merely cutting off their big toes, why not the big toe and two other toes and leaving the two remaining toes there to console each other. After all, two's company whilst three's a crowd."

"This brilliant scribe happily concurs!"

"I thought you would," purred Maebelle. "And now, the million-cum-zillion-dollar-cum-billion- euro question. When?"

THE PALM - BEVERLY HILLS

"Apologies for having to cancel our previous dinner engagement at the last minute," said Malcom giving Boysie a hug.

"No problem as we're here now," grinned Boysie. Holding Malcom at arms-length he added with a laugh. "Christ! You get better looking by the day, my handsome friend. No wonder all the girls fall for you!"

"Girls *and* boys," chuckled Malcom. "Don't forget the boys! Now, let's find our table and arm ourselves with a couple of drinks before we order and get down to business." He gave Boysie a playful dig in the ribs. "But before business, a bit of gossip. I want to hear all about your subtle seduction of the dreaded Dee-Dee Devereaux!"

"I can assure you there was nothing subtle about it," sniggered Boysie. "Dee-Dee Devereaux" - he made air quotes – "is what Mama Matildia, our cook back in Atlanta, would have described as someone who 'rapes easy'. Christ, the little bugger is insatiable! But enough about him, as I know it's that Maebelle woman, you're more interested in." He gave another snigger. "You have to agree, she's one helluva looker, but what a cow! Added to which, she and your little friend, Devereaux are, for the moment anyway, positively conjoined!"

"Tell me about it!" replied Malcom as they were shown to their table. "There was a time when you didn't dare mention one to the other, but - like most sparring couples - they were constantly falling out and making up."

"Rumour has it she's being lured away from the catwalk and fully into films and, if all the hype about Bromeando's forthcoming *High Jinks in High C!* proves to be correct, she'll go from strength to strength. As could Devereaux seeing he's now Sylvester Steinberg's golden boy in all senses of the word."

"God help Hollywood is all I can say," snorted Malcom as they sat down "But, like the Hindenburg, one moment you're up there, full of hot air, and the next moment you're back on *terror* firma - pun intended - in all senses of the word!"

"I take it we're talking about both esteemed passengers?"

"We are indeed, but let's deal with Devereaux first," continued Malcom. "My suggestion is we use him as a hint of tint, a warning-cum-appetiser of things to come concerning the two of them. As both are blessed with fairly formidable IQs, it shouldn't take them long to get the message. This should lead to Dee-Dee Devereaux becoming an exceedingly damp squib in L.A.'s exalted but precarious film world.

"As for Maebelle, we'll wait until her triumphant return to London for the premiere of *High Jinks.* Her entry into Leicester Square making Liz Taylor's entry into Rome as Cleopatra look lilliputian in comparison! But, unlike the conniving Cleo, it won't be randy Mark Antony waiting for her, but an uber-unpleasant surprise instead."

"I can't wait," chortled Boysie. "But back to Dee-Dee Devereaux; how do you plan to *dampen* him?"

"Think of the term, 'don't throw the baby out with the bathwater' so, how about this?"

DEE-DEE DEVEREAUX'S BUNGALOW - BEVERLY HILLS HOTEL - THREE DAYS LATER

"Can you sashay your way over to me within the next bewitching hour?" cooed Dee-Dee into the phone. "I've been in touch with one of Sylvester's dubious contacts in London who would be more than happy to assist in our *Toeless in Gaza* campaign." Dee-Dee's suggested code words for their proposed plan in case "in case of being overheard".

"I have a charity luncheon to attend," crooned Maebelle, "so it will have to be a quick in and out!"

"How very unsatisfying," trilled Dee-Dee. "But then I've never been a fan of the three W's."

"The three W's?"

"Whip it in. Whip it out. Wipe it!"

"At times, Dee-Dee Devereaux, you are too, too disgusting!" chortled Maebelle. "I'll see you in about thirty minutes."

*

"So, tell me all as if racing for gold," crooned Maebelle as Dee-Dee greeted her with a chaste kiss on the cheek.

"In best fast-talk I spoke to Sylvester's contact in London - a strange sounding creature named Tommy Trew - and I explained somewhat vaguely what we required . . ."

"You mean what Mr. and Mrs Gaza required!" interrupted Maebelle.

"Of course, I said Mr. and Mrs *Gaza*," said Dee-Dee petulantly. "To cut a long story short, once we'd agreed a fee - not as high as expected - he then asked me to leave the details on another number. Once he'd had a chance to study them, he'd think it over and then get back to me with a yea or nay and, if the former, details regarding payment blah blah. A bit iffy, methinks."

"Hmm," murmured Maebelle. "I agree. Therefore, I don't think any further contact with this Tommy Trew would be wise. I say we forget him and look around for someone else. Someone else who doesn't expect us to play by *his* rules when he's being paid to play by ours!"

"I knew, just *knew* that's how you'd react, Maebelle dearest," crowed Dee-Dee, "so, being the artful dodger I am, I then rang the telephone number Boysie gave me: the number for someone who could help me with" - he made air quotes - "a tiresome problem."

"And?"

"I spoke to a pleasant enough sounding guy - for one heart stopping moment I thought I was talking to Malcom Duval, but a Malcom Duval with an of American accent - who introduced himself as Dillon Digberry," said Dee-Dee. He added smugly. "I've arranged to meet him for a drink at the Beverley Wilshire at six this evening. I'll call you after I've seen him."

"No, call me first thing in the morning," trilled Maebelle, "as I plan to be otherwise engaged,"

"Oh? With whom, and how?"

"None of your beeswax, Mr. Artful Dodger!" crooned Maebelle. "All I'm prepared to say is that it's nobody you know, but someone Oscar insists I meet. We're having dinner at Providence before going on to trip the light fantastic - ha! - at Avalon or someplace similar. So, who knows?"

THE NEXT MORNING

"How strange," murmured Maebelle to the smirking Tyler Hoechlin lookalike and one of Oscar's "potential leading men" as they sat having breakfast. Maebelle wearing a luxurious cashmere housecoat and her guest, freshly showered and wearing his clothes from the night before. "No messages on my phone nor with reception from my friend s few bungalows along; and now he's not answering." She gave a madcap laugh. "Unless, like *moi,* handsome, hunky . . . er . . . Zorba . . ."

"Torba. Torba Toutakis," said the handsome young Greek with a cat that got the cream smile.

"Of *course*, Torba dear," cooed Maebelle. "As I was about to say, unless, like lucky me, he too got lucky last night."

"Yeah, you certainly did, Miss Maebelle," drawled Torba; his accent a mixture of American and something decidedly European. "I'm good, huh? An' I bet you 'aven't been fucky-fucked with such a beeg, beeg cock before, huh?"

Giving Torba a glare which would have felled a lesser man, Maebelle said crisply. "I am sorry, *Zorba,* but I must ask you leave as I am far too concerned about my friend and really don't give a monkey's about your *beeg* cock - not the biggest *I've* seen, not by a longshot - and I am sure Mr. De Sade will have no trouble finding you a *bit* part in a film, so I really must ask you to leave." Rising from the table she moved to where one of the house phones sat on a nearby countertop. "Unless you insist on being escorted from the premises. The choice is yours."

"Fuck you, beetch!" yelled Torba as he leapt up from the table and headed for the door. "Fuck you and fuck Oscar De Sade!"

"Well, you may have gotten away with fucking me, but fucking Mr. De Sade could prove to be a bit of a problem," called Maebelle as Torba slammed the door shut. "Now, let's see if I can get hold of dear Dee-Dee and find out what he and the mysterious Mr. Dillon Digberry have come up with; apart from the obvious!"

ELECTRIC FOUNTAIN - BEVERLY GARDENS PARK

"A van in the gardens? Surely that's not allowed?" exclaimed Debbie Alyson, pointing to a small, black van as it skidded to a halt next to the fountain. "Janey! Janey! Look!" she called to friend attending to her child in a pram. "What on earth are they doing?" she cried as two men leapt from the driver and passenger doors, raced round to the back of van, pulled out a large pink bundle and threw it into the fountain before getting back into the van and driving off.

"Damn litter louts," she hissed. "It looks as if they've thrown an old mattrass or something similar into the fountain. Honestly, some people!"

"Oh, my God!" screamed Janey Russell having left the pram and joined her friend. "It's not a mattrass! It's man! An almost naked man apart from a diaper and what could be some sort of eyepatch!"

"I'm calling for help!" shouted Debbie as the two young women ran over to where Dee-Dee, naked apart from what looked like an incontinence diaper, sat floundering in the fountain; his movements impeded by a pair of rattles taped to his hands with a further piece of tape across his mouth. Adding insult to injury, Dee-Dee was completely bald: his shaven head and brass eyepatch gleaming in the sunshine.

As a breathless Debbie said to a reporter. "The poor man looked rather like a very large pink baby!" Despite trying to look serious, she was unable to stop herself and said with a giggle. "God! He was *so* embarrassed when Janey and I finally managed to get him out but, because of all the struggling in order to haul him out, he lost his diapers, so all was revealed." Debbie could resist a further giggle. "According to what I overheard, the reason why he had *no hair down there* is because they'd shaved *down there* as well!"

A deeply embarrassed and furious Dee-Dee, fully wrapped in a hastily produced blanket, calmy informed the police officers called to the scene that the whole incident was nothing more than a drunken prank that had "gotten out of hand", and no, he wouldn't be pressing charges.

On the drive back to the hotel, Dee-Dee steadfastly ignored the curious (and obviously amused) glances in the rear-view mirror by the officer behind the wheel; his mind focussed on Malcom Duval and associates and how they would pay for the gross indignity they had put him through.

TWENTY-FOUR

MAEBELLE'S BUNGALOW - BEVERLY HILLS HOTEL

"If they can do this to you, Christ knows what they could have planned for me," croaked Maebelle as she sat eyeing a sheepish Dee-Dee sitting opposite, his bald pate sporting a hastily borrowed peaked cap. "But what I don't understand is why, despite the caller sounding suspiciously like Malcom Duval, you agreed to meet him for a drink and furthermore, when he did a no show, alarm bells didn't start ringing in your former coiffed head! It's pretty damn obvious Duval and his henchmen would be waiting outside for you to do exactly what you did."

"I wouldn't be at all surprised if that wretched Baz Malone was somehow involved as well," said Dee-Dee sulkily, "seeing he never got over me ousting him role wise and every otherwise with *High Jinks in High C!*"

"Pah!" spat Maebelle. "Baz Malone isn't capable of even a wank! No, it's Malcom Duval who's responsible and we - yes, *we* - know it!" She gave a snicker. "It's been puzzling me who, with your new *hairless* do. You remind me of!"

"If you say Baldy Brynner, I swear I will never, *ever,* speak to you again!" squawked Dee-Dee.

"No, not Baldy Brynner! I'm not *that* unimaginative!" crooned Maebelle.

"Who then? Prince William?" camped Dee-Dee.

"No, not Prince William! He's far too young!" shrieked Maebelle. "Think action man Jason Stratham!"

"Jason Stratham!" shrilled Dee-Dee. "Have I ever told you how much I love you. Maebelle? Jason Stratham, eh? Talk about a lucky dip!"

"As I said before, and I'll say it again, first you and then me," murmured Maebelle. "Therefore, before we do anything else, we must inform Oscar of what happened to you. I will insist Bromeando Films make suitable arrangements for us to have personal bodyguards, twenty-four-seven, until our return to London. But before I ring him, are you quite sure about *not* involving the police?"

"Quite sure," replied Dee-Dee. "First of all, I have no proof it *was* Malcom Duval who had me snaffled away, and secondly, I would much prefer to have Sylvester's very capable head of security deal with this. His name is Rhett La Maar and, according to Syl, is unbeatable at persuading someone to say they're sorry!"

"Sylvester appears to be a man of many hidden, talents," snickered Maebelle.

"That he is, Maebelle dear, that he is," purred Dee-Dee. "Not only talented, but *uber*-talented, and a good friend in both need and deed." Tapping his nose with his forefinger he added slyly. "According to delicious rumour, a few years ago your now discarded Mr. Preston Pulmonary was taking great delight in boasting here, there, and everywhere, that all he had to say was 'Ophelia, may I feel ya' and Mrs De Sade's panted reply would be an ecstatic 'Is this a dagger I see before me?' At Mr. De Sade's request, Sylvester's Rhett La Maar made sure Mr. Pulmonary removed such a request from his repertoire!"

"Preston Pulmonary?" chortled Maebelle. "Please tell me you're joking!"

"Of course, I am!" trilled Dee-Dee. "What's more, I've got you laughing!"

"Why don't you mix us a whacking jug of martinis whilst I telephone Oscar," crooned Maebelle reaching her mobile. "Hopefully I will not have a fit of the giggles due to an unexpected vision of Oscar De Sade in doublet and hose - or even a kilt - springing to mind! Hose or Oscar-winning night fighter being the operative words!"

GODFREY STREET

"Leo or Lobie! Could one of you see who's at the door, please! Bloody sneakers! I'll be down in a second!" called Lulu from where she sat on the stairs dealing with an errant lace on one of her trainers.

"I'll deal with it!" yodelled Leo as he headed for the front door.

"Pizza for Mayhew," grinned the young man standing on the doorstep.

"Er . . . okay . . . thanks," smiled Leo. "Anything to pay?"

"No, I'm simply the delivery boy," said the young man. "Enjoy!" he called before jumping on his scooter and disappearing down the street.

"Pizzicato Pizzas," muttered Leo looking at the box he was holding. "Never heard of them, but Lulu obviously has. Better take it down to the kitchen."

"Who was at the door?" asked Lulu on entering the sitting room.

"Pizzicato Pizzas," replied Leo. "I left the box in the kitchen."

"Pizzicato Pizzas?" said Lulu. "I never ordered a pizza, and, if I do, I always order from Domino's. So, who the hell are Pizzicato Pizzas?"

"You left the box where?" said Lobie glancing up from the *Evening Standard.*

"In the kitchen. Why?"

"Because we're supposed to be extra vigilant, that's why," snapped Lobie tossing the paper aside and rising from his chair. "And if an unknown pizza company delivers a pizza which Lulu didn't order, we'd better check it out."

"Then I'd better go and fetch the damned pizza and a knife so that we can examine the wretched thing," said Leo a touch sarcastically.

"Yes, you better," sniped Lobie.

"Okay," carolled Leo on his return. "Herewith the ticking pizza!"

"Ticking pizza?" cried Lulu. "You never said anything about it ticking, you idiot! For God's sake, get the fucking thing out of here!"

"Jesus, Lulu, I was only joking," said Leo rolling his eyes, "Obviously I would *not* have brought the bloody box into the house if it was *ticking*! Jesus! Get a life!" He nodded toward Flip Flop who was sitting eyeing the box, "At least someone's keen to have a slice!"

"Don't you *dare!*" shrieked Lulu. "As I never ordered any pizza, whoever did could have easily put poison in it!"

"Now you're being doubly paranoid," said Leo with another rolling of his eyes. Opening the box, he said mischievously. "It looks a perfectly normal pizza to me so, in order to put your bestselling, uber- active mind to rest, Lulu dear, allow Leo the Braveheart to try a slice."

"Leo, please don't," pleaded Lulu, almost in tears.

"Too late," grinned Leo as he sliced the pizza.

"Did you hear that?" hissed Lobie.

"Hear what?" said Leo about to take a bite.

"When you sliced the pizza, I'm sure I heard a slight clicking or a crunching sound. Here, give me that!"

Snatching the slice from Leo's hand, Lobie placed in onto a side plate and began to gently scrape away the filling from the crust. "Bloody hell." he muttered. "I don't believe it!"

"Believe *what*?" cried Lulu.

"Slivers of glass," murmured Lobie. "The filling is filled with slivers of glass! Jesus! Imagine what that could have done to your insides on swallowing it!"

"But who . . ." stammered Lulu.

"But who? But who?" shouted Lobie. "How about Dee-Dee? How about Maebelle? How about Andy McCulloch Robert Apps or Macom Duval! That's who! And that's for starters!"

"Shouldn't we call the police," said Leo nervously.

"And what good would that do?" snapped Lobie. "Apart from the fucking pizza itself, what leads do we have? You can bet on it that Pizzicato Pizzas don't exist." He pointed at the discarded box. "What's more, I bet the delivery boy was wearing gloves. Added to which, there must be endless other fingerprints on the box."

"So, what *are* you suggesting?" snapped Lulu.

"What am *I* suggesting?" echoed Lobie. "I'm *suggesting* it's time we take off the kid-gloves and teach those various arseholes a lesson for once and for all. Not necessarily fatal; but as near as damnit."

"Easier said than done," quipped Leo, "seeing they're all out of the country."

"Out of the country, maybe, but still on the planet," said Lobie sarcastically. Turning to Lulu, he pointed again at the discarded box. "A pizza, to me, means Italian; so, let's start with your writer friend. Only this time it'll more than ineffectual fireworks."

"Hear! Hear!" chorused Lulu and Leo.

Giving the two a thumbs up, Lobie said cheerfully. "Okay, my friends, whatever we decide to do must be carefully thought out, checked and then double-checked as we can't afford any slipups."

"Hmm," pondered Lulu. "I know I keep banging on about a personal attack on Apps, Andy, whatever, but instead of attacking *him* why not attack what I see as his Achilles hell; the heel, in this case, being the bland Dr Cordell."

"Go on," said Lobie admiringly.

"First of all, he's local which cuts out having to rely on someone over in Italy and, secondly, if we kidnap the doting doctor, we then ask for a substantial ransom or else." Lulu gave a giggle. "In order to prove how serious we are; on sending the ransom demand we include a Vincent or a Getty!"

"A Vincent or a Getty?" said Leo. "I don't quite follow?"

"We include one of the doctor's ears!" carolled Lulu.

"You mean we cut off one of his ears?" said Leo with an audible gulp.

"I think what Lulu means is that we explain to the doctor it's a case of either or," interrupted Lobie with a chuckle. "Either he, the doctor, tells us how we can get an ear from the local morgue; the alternative to *him* being the donor!"

"You took the words right out of my wicked mouth," chortled Lulu. "However, when it comes to Malcom Duval, that's a very different kettle of fugu fish!"

"Fugu fish?" questioned Leo. "Once again, I don't quite follow?"

"Fugu fish also known as puffer fish and highly poisonous," said Lulu deadpan. "In other words, a kettle of *poisonous* fish."

"Oh," said Leo, looking none the wiser. "I take it that was meant as a joke?"

"Maybe, Leo; maybe not," said Lobie dryly. "So, Lulu dear, tell us more." He gave a chuckle. "No doubt the *fugu* - read fuck you - plot thickens!"

DEE-DEE'S BUNGALOW - BEVERLY HILLS HOTEL

"Mr. Devereaux?"

"Speaking!" carolled Dee-Dee who had early been waiting for the call.

"The name's La Maar, Rhett La Maar, head of Bromeando Studio security," said a deep bass voice. "A Miss Maebelle called me earlier and explained that you were associates of Mr. Sylvester Steinberg, the film director, and about a situation troubling you. Miss Maebelle emphasised the situation had nothing to do with the studio and whatever is said between the three of us, is strictly confidential."

"Absolutely correct, Mr. La Maar," replied Dee-Dee. He allowed for a few seconds to tick by before saying in a no-nonsense voice. "Mr. La Maar, if I were to ask you ask you about the possibility of undertaking a contract which some may - I stress the may - may involve something a tad shady, would you still be interested?"

"Suggest a time and a place," replied La Maar. He gave a chuckle. "I take that answers your question?"

"Seven o'clock at my bungalow at the Beverly Hills Hotel," cooed Dee-Dee, followed by the number for the bungalow plus his mobile number.

*

"Mr. Rhett La Maar, I resume?" carolled Dee-Dee on opening the door. "Dee-Dee Devereaux," he added, proffering his hand. "I do like a man who is spot on time. Pray, *do* come in."

"We have met before, Mr. Devereaux," smiled Rhett La Maar who, as if to justify his first name, was the splitting image of Clark Gable, the original Rhett Butler of *Gone with the Wind* fame; even to the protruding ears, but without the moustache.

"We have?" questioned Dee-Dee. *If we have, then I'm quite sure I would have remembered you Mr. Rhett Clark Gable La Maar!* he thought with an inward snicker.

"On the set of *High Jinks.* I was introduced to you and Miss Maebelle."

"But of course! Silly me!" crowed Dee-Dee. "How could I forget!"

Just testing and one down for you, Mr. Devereaux, thought Rhett La Maar. *We've never met before. However, Sylvester did warn me you were somewhat liberal with the truth!*

"So, how about you tell me all," said La Maar with a whiter than white smile.

"That I shall," crooned Dee-Dee. "But before I do, I have something I'd like you to peruse *after* our meeting." Reaching for a package on the coffee table he handed it to his bemused guest. "It's a book by someone named Robert Apps. A book titled *The Omnipotent,* and a book that speaks for itself."

"Thank you, Mr. Devereaux! - "Dee-Dee, per-lease" - "thank you, Dee-Dee, and please call me Rhett. (*Call you Rhett?* thought Dee-Dee mischievously. *Does that mean I may become your Miss Scarlet O'Horror?*) Now, if you would care to explain what you require of me; something you referred to as" - he made air quotes - "a tad shady. Once I have an idea of what could be involved, I will need a day or two to consider the pros and cons before I give my answer."

"A day or two to consider your answer and a day or two in which read Apps's book," trilled Dee-Dee. "May I quickly say I appreciate your fee will be substantia due to *two* people being involved as opposed to one. Happily, the fee will be agreed to without any quibbling."

"As Mr. Steinberg would have told you, once we agree a fee - any expenses are extra - I will require fifty percent paid into an overseas account, the balance on completion," said Rhett in a no-nonsense voice.

"Take it as done," said Dee-Dee with a coquettish smile. He gave a start. "Manners! Devereaux! Manners!" he trilled. "Forgive me *Rhett.* A libation of sorts? A martini? A glass of wine? White or *rouge.* If I don't have your preference here, I can easily whatever you wish from the hotel."

"A glass of white wine would do nicely, thank you," replied Rhett. *Do nicely?* he thought. *Christ, what gives with this guy and his la-di-dah talk. My 'do nicely' sounding exactly like the sort of reply* he'd *give! Unbelievable!*

"Your wine, sir," crooned Dee-Dee handing Rhett a brimming wine glass. "A chilled Pinot Grigio which, I feel sure, will titillate those discerning taste buds! Ha ha! I, true to my decadent fashion, am making do with a martini!"

Settling himself on a chair opposite, Dee-Dee took a long sip of his martini, placed his glass down and said matter-of-factly. "Now we're well-armed and sitting comfortably, it's time for me to reveal all."

Hopefully that's an understatement, thought Rhett, *otherwise you'll have a great deal to apologise for, Mr. Sylvester!*

Raising his glass, Rhett said with a grin. "Fire away, Dee-Dee! I'm all ears!

That you most certainly are, Mr. Rhett La Maar, thought Dee-Dee lewdly. *And if your* ears *stick out like that, I wonder what else can. Down, Devereaux! Down. In all senses of the word!*

Rhett sat listening, his face expressionless, to what Dee-Dee had to say.

"So, that's it in a nutshell, said Dee-Dee smugly," on ending his recitation. "Mr. Duval toeless in San Francisco or here in L. A. with Mr. Apps toeless in Italy. So, the proverbial ball is now well and truly in your court."

"Yes, in my court and well and truly caught," replied Rhett with an indiscernible smile. "Right," he said, simultaneously rising to his feet and taking hold of the book. "Thank you for the wine, Dee-Dee, and, as I said, I'll give you a call or text you within the next day or two. Now, if you'll excuse me."

Before Dee-Dee could clamber to *his* feet, Rhett had already reached the front door and let himself out.

"Well, fuck you too," muttered Dee-Dee. "Talk about a dramatic exit! A sure-fire sign of *arrivederci*, Italy and piss off San Fag Crisco or L.A. methinks. So, let's wait and see. However, I have a strong feeling Maebelle and *moi* will have to think again."

Two days later received a text as promised.

"Bastard!" screeched Dee-Dee on reading the succinct message. "Bloody bastard!" he shrieked hurling his mobile onto the floor where it lay unscathed, Rhett's message, *Unfortunately I am not a podiatrist and therefore cannot help you. Good luck. Rhett,* still visible.

Taking several deep, slow breaths, Dee-Dee finally managed to calm down. Muttering a seemingly endless torrent of expletives, he poured himself a large Remy Martin and, after a few restorative swallows, rescued his mobile from the floor, deleted Rhett's text and called Sylvester.

"Aha!" cried Sylvester on promptly answering. "I've been waiting for our call!" He gave a chuckle. "A screenwriter as well as a closet podiatrist! Whatever next? A closet gynaecologist?"

"Jesus! Sylvester!" shrieked Dee-Dee. "It's not fucking funny!"

"I find it fucking hilarious," said Sylvester. "Fucking hilarious and fucking ludicrous. Please don't tell me you seriously expected a man of Rhett's calibre to cut off someone's toes? Whatever next? Perm their pubes?"

"As I said, it's not fucking funny, Sylvester!" shrilled Dee-Dee.

"Well, it certainly got me, Rhett and a few others laughing," chuckled Sylvester. "Sorry I am unable to be of any help despite me being a deft hand at carving the Thanksgiving turkey." Unable to stop himself, Sylvester burst into further peals of laughter.

"Arsehole!" snapped Dee-Dee terminating the call. "Now, I'd better call the gorgon herself. But before I do that, another swallow of Remy goes without saying, for God only knows how she'll react!"

TWENTY-FIVE

MAEBELLE'S BUNGALOW - BEVERLY HILLS HOTEL

"What you've told me comes as no great surprise," said Maebelle airily.

Taking a dainty sip of an unusually early martini - Dee-Dee having advised her she should have one in preparation for what he was about to tell her - she added snappily. "It only goes to prove that the likes of Mr. Rhett La Maar, Preston Pulmonary and that ghastly Ophelia De Sade are all the same; narcissistic and two-faced!"

"Oh," murmured Dee-Dee, unable to contain his disbelief and relief at Maebelle's unexpected response to Rhett La Maar's text. "Oh," he repeated. "So, you're not pissed off with me?"

"Why on earth should I be pissed off at you?" said Maebelle in a tone more Mary Poppins than Cruella de Vil. Her surprised response interrupted by a ringing of the front doorbell.

"I'll get it!" chimed Dee-Dee hurrying to answer. "It's a delivery of an enormous bunch of red roses!" he called from the front door. "An entire field to be exact!"

Re-entering the sitting room, the size of the bunch he was carrying literally covering his whole frame, he barely managed to peer round the bunch in order to say mischievously. "There's a card from this extravagant, obviously *disillusioned* admirer!"

"Gimme! Gimme!" yodelled Maebelle. "If it's from who I think it is, it could be the answer to our tiresome little hiccup!"

Tearing open the envelope with her teeth, Maebelle gave a loud whoop. "As I thought! Extreme apologies from Mr. Pulmonary along with a heavily - underlined in red - please, please call me!" Eyeing Dee-Dee, she said smugly. "As I so rightly predicted, a very possible answer to our present predicament. Therefore, without any further ado, let me call the pathetic, panting creep!"

"Is that wise? Shouldn't you let him suffer a bit?"

"Is that wise?" repeated Maebelle. "Let him suffer a bit? It's more than wise Dee-Dee Devereaux, when what we have in mind for Messrs. Duval and Apps could see them hobbling for the hills: if they were able! So, don't be such a wuss! Hand me my mobile so I can call Mr. Please-Please and have him come crawling back not only for my forgiveness, but to do my - our - wicked bidding! And then some!""

"Preston, it's Maebelle," said Maebelle on the call being promptly answered. Ignoring Preston's gasped "Maebelle? Oh, thank you! Thank *God* you've called!" Maebelle said crisply. "I'm calling to thank *you* for those totally unnecessary roses. So, thank you, and please don't bother me with anymore such plaudits as they will not be appreciated!"

"Oh, Maebelle! Maebelle!" wailed Preston. "I've been wracking my brains trying to work out what I could have said to offend you, whatever . . ."

"Wracking your brains?" interrupted Maebelle with a snort. "That must be a first!"

"Oh. Maebelle! Whatever it is I'm guilty of, I'm so, so sorry. Please forgive me and tell me what I have to do to make amends!"

"First things first, Preston," crooned Maebelle, "I was given to understand that *artists* were of a sensitive disposition but not once, not *once*, did you take into account that I could be worried about how my film, *High Hinks in High C!* would be received by the critics, and more so, by the discerning public! Not *once* did you take into account that the most minor of upsets could trigger off a major upset!"

"But what did I *do* or say for you to come up such dreadful misunderstandings?" wailed a bewildered Preston.

"If you don't know now, then you never will know," purred Maebelle, giving a bemused Dee-Dee a thumbs up. "Now, if you'll excuse me . . ."

"Maebelle! Maebelle! Please don't hang up!" implored Preston, cutting in. "All I ask is that you have a final dinner with me, tonight if possible: a last supper as it were. But at least give me a chance to apologise in person and, sadly, present you with a farewell gift."

"A last supper and farewell gift you say," murmured Maebelle giving a now doubled-up Dee-Dee a wink. "Sounds a touch ominous to me. However,

I'll unhappily agree to your invitation but only on condition Dee-Dee Devereaux, my port in any storm, joins us."

"Jesus!" gasped Dee-Dee, now lying on the carpet, clutching his stomach. "Put the poor guy out his misery before I wet myself!"

"Dee-Dee Devereaux join us?" said Preston weakly.

"Yes. Dee-Dee Devereaux joins us for dinner or else no dinner. *Capiche?*"

"Yes, I understand," came the sullen reply. "Er . . . which would you prefer? Dinner here at Malibu or in a restaurant."

"Definitely a restaurant," snapped Maebelle. "I suggest you leave a message with the hotel saying where we should meet and we'll see you there, *No*, Preston! Do. Not. Interrupt! I have no desire to be collected by you or Tubby the Tuba-cum-Turbo! We'll see you when we see you at whatever place you instruct reception. Talking of reception, be prepared for a suitably cool one from both of us as Dee-Dee Devereaux is not all amused by the cruel manner and the way in how you upset sensitive me."

Before Preston could respond, Maebelle clicked off and, shrieking with laughter, joined Dee-Dee on the floor.

Ten minutes and another martini later, Maebelle received a call from reception saying Mr. Pulmonary had confirmed their meeting for dinner for eight o'clock that evening at nearby *Il Cielo,* a popular Italian restaurant known for its exceptional cuisine.

"*Il Cielo?*" carolled Dee-Dee. "All that delicious pasta! Yum! Yum! Happy tum!" He gave a giggle. "These include a dreamy, *pappardelle al cinghiale* - pasta flavoured with wild boar - and therefore the total antithesis of our *boring* host!"

His comeback causing the two to burst out into further paroxysms of laughter.

VILLA CASA DEGLI ARCHI

"Good morning, Mr. McCulloch, it's Dr Cynthia Woodhouse calling."

"Dr Cynthia Woodhouse?"

"An associate of Dr Cordell's."

"Of course!" replied Andy, "Forgive me for not recognising your voice. Er . . . is something wrong? Has something happened to Andy - Mr. McCulloch?"

"Well, yes and no. I don't wish to alarm you, Mr. McCulloch, but Dr Cordell didn't turn up at the hospital today. I've tried ringing the house, but without success, so I was wondering if you had heard from him." Dr Woodhouse gave a forced laugh. "Unless he's there with you!"

"No, he's not here," said Andy tersely. "I was beginning to wonder why *he* didn't call *me* earlier as he usually calls dead on seven before leaving for the hospital. However, as I've been working nonstop on a new novel, I wasn't duly concerned." He gave a forced laugh. "But, as you say, Clive - Dr Cordell - is known for going walkabout now and then."

"Like you, I'm sure he'll turn up," said Dr Woodhouse, doing nothing to hide the concern in her voice. "Once again, my apologies for disturbing you, Mr. McCulloch, as I know you're a busy man."

"It's no problem, Dr Woodhouse. Please ask Dr Cordell to call me should he get in touch with you, and vice versa."

"How very odd?" murmured Andy replacing the receiver. "I'd better try the house and see if *I* get any response. However, if Woodhouse has been trying, it's more than likely to go to voicemail." He gave a wry chuckle. "Well, whatever devious mischief you're up to, Clive, my love, you'd better have a bloody good explanation or heads will roll!" Andy gave a further chuckle. "Maybe old Andy's a tad jealous, but hopefully your explanation will erase any nasty, niggling suspicions."

A deeply worried Andy received an anonymous text early the next day. Gazing in disbelief at the message on the screen of his mobile, it took him several minutes to absorb what he read.

If you wish to see Clive Cordell again, we will require a cash payment of £50,000 in used £50 notes left at address to follow. Once you accept our demand you will receive a telephone call later as to your decision and, if your decision is favourable, details as to where the exchanges can take place. The money in exchange for Clive Cordel. Do not contact the police. If you do, you can expect parts of Clive Cordell to be delivered to you over the coming days.

"Lulu fucking Mayhew!" roared Andy, his face distorted with fury. With trembling fingers. he dialled Lulu's mobile number. "Idiot," he muttered. "No doubt when she sees who's calling, she'll ignore it. However, as I do have three other lines, let's call *all* her fucking numbers and let them keep on ringing until she, or someone else simply *has* to answer!"

"*Yes*? Damnit!" snapped Lulu on answering her second landline; her two lines other lines ringing in the background.

"You know *exactly* who's responsible for those other phones I can hear ringing in the background, you devious bitch, you!" stormed Andy. "Don't call the police if I wish to see Clive Cordell again? Fifty thousand pounds in used, fifty-pound notes. Jesus. Mayhew, how your fucking, trite, so-called novels ever sell, is more of a mystery than even Robert Apps can ever write!"

"I have no idea what you're talking about, Mr. McCulloch-Apps," purred Lulu. "And if you continue to be so abusive, I shall have no alternative but to report you."

"You do that, Miss Mayhew and you can bet on what you have the audacity to call your talent, you'll never type or print another word ever again. And no, you are not getting one penny, and yes, you will be releasing Clive Cordell without delay. If I don't hear from Clive within the next hour, you have only yourself and your two equally laughable cronies to blame. Finally. Miss Lulu Mayhew, please note this is not a threat. It's a fact."

Andy hung up, took a deep beath and dialled another number. On hearing a cheerful "Altitude Air Services" he said in a no-nonsense voice. "Alan, it's Andy McCulloch. I need someone - preferably Collie who knows the ropes - to collect me from Christoper Columbus Airport, Genoa, asap and get me back to London. I'll be leaving the villa within a matter of minutes and be at the airport in a couple of hours."

"Collie just happens to be here in the office with me," said Alan, "so, consider it done!"

GODFREY STREET

"As Robert Burns so rightly wrote, 'the best laid plans of mice and men so often go awry: the mouse on this occasion being Andy McCulloch who, on receiving our text, immediately morphed into the mouse that roared," said Lulu dryly as she, Leo and Lobie sat having what she described as a "hastily arranged pow-wow" following Andy's incensed telephone call.

Staring at the two men, she added matter-of-factly. "Knowing Andy McCulloch as I do, we shouldn't take his words lightly so, sad as it may seem, we'd better let Clive Cordell go."

"Let him go?" exclaimed Lobie. "C'mon, Lulu! This is not the Lulu we know and love! I say we keep him locked up in that crummy Pimliico bolthole of mine; send McCulloch the borrowed ear if he doesn't come with the money or an offer for sorts and see what happens."

"Sorry, Lobie, but I agree with Lulu," said Leo fiddling nervously with his Pinky ring made in the shape skull with green agate eyes. "Andy McCulloch is not someone to be trifled with seeing he immediately put two and two together and came up with a resounding us. What's more, it wouldn't surprise me if he wasn't on his way back to London as we speak!"

Giving Leo a glare, Lobie turned his attention back to Lulu. "Lulu?"

"Sorry, Lobie, I'm with Leo," said Lulu. She gave a shiver. "If you'd heard Andy McCulloch's voice when he said I'd never type or print another word ever again . . . it was terrifying! So, we let Clive go and hopefully he won't kick up too much of a fuss at what we can try to pass off as some stupid caper."

"Jesus, talk about caving in," sniped Lobie. "And if you and Leo think McCulloch will forgive and forget and walk off, hand in hand, with Cordell into the proverbial sunset; you've another think coming. You've only got to read one of his books, for Chrissake!"

"I'm still willing to give it a try," said Lulu solemnly. "So, Leo dear, if you wouldn't mind, please go and collect Clive, apologies profusely and, if he agrees, drop him back at the flat."

"As Big Arnie said, I'll be back!" replied Leo with a grin as he made for the door.

Lobie sat glowering at Lulu before saying in a strained voice. "I swear you'll regret what you've just gone and done, Lulu. Christ, you're going to regret it!"

"I'm already regretting it," said Lulu reaching for Lobie's hand. "Oh, Lobie, what have I done!"

"Hopefully I can get hold of Leo before he gets to the flat," muttered Lobie reaching for his mobile and punching Leo's number. "C'mon! C'mon!" he growled, "Answer your fucking phone!" After what seemed an eternity, he turned to Lulu and said softly. "It keeps going to voice mail."

"Let's keep trying," said Lulu in a strained voice. "Let's keep trying!"

After ten minutes Leo picked up. "Needless to say, a highly indignant Clive refused to accept any apology whatsoever and as for my offer to drive him home" - Leo gave a snigger - "forget it. I have to say I never realised there were so many alternatives for fuck off and fuck you!"

"Oh, my God!" gasped Lulu,

"That's fucking torn it" muttered Lobie.

*

Andy was about to board the Phenom 300 when his mobile rang. On seeing the name of the caller, he gave a huge sigh of relief. "Clive!" he shouted on answering. "Are you okay? Did those fuckers hurt you?"

"Andy! Darling Andy! I'm fine. Pissed off but unscathed!"

"Thank Christ for that! Look, my love, I'm about to board my plane and will be landing at The City Airport in a couple of hours' time."

"I'll be there to meet you!" cried Clive. "Jesus, Andy, that lot are going to pay for this!"

"And how!" vowed Andy. "Darling, Collie's beckoning so I must go. I'll see you at the airport. Love you!"

TWENTY-SIX

IL CIELO RESTAUARNT - BEVERLY HILLS

"I thought you said he was a doppelganger for Gary Cooper?" hissed Dee-Dee in an aside as he and Maebelle were shown to a table where a nervous Preston Pulmonary rose nervously in order to greet them. "Not Gary Cooped-up!"

"Hush ya mouth, mother-*fukka*!" whispered Maebelle. "The hombre may look cooped-up, but he could also be the solution to our *Toeless in San Franciso* manoeuvre!"

On reaching the table, Maebelle gave a theatrical shriek. "Preston *darling*! Divine to see you again after so few hours! This *stunning* young man with me is *not* a one-eyed reincarnated Truman Capote but Dee-Dee Devereaux, an equally naughty hee-hee T.C. type scribe!"

She glanced round the attractive restaurant. "I've always wanted to experience what it must be like to be an actual *pasta* and perhaps you, dear Preston, are about make such a *fulfilling* dream come true!"

"I am so pleased to see you, Maebelle," croaked Preston, his face reddening. "And a pleasure to meet you . . . er . . . Dee-Dee." He gestured at an ice bucket. "I appreciate champagne is not usually served with pasta, but as this is a celebration . . ."

"Champagne sounds divine!" crooned Maebelle.

"Too, too divine!" carolled Dee-Dee.

"Er . . . spl-spl-splendid!" stammered Preston giving the hovering waiter a nod. "Champagne it is!"

"Yes, so it is! Unless my heavenly peepers deceive me!" camped Maebelle. Sitting down she eyed the increasingly confused Preston and said with a typical model Maebelle smile. "Forgive us, Preston, dear, we're only teasing! It really *is* good to see you. I can see I'm going to enjoy my dinner, despite not having had a nibble of anything they have to offer! I can tell, just tell, it's going to be a super, duper evening!"

The next half hour was spent in light-hearted small talk during which Preston was happy to take the lead telling wild tales of walks through the Amazon jungle in order to photograph and sketch various wildflowers and orchids he would later replicate on canvas.

"Badly," mouthed Maebelle discreetly at a snickering Dee-Dee.

"So very Bunthorne," carolled Dee-Dee rapturously when Preston paused to take a breath.

"So very Bunthorne?" repeated Preston a touch querulously.

"You in the Amazon jungle clutching an orchid reminded me of Gilbert and Sullivan's Bunthorne in *Patience* and his delicious ditty, *If you walk down Piccadilly with a poppy or a lily in your medieval hand*! And the thought of *you*, Preston, walking alongside the mighty Amazon, a rare *orchid* in your hand! A happening I would truly love to see!"

"We're here for dinner, Dee-Dee, dear," interrupted Maebelle on seeing Preston starting to visibly wilt in front of them. "Not a walk on the wild side or a jungle trek!"

"Er . . . more champagne, anyone?" croaked Preston looking thoroughly confused by Dee-Dee's interpretation of his artistic forays into the jungle.

"Why don't we order?" suggested Maebelle brightly. "Dear Dee-Dee strongly recommends the *pappardelle al cinghiale - roasted wild boar in Barolo wine . . .*"

"Hopefully I'm not seen as a competitor!" quipped Preston as if suddenly coming to life. His reaction causing Maebelle and Dee-Dee to burst out laughing.

"Oh, Preston, you are a one!" shrieked Maebelle; her comment resulting in a guffawing Dee- Dee to fall from his chair onto the floor.

"Sorry about that," said Dee-Dee after two concerned waiters had helped him back onto his chair. "It's just this evening is proving to be such fun that I simply lost control of my naughty, naughty frame!"

Giving Dee-Dee her version of the evil eye, Maebelle turned to Preston and said with feigned interest. "Preston, dear, have you ever participated in the manly sport of big-game hunting?"

"Big-game hunting?" echoed Preston, obviously confused by the change of topic. "No, why?"

"Are you interested in gardening? Especially *topiary*?" carolled Dee-Dee.

"Big-game hunting? Gardening? Especially topiary?" repeated Preston. "Forgive me, fellas, but I am now completely lost at what this is all about, so, if you would care to explain."

"Oh, have no fear, Preston dear, we're more than willing to explain, but only after we finish our delicious dinner and you, dear Preston, have downed your nth grappa!"

"Sounds good to me!" enthused Preston, "so, let's tuck in!"

*

"Just as well he has Tubby the tuba waiting there for him in order to take him back to Malibu," snorted Maebelle as she and Dee-Dee watched Preston walk away with exaggerated care from the table toward the entrance of the restaurant.

"Do you think he really *is* on board. More importantly, is he reliable?"

"With the thought of a weekend with me at the Sands, Barbados, he's more than reliable," crooned Maebelle. "He's firmly caught; hook, line and sinker!"

"Yes, provided it doesn't turn out to be a case of hook, line and *stinker,* then I have no alternative but to agree with you," snickered Dee-Dee. "But methinks yon drunken wannabe painter is more pillow squawk than action!"

"We can only wait and see," murmured Maebelle, "and as this could very well be a rehearsal for our waiting and seeing, why not another nightcap afore we go?"

LONDON - CHEYNE WALK

"We know Lulu Mayhew was the one behind this particular little plot; she and those two arse-lickers, Maseko and Murrain," growled Andy. "But, back to the actual kidnapping; any idea as to the actual abductors?"

"One was definitely Murrain," replied Clive without hesitation. "Despite wearing a mask and gloves, the glove on his left hand couldn't disguise that skull ring of his; a ring which was glaringly on show today."

"A prime example of how simple *slips* sink ships," muttered Andy, "and a definitive way in which Lulu Mayhew can be given a taste of her own medicine."

"What? You surely can't mean we get someone to cut-off Murrain's ring finger and send it to her?"

"Why only his finger? Why not his whole hand?" replied Andy. "After all, I did warn her that she would never type or write again had she harmed you by sending me your ear - false or not - so, what better way to validate my threat of things to come."

"Brilliant!" chortled Clive. "The very thought of what she had mind causing my still intact ear to literally tingle as we speak!"

"Well said," chuckled Andy. "Seeing her latest little plot was well and truly nipped in the bud, it got me thinking. You may or may not remember - it was in the news some time back - something about an estate agent who mysteriously disappeared and something I made a note of as potential fodder for a novel. Interesting to note that the agent - Morden or something like what - was at school with Mayhew and her lot, so it wouldn't surprise me if she didn't have something to do with Morden, Motcomb or whoever's disappearance."

"Aw, c'mon Andy! Now you're letting your author mind really take over! Morden, Motcomb, whoever, is more than likely living it up on embezzled funds in some exotic venue and not necessarily feeding worms or fishes!"

"You're probably right; although I wouldn't put it past her!"

"Getting back to what we were talking about. So, instead of 'off with his head' you're now suggesting we change this to 'off with his hand?" Clive gave a snigger. "Cleeever, Andy, my love. Very clever. Have you any one in mind who could possibly do this for you? Us?"

"I most certainly do," said Andy smugly. "A somewhat fey ex-con who is a hive of information when it comes to what's going on in the secret, sordid underworld of today's society." He added with a grin. "He goes under the name of Dorain Beige."

"Dorian Beige?" exclaimed Clive.

"Wait until you meet him! I'm sure you'll agree with me when I say he should have called himself Dorian *Coelacanth*! Christ knowns where the beige comes from!"

"So, when do I meet this coy fish?" giggled Clive.

"This evening as a matter of fact, seeing I've invited him and his sidekick, Chucky Craven - I joke not - to dinner!"

"Dorain Beige and Chucky Craven? They sound like two characters from one of your chiller thrillers," chortled Clive. "These two I can't *wait* to meet. Are we dining in or out?"

"Oh, definitely in. I've organised the uber-efficient Bernie Law and hubby Ralph to deal with it."

"I take it Ralph will *not* be serving Bloody Marys as an aperitif and Bernie will be avoiding her usual mouth-watering rare roast beef accompanied by a beefy Bordeaux followed by strawberries or raspberries!"

"Strawberries or raspberries no; but blood orange slices in cognac, yes," chuckled Andy. "Er . . . where are you scurrying off to?"

"Off to pop my red cords in the trouser press," replied Clive. Pausing momentarily in the doorway he said with a feigned frown. "Do you think if I also wear my red shirt from Turnbull & Asser it could be a bit much?"

"Far too much," chuckled Andy, "so I suggest you simply wear your red skants and leave it at that, as I am quite sure Dorian and Chucky will find a pair of bulging skants much more their taste!"

*

"They're here!" whispered Clive on hearing the front door buzzer,

"And right on time," grinned Andy. "Give me a sec as I told Ralph not to answer the door as I'd prefer to let them in myself." On his way toward the entrance hall, he said with a wink. "*Love* the dark blue chinos and cream rollneck *Very* scary!"

"My thoughts exactly," giggled Clive craning his neck in an attempt to get a glimpse of the two mystery guests once Andy opened the door.

"Oh?" he muttered as Andy warmly greeted the couple. "Dorian Beige and Chucky Craven? There must be some mistake because I'm quite sure the couple Andy's just welcomed are none other than Messrs. Mutt and Jeff!"

A smiling Andy introduced the two arrivals to a grinning Clive. Gesturing toward a beaming Ralph he added cheerfully. "A welcome drink? Clive and I are having our de rigueur martinis but please ask Ralph for what you'd like."

"A Bloody Mary for me. please, er . . . Ralph," croaked Dorian.

"The same for me, thank you Ralph," rasped Chucky. The two guests unaware of the ensuing looks between their hosts.

Whatever you do, whatever you do, repeated Clive to himself. *Do* not *refer to them as Mutt or Jeff,*

*

As expected, Bernie's dinner proved to be delicious, the wine intoxicating while the conversation flowed with Dorian and Chucky keeping their hosts entertained with endless stories of putting irritating situations to right. Or, to quote a cheerful Dorian. "Presenting the chosen one with a colourful *Colombian* necktie instead of a boring run-of-the-mill bowtie."

"Right!" said Andy in a no-nonsense voice. "It's showtime! Time to tell you chaps what we'd like you to do for us. We have two tasks in mind: both are local and, as always, are to be carried out as if by a pair of ghosts."

"In other words, *not* a pair of your regular Caspers," croaked Dorian deadpan.

"Pair of regular Caspers?" questioned Clive.

"Unfriendly as opposed to friendly ghosts," rasped Chucky.

A grinning Andy rose from the table in order to collect two envelopes from the sideboard. "Explicit details are all in here. The envelope marked One is to be dealt with a.s.a.p. while the envelope marked Two should be dealt with approximately three months after envelope One. I suggest we show you to the study and leave you for a couple of minutes to quickly through what we have in mind. I have also suggested a substantial fee. If you agree to both the fee and the task, a fifty percent deposit will be immediately paid to you as instructed."

"Do you require our answer now or later?" croaked Dorian.

"If by later you mean after we four meet-up for after-dinner brandies and cigars, that would be perfect," said Andy. "So, gentlemen, if you'd like me to top-up your wine glasses, I'll then show you to the study where, as I said, Clive and I will join you later." He gave the two men a tight smile. "Will thirty minutes give you enough time to come to a decision?"

"More than enough," croaked Dorian, taking hold of his topped-up glass and rising from his chair. "Show us through to the study, my friend, where I am sure Chucky and yours truly will be more than happy with your proposals." He gave a scratchy laugh. "A delicious dinner, an anticipated agreeable fee and the promise of endless brandies and cigars? A perfect evening, wouldn't you say?"

"Hear! Hear!" rasped Chucky. "I can almost feel my hands on the steering wheel of the latest BMW coupé!"

"A simple BMW coupé as opposed to a Ferrari *Stradale*?" exclaimed Clive. "Tut! Tut! Chucky. You do surprise me!"

LOS ANGELES - PREVIEW SHOWING OF *HIGH JINKS IN HIGH C!*

"Are you ready for your close-up, Miss Maebelle?" carolled Dee-Dee. "Are you ready for your launch into the Hollywood galaxy of superstars?"

"Ready as I'll ever be," murmured Maebelle taking hold of Dee-Dee's hand as their limousine made its way toward the cinema for the first showing of *High Jinks in High C!* "Oh, Dee-Dee!" she wailed. Tell me I'm a star!"

"Miss Maebelle, you are not only a star; you are a double *superstar!*" carolled Dee-Dee. "Superstar of the catwalk and, as from tonight, superstar of the film world! So, let's see that famous smile and, better still, let's have those superstar thoughts that it's even going to get better than this!"

Lowering his window slightly. Dee-Dee said with a grin. "Can you hear the cheering? I certainly can and don't forget for one teensy-weensy second, Maebelle dearest, that they're cheering for you!"

GODFREY STREET

"Of course, the fucking film's a fucking triumph!" cursed Lulu glancing up from her laptop. "Maebelle Magic is what some wag's dubbed the event. Not only that, one fucking newscaster has the temerity to call her a new star in the glittering galaxy of talent! Grotesque Gorgon or garbage would be nearer the truth. I think I'm about to throw up!"

There's no need to be upset, Lulu dear," said Lobie who had arrived earlier with an armful of papers saying much the same. "It was inevitable that Hollywood would take her to its perverse bosom and, though you may not like it, former model Maebelle now actor Maebelle, is here to stay."

"Thanks for you reassuring words," hissed Lulu. "Oh, Cymbeline-cum-Maebelle, you have no idea; no idea at what new little upsets await you!"

GODFREY STREET - SEVERAL DAYS LATER

"Jesus, Lobie," grizzled Lulu stifling a yawn on answering the phone. "For fuck's sake, it's not even six bloody o'clock!"

"Bad news, I'm afraid. Terrible news, in fact," said Lobie without preamble. "I've just had the police on the phone, Leo was anonymously dropped off at the entrance to your local A & E about an hour ago. As I'm listed as the person to be contacted in an emergency; hence the phone call."

"Oh my God!" exclaimed Lulu, wide awake and sitting bolt upright. "A & E you said. What happened? Is he alright?"

"*It's* happened," said Lobie hoarsely. "His condition's stable but he's still unconscious." He took a deep breath. "Having asked me if Leo wore an expensive watch and I told them he owned a twenty-two thousand gold Rolex plus, the police then said it's obviously a robbery gone wrong because not only is his Rolex missing: his whole fucking *hand's* missing!"

"Wha . . . what did you just say?" asked Lulu in a strangled voice.

"Whoever attacked him cut off his hand, is what I said," rasped Lobie.

"I think I'm going to be sick," hiccupped Lulu clutching hold of a concerned Flip Flop who had joined her on the bed. "It can only be bloody Andy McCulloch who's responsible. I take it you informed the police of his threats?"

"No, Lulu, I did not," came the emphatic reply.

"And why not?" said Lulu imperiously.

"Because of that threatening letter and ransom demand *you* sent to McCulloch and *my* involvement," yelled Lobie.

"No need to *yell,* Lobie," hissed Lulu. "My - our - main concern is what happens next? What do we do now."

"We do nothing for the moment until I've spoken to Leo," said Lobie. "You do know what this means?"

"Yes, I do," muttered Lulu pulling on her stylish Bonsoir of London dressing gown. "Another anonymous delivery from the likes of the non-existent Pizzicato Pizza!"

"Are you prepared for that?"

"Oh, yes, Lobie," said Lulu through gritted teeth. "One hundred and fifty present ready!"

*

Four days later, as anticipated, on hearing the front door buzzer and getting no response when asking who was there, a grim-faced Lulu opened the door to find a brown paper package sitting on the top step.

Rushing to the phone she immediately alerted Lobie who told her to don a pair of kitchen gloves and carefully place the package somewhere safe until he arrived so that they could open it together.

Overcome by curiosity and watched by a tail wagging Flip Flop, Lulu nervously opened the package to reveal a clear plastic food container displaying Leo's hand: the silver skeleton ring proudly on display.

MAEBELLE'S BUNGALOW - BEVERLY HILLS HOTEL

"Goodness, talk about an example of perverted plagiarism," crooned Mabelle on being told by a gleeful Dee-Dee about "poor Leo's unfortunate mishap." Eyeing the giggling little man, she added acerbically. "Not that dear Preston has come through with the first part of our Toeless in Gaza romp *despite* my promised, acrobatic-cum-contortionist performance at The Sands Hotel, Barbados!"

"A tad harsh, don't you think, cutting off the poor sod's whole hand?"

"You did say it was his *left* hand, didn't you?"

Dee-Dee gave a nod.

"So?" trilled Maebelle.

"So, what?"

"I take it he's right-handed which means he can still *do* what all you naughty boys *like* to do!"

"Honestly, Maebelle, dear. You are too, too much," snickered Dee-Dee, his brass eyepatch twinkling in the early morning sunlight.

"That's exactly what Preston said," purred Maebelle. "However, here we are, still waiting to go Toeless in San Francisco. As for Toeless in Italy, we'll more than likely witness another Pompeii before that happens!"." Reaching for her mobile she said mischievously. "Maybe it's time for dear Preston to suffer another pulmonary attack!"

"Careful, dear," said Dee-Dee snatching the mobile from her hand. "Remember we have a mega meeting tomorrow where Oscar et al will be discussing your next film role, plus we have to be in London the week after for the Leicester Square premier of *High Jinks!* So, why not let sleeping tootsies lie, and we can deal with all our return."

"Your words, Mr. Scriptwriter extraordinaire, are words of wisdom indeed," crooned Maebelle. "So, how about an extra-large martini to celebrate such a cerebral happening?"

"My thoughts exactly," crowed Dee-Dee. About to do the honours, he said contemplatively. "Why not invite Preston to the London premier? Who knows, he may even end up buying you The Crown Jewels!"

"A splendid idea!" crooned Maebelle, "seeing I'm far prettier than Charles or Camilla! Now, whilst you're busy organising those martinis I plan to be busy billing and cooing with 'time to pull yer finger out' Preston." She added with a trill. "Maybe we'll avoid Eaton Square and make do with the likes of The Berkeley, The Dorchester or The Lanesborough instead?"

"No, no! None of those and, if the truth be known, why *not* Eaton Square?" yodelled Dee-Dee. "I, for one, can't think of anything more satisfying than *cleaving* one's way through all those clamouring photographers as we head toward Colbert in Sloane Square for a champagne brunch! You, wearing The Crown Jewels; me drenched in Pucci and Gucci, and Preston sporting a custom-made painter's smock from Tom Ford!"

"In the words of your favourite Mr. Gilbert and Mr. Sullivan, one little maid - me - and two other little maids - you and Preston - from Eaton Square can be viewed tripping their way to stylish Colbert!" crooned Maebelle. "Dee-Dee, darling you're on! Eaton Square it shall be! I'll give Mrs Edwards a call later so that she and Briggs can get things organised for our impending arrival."

"I take it the passionate . . . er . . . painter will also be staying with us?" tittered Dee-Dee.

"Obviously, seeing he's not only part of our grand parade when we descend upon lucky Colbert but a vital cog in our wicked spinning wheel!"

*

"Accompany you and Dee-Dee to London for the premiere of your movie, Maebelle?" enthused Preston. "Why, I couldn't think of anything nicer!"

"You obviously don't know Bond Street," said Maebelle dryly. "So, Preston dear, if you're at a loose end this evening, why not join the two of us for dinner here at The Polo Lounge for dinner. We'll be dining at eight."

"I'll be there, Miss Maebelle, polo stick and all. Ha ha!" guffawed Preston. "London, eh? Wow! Just wait until I tell my latest canvas!"

COLBERT - FRENCH CAFÉ RESTAURANT - SLOANE SQUARE

"I know just what that poor Marie Antoinette must have felt like on her way to the guillotine," crooned Maebelle eyeing the growing sea of well-wishers and gawkers gathering outside the popular eatery in order to catch a glimpse of Hollywood's latest darling.

"Don't be so presumptuous, Maebelle darling," chided Dee-Dee. "At least when you return to Eaton Square, you'll still have your head, never mind that dazzling diamond bondage collar!"

TWENTY-SEVEN

AN ELEGANT DUPLEX APARTMENT OVERLOOKING EATON SQUARE

MAEBELLE PUTS THE GREAT BACK INTO GREAT BRITAIN! blazed one effusive headline. *ENGLAND'S ANSWER TO HOLLYWOOD TALENT & GLAMOUR!* sang another.

"I *told* you you'd be an absolute sensation," crowed Dee-Dee as he, Maebelle and Preston sat having a leisurely the morning after breakfast while flipping through the morning papers.

"How about this?" guffawed Preston. "*LEICESTER SQUARE GREETS A LIVING LEGEND.*"

"Aha! But what about *this* one," camped Dee-Dee. "*MAEBELLE - THE TRUE BELLE OF THE BALL.*"

"Hmm," said Maebelle with a Cruella de Vil smile. "No doubt if that dreadful Lulu Mayhew reads any of these - especially that last one - she'd be wishing the headline had been *MAEBELLE - THE TRUE BALLS-UP OF THE BALL!*"

"The balls-up of the ball?" echoed Preston in a deep, belly rumble. "Oh, Maebelle, you never fail to surprise me so, now it's *my* turn to surprise *you*!"

"Surprise me," crooned Maebelle. "After what you greeted me with earlier, it'll have to be something extraordinary to even catch a glimmer of a surprise!"

"Well then, how about this?" grinned Preston delving into his dressing gown pocket and producing an instantly recognisable blue box. "You did say I may not know of your Bond Street, but then I *do* have my spies!"

"Goodness," crooned Maebelle reaching for the tantalising blue box. "How very *Breakfast at Tiffany's.* Or should I have said *Breakfast at Eaton Square*? Well, I never!"

"Don't just sit there; open it, Audrey!" camped Dee-Dee.

"Audrey?" questioned Preston.

"He means Audrey as in Audrey Hepburn who played Holly Golightly in the movie!" trilled Maebelle on plucking the sparkling diamond necklace from its box. "Oh, Preston," she breathed. "It's beautiful, but you really shouldn't have!" Her bogus response resulting in Dee-Dee having an unexpected coughing fit.

"Maybe I shouldn't have but then I just have," grinned Preston.

"I love it! Simply love it!" crooned Maebelle as Preston gently helped her fasten the necklace round her slender neck. Eyeing Dee-Dee, she added mischievously. "If this isn't a direct answer to Colbert, here we come, then I'd like to know what is!"

"The answer to *that,* Maebelle dearest, if for the three of us to get dressed and make it a glittering Colbert, here we come, *à la* your arrival at Leicester Square last night," carolled Dee-Dee. "But not until I've spoken to Donna Tattle, Bromeando's razor-sharp PR person here in London and given her an update!"

COLBERT - SLOANE SQUARE

"Talk about a veritable Athena! Donna Tattle would have made Homer proud!" carolled Dee-Dee as they sat down. "By the time we arrived, she swore that not even an amber alert would have prepared Sloane Square for what it was about to perceive! She vowed to 'spread the word' via a couple of nearby girls' schools, taxi ranks et cetera! And as you can see, Miss Donna Tattle is a force to be reckoned with!"

"Oh, yeah?" twanged Maebelle slipping into Mae West mode. "And what about *me*? Ain't *I* a force to be reckoned with?"

"Goodness, Maebelle," carolled Dee-Dee. "Do I detect a touch of old timer's here? Please don't tell me you've already forgotten those immortal words referring to you in one of today's rags. The uber-perceptive 'Leicester Square greets a Living Legend'. So, instead of posturing and pouting for the likes of Preston and *moi*, I strongly suggest you put on your best Maebelle smile in order to face the inevitable."

He glanced toward the entrance. "Oh dear, methinks I have just seen the first of the brave autograph hunters daring to challenge the sharp looks of the majestic maître d'! A dreadful little Matilda lookalike! I take it you have at least a dozen biros in yon Prada handbag,"

"Two dozen at the last count," quipped Maebelle. Turning to face a bemused, if not somewhat taken aback Preston, she added waspishly. "Take a good look, Preston dear, as this is the *real* fame game; something which the likes of that strange, sizzling Mr. Bacon, nor Mr. Hirst, would never have experienced - or will ever experience by hanging in a gallery - compared to the glamorous Maebelle sitting here, wallowing in all the adulation; the very *real* McCoy!"

Ignoring Preston's stunned expression, she turned to the impatient young Matilda lookalike now standing next to the table and said with a strychnine smile. "How *sweet* of you to want my autograph. What is your name, dear?"

"Hyacinth," giggled the young girl.

"How charming!" purred Maebelle, busily scrawling: *To Blossom. Best wishes, Maebelle.* "Next?"

"I strongly suggest, Preston, you'd better ask for the bill so that we can make our exit before Madam is completely swamped," hissed Dee-Dee. "Once you've done the necessary, we'll do what I call a surprise up and scuttle. Maebelle and I got quite good at this back in L.A! We call it our 'up, up, and away' manoeuvre!"

Preston promptly did as Dee-Dee requested, his action followed by Dee-Dee's muttered aside to a graciously smiling Maebelle signing yet another scrap of paper or autograph book with a flourish.

"Time to get your skates on, Lois! Allow yourself another two or three squiggles and then it's a sure-fire case of us three up, up and awaying!"

"Gotcha Superman!" came the furtive reply followed by a cheerful "Sorry darlings! I love you all but no more signing today as I am due at the Southbank Centre and dare not be late! So, bless you and thank you! Love you!"

Grabbing hold of Preston and Dee-Dee, Maebelle literally frogmarched the two grinning men through the eager mob outside where, fortunately for her a couple were just climbing out of a taxi, and as the couple got out, Maebelle, Dee-Dee and Preston clambered in.

"We're only going as far as Eaton Square, cabbie!" crooned Maebelle. "However, as the situation is dire, I am sure one pf these charming gentlemen will be happy to present you with a fifty-pound note for coming to our rescue!"

GODFREY STREET

"I must have a stronger stomach than I thought," murmured Lulu as she and Lobie sat having a catch-up mid-morning martini. "Did you see, did you just *see* those photographs and films of her, Dee-Dee bloody Devereaux and that smug Andy McCulloch as the preened and posed at last night's premiere? As for those fucking headlines, as they so happily say in the U.S. of A. 'No comment'."

"I have to say she - they - did get an enormous amount of coverage thanks to Bromeando's highly competent PR people," replied Lobie. Eyeing a glowering Lulu, he added sotto voce. "Er . . . any further news on Leo?"

"According to the doctor I spoke to he's still heavily sedated," said Lulu. Giving a grimace she added harshly. "Though the deeply embarrassed doctor went on to inform me that Leo was lucid enough to inform him that no matter what we said, he had no wish to see either of us."

"Well, can you blame him, seeing what happened to him is all our fault," snapped Lobie. "No, I stand corrected: more *your* fault, seeing you not only had us kidnap Clive and then threaten McCulloch as to what would happen to the poor guy if he didn't adhere to *your* damn instructions, you then had to go and turn bloody McCulloch's response to your threats into fact!"

"Aha! So Lobie Maseko shows his true colours at last!" cried Lulu. "A case of put the blame on Lulu Mayhew as opposed to Gilda's *Put the Blame on Mame*! Well then, Mr. Loyalty Maseko, as you're blameless and have nothing to hide, I suggest you take your dismal *hide* out of here! Any follow-up that may need doing will be done by the guilty as charged Miss Mayhew. A very disappointed Miss Mayhew I may add."

"Aw, c'mon Lulu, there's no need to be like that."

"Just as there's no need for you to remain sitting here," said Lulu. She turned to where Flip Flop, an ear cocked, sat watching the two. "And I'm sure my loyal Flip Flop will agree with me, the guilty Lulu Mayhew, that you - like namby-pamby, one handed Leo - are no longer wanted on Lulu Mayhew's next voyage. I take it you can *steer* your limpid self toward the front door. Now, fuck off!"

On hearing a furious Lobie slam the front door shut behind him. Lulu turned to Flip Flop and said nonchalantly. "So, my darling Flip Flop, yet another zipper gets pulled well and truly down which means it really *is* up to you and me, Cheslea's answer to the Lone Ranger and her uber-reliable

Tonto! However, first things first, which means another lethal martini for yours truly and an avalanche of doggy treats for you, before we head down to the office and I don my thinking cap. Talking of which, perhaps Aye! Aye! has an idea or two, so why don't I ask him to suggest something that not even *he* would deem possible to solve, but inevitably does! Which still leaves the million euro question unanswered. Who the hell do I get to assist me when the time comes?"

Taking a sip of her freshly mixed martini Lulu sat staring contemplatively at Flip Flop busy with a doggy chew. "What I really need is the return of Dan the Man or else a pair of conjoined twins called Dee-Dee and Niccolò - I'm referring to the dreaded Devereaux and Niccolò Machiavelli if you're at all interested, as I do believe this wily author is experiencing a severe case of the dreaded writer's block!"

About take another sip of martini, Lulu gave a sudden start at the sharp ringing of the red telephone on her desk. "Jesus wept!" she cried, dabbing herself with a quickly snatched tissue having spilt most of her drink. "Who the fuck can this be calling on my hot line seeing nobody, but *nobody,* wishes to converse with the lovely me at the present moment. Zazu Pitts speaking." she cooed on answering. "How may I not help you?"

"Lulu it's Dan the Man calling from the now cured Cape Town. Some little witch doctor as opposed to the usual little bird tells me there's a possibility you may need me to assist you in casting some of those old bones and rattle some gourds due to a few problems which appear to have made themselves known during my absence."

"But . . . but how *did* you know?" gasped Lulu.

"Lulu, dear, you know me, I was only joking, but if you are still having problems with the usual team, I am not at all surprised. Why I was calling was to say I'm back in London early next week - I've yet to confirm which day but should know tomorrow latest- arriving at Heathrow around sixish and, if convenient, may I doss down not quite in Godfrey Street itself - the house being somewhat preferable - for a few nights?"

"Doss down for a few nights?" shrieked Lulu. "Dan! Dan! You darling man! Not only are you a glorious, gorgeous, handsome, hunky mind reader, but you are permitted to doss down here with me and Flip Flop for as long as you can bear us! What's more, give me your flight number so that Flip Flop and the lovely Lulu can collect you from the airport."

CHEYNE WALK

"Not a word about Murrain from anyone," chuckled Andy. "What's more, when I rang the hospital saying I was a concerned relative and simply checking up on him, I was told in no uncertain terms that Mr. Murrain was resting and furthermore, had given strict instructions that he had no wish to have any visitors. Obviously, he was obliged to talk to the police."

"I would have loved to have been a fly on the wall when he explained the mystery of his missing hand - sounds *very* Enid Blyton - to Mr. Plod," sniggered Clive.

"As a robbery gone wrong, what else?" said Andy calmly. "He wouldn't dare say otherwise knowing it would all come back to Lulu, him and Maseko." He gave a chuckle. "One thing we can be certain of is that Lulu Mayhew must be wetting her pants seeing she's astute enough to realise this is only the beginning. The big question being who's next?"

"And who *is* next?" questioned Clive taking a hefty sip of his G and T.

"Why, the I'm so smug Mr. Maseko, of course," replied Andy. Reaching for his G and T. he added mischievously. "I wonder if he's had the snip?"

"Had the snip?" exclaimed Clive. "Christ! You're not suggesting we cut off his dick!"

"No, not his dick," chuckled Andy, "his foreskin, which could then be delivered to Madam Mayhew via regular post."

"Very amusing, Andy, but being serious for a moment, what do you suggest we really *do* with Maseko?" Clive couldn't resist a snicker. "Another hand job would be a touch unimaginative don't you think?"

"A double Vincent," said Andy. "We have Dorian and Chucky somehow get to cut off both his ears and send them by regular post to Godrey Street. How Maseko will explain his unexpected surgery to A & E *and* the police - as this time they will *have* to be involved - will be interesting to see."

"And after Mr. Maseko, the crème de la crème herself, Madam Lulu Mayhew," enthused Clive.

"Madam Mayhew herself, in a situation which could be easily titled *The Mystery of The Burning Tyre.*"

"I take it you're referring to something you can't actually buy from Cartier," snickered Clive.

"I am indeed," replied Andy with a grin. "A bona fide Winnie Mandela twinkling necklace. I.e., a tyre filled with petrol placed around her upper regions and duly set alight." His confirmation causing the two men to burst out laughing.

"Beats a run-of-the-mill skyrocket!" gasped Clive.

"The only problem," gulped Andy drying his eyes, "is that this can't happen for at least a year and then, it will have to take place somewhere abroad; preferably *not* Italy!"

"Don't!" cried Clive, clutching his stomach. "Another crack like that and *I'll* be the one wetting my pants!"

Andy gave a further laugh. "Maybe after a cleverly orchestrated kiss and make up following the two mishaps in her miserable existence, we'll invite her to join us, along with Dorian and Chucky, on a Mata Hari safari."

"A Mata Hari safari?" chortled Clive. "I can't wait!"

"Once we've dealt with the dreaded Lulu, I think we can finally write *The End*," said Andy pouring himself another G and T. "Another?"

"Aren't you forgetting something? No, not a *something* but a few somethings?" replied Clive handing Andy his glass.

"Am I?"

"The other irritants, ne'er-do-wells, arseholes or whichever epithet flatters them best. I'm thinking of Maebelle, Dee-Devereaux and Malcom Duval for starters. Maebelle being the pièce de resistance if ever there was."

"So, go ahead and add them to our list as well and, once *they* too are all ticked off, we can finally write *The End*!"

*

Andy received a cheery telephone call from Dorian a mere three days later.

"You'll be chuffed to hear, Mr. McCulloch, sir, that your Mr. Maseko will now have to wear a turban when appearing in public."

"Well done, Dorian! That's splendid news and thanks for letting me know," chuckled Andy. "As usual, the balance of your fee is here whenever you wish to drop by - maybe have a drink - and collect it."

"Would tomorrow lunchtime be okay for me and Chucky to drop by? I say Chucky and me, 'cause you know what he's like if there's a chance of a free drink!" croaked Dorian.

"The two of you dropping by around lunchtime would be perfect, Dorian," replied Andy. "See you then!" Turning to face Clive he said with a grin. "As you must have gathered that was Dorian confirming a job well done." He gave a chuckle. "Despite *not* being an authentic Sikh, Mr. Maseko will have no alternative but to start wearing a turban. A prime example of a Sikh who may *Sikh* but never find his missing ears!"

TWENTY-EIGHT

ARRIVALS - TERMINAL FIVE - HEATHROW

"Now that's what I call a brilliant sight for tired eyes!" beamed Dan giving a smiling Lulu and all-embracing hug. "And as for your handsome, tail wagging escort, I should be jealous but what can I say!"

"Welcome, dearest Dan! Welcome!" cried Lulu smothering Dan with kisses. "If I say we're glad to see you, it'd be not nearly enough! I could almost burst out into hives and Flip Flop - I'm quite sure - into a fit of massive scratching!"

"Well, that would never do!" laughed a delighted Dan. "So, let's all settle for a double it's good to see you recurring!"

"I have a limo waiting so let's leave this madhouse and head back into town. Plus, you don't even have to ask. The limo boasts a well-stocked bar so it's champagne or whatever you wish all the way to Godfrey Street!"

Once they were settled in the comfortable Mercedes limousine speeding toward London, Lulu gently asked Dan if he'd heard what had happened to Leo. On Dan's nondescript "not a dickie bird, why?" she gently brought him up to date.

"Someone *cut off his hand*?" shouted Dan. His violent reaction causing a dozing Flip Flop to jump up and give a bark. "Jesus Christ! Any ideas as to who the culprits are?"

"Andy McCulloch for starters," said Lulu without hesitation before going on to sheepishly explain the whole saga. "In other words, I blame myself," said Lulu forlornly. "And even though it's been swept under the carpet as a violent robbery gone wrong, *I* know, and I'm sure you'll agree after what I've just told you, it can only be the work of Andy McCulloch - egged on by Clive Cordell - with a distinctive V-sign for me!"

"You know what I'm about to say, don't you?"

"Yes, who's next," said Lulu with a sigh. "Hopefully the answer is no-one else, but I feel that's wishful thinking. If Andy McCulloch and whoever have already gone for Leo, it's pretty damn obvious that Lobie or I are next in the firing line."

"Out of interest, what was Lobie's reaction to all this?"

"I have no idea seeing he's in a mega sulk with me," replied Lulu. "But you know Lobie, give it few more days and he'll be as good as new. Seeing you alive and kicking should definitely put matters to right."

"I'll give him a call. In the meantime, I'll see if I can meet up with Leo. Is he still in hospital?"

"As far as I know, However, you can sort all that out once we're back at the house. Meanwhile, a top-up wouldn't go amiss!"

*

"The hospital informed me that Leo was discharged a few days ago," said Dan. "I tried both his landline and mobile, but both went to voice-mail, so I left a message asking him to call me."

"Did you leave my private number?"

"Yes, I take it that's okay?"

"Fine by me, but you do realise on recognising the number as that of my hotline, I very much doubt he'll call back."

"It's that bad, is it?" chuckled Dan, his eyes twinkling. "Honestly, Lulu, the three of you are at times are the antithesis of the three musketeers in that you take - when it suits you - the term bickering to a new high!"

"Talking of which that's my red phone, my hotline ringing," interrupted Lulu on hearing the distant ring. "Maybe it's one of the gruesome, twosome - oops, forgive me Leo - returning your call. Let it go to go to voice mail and we'll deal with it once we've finished our drinks."

"I'd prefer to deal with it now, if I may," replied Dan. "Strike while the iron's hot, as they say. Unless the call was for you."

"It could be my agent who thinks nothing of calling at all hours," smiled Lulu. "But you're right. I'd better listen to the messages; if any. Follow me."

On hearing Leo's strangled "Lulu or Dan, it's Leo. The most dreadful thing has happened to poor Lobie so please, *please,* call me! I'll try your mobile!" As if telepathic, Lulu's mobile started to ring.

Lulu, her face paling, stood looking at Dan before reaching for her mobile. "Leo," she cried on answering. "What's happened to Lobie?"

"Lulu! Lulu! Thank Christ you answered!" sobbed Leo. "Its Lobie! Poor bloody Lobie! Someone's gone and cut off both his ears!"

"What the fuck?" exclaimed Dan as Lulu dropped her mobile and slid down on to the floor in a dead faint; a concerned Flip Flop giving her a gentle while whimpering softly. Picking up the mobile he said tersely. "Leo its Dan Crozier. Sorry to hear about you hand! What was that you said about Lobie's ears?"

Dan listened in growing horror and disbelief to what to an almost incoherent Leo had to say. After finally calming him down and promising have Lulu call him as soon as she was able to, Dan helped her up from the floor and gently sat her on a nearby chair.

"Here you are, take a sip," he said holding a hastily poured brandy to her lips.

"Thank you," said Lulu weakly before doing as instructed.

"Better?" asked Dan.

"Much better," murmured Lulu. Glancing up at Dan she added tearfully. "Jesus, Dan, what will they do next? His *ears*? That's so, so barbaric!"

So is cutting off Leo's hand, thought Dan. "I need to speak to Andy McCulloch right now!" growled Dan. "I don't give a purple fuck for what's going on between the lot of you but it's going to stop; and stop *now*! Do you have a number for McCulloch?"

"He's in my mobile," mumbled Lulu, "but I don't think you should call him."

"It's got beyond *thinking*, Lulu!" snapped Dan reaching for her mobile. "Where is it? I can't see any bloody Andy McCulloch listed!"

"He's under Apps; Robert Apps," whispered Lulu.

"Found it! Okay, let's see what Mr. Apps-cum-McCulloch has to say for himself. Hello? Is that Andy McCulloch? Good evening, Andy; it's Dan Crozier, a friend of Lulu Mayhew's. I've just got back from South Africa and heard about what happened to Leo Murrain and, a few minutes ago, what happened to Lobie Maseko; two great friends of Lulu's. I am going to ask you a question, Andy; but before you answer I'm well aware of what you said to Lulu on the phone about any future typing et cetera, so tell me truthfully: are these two appalling attacks anything to do with you?"

"Anything to do with me?" exclaimed Andy. "It may have escaped you, *Mr.* Crozier, I am a *writer* of fiction: *not* a participant. Therefore, in answer to your ridiculous question, no, it has *nothing* to do with me. Perhaps you should cast your somewhat jaundiced eye California-wards instead of dithering around in your own back yard. Call me in the morning, Mr. Crozier, after you've had time to think again before jumping once again to such wild conclusions. Now, if you'll excuse me, I have dinner guests requiring my attention Goodnight, *Mr.* Crozier!"

"Sarky bastard," muttered Dan staring at the phone in his hand.

"I *told* you it was a bad idea to call him," sniped Lulu.

"Sorry Lulu, I disagree! Instead of all this continual backstabbing it's time we all sat down and cleared the air, once and for all. I appreciate I'm a guest in your house, but, whether you like it or not, when I speak to Andy McCulloch tomorrow - which I will do, contrary to all your sighs and grimaces - I'm going to suggest we meet for a civilised lunch and - as I said - clear the air like civilised people and not a bunch of screaming yobbos!"

"Good luck with *that* but I can tell you here and now Andy McCulloch will never agree to a lunch with us; not after what you said to him on the phone,"

To Dan's surprise his invitation to lunch was promptly accepted by Andy along with the words "I take it Clive - if he's not on duty - is also invited?"

"But of course!" exclaimed Dan giving a startled Lulu a thumbs up. "Cecconi's at one?"

"We'll see you there!"

CECCONI'S RESTAURANT

"Well now, don't you look swell!" commented Andy with a phony American accent and a questionable smile as he and a similarly smiling Clive approached the table where Lulu and Dan were sitting. "Despite your recent, highly setbacks, I take it the new book is going well?"

"Even better than expected, thank you, Andy," replied Lulu with a tight smile. "Unlike the fact, not the fiction, regarding Leo Murrain and Lobie Maseko."

"Before Clive and I sit down, Lulu dear, as I said to your friend here on the telephone last night, whatever happened to those two has nothing to do with me, and certainly nothing to do with Clive. Now. either you accept that - a simple 'I agree with what you say' will suffice - which will see Clive and myself joining you for lunch, or you continue with your totally unjustified comments and rantings, but without your guests. Guests who happily accepted *your* invitation, I hasten to add."

"So, who do *you* see as the guilty party, or parties?" said Dan giving Lulu a discreet "zip it" look.

"As I said to you on the phone, Dan. Look California-ward instead of dithering about in your own backyard." Andy turned to Lulu. "C'mon, Lulu. You know damn who's abroad - or should I say who *are* abroad - your nemesis now superstar Maebelle and the dreaded Dee-Dee Devereaux! It'd never been proven but Clive and I are pretty damn sure they were the ones behind the skyrocket attacks on our Italian villa.

"Think back, Lulu. The defacing of the bookshops promoting your latest book; the spray painting to the front of your house and more. Now, do we sit down or do we leave."

"Please sit down," said Lulu quietly. "And Andy, if it's not too late, I can only apologise for my frantic finger pointing. The truth of the matter is that I am now literally wary of everyone I meet!"

"Well, don't be," said Andy on sitting down. "I see you and Dan are drinking wine, so I'll join you."

"We've got a couple of bottles of Pinot Grigio on ice," said Dan. "Clive?"

"Pinot Grigio sound good, thank you."

"Clive and I have prepared a formal statement which I would now like to read to you whilst we enjoy our wine and before we order," said Andy solemnly, reaching for a folded sheet of paper from inside his jacket.

"A statement?" repeated Lulu, raising an eyebrow.

"Yes, a statement," repeated Andy. He took a sip of wine. "You ready?"

"As ready as I'll ever be," muttered Lulu.

"I'm more than ready," said Dan.

Andy unfolded the sheet of paper and started to read. "To whom it may concern. I, Andrew McCulloch and my husband Clive Cordell, wish to state, once and for all, that we remain totally blameless regarding the recent attacks on Mr. Leo Murrain and Mr. Lobie Maseko. There is no evidence, whatsoever, to substantiate such claims and both Mr. McCulloch and Dr Cordell are willing to testify in a Court of Law, if necessary, to prove their innocence."

Andy glanced up at Lulu and Dan. "Signed: Andrew McCulloch and Dr Clive Cordell. Any questions?"

"No, Andy, no questions," purred Lulu. "I take it that copy is for me?"

"It is."

"Good," said Lulu with a cat that got the cream smile. "Now, first on the agenda - and I'm sure you'll agree - is that we order, and second on the agenda; we discuss - *in detail* - what is to be done with Maebelle and her poisonous little sidekick. Again agreed?"

"Agreed!" chorused Andy and Clive."

"Double good," purred Lulu picking up a menu. "So, team; what shall we order, apart from Maebelle and Dee-Dee's heads on a plate?"

*

"So, what do you *really* think?" asked Dan as he and Lulu stood on the corner of Burlington Gardens and Bond Street looking for a taxi.

"What do I really think?" echoed Lulu. "I think it's - without a doubt - another case for the uber-wily PI Aye! Aye! A case even stranger than *The Strange Case of Dr Jekyll and Mr. Hyde* or, to put it bluntly, *The Strange Case of Dr Cordell and Mr. I Will Not Abide*! I wouldn't trust those two as far as I can throw a stick for Flip Flop: which isn't very far!"

"As Dan the Man always says, dear Lulu, it takes two to tango, and best to practice your dance steps before the dance floor becomes too crowded! Taxi!"

*

"Your honest opinion?" said Andy to Clive as their taxi stop-started its way toward Cheyne Walk.

"My honest opinion?" echoed Clive. "The sooner we get those two on a swinging safari, the better." Giving Andy a wolverine smile he added slyly. "However, lunch was fun with the ice well and truly melted. And I'm sure, when the time comes, you with your vivid imagination and me, with my medical skills, will *colourfully* prove that time does heal the most serious of wounds."

"Well said, lover!" chuckled Andy. "And if all goes well with our severely disjointed and twisted plan which sees Maebelle and Devereaux also aboard and where Dee-Dee realises - to his cost - that crocodiles aren't necessarily handbags. Likewise, Maebelle, when she realises leopards are better stroked when a coat and not the real McCoy!" He gave a further chuckle. "I feel the stirrings of a new book. Something along the lines of *Deceivers and Grievers*!"

"The only problem is that Maebelle and Devereaux, with their increasing American commitments, could be strictly *Out of Africa* for God only knows how long," chortled Clive. "Which means man-eating crocodiles and fearsome leopards are seriously out." He gave a further chortle. "Unless one switches locations and makes do with a couple of homegrown Florida alligators and a willing panther or two."

"*Not* the most brilliant of substitutes, but a nice try," chuckled Andy. Staring pensively at Clive he said cheerfully. "Maybe an unscheduled visit to a local zoo?"

"Need it be a repeat performance of *Deceivers and Grievers* when we have the time and so much to play with out there," replied Clive. "Why not an unexpected dip in one of the many aquariums in the area?" He gave a snigger. "The thought of Maebelle having to fight off a genuine shark as opposed to the usual two-legged version could see *Jaws* in a mega sulk! As for Devereaux: a wild struggle with a giant octopus would surely fulfil his wildest, twisted fantasies!"

"Take it as done," chuckled Andy. "But first, our schedule for the continued wooing of Lulu Mayhew. Okay. Lunch wasn't exactly headline-worthy, but, as you so rightly say, we've time to fix that. Our next step will be to throw a cocktail party for a dozen or two agreeable souls where Madam, along with Mr. Crozier, can happily mingle with the likes of Messrs. Beige and Craven. Next thing, we get Dorian and Chucky to invite them to lunch or dinner at Castle Dracula."

"Castle Dracula?"

"The name I use when referring to their turreted Victorian horror of a house near Petworth in deepest Sussex." Andy couldn't resist a further chuckle. "You may think I'm having you on when I tell you *they* named the place *Notre Trésor*, but I joke not!"

A MANSION IN BEL AIR

"Not that I could fault the hotel, but this is much more my style - oops! *our* style," crowed Dee-Dee taking in the rival to Tara basking in the sunshine as he and Maebelle stood smiling smugly at the spectacular homestead. "And most fitting for Hollywood's latest 'go get 'em' goddess!"

"Oh, Dee-Dee Devereaux, you are *such* a tease!" crooned Maebelle. "And yes, I agree, far more me - us - as we continue to ascend those slippery steps taking us to the very top of the Tinseltown firmament! Ah, this must be her, the estate agent who goes under the somewhat bizarre name of Miss Bendy Lymetick!"

"Miss Bendy Lymetick?" tittered Dee-Dee. "Sounds very catchy to me; Lyme disease and all that! The mind boggles!"

Watching the tiny, Liza Minelli lookalike spring sprightly from a shiny, yellow Toyota GR89 sports car, he added camply. "I'm Bendy with a B. *Bendy*!"

Half an hour later, Maebelle was happy to claim the spacious house as hers.

"I love it! Simply love it," she told the beaming Bendy with a B (Dee-Dee's tongue in cheek nickname instantly sticking). Nodding to where a couple stood waiting, Maebelle said with a gracious smile. "I take it the lady and gentleman waiting to be introduced are the major domo and his wife, the much-lauded cook?"

"They are indeed Miss Maebelle," simpered Bendy. "Their names are Brandon and Freda Carp, and they are most anxious to meet their new employer. Let me call them over so that I can introduce you."

"Talk about Mr. and Mrs Jack Sprat!" tittered Dee-Dee in an aside the odd-looking couple approached.

"I sincerely hope he's not a tottering advert for her culinary skills," hissed Maebelle in reply.

"Unless she can't resist tasting everything she cooks before serving the results to her employers whilst keeping him on a strict diet of leftovers!" giggled Dee-Dee in response.

Continuing to smile graciously as Freda Carp harped on about how much she and Brandon had enjoyed *High Jinks in High C!* and how clever Mr. Devereaux must be to have written such a fun script, the couple left in order - as Freda wheezed - "to keep on doing what we do so as to make sure everything remains tickety-boo for you!"

Giving Dee-Dee an "are they for real" look, a relieved Maebelle and Dee-Dee saw Bendy to her car before returning to the house.

On entering the elegant entrance lobby, they were greeted by a beaming Brandon and Freda; Brandon carrying a tray bearing two sparkling flutes of champagne and Freda, a tray holding a plate of triangular pieces of toast topped with caviar."

"Our little welcome present," said Brandon, a Charles Hawtrey lookalike, in a choir boy's falsetto. "Welcome to your new home, Miss Maebelle and Mr. Devereaux."

"Yes, a very warm welcome, Miss Maebelle and Mr. Devereaux," warbled Freda. "Brandon and me, wish you both many happy times ahead here at Shangri-La!"

"Goodness!" exclaimed Maebelle, reaching for a flute. "Silly me! I was *so* carried away by this lovely house that I never asked or homed in on the name, even when signing Miss Lymetick's various papers! Shangri-La? How apt!" She gave a madcap laugh. "Goodness, Dee-Dee, darling! Hopefully I won't be subjected to the real you when we have to leave Shangri-La and return to the hotel in order to pack!"

"Really?" sniped Dee-Dee. "If I remember the film of Mr. Hilton's *The Lost Horizon* correctly - it's aeons since I saw it - it was Lo-Tsen who collapsed and showed her real age on attempting to leave. Added to which I would never have done a Robert Conway and left Shangri-La. I would have stayed put and continued to be as lovely as I am!"

"Maybe I should call Lulu Mayhew," cackled Maebelle determined not to be outdone. "After all, plagiarism does appear to be her forte, so she'd have no problem *embroidering* Mr. Hilton's ending with you replacing the reckless Lo-Tsen!"

"And why should I care?" carolled Dee-Dee, "seeing I never travel without my L'Oréal anti-wrinkle cream!"

"No comment!" shrieked Maebelle. Taking a sip of champagne, she paused for a moment before saying a touch sombrely. "And how clever of you, my darling, thoughtful, younger than springtime Dee-Dee Devereaux, to have that discreet meeting with *darling* Oscar's lawyer and make arrangements for when it *is* our final curtain, you and I be interred at Forest Lawn among all those harpists and coal shovelling Hollywood greats!"

"And should you go first?" tittered Dee-Dee.

"Then I'll be there, lying in wait for you, or vice versa!" crooned Maebelle. "God only knows what you'll be wearing!"

"Certainly *not* a chastity belt seeing I could well meet up one of those very friendly ghosts!"

TWENTY-NINE

GODFREY STREET

"Now that was a surprise," said Dan looking a Lulu. Placing his mobile down on the coffee table he said with a wide smile. "A call from Mr. Murrain himself; a very contrite and apologetic Mr. Murrain. Not only that, he and Lobie wish to meet up with us a.s.a.p. and sort matters out."

"Thank God for that," replied Lulu. She gave a deep sigh. "I *know* I've a lot to answer for and because we have been friends for such a long time, I have been feeling so full of remorse and so *guilty* as to what happened to the two of them, and what they must be feeling. Added to the fact, they must also realise that more is sure to happen.

"However, we can talk about all over dinner so, please call Leo and see if they are free for dinner this evening." She gave a light laugh. "Tell Leo to inform Lobie that I'll be making his favourite cheese soufflé followed by his favourite Coq Au Vin!"

"And mine!" chuckled Dan. "I'll drop into Blanco and Gomez and get a few bottles - no, make that a case - of their splendid Chianti Colli Fiorentini; the least I can do in my role of a maybe referee!"

"Just as well you included the words 'maybe referee'," giggled Lulu, "otherwise I could have taken umbrage at your suggestion the Mayhew wine cellar wasn't good enough!"

"I wouldn't dare," chuckled Dan. "Happy now?"

"More than happy," said Lulu teasingly. Turning to where Flip Flop lay softly snoring, she said with faux seriousness. "Should we wake Flip Flop and tell him the good news or - as the saying goes - let sleeping dogs lie."

"Let's do as the saying goes and leave Flip Flop happily chasing imaginary rabbits," chuckled Dan. "Now, let me give Leo a call and see if he and Lobie are able to join us for dinner."

On hearing Dan's cheerful laughter on ending the call, Lulu said curiously. "From the sound of it, they will be joining us and happily so, Care to explain the jollity?"

"By 'they' I take it you're referring to a ruling figure and a touch of J.M. Barrie?"

"A ruling figure and a touch of J.M. Barrie?" questioned Lulu. "What on earth are you going on about?"

Dan gave another laugh. "Leo, because of his missing hand, and Lobie, now sporting a turban because of his missing ears, announced that both Captain Leo Hook and the Maharaja of No Ears are delighted to accept Miss Lulu *Mayhem's* kind invitation to dinner!"

"Captain Leo Hook and the Maharaja of No Ears?" giggled Lulu. "They sound even better than back to their old selves; they sound bloody wunderbar!"

Smiling broadly at Dan she added with a wink. "I wonder what colour turban the Maharaja of No Ears will be wearing. Gold, no doubt."

"Either gold or blood red," chuckled Dan, "but if I were you, I'd put my money on red."

"Lobie in a blood red turban?" shrieked Lulu. "Not only is he a gorgeous Boris Kojo lookalike, but the thought of the dishy Boris in a turban is almost too much for this hard to please woman! Talk about turning the vicious world topsy turvy. And well done Lobie, for turning a tragedy into a triumph!"

"The same can be said for Leo," said Dan admiringly. "When bringing me up to date about himself he said the great thing about having a prosthetic hand is that you can play 'I spy' on all and sundry without the worry of getting your fingers jammed in a doorway or a window!"

"I can hardly wait to see them," giggled Lulu. "Now, off you go on your wine buying spree whilst I return to see what PI Aye! Aye! Golden Eye and co are up to! What with Cymbeline now even more scheming and flighty than before, even I, the intrepid Lulu Mayhew, am having difficulty in seeing what happens next!"

*

"I knew it! Just knew it!" cried Lulu on greeting Lobie with a hug, "Lobie Maseko sporting a turban, and a red one at that, puts any Bollywood hero to shame! Oh, it's so good to see you!"

Turning to give Leo a hug she said with a laugh, "And you to, lovely Leo! I take it the red glove is in keeping with the Maharaja's magnificent turban?"

"It most certainly is!" chuckled Leo. "Captain Leo Hook usually wears a black glove, but as tonight is special. Ta da!"

"And here's poor Flip Flop having to make do with a boring tan collar," giggled Lulu, "and me in a simple Stella McCartney."

"And just get an eyeful of Dan the Man!" chuckled Lobie. "Please don't tell me that really *is* you wearing a tiger print onesie?"

"At least somebody's noticed it," chuckled Dan. "Now Mr. Tiger would like to know what you guys would like to put in your tanks."

Amidst groans from Lobie and Leo and Lulu's cried "You don't get any cornier than that", Lobie added with a smile. "It's really great to see you again, Lulu, and as I said to Dan on arrival, no recriminations, and let us simply enjoy ourselves as old friends should on meeting again." As if to give further credence to his words, he moved forward and embraced Lulu in another warm hug.

"Bless you, Lobie, and again, I'm so sorry," said Lulu in a tearful voice.

"Uh-uh!" said Lobie stepping back and waving an admonishing finger. "As I said, no recriminations." Pointing to one of the Barcelona chairs he added matter-of-factly. "May I?"

"Oh, God yes!" exclaimed Lulu. "Please sit down!"

"As I was saying," continued Lobie as he and Leo sat, "no recriminations. Instead, tell me your reaction to my new look! A worthwhile answer to a wannabe Maharaja, wouldn't you agree?"

"More than worthwhile," giggled Lulu, "I'd even go so far as to say a hundred percent *zowie!*"

"And me, with my matching glove?" asked Leo with a grin.

"Another one hundred percent zowie!" cried Lulu. "Now, instead of telling Tiger Dan what you'd prefer in your tanks, may I suggest a glass of champers to toast this absolutely *splendid* reunion and in celebration of happier times to come!"

"As Aye! Aye! Golden Eye, your favourite sleuth would say," added Dan, "*I* also say aye, aye to that very noble suggestion!"

"Aye! Aye!" chorused Lobie and Leo.

LOS ANGELES

"That's not only interesting its fucking mind blowing!" laughed the other party. "So, thanks again for the catch-up call and I look forward to seeing you at Apotheke, Chinatown, tomorrow evening. Go well!"

"You to," said the caller. "See you tomorrow!"

GODFREY STREET - THREE MORNINGS LATER

"I knew it! I just fucking *knew* it!" shrieked Lulu looking up from the news channel on her laptop.

"Knew what?" said Dan about to take a mouthful of coffee.

"Look! Dan look!" she cried, turning the laptop so that he could see the screen. "Look! Just look!"

"Christ!" exploded Dan, almost dropping his coffee mug. "Jesus! I don't believe it!" he yelled on seeing the headline: *FAMOUS MODEL/ACTRESS AND COMPANION BRUTALLY SLAIN!*

"I can't believe it!" gasped Lulu reaching for Dan's hand. "Maebelle and Dee-Dee *murdered*? And not only murdered, but horribly mutilated as well? Oh my God! Oh my God! I think I'm going to be sick!"

As Lulu dashed from the breakfast table, Dan reached for his mobile and called Lobie. On hearing Lobie's cheerful "Good morning, Tiger Dan! I trust the esteemed Maharaja of No Ears finds you well?"

"Jesus, Lobie have you been watching the news? I mean the *latest* news such as Sky?"

"No, I've been busy clipping my toenails if you must know. Why?"

"Why? Because it appears Maebelle and Dee-Dee were murdered last night, that's why!"

"Did you just say *murdered*?" said Lobie in a strangled voice.

"Look, have a word with Lulu who has just joined me," added Dan. "Have a word and, if you can get away from the office, join us as soon as you can."

"I'm about to go into a mega meeting so it won't be until much later," replied Lobie. "This also means I won't be able to get hold of Leo to see if he's able to join us."

"Great. Whatever" said Dan grimly. "Here's Lulu,"

"Oh, Lobie!" wailed Lulu. "I know I never liked the woman *or* Dee-Dee, and I know it was a rather childish vendetta between us, but this absolutely dreadful. For all his faults I'm quite sure this has nothing to do with Andy McCulloch so, who on earth could be responsible? Nobody *I* can think of."

"Let's wait until we're all together and talk about it before we jump to any conclusions," said Lobie. "As I said to Dan, I'll be with you as soon as I can, and if I can get hold of Leo, so much the better!"

Instead of agreeing with Lobie, Lulu gave out an un-Lulu like cry. "Can't you morons understand what I'm going through? Every time the post arrives, or I hear someone press the front door buzzer, I expect to find an envelope or package containing your *ears,* Lobie! Can't you understand that every time I answer any of my phones I expect a deathly silence, heavy breathing or someone whispering vile threats?"

"Whoa! Whoa! Lulu! Hold your horses!" called Dan, moving over to give her a hug. "Whatever happened to Maebelle and Dee-Dee has nothing to do with you; us. It happened in Los Angeles, for God's sake, and not even Andy McCulloch could have organised such a cruel happening despite its connotations! Disturbing acts, yes: but murder? Never! *Despite* his impassioned threats over the phone."

"Talk is cheap," sniffed Lulu, "yet it can still be soul destroying." Turning her attention back to her conversation with Lobie, she said tearfully. "I keep trying to get back to my writing but all I can think about is after what happened to you, Lobie, and to Clive, what's going to happen to me! And yes, Dan could be in the firing line as well! Oh God! Oh God!"

"Jesus, Lulu! calm *down!*" snapped Lobie. "You have Dan staying with you and nobody, but nobody, can harm you if he's there. Look, I have to go as I have a client arriving about now, so I'll leave you in Dan's capable hands. I'll see you later. Okay?"

"Yes, okay," murmured Lulu. About to replace the receiver she said with a whisper. "It's at times like this I really miss Maddy. Not only do I miss her I *need* her as she is the one person who really understands me. Do you still have a contact number for her?"

"I've got it here somewhere," muttered Lobie. "Look, may I have another quick word with Dan and then I really must go!"

"Hold on, here he is."

"Dan, can she hear us?" whispered Lobie.

"No, she's gone to the loo so say what you want to say but make it quick!"

"I'm really worried about Lulu, you don't think she's losing it, do you? I'm seriously concerned that she now wants to contact Maddy Thompson again," said Lobie. "Surely she must be aware that Thompson and Duval are - or were - close friends?"

"Maybe, maybe not," replied Dan, "but best we play along. Who knows, seeing Maddy may help get rid of this ever-growing paranoia."

"You wish," muttered Lobie. He gave a sardonic chuckle. "I sincerely hope she's wrong about my ears arriving in the post or making themselves known by turning up on her doorstep!" He gave a further chuckle. "At least you didn't say ear, ear! See you later, Dan the Man!"

*

A week later, as if dozing in the wings while waiting for its cue, a white, standard envelope, was delivered along with the usual daily wad of fan letters, business letters, bills, and general what have you. On opening the innocuous-looking envelope with its typed address, Lulu let out a shriek as two small, black, leathery items, namely Lobie's ears, fell onto the desk.

Letting out a further shriek that could be heard in nearby Chelsea Green, a horrified Lulu - much to the consternation of a startled Flip Flop - collapsed onto the floor in a dead faint.

*

"With luck the neurotic cow will accept it as the last of any nasty post," sniggered Leo on being told the latest drama by a resigned Lobie.

"Oi!" said Lobie with mock severity. "Those are *my* ears you're talking about, and as far as I remember, my ears were nigh on perfect!"

"My apologies, *Vincent*!" chortled Leo. "Of course, they were. Two perfect curlicues which - so I *hear* - endless girls couldn't wait to nibble!"

"Fuck off, Leo!" grinned Lobie. "Fuck off before I really give you something to smile about!"

"Promises! Promises!" cried Leo. "Luckily for me I am *not* another Clive Cordell!"

CHEYNE WALK

"Give my *amore* to the villa," said Clive as he sat watching Andy pack a small holdall.

"I will," replied Andy. "And again, congratulations on your new administrative post! We'll certainly celebrate when you join me this weekend!"

"Unfortunately, I simply could not find a patient wiling to be examined with an artificial hand despite everyone thinking there would always be a willing, kinky soul out there." chuckled Clive, "so the hospital thought it better to" - he made finger quotes with his right hand - "*promote* me rather than get rid of me!"

"Tut-tut!" said Andy with a grin. "How many times do *I* have to tell you that I absolutely *adore* you making love with your highly intrusive leather glove!"

"Touché douche!" tittered Clive. "As for the lovely you and bearing in mind all that's happened, will you be starting a new book, inspired by what happened to Maebelle and Devereaux:"

"No, Clive, not at the moment as I'm already working in something else," replied Andy. Looking at Clive he added mischievously. "However, it's inevitable that Maebelle Manson and Dee-Dee Devereaux-Nielsen will eventually appear in a book as a pair of bizarre serial killers. Two *exceptional* serial killers whose selection of victims would make Dubai's Burj Khalifa look like a minor abscess!"

LOS ANGELES

"Malky, she's gone and done exactly what you said she'd do. Approach we with a verbal white flag-cum-begging bowl which means as from tomorrow, I'll be back living with Madam Mayhew in glamorous Godfrey Street!" Maddy gave a giggle. "Nota bene; not only as her secretary but also as a much-missed friend!"

"Well done, Maddy," said Malcom. He gave a snigger. "As you haven't mentioned it, I take it, because of all the recent excitement, you haven't had a chance to deal with Noddy and Big Ears?"

"Big Ears *sans* Noddy is due to make his surprise arrival the day after tomorrow with me there to help deal with the ensuing shrieks and squeaks."

"Lucky you, lucky *her*!" chuckled Malcom. "Let me know how it goes. Hold on a sec! Rhett has just blown you a large kiss and sends reams of unbridled love!"

"Likewise," tittered Maddy, "along with an extra-large helping of love and kisses for *you*, my darling! Oh, Malky! Your Maddy does miss you!"

"Not nearly as much as your Malky misses you!" said Malcom softly. "Remember, this is only the beginning and, if all goes as planned, you'll be joining me in sunny California before you can say 'what's that ya hidin', Mr. Biden!"

GODFREY STREET - THREE MORNINGS LATER

"I don't like the look of that package or box which must have been left by the front door while we must have been having breakfast," said Maddy crisply. "Knowing what you've been going through recently, I suggest you take a seat in the sitting room while I take it downstairs to the office and open it!"

"Oh my God," murmured Lulu, nervously twisting het hands, "I can't bear it! Yes, please open it in the office. I know I'm being a wimp, so please forgive me."

"There's nothing to forgive, Lulu love," said Maddy though pursed lips. Picking up the package she added reassuringly. "It's not at all heavy so maybe it's something perfectly innocent." She gave a mischievous giggle. "Give me a couple of minutes to check it out and, if I don't come back with a call of 'all clear', call Lobie." Pausing for moment, Maddy added almost as an afterthought. "I take it Dan must be at the gym for his daily workout?"

"Where else," replied Lulu with a forced smile. "After all, he *is* Dan the Man, Now, off you do, Maddy dear, and do what you have to do!"

A few minutes later Maddy called from halfway up the stairs leading to the basement kitchen and office. "*Not* a bomb, I'm happy to say, but another irritating prank, I'm afraid!" She added hastily. "A silly prank more irritating than nasty!"

"For God's sake Maddy! Stop beating around the fucking bush and tell me what was inside the fucking package!" shrieked Lulu.

"Er . . . the package containing a pair of jumbo fake ears and a pair of gloves!" replied Maddy lamely.

"Oh my God!" wailed Lulu jumping up from the Barcelona chair. "Oh my God! I can't bear it! Will it never stop!"

"Hold on, Lulu, I'm right here!" puffed Maddy having sprinted up the remaining stairs and back into the sitting room. Placing her arm around the hyperventilating Lulu she said firmly. "Come and sit down and let me get you a stiff brandy before anything else!" Within seconds she had opened the

Parzinger cocktail cabinet and half-filled a brandy snifter which she quickly handed to Lulu.

Having gulped down a hefty mouthful, Lulu said with a frantic gurgle. "Show me! Show me!"

"I left them in the box downstairs," said Maddy calmly. "In other words, out of sight, out of mind. And there they'll stay until Lobie arrives or Dan gets back! Like myself, Lulu dear, and I'm sure they'll agree it's time you spoke to the police."

"No! No police!" snapped Lulu back to her old self. "If Lobie Maseko, Leo Murrain, and Dan Crozier and bestselling author Lulu Mayhew can't get to the bottom of this, then nobody can."

Talk about an ungrateful cow, thought Maddy, biting her tongue. *Stange how Wonder Woman aka Maddy Thompson suddenly becomes the Invisible Woman within a few days. Just wait until I tell Malcom and Rhet about Madam Defarge's latest plots and ploys!*

"Now, *that's* the Lulu Mayhew we know, so admire and love!" said Maddy with a tight smile. "What's more, this about to do battle Lulu Mayhew deserves a top up; and not only a top up of brandy but, if I may be so bold, an additional top up of champagne!"

"But only on condition a certain Maddy Thompson joins me," replied Lulu with a tremulous smile.

THIRTY

LOS ANGELES

"Big Ears has well and truly landed!" giggled Maddy over the phone. "As predicted, shrieks galore, followed by soothing words from Dan Crozier and, as you've probably guessed, an earlier serious - all is forgiven - conflab with Messrs. Maseko and Cordell from which I was well and truly excluded."

"Hold on, Maddy, you're doing great," said Malcom smoothly. "Simply, as I've said before, see it as the calm before a very nasty final storm!"

Maddy gave a sniff. "And not only is she all chummy, chummy with Maseko and Murrain, she's also in cahoots with McCulloch and Cordell. So much so that they're even talking about the three of them going on *safari* in Africa sometime next year!" She gave a titter. "At least that's what it sounded like. Obviously, my eavesdropping skills require a bit more practice!"

"As I said, Maddy, you're doing great plus - and I'll say it again - time is no longer the essence." There was a pause before Malcom said a touch curiously. "Is she still in a zombie-like state or has she managed to overcome her so-called writer's block?"

"Oh, she's well and truly over that and beavering away on a new novel" snorted Maddy. "I haven't managed to have a shifty at her computer, but I believe it once again revolves around the latest shenanigans of that PI with the ridiculous name."

"Any news on McCulloch and Cordell?"

"McCulloch is back in Italy while Cordell seems to have taken on the personality of a yo-yo and travels between their villa and the house in Cheyne Row as if there's no tomorrow!"

"As there may well not be," sniggered Malcom. "Now, something which may tickle your fancy - apart from me, that is" - Rhett La Maar may be in London within the next day or two. I'll ask him to give you a call and, better still, I suggest you two should meet as I'm a great believer in being able to put a face to a voice." He gave a chuckle. "Who knows, perhaps you could even introduce Rhett to Mayhew, but on the understanding that neither you nor Rhett let on that Rhett, in a future role as a big white hunter, could very well be the irresistible, charismatic gentleman she, McCulloch and Cordell just happen to meet while on safari." He gave another snigger. "Pity they get caught up in a manmade stampede of endless, desperate wild animals escaping from a beautifully *executed* bush fire!"

"I look forward to meeting the charismatic Rhett," giggled Maddy, "albeit in the tole of big white hunter, arsonist or simply as your comrade in harms; a much-used Mayhew saying. I'll let you know how I get on."

GODFREY STREET

"Morning, Maddy," yawned Lulu as she swept unto the kitchen in a billow of Janet Reger, "you're up early."

"Busy day," replied Maddy about to pour herself a cup of coffee. "Coffee or tea?"

"Tea, please. A busy day for me as well seeing I'm determined to finish the first draft of my latest, so I'll be needing you to run a few errands," said Lulu matter-of-factly." Eyeing Maddy over the top of her teacup, she added waspishly. "*That's* if you don't mind!"

And if I did? thought Maddy, *what then?* "Of course, I don't mind, after all that's what I'm here for," purred Maddy. "Anything particularly urgent? When I said I have a busy day I was referring to my having to take Flip Flop to the vet for his regular check-up, plus my meeting with the kitchen people back here seeing you suddenly find it imperative that the kitchen gets a new look; despite it being totally refurbished during the time I was persona non grata."

"I want all the kitchen cupboard fronts changed because I no longer approve of their non-colour; okay?" sniped Lulu. "They say white is right, but after seeing Gerald and Tabitha Collis's kitchen the other evening *I* decided white is *not* quite right and a zap of colour in *my* kitchen could do wonders! So, a touch of jasmine yellow and cerulean blue will be my new thing!"

"In other words, a touch of Vermeer," said Maddy with a grin.

"A touch of Vermeer?" cried Lulu clapping her hands. "At times Maddy Thompson you should be considered the genius in this house; not *moi*!"

"Whatever you say, Lulu dear. Whatever you say." Maddy gave s grimace as her mobile started to ring. "Oh, I wonder who that could be seeing I don't recognise the number. Excuse me a sec. Hello. Maddy Thompson speaking," she said on answering. "Oh, hello Mr. *Maar*, how nice of you to call. Sometime today? I could, but only briefly as I'm not only acting as chauffeur for Mr. Flip Flop, *a very important dog,* but I'm also meeting a representative from a kitchen supplier. Sorry, I missed that. A quick drink at The Connaught or wherever's convenient simply to introduce ourselves? Yes, I'm sure I could manage that. The Connaught at one. I look forward to meeting you, Mr. Maar."

On seeing Lulu's questioning look. Maddy clicked off the phone ad said brightly. "A friend of Helen Minter's from secretarial college; a Rick Maar. Helen now lives in New York and as its Rick's first visit to London, she suggested he look me up."

"His first visit to London?" carolled Lulu. "When you meet him and given the man's presentable, why not invite him to dinner as I'm sure he'd be delighted to visit a typical Chelsea house."

Typical Chelsea house? thought Maddy stiffing a laugh. *That'll be the day!*

"What a lovely idea, Lulu!" she cooed. "You are too kind. But only if he's presentable as you so rightly say!"

*

Waving Flip Flop and Maddy goodbye as they drove off in what Lulu glibly called her "chariot of desire" - a pink Mini Clubman - Lulu quickly made her way back to the downstairs office and called Lobie.

"Morning, dear," she cooed. "I won't keep you as I know you're a busy bee, but could one of your more unscrupulous contacts check out a Rick Maar and a Helen Minter for me, both of them supposedly living in New York, and get back to me as soon as poss. To quickly put you in the picture, this Rick Maar called Maddy earlier and they've arranged to meet at The Connaught for a getting to know you drink. I've suggested she invite him here for dinner this evening, but I can soon change that if what I think is true."

"If what you think is true?" chuckled Lobie. "And what is that of I dare ask?"

"It's that famous tried and true Mayhew gut feeling," replied Lulu in a no-nonsense voice, "that Mr. La Maar could be a no-gooder, so better to be safe than sorry!"

"I'll call you back."

EARLY MORNING - LOS ANGELES

"I met up with Maddy as arranged," said Rhett over the phone. "She's quite a stunner, isn't she? Much to her surprise, and mine, Lulu Mayhew has invited me - introducing myself as *Rick* Maar - to dinner this evening."

"Cancel! It."

"Cancel it?"

"Yes, c-a-n-c-e-l. You know my opinion of Mayhew; she's not to be trusted, and should Maddy slip-up and address you as Rhett, it'll lead to alarm bells ringing. Furthermore, she'll no doubt invite Maseko and Murrain to literally vet you, and I can assure you, those two are more dangerous than a pair of hissing cobras!"

"I'll do that as soon as we finish talking." Rhett gave a snigger. "How convenient a distant cousin should also ring to welcome me to London. plus invite me to a dinner dance at The Savoy in celebration of her son's twenty-first this very evening. Something I simply couldn't refuse!"

"I always knew you were a closet Fred Astaire," chuckled Malcom. "When you cancel Mayhew, invite her and Maddy for lunch if possible. I need you to check out any future travel plans et cetera: plus, I'd be interested to hear your frank opinion of Madam Bitch Supremo!"

GODFREY STREET

"Lulu, dear, need I tell you the tried-and-true Mayhew gut feeling was - as per usual - one hundred percent correct. An uber-reliable 'I'll see and definitely find' super sleuth New York contact was unable to find a Rick Maar nor a Helen Minter living in the city. What he *did* find was a *Rhett* La Maar based in Los Angeles and get this, known as a ruthless mercenary for hire and an equally ruthless Mr. Fixit!"

Lobie gave a chuckle. "And before you even ask, Leo and I would *love* to join the three of you for dinner this evening!"

"A zillion thanks, Lobie," said Lulu, "and thank your New York super sleuth on my behalf next time you speak to him." She added grimly. "So much for your loyalty, Maddy *dear.* Talk about biting the hand that feeds you! Now, I simply must ring the caterers as I feel Miss Madelaine Thompson and Mr. *Rhett* La Maar deserve a last supper to remember - does one *remember* a last supper? - a last supper which sees her spluttering out like a damp squib and he, as befits a slimeball, ending up a well and truly deflated one! Hold on a moment, Lobie, as one of the other phones is ringing so I'd better let you go. See you and Leo later around eight."

Lulu hastily picked up the ringing phone. "Hello? No, it's not Maddy Thompson, this is Lulu Mayhew whom she works for! Who? Oh, Mr. Maar, how nice to talk to you, and need I say how much I'm looking forward to meeting you this evening. What's that? You can't make it? What a pity! No, no, there's no need to explain, Mr. Maar, another time perhaps. Sorry, I didn't quite catch that. Lunch or dinner? I'll have to get Maddy to confirm that with you, Mr. Maar as I am busy working on a new book and, if the muse is *musing*, we wouldn't like to be *un*-musing, would we? Whatever, I'll tell Maddy you called in order to cancel dinner. No doubt she'll want to call you back. Goodbye, Mr. Maar."

"Sorry, I couldn't help overhearing," carolled Maddy on walking into Lulu's office. "Was that Rhett - I mean Rick - cancelling dinner?"

"Yes, Maddy, it was. Rather rude of him I have to say as he could have told you then and there at The Connaught that he wouldn't be able to join us, instead of coming up with some pathetic excuse! A surprise twenty-first dinner dance? Pull the other!"

Giving Maddy a tight smile, Lulu added snidely. "But as Margaret Mitchell's *Rhett* said to Scarlet. 'Frankly, my dear, I don't give a damn!'"

As Rhett Butler said to Scarlet O'Hara? thought Maddy inwardly panicking. *Just* what *is the bitch implying?*

"However," continued Lulu, "all is not lost as Mr. Maar - he sounded positively *presentable* on the phone - did say he'd do his best, and, if a break comes up in his very busy, to invite *us* to lunch or dinner. Silly man! Little does he realise Lulu Mayhew can sniff out a bluffer likes there's no tomorrow." She gave a derisive sniff. "Unlike you, Maddy dear."

To Lulu's dismay, Maddy's response was a placid "Whatever you say, Lulu" instead of some acidic comeback. Giving a tight smile she said matter-of-factly. "Now, if you'll excuse me, I have another *errand* to run. Namely to collect some essentials from the Chelsea Green Pharmacy. I won't be long."

"Take as long as your wish. Maddy dear," murmured Lulu looking at herself in the stylish Maximus Art Deco wall mirror behind her desk. "Hm, not bad Miss Mayhew, not bad at all, so why don't *I* also pay a visit to The Green. Who knows, maybe Madam Maddy has a clandestine rendezvous at

Finns or The Pie Man with the mysterious I'm no Rick Maar but a living, breathing Rhett La Maar; a mercenary and Mr. Fixit. What a hoot!"

Much to Lulu's chagrin she bumped into Maddy on her way back to the house. On seeing Maddy's surprised expression, she said gaily. "I was hoping to catch you in the chemist before you got back so that we could have a coffee and one of those delicious, calorific pastries at Finns. Could you maybe do an about turn?"

"Why not?" cooed Maddy, "as a coffee and a calorific pastry sounds just what the dietician ordered!"

Thank God you weren't out stalking me a few minutes earlier, she thought, *otherwise you would have caught me on my mobile to Rhett. A conversation that would have made you ears - unlike Lobie Maseko's - positively go up in smoke instead of being cut off!*

FIVE MINUTES EARLIER

"Rhett, it's me and this has to be super quick! She's definitely on to us so I don't know what you want to do next."

"I *do* have to meet up with a business associate later today - the main reason I'm over here - and as our meeting could go on for some time, let's meet up tomorrow at a time and a place convenient for you. If you could manage lunch, even better! Plus, you may remember me telling you I am flying back to L.A. tomorrow evening."

"Lunch tomorrow would be brilliant as Lulu has an interview with some TV hotshot over from Holland. They're lunching at her favourite Cecconi's which means I'll have several hours off the leash!"

"Do you have a particular restaurant in mind. One where we can bill and coo without startling the locals?"

"Goodness, Rhett! You've got me blushing," giggled a delighted Maddy. "I simply adore Daphne's on Draycott Avenue, a ten-minute walk from Harrods!"

"I'll see you there, Maddy Paddy, and can hardly wait!" replied Rhett with a chuckle. "In the meantime, I need to speak to Malcom as it appears Lulu Mayhew is becoming more of a problem with each passing minute; a problem which needs to be nipped in the bud before it's allowed to bloom."

"Oh, Rhett! Just hearing you say that sends tingles down my spine," giggled Maddy. "Fill me in tomorrow! Byee!"

Fill you in tomorrow? thought Rhett with a grin. *Dear Maddy, it wasn't on my original agenda but having met you, who knows what may happen. I know Malcom goes on saying you'll eventually be joining him in L.A. but why not join me instead? Talk about love - along with a soupçon of lust, of course! - at first sight! Rhett and Maddy instead of Rhett and Scarlet? Sounds good to me!*

*

"So, what happened to your mystery guest?" quizzed Lobie as they sat down to dinner.

"Mr. Maar cancelled at the last minute, claiming he had no alternative seeing he'd forgotten about a twenty-first birthday party he had been invited to weeks ago," replied Lulu in a disinterested voice. "As I said to Maddy, he could at least have come up with something a bit more believable instead of such a lame excuse and obvious bluff."

"I really do believe he *is* attending a twenty-first unforgotten birthday party," snapped Maddy. "Honestly, Lulu, you haven't even *met* the man so how can you be so sure he blatantly lied to you?"

"Blatantly lied to me?" snickered Lulu. "I'd mind your mouth, if I were you, Miss Thompson. If you're so insistent on spreading the good word regarding your Mr. *Rick Maar*, maybe you'll so the same for his" - she made finger quotes - "*almost* namesake, Mr. *Rhett La Maar!*"

"As usual, Lulu. I have no idea what you're going on about," said Maddy casually folding her table napkin, "nor am I prepared to sit here and listen to you purposely malign - yes, malign *and* destroy, as is your wont - everything and everybody! So, excuse me and, if possible, do your best to enjoy your dinner!" Glaring at a stunned Lulu, she added through clenched teeth. "And if, yet again, this ends with another of your bosom beating déjà-vus with you telling me to get out, I'll be happy to do so! The choice is yours."

"Oh, don't be such a silly billy," replied Lulu with a forced smile. "You *know* my bark's worse than my bite! So, *dear,* please sit down and I promise not to say another word about Mr. *Maar.*"

"If you insist," muttered Maddy, sitting down and unfurling her table napkin.

DAPHNE'S RESTAURANT - THE NEXT DAY

"God! Poor you," said Rhett sympathetically after Maddy had finished telling him about the dinner he was fortunate to have missed. "Lulu Mayhew seems to get worse by the minute."

Without any warning Rhett reached across the table and said in a determined voice. "Maddy, may I hold your hand?"

"Er . . . yes, of course," stammered Maddy placing her hand in his.

"I had a long talk with Malcom about you," continued Rhett, "and what I'm about to say may come as a bit of a shock, but when we leave Daphne's, I'd like to come back to Godfrey Street with you, wait while you pack a few items of clothing and necessities, and then travel back to L.A. with me. I know you hold a visitor's visa so, apart from saying yes, and being brave enough to put up with the likes of me, you'll not only working with us - Malcom and me - but hopefully living with me!"

"Rhett! Dear Rhett! I really don't know what to say!" gasped Maddy.

"Simply say yes; nothing else," smiled Rhett. "As for Lulu Mayhew; a polite note implying she can go fuck herself should suffice."

"After such a proposal," said Maddy with a beatific smile. "How can I *not* say - yes! Yes! *Yes!*"

*

Lobie's response to Lulu's hysterical tirade about "that ungrateful, duplicitous, cheating bitch" was a laconic, "Lulu, dear, don't you have the teensiest feeling you could be guilty party here and Maddy's sudden departure is more than justified. Your outrageous behaviour at dinner last night being the straw that finally broke the camel's back!"

"Oh, piss off! Lobie!" snapped Lulu. "Better still, why don't you take your earless self and your one-handed friend and get the fuck out of my life!"

"With pleasure, Lulu: with pleasure," said Lobie before terminating the call. Taking a deep breath, he poured himself a large whisky soda and called Leo.

"You mean Maddy is actually on her way to L.A. with the mysterious Rick, Rhett, whoever?" chortled Leo. "Good for her! It may not be L.A. but I am sure you'll agree that London *sans* the cloying Lulu and all her endless vendettas is something not to be sniffed at!"

"Could you please repeat that," chuckled Lobie. "Because, once again due to my turban, I didn't quite ear!"

*

"Damn and blast all of them!" snapped Lulu giving Flip Flop's head a rub. "It now looks as if it's you and I left to face this madcap world of ours! Ah! That must be Tommi Denning, a ghastly creep who will simply have make to do as my new secretary and major homo for the time being until I find someone else less drenched in Aramis!"

"Mr. Denning, he is here," announced Trini Lulu's no-nonsense Filipino cleaning lady, as she showed a bald, stick-thin, leather-clad young man into the sitting room.

"Tommi, my dear. How lovely to see you, and how sweet of you to come to my rescue at short notice," cooed Lulu, proffering her hand which Tommi promptly kissed.

Eyeing Lulu, Tommi Denning replied mischievously in a high, fluty voice. "Oh, c'mon Lulu! You know it's Flip Flop who really enticed me here!" Bending to give a tail wagging Flip Flop a resounding kiss on his muzzle, he added a shrill, "Hello, Flippy Floppy! Look what Uncle Tommi's brought you! A whole bar of delicious white choccy woccy! That's if, of course, your wicked mummy wummy doesn't nick it for herself!"

"Of course, mummy wummy won't nick it," replied Lulu rolling her eyes. "Now, if Tommi *wommi* doesn't mind following Flip Flop's mummy wummy downstairs to her study, wuddy, she has several letters for him to dealy weely with!"

LOS ANGELES

"Interesting to note that there's been a major rift between Lulu with Lobie Maseko and Leo Murrain," said Maddy to Rhett and Malcom as the three sat in Malcom's state-of-the-art office in Century City. "Talk about having the knack of falling out with all and sundry, no matter how useful they may have been in the past."

"You said it," growled Rhett. "Did you happen to show Malcom any of those vitriolic emails she sent you? Even I was somewhat taken aback by some of the comments. Especially the one that read '*having your guts turned inside out is far too good for you*'. And another one. '*I strongly believe you have stolen a copy of my latest book with the intention of publishing it under your name or a pseudonym. If I find out I am right, prepare yourself for the biggest court case in history!*'"

"As if I'd *deign* to pollute my fingers by even *touching* her wretched book," snickered Maddy. "God only knows what she'll come up with next. Another snippet of good news from across the water is, that on approaching Andy McCulloch - aka Robert Apps - about the possibility of working on a book together, she was told in no uncertain terms to forget it!"

Rhett sat staring adoringly at Maddy before clearing his throat and saying casually. "Malcom and I were talking to Dax Jefferson in London before you joined us. Dax asked if either Malcom or I could do a quick in and out to London in order to speak *kindly* to a certain City gent who's becoming a bit of a problem. Would you mind if I left you in the safekeeping of the lovely Jasmine and the ferocious Bim Bim while I dash over there for a day or two and give Mr. City gent a severe talking to?"

"A couple of days being pampered by the glorious Jasmine, the most revered cook and housekeeper in Beverly Hills and guarded by Bim Bim, the most ferocious chihuahua in the whole of Los Angeles? Why would I mind?" carolled Maddy, blowing Rhett a kiss.

"Good, darling, because I'm flying over tonight!"

GODFREY STREET - THE FOLLOWING EVENING

"Bugger, of course it would be Trini's day off and of course Tommi is out, and as you, darling Flip Flop, can't be bothered to ever answer the door, I suppose your long-suffering mistress better go and see who's come a buzzin'! But of course! Ho Lin with my Chinese takeaway!"

"Yes?" said Lulu imperiously on opening the front door and seeing a tall stranger instead of the smiling Chen from the local Chinese takeaway.

"Miss Mayhew?"

"Yes, I'm Miss Mayhew. Who are you, and what do you want?"

"Good evening, Miss Mayhew. We haven't met before, but we have spoken on the phone."

"We have?"

"Yes, Miss Mathew, we have. My name's La Maar, *Rhett* La Maar: though you may remember Maddy referring to me as *Rick* Maar."

"I'm sorry, but I don't have any recollection of a Maddy or speaking to a Rick Maar, Mr. Whoever you are claiming to be!" snapped Lulu. "In other words, I can't help you!" Adding a curt "Goodbye Mr. Whoever you are," Lulu's attempt to close the door was thwarted by Rhett giving it a violent shove resulting in a startled Lulu staggering backwards into the entrance hall.

"Thank you, Miss Mayhew," said Rhett with a smile on following her inside. "But I don't require any help seeing this is by no means a social call as I'm here to kill you on behalf of Maddy Thompson and doubtless, numerous others, and quite capable of doing so unaided."

THE END

ABOUT THE AUTHOR

Robin Anderson, a successful independently published author and a former internationally acclaimed interior designer, was born in Prestwick, Scotland, but spent his childhood and teenage years in the former Southern Rhodesia (now Zimbabwe) and South Africa. Before attending Rhodes University in the Eastern Cape, he hosted his own radio programme in Rhodesia (where he was duly dubbed "The Golden Voice of Teenage Half Hour"!) and worked as a reporter on The Bulawayo Chronicle (still going strong!) during his gap year.

Leaving South Africa, he spent the early sixties working with interior design companies in Paris, New York and London. He set up his own London-based design company - **RAD** - in 1970. Commercial ventures have included such names as Gulf + Western and the former Merseyside Development Corporation (the total refurbishment of the magnificent Royal Albert Dock in Liverpool) and private clients such as Ivana Trump; actress Coral Browne and husband Vincent Price (fondly referred to as Mr and Mrs Horror), impresario Mark McCormack and author and theatre producer Sally Burton.

Although interior design has been Robin's first interest, he has never stopped writing.

The former designer-now-author lives in a spectacular Chelsea apartment "overlooking endless lush private gardens" which he shares with Miss Abel Mabel Mortis: a glamorous skeleton of questionable years with a penchant for metal studded leather bondage collars.

To read more about Robin visit please visit his website:

www.robinandersonauthor-ott.com

BOOKS by ROBIN ANDERSON

www.robinandersonauthor-ott.com

AUTOBIOGRAPHY

Never a "Craft" Moment

NOVELS

Regina
Red Snapper
Sebastian & Seline
Versus
The Gallery
Divoon Daddy
Neos Helios
Amo, Amas, Amassive
Ceruse - A Cover-Up Extraordinaire
The Grin Reaper
The Go Blow Go Bar
Bobette - The Ups & Downs of a Total (Male) Tart!
Jan Unleashed!
Still Life - The Resurrection
Bruised Fruit
Defunct Gristle
Paul Dot Go
Crisp & Golden
Too Good to be Trué
I Give You My Heart
The Evil That Men Do - The Evil I Have Done
High Jinks in High C
Five Caballeros
Et Tutu, Brute?
Pillow Squawk
Pits, Privates, & Feet
Leo, Lulu, Lobie, & Mae

TREYTON TEMPLETON series

The Omnipotent
Colosseum
Who Scares Wins

LA DI DA DI BLOODY DA! series

La Di Da Di Bloody Da!
Trannys to Tiaras!
Maharajas, Mystics & Masala!
Wow! Pow! & Persuasions!
Oysters Aweigh!
Triple Oh Heaven!
Rootin' Tootin' Khamun!
Aliens & Arabesques - Blast Off!

NOVELLAS

The Burning Bush
Bel Ragazzo - Beautiful Boy?
Swallow Dive

SHORT STORIES

6 + 6 + 6 - Eighteen Tales of Textual Titillation (Volume One)
6 + 6 + 6 - Eighteen Tales of Textual Titillation (Volume Two)
She Married a Zombie Truck Driver & Five other "Trucking" Tales
Three on a Match Plus Three

CHILDREN'S BOOKS

Four Zimbabwean Adventure Tales
The Adventures of Tumble the Clumsy Tree

PLAYS

The Burning Bush

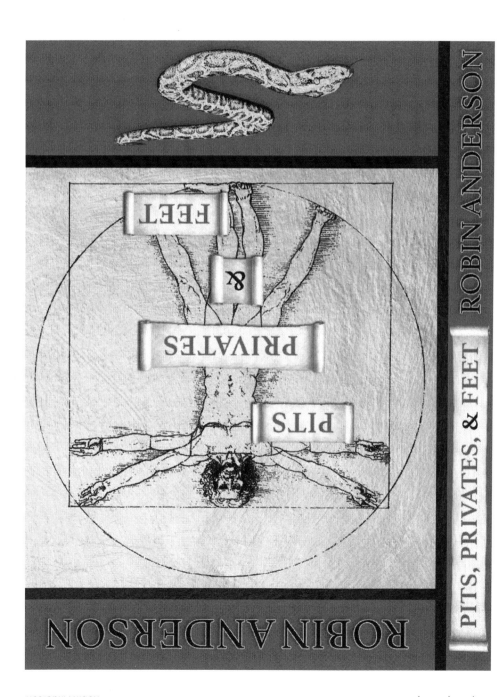

PITS, PRIVATES, & FEET ROBIN ANDERSON

ROBIN ANDERSON

FEET

&

PRIVATES

PITS

PROLOGUE

OBVERSE OPINIONS

THE CONFERENCE ROOM - *PAVONIA FASHION MAGAZINE* -
IMPERIAL WHARF - CHELSEA

LONDON

"To me armpits could never, ever be charm pits," giggled Barry "Belladonna" Babbage, a Macauley Culkin lookalike, wrinkling his retrousse nose (eight thousand pounds plus from one of Harley Street's most revered rhinoplasty surgeons). 'As for all that tangly, sweaty, smelly hair? No thank you!"

"You're such a phony, Babbage," drawled Magna Carter the glamorous forty going on sixty sub-editor who - despite looking like an over-the-top drag queen - was mother to three raffish teenage boys and happily married to millionaire stockbroker Jeremy Carter whom she described as "utterly divine in every which way: so there!"

Taking a fortifying swallow of her de rigueur eleven o'clock G & T, she added mischievously. "The whole magazine *knows* how you were caught sniffing all those discarded sweatshirts in the men's changing rooms at our local health club the other week! 'Armpit ambrosia' is what Timbo said you called it!"

"At least I wasn't caught sniffing any discarded jockstraps or socks," trilled Barry, "which, if the truth be known, was what yours truly caught little tattle Timbo Myers doing! Something the irresistible Barry Babbage would never, ever do!"

"May I remind you, one and all," interrupted Laurence Ward, the editor, a bald Mr. Magoo lookalike usually referred to as Larry but behind his back as LOL, Doll, "we're here to discuss the layout for Cyril Cristal's forthcoming fashion show and not Barry Babbage's perverted preferences so, if it's not *too* much of a strain on what limited grey matter you lot claim to possess, could we perhaps try and do just that."

"If anyone's into armpits its Cyril Cristal," hooted Bob Miller, a doppelganger for Michael Fassbender and the magazine's top photographer.

"Come to think of it, he even looks like one. As for his amorous aroma, I prefer to remain blissfully ignorant. Ha ha!"

"*Enough!*" boomed Laurence, who despite his timid looks and size, could - when pushed - make a foghorn sound inadequate. "Enough of this puerile crap: we have a magazine to deliver!"

"Keep your invisible hair on, Tony dear," giggled Vanessa Loos his pert, Lady Gagga-playing-Patrizia Reggiani in *House of Gucci* lookalike, and uber-efficient secretary. "Everything, as always, is well under control. Cyril Cristal finds the proposed layouts 'orgasmic' - his utterance, not mine - and is, in fact, blessing us with a visitation this very afternoon in what's supposedly a surprise happening."

"Thanks for the warning!" grinned Murray Griggs, head of sales and known as Mountain Murray due to his Charles Atlas-like frame and passion for rock climbing. "I'll make damn sure I'm well away from the office when he vaporizes by later."

"He's expected to be bringing Vestal his top mannequin with him," added Vanessa slyly.

"You mean Vestal Verona? The six-foot Aphrodite lookalike?"

"The very undulating one."

"If that's the case then a definite change of plan," chuckled Murray. "Make sure you introduce the elegant Aphrodite-cum-Vestal to me, Vanessa love, even though I'm pretty damn sure she isn't!"

"Isn't what?" tittered Vanessa, feigning ignorance.

"Vestal," quipped Murray.

"One thing that's certain is you can *definitely* count me out," yawned Perry Stalsis, *PAVONIA's* food writer and restaurant critic, "seeing this Vestal resembles nothing more than a walking, talking, stalking skeleton and therefore of no interest to me at all."

"So sports a matching, walking, stalking cadaver," tittered Barry. "As the vintage saying goes: 'Look in your own back yard before you look abroad!'"

"Will you loquacious lot just fucking zip it up so can get on with the double-fucking job!" yelled Laurence. "Here, gimme that," he added grabbing hold of Magna's G & T. Downing the contents of the glass he added deadpan. "Promise me, Magna, you've another bottle stashed away, plus a load of Anadin!"

MORTEM & POST - DETECTIVE AGENCY

"Joe the head porter appears to have got his Y-fronts into a right old twist," chuckled Dick Mortem, a striking thirty-year-old Jack O'Connell lookalike.

"Nasty thought that, seeing Joe's famous for continuously scratching himself and anything else living down there," grinned Pat Post, the other half of the agency who - unlike his raffish colleague - was seen by his doting mother as a Raphael cherub brought to life.

"Jesus, Pat! Not when I'm about to attack my M & S sandwich!" quipped Dick. "However, despite a *total* lack of interest, why the twisted Y-fronts?"

"*PAVONIA* is expecting fashion royalty around threeish; or so he said on waylaying me on my way in."

"Fashion royalty? Who else apart from Vestal Verona will be visiting the Wharf?" questioned Dick.

"Vestal Verona's Svengali, muse, fashion designer whatever; the very questionable Cyril Cristal himself."

"Also known as the best glass blower in the business," chuckled Dick.

"I sincerely trust that doesn't come from personal experience," tittered Pat.

"Speak for yourself! You lecherous old sod!" snorted Dick. "You know very well Miss Belinda Bowden is the only personal experience in my life and has been since we were weeny boppers," replied Pat loftily. "As for glass blowers, the only experience *I've* had was when Bell and I visited the glass works on Murano during a trip to Venice a few years back."

"Asking, only asking," chortled Dick. He glanced at his watch. "Shall we go and have a sneaky looksee?"

"I thought you'd never ask!"

ATELIER PIEDI FAVOLOSO - EARLIER THE SAME DAY

Alexander Etherington-Smythe - a Quentin Tarantino lookalike otherwise known as *il direttore* Alessandro Esposito-Amore to the long-suffering staff of the fashionable Italian ladies' shoe shop - stood pouting, hands on scrawny hips, as he surveyed the display of strappy, high-heel summer sandals.

"Looks like a pyramid of liquorice allsorts," he said prissily in what he considered an accent worthy of Raoul Bova, his secret lust. Turning to face Lily Stump his acerbic assistant - referred to as Stump the Frump behind her skinny back - he added bitchily. "Strappy, scrappy and a veritable pile of you

333

wouldn't even want to fuck-me pumps! The display takes hideous to a new low, Lily. It's ghastly! It's grotesque! Even Signor Roget would have a problem describing it'

So why didn't you get off your scrawny, much-abused arse and do the fucking display yourself, Alexander, you ludicrous fucking phony, instead of insisting Timmy Longwire of legendary eight-inch cock fame have a go! thought Lily waspishly.

Giving Alexander a strychnine smile she said in a diplomatic simper, "I rather like it myself, Signor Alessandro. To me it seems to say let's have fun in the sun. Being quite honest and having graciously suggest Timmy deal with display, I would have said he's *done* you proud." The "*done* you proud", said deadpan.

"Oh, you do, do you?" pouted Alexander, a manicured nail pressed to his butt chin. "Hmm . . . I have to say looking at the garish pile a second time it does seem to have a certain *non so che*. *Si*, you could be right for once, Lily. So . . . o-k-a-y . . . let's leave it. Now what's next on my silver platter for today?"

"You have an appointment with fashionista Cyril Cristal and Vestal Verona at three o'clock. Cyril Cristal naturally asked for you to be in attendance."

Lily gave an inward snicker. *Two painted, insufferable queens battling for centre stage! I wouldn't miss it for all the coke in Colombia.*

"Vacuous Vestal and her desperately fallen arches," tittered Alexander. "Oh, what we inexhaustible Svengalis of fashion have to put up with when you're in charge of one of Chelsea's most fashionable ateliers, Imperial Wharf must be *così* proud to have you as one of their most exclusive inquilini!"

Thank you for reading my book and - having reached this page - which I trust you enjoyed; as an independently published author, I rely on you, the reader, to "spread the word". So, if you enjoyed the book, please tell others and, if it's not too much trouble, I wouldn't say "no" to a notification (or review) on AMAZON.